the

quiet

and   the

loud

the quiet *and the* loud

HELENA FOX

Dial Books

DIAL BOOKS
An imprint of Penguin Random House LLC, New York

First published in the United States of America by Dial Books,
an imprint of Penguin Random House LLC, 2023

Visit us online at penguinrandomhouse.com.

Library of Congress Cataloging-in-Publication Data is available.

Printed in the USA

ISBN 9780593354582

10 9 8 7 6 5 4 3 2 1

BVG

Design by Cerise Steel
Text set in Alkes

Epigraph quoted from Arundhati Roy's *Capitalism: A Ghost Story* and used here with
thanks.

for Mom

Another world is not only possible,

she is on her way. On a quiet day,

I can hear her breathing.

—ARUNDHATI ROY

summer, *nine*

When I was small, almost ten years old, I rowed out with my father to the middle of a lake. It was after midnight—owls prowled, lizards hid, and Mum lay sleeping in the tent beside the water.

We'd arrived at the lake in late afternoon, unpacked the car, and set up camp—a big tent for Mum and Dad, a small one of my very own, for me. Mum banged in pegs with a hammer. Dad fluffed around with the fly and guy ropes, swearing. The lake *lap-lapped*. I clambered over the shoreline, found flat rocks, and skipped them.

At dusk, we three stood at the water's edge. I held Mum's hand and we looked out at the lake, the mist, the quiet, fading light. Birds squabbled and settled. The dark dropped in.

Then Mum cooked sausages on the fire while Dad blew up our inflatable dinghy with a foot pump. After dinner, we turned marshmallows on our sticks, watching the skin bubble and blacken. The flames crackled and licked. I crawled into them, listening for stories.

Mum drank her tea. Dad pulled out a beer, hissed the can open. Took a long draw. Mum touched my leg, stirring me. "Time for bed," she said.

I brushed my teeth with bottled water and spat paste onto the dirt. I kissed Mum and Dad good night, crept into my tent, snugged into my sleeping bag, and went to sleep.

Dad woke me with a shake.

"Georgia!" he whispered. "Let's go have an adventure!"

I could see his glassy eyes, his toothy grin in the dark. I stared at him, confused. I'd been dreaming of apples, of underwater trees? I glanced left, at the canvas wall—just a few steps away was Mum.

"Don't wake her," Dad said. "Come on!"

There was something in his voice, something sparking. *Say yes,* the spark said. Dad's eyes glittered.

I sat up, shivered out of my bag, and scooted out of the tent. Dad handed me a jacket. We tiptoed like burglars over to where the boat waited. We lifted the dinghy, laid it onto the water, and clambered in.

Then Dad pushed us out into the nothing.

The lake was inky. Gum trees ghosted the shore. The moon ticked across the sky, and the stars blazed.

I looked up. I felt wrapped in it, inside the immensity, the space and silence all around. But I didn't have the word for that then— *immensity*—so I said, "It's really pretty."

Dad beamed. "Isn't it just?" he said.

He rowed us until we were nowhere and everywhere. I dipped my hand into the water, scooped and trickled moonlit drops through my fingers. Dad did too. He rested the oars, leaned over the dinghy side, and looked into the lake. He looked into it so long, maybe the sky fell into the lake and the lake fell into the sky, because then Dad looked like he wanted the lake to eat him up.

He said, "Hey, buddy, you can row back, can't you? Just head for those trees." And with a plop and a splash, he hopped into the water and swam away.

Oh.

Dad hadn't surprised me like this in a while. It had been months of a sort-of calm, a sort-of easy, a sort-of happy. I'd seen Mum kissing Dad in the kitchen and smiling into his eyes, and it had been a long time since she'd done that.

But all of Dad was gone now.

I could hear him *splish-sploshing* through the water. I grabbed the oars and tried to follow the sound. The oars knocked my knees, and I lost one. Then I called and called over the solid lump of lake, but the lake didn't answer and neither did Dad.

I tried to row back with one oar. I slipped in dizzy circles and all I could hear then was the oar clunking at the lake like a spoon on an empty bowl: *scrape, scrape, scrape.*

I slumped against the boat side. I would die out here, I knew it. Dad had already drowned. He must have. Lakes could swallow you whole, skies too.

I huddled, knees to chin, and cried with the mucky hopelessness of going in circles and waiting to drown, cried over the water and up. My tears clanged the branches of the sorrowful trees and hissed at the stars.

When I took a breath, I could hear I wasn't alone.

Mum stood, shouting and screaming, from the shore.

summer, *eighteen*

1

Cool air. Slight breeze and sun, rising.

Sydney Harbour lies belly up—made of glisten, glass, and water—and I'm on it, in the kayak Mum and my stepmum Mel gave me for my eighteenth birthday. My body snugs the boat like a seed in its pod. My paddles cut and pull, leaving ripples. Above me, a sea hawk spirals; a gull glides, dipping down, and ahead of me, a duck, flipped over, waggles its feet and rummages the wet for breakfast.

The water is polished flat. If I wanted, I could lay my palm on the harbor's skin and rest it there. No big boats go by this early: no ferries, no sailboats, no water taxis. Nothing on the surface but the sheen of early light, a distant clump of rowers, and here and there, a bird.

Below lies everything else:
bull-sharks roaming the muddy dark,
fish and cans and plastic bags,
fallen boats and rusty fishing rods
and all the other lost things.

Behind me, my house on the peninsula drifts out of sight. Flanked by mansions, the house is old, tin-roofed, and jittery. The windows stick, white paint flecks from the eaves, and the barnacled dock at the end of the yard is slowly sinking into the seabed. The house belongs to Mel—her family has owned it since houses were being built on the peninsula. It hasn't been smashed or remade yet.

Mum, Mel, and my grandfather rattle around the worn house, clacking and pecking at each other. Gramps is eighty-four and always losing something—his teeth, his shirts, his shoes, his pills. He spindles the rooms, circling upstairs, downstairs, shouting. It drives Mel crazy. She's always saying, "Sara, that man scrambles my mind."

"Tell him, don't tell me," Mum always says back.

"He's *your* dad," Mel says.

"He's his own person, Mel."

And round and round they go.

Life in my house is like one of those black-and-white movies where people run fast through one door and out another. Music jangles; everyone's limbs jerk and bolt. My best friend Tess said once, "Your house is like a carnival ride, George."

But I confess: Sometimes I sit in my room, there on the top of the higgledy-piggledy house, stare out the window, and dream of quiet.

I paddle west and upriver. I sweep past sleepy coves and boat shacks, past rotting piers and rowing clubs, past apartment buildings and fancy gold-brick houses with their gold-brick swimming pools. I pass parks and yachts and slatted rocks.

In time, I turn into a bay and pause. I trail one paddle, carving a thin path of bubbles, coasting. A single cloud scooches over the sky, teasing rain. A crow calls from a tree. I rest the paddles across the boat. And breathe.

My phone buzzes in the front pocket of my life jacket.

It's a message from my father in Seattle.

Georgia, it's Dad. I have some news. Please call me back.

A pulse moves through my body—old, murmuring, like the thrum you feel when tectonic rocks turn over in their sleep. News from Dad could be anything—he's surprised me before.

I don't like surprises. When did we last speak? My birthday, I think. Dad and I don't really talk.

I flick the message away with my thumb.

The sun eases upwards, gathering heat. Trees wave from the park, by the shoreline. The sound is *hush-hush*, a *hellohellohello*, a soft listing in the leaves. I have lain on the grass under those trees before. I've sketched their twisting branches, made patterns on the page.

I close my eyes. Listen to the slap of water against the side of the kayak, listen to the trees.

My phone buzzes again.

I check it. It's Dad. Again.

Georgia. If you could please reply I would appreciate it.

It hasn't even been three minutes.

My stomach squeezes. I should have eaten before I left. Or brought along one of Mum's granola-bar experiments—Mel always brings them whenever we paddle together. "Always be prepared, George," she says. "What if we get marooned?"

My thumb hesitates over the phone. What should I write back?

Sorry, Dad, can't call. Am marooned. Need to use all battery power to Morse-code passing sailors for help.

A jellyfish glides under the boat.

Or: *I'm busy, Dad. I'm paddling to Hawaii. Call you when I get there.*

The crow rattles the air from his faraway tree.

Or: *Dad, listen: I'm in my happy place right now. Do not disturb.*

I put my phone away without replying.

The bay tilts and shivers.

It's too late—I'm disturbed.

● ● ●

The night Dad left me in the middle of a lake, it took a while to get me back.

"George! George!" Mum cried from the shore.

"Mum! Mum!" I cried from the boat.

"Coooo-ee!" called Dad. He must have slithered out of the lake and slopped over to Mum.

"Come this way!" Mum waved with her flashlight. She was a reedy voice and a thin pinpoint of light. I wanted to fly over to her like a bird.

But I couldn't *come this way*. I swiped at the lake surface. My oar skipped like a stone. The boat wobbled; I screamed and Mum screamed. We woke all the bugs and all the birds. We woke the sleepy moon. The lake heaved and shivered and I couldn't breathe. I felt crinkly with fear, eaten up. I couldn't stop crying.

I heard a sound then—a boat, coming. A spotlight lit me up. A shadow sat behind the light.

"Hey, darlin', we've got you," the shadow said. His voice was broad, like a pancake. I couldn't see his face.

"Mum!" I cried.

Another shadow at the back said, "It's okay, it's okay," but his voice sounded gravelly, and my best friend Tess said strangers took people and kept them in cages in their basements and maybe these shadow men were going to kidnap me and keep me in a cage?

The men's boat bumped against the dinghy. It rocked. I yelped. I saw a hand, reaching—

so I jumped into the lake and swam away.

Water sucked at my legs. My arms flailed, and the monsters rose. The men's boat followed, the spotlight chasing me.

They were coming! They were coming!

I thrashed away and all around me I felt the fingers of the water pulling at my skin. I could hear the screaming eels, coming to scissor off my flesh.

I gulped in a breath—and gulped in the lake instead.

I choked, coughed. Twisted.

And sank.

Then came the feel of water, the weight of water. My arms rose up. My eyes were open. I could see nothing. I could see *everything.*

A shadow man dove after me like a seal. Before I could die, fingers grabbed my body; I felt a *whoosh* and we rose till our heads broke the surface. The man lifted my face out of the water. I could feel his hands on my skin—a stranger, a *stranger!*—I cried and beat at his hands.

"Leave it alone, you wriggler," the man shouted, and his eyes shone like stars into mine.

I was hauled onto the flat of the boat. I coughed out lake water under the empty moon, then lay on my back, blank. Too shocked to cry, too drowned to scream.

● ● ●

The crow calls again.

Aaark.

Aaark.

Aaark.

I look around—

No lake. No night. No strangers, no Dad. Just me and a bird and a bay and a boat. Wind plucks water and sprays me. The hair on my arms stands up.

I breathe in, shake my head to clear my father out. It's time to move and keep moving; you can get stuck sitting still. I pick up the paddles, start turning, when I see a shift on the shore, someone coming from behind the trees and trotting down towards the water.

I squint—it's a girl, I think, wearing a red sundress. She stops, pulls a camera and tripod out of her backpack, sets them up, and now she kicks off her sandals and jumps, fully dressed, into the bay.

Into this water? With the muck and the jellies and secrets and sharks?

Yes. But not too deep; she's okay.

The girl does a handstand in the shallows. Now she flips back upright. Now she's running through the water, kicking up a spray. Now she's doing *cartwheels*.

I can't stop watching. The girl whirls on the beach, drops flying, sundress riding up. She's like a picture I might draw when I can't sleep. Her dress flaps—it pins itself to her body as she spins.

I seem to have paddled closer. Now I can see the girl's brown skin, her tangled hair and wide shoulders. She's about my age. She's upside down, right-side up. Bright drops flick from her body. She's all movement and muscle, curves and motion. My breath catches, like in those books where they say, "Her breath caught. Her bosom heaved—"

The girl pauses, looks out over the water, spots me and laughs. Her sound shivers the river, tingles me. She lifts her hand and waves. Her face is wide open, her arm like a flag . . .

And I'm waving my hand right back at her.

Why am I waving?

Why am I *staring*?

I drop my hand, scrunch it in my lap. *Très embarrassment,* my friend Laz would say. I turn the kayak, start paddling away. But then, like in those movies where the spaceships are being drawn by some enormous gravitational pull, I slow, and turn back to see the girl.

And she's disappeared.

I look around. How did she leave so fast? Did she duck behind the trees? I paddle forward, almost to the beach, but the girl is nowhere to be found.

I even look up, in case she's in the air and flying.

But if she is, she's going much too fast to see.

2

I'm out of the bay, heading west again, upriver. My paddles cut and pull. I fly over water, *quickquick*. It feels so good to move fast, to feel wind and spray, to think about a girl cartwheeling, to not think about Dad, to feel the sun on my back—

My phone buzzes again. This time, it's ringing. The *burr* vibrates up to my chest.

Is it Dad? Done with waiting already? What will he say? What will *I* say?

I check.

It's Tess.

"You up?" she says.

"Yeah. I'm in the kayak—I just saw—"

"I'm so fucking tired!" she says. "Got my assignment in, with like five minutes to spare. And then the baby kicked all night."

Tess is six months older than me. She's almost finished her first year of uni, unlike me, who is not at uni—I am on a gap year, which Tess didn't love because it meant we wouldn't graduate at the same time. Also, Tess is pregnant. *Resplendent with child,* Laz likes to say.

In about a month, Tess will be a mum. I've known her since we were babies, and now she's about to launch an actual baby out of her actual vagina.

I can't even imagine.

"Hey, Tess, I'm in the middle—" I start.

"Want to get coffee?"

"Um. Sure. When?"

"Now. Well, like, soon?"

"I'm paddling."

"Well, I need coffee. And I'm starving—there's nothing good to eat here. Come to our café at eight?"

I look around. The water hums. The sun arcs upward. Birds flit, dip, duck under. I'd have to sprint back downriver, then run to the café to make it in time.

"There will be pastries, George," says Tess. "When have you ever said no to a pastry?"

That would be never. Tess knows all my wants and weaknesses.

"I might be late," I say, wavering.

"That's okay. I'll wait."

I give in. "All right. I'm coming."

"Great! See you in a sec." Tess hangs up.

I pocket my phone. Turn the kayak.

The sun calls: *Leaving so soon?*

The water says: *But we were just getting started.*

I ignore them. I dig the paddles in and run the river path home.

Tess and our friend Laz are in the corner of the café when I get there, drinks already on the table.

"Perfect timing! Here you go," Laz says, pushing a latte towards me.

"Hey, George." Tess shoves over the sugar bowl.

"My heroes." I bend and plant kisses on their cheeks.

Tess makes a face. "Yuck, you're sweaty."

"Well, duh," I say.

"That's what happens when you run, dear," says Laz to Tess.

She sticks her tongue out at him.

I peel off my wind-jacket and sit. I've jogged from home. I didn't have time to shower or change. I dragged the kayak onto the dock, ran up the side path out to the road—past the picket fences and the park and the Johnson's dog, *bark-barking*—zigzagged right and down and left and up, and now I'm here. Sweaty and ready for coffee.

"I didn't know you were coming," I say to Laz. I take a spoon and start sugaring my drink.

"You didn't?" Laz looks over at Tess. "You didn't tell her I was coming?"

"I didn't tell her because I didn't know," she says. "You woke up after I rang."

"Oh, you slept over?" I say to Laz.

"Yeah. It was horror movie night." Laz stares over at Tess. "As though I wouldn't want to come."

"Sometimes you sleep till the afternoon, Laz." Tess flicks her red hair; it ripples like it's on fire.

"I only did that *one* time."

"Well. I was hungry. I needed to eat—"

I sip my coffee—it tastes of sugar, milk, and just a hint of coffee. "Perfect," I say, interrupting the Laz-and-Tess show.

"You're welcome!" Laz says, and grins at me. He's ridiculously beautiful. Smooth, tanned skin, sleek Greek cheekbones, and gray-blue eyes. I'd probably swoon if I were into boys. And maybe he'd flirt with me if he were into girls.

Tess leans over the table, her hair swishing forward. She mock-whispers: "*Also*. The pastries are on their way."

"*Nice!*" I say.

Tess grins. And it's like she's clicked her fingers and summoned them, because a plate arrives just then—six pastries, all chocolatey and shiny.

I lean towards Tess and lay my palms on her cheeks. "Marry me."

"You're too young," Tess says. She grabs a pastry and rips it in half. "Anyway"—she points to herself—"not gay."

"Close enough. Gay adjacent." I point to myself and Laz.

"Adjacent. Ha," Laz says to me. "Her overlap length is huge. Remember that girl last year?"

"Overlap length? Don't start your engineer speak, Lazaros. It's too early," says Tess.

But Laz continues. "Imagine you're a beam, Tess, crossed with significant length over another beam. That's you and that girl at the pub last year." Laz sits back. "Your gay overlap is strong, my friend."

"Jesus," Tess says, shaking her head.

She and Laz start talking over each other, as usual.

"It wasn't like anything even—" says Tess.

"Dude, you basically—" says Laz.

"Let me talk, shithead," says Tess.

"Same to you, lumpy," says Laz.

Here we go.

Laz and I met in art class three years ago; I introduced him to Tess. Within seconds, she decided Laz was her emotional twin, or emotional punching bag, or something in between, and Laz decided the same. Watching them is like watching a TV series that never ends.

"Anyway," says Laz, putting a hand in front of Tess's face. "This is not important. I have news."

"What?" Tess says. She has chocolate on her cheek from the pastry.

"Adesh told me he loved me last night." Laz wipes the chocolate off with a thumb.

"He did?" I say.

Laz nods, grinning. Adesh, Laz's boyfriend, has been in the picture for four months. They met through Laz's climate group at uni. They've gone on marches, posted flyers, shouted in corporate atriums together. The two of them are pretty inseparable. It's impressive Laz is even here with us now.

Tess says, "So what did you say?"

Laz smiles. "I said, 'Same.'"

"Awwww," Tess and I say together.

Laz looks soft and vulnerable for a second. Then he says, "So, when are you losers going to catch up?"

Tess chucks a chunk of pastry at him. "I don't want to be with anyone right now."

"Liar." Laz picks the pastry off his lap and pops it into his mouth.

"Not lying."

"I'm all good too," I tell him.

"Liars, both of you," says Laz.

"Well, I met someone at the shops yesterday," says Tess. "We had a moment."

Laz leans back in his chair. "Was that before or after he saw your elephant-sized arse?"

Tess frowns. She squints at her half-eaten pastry. "Okay, I know I'm enormous right now . . . but they said not to worry about the weight gain—" She stops, looks uncertain.

A darkwater feeling hums inside my body. I touch Tess's hand. "You're super pregnant, Tess. You look totally normal. And anyway, what's wrong with having a big arse?" I stare at Laz.

Tess stares too.

Laz twitches under our laser beams. "Sorry. Shit. That was probably a dick thing to say?"

"Yeah," says Tess.

Laz reaches over, squeezes Tess's hand. "Sorry, T."

"Thanks."

"Really though, I am."

Tess lifts her shoulders, drops them. "Don't worry. It's fine." *Fine* comes out glittery, like Tess has just tried to polish it, make it shiny enough we can talk about something else.

So I talk about something else. "Hey, so I saw this gir—"

Laz's phone rings. He glances down. "Oh! It's Adesh!" He gets up, motioning to the phone. "He auditioned for this play and he's been waiting to hear—" Laz presses answer. "Hey, lover," he says, and walks outside to the café veranda.

Tess looks at me. "You saw a who?"

Oh good. She was listening. "A girl. By the river. While I was out in the kayak before."

"Oh, yeah? What was she doing out at dawn? Burying a body?"

"Cartwheels," I say.

Tess tilts her head. "Really?"

"In the water. It was cool," I say, and I'm about to tell Tess about the way the girl's sundress flapped and clung, and the way the water flicked from the girl's skin, and the way time seemed to slow—but now Laz is bouncing back to our table, and he's saying "We've got to go! It's an emergency!"

"It is?" says Tess. Instinctively, she puts her hand on her belly.

"It's Adesh. He just got into the play! He's going to get naked. There'll be a horse, I think? I can't remember the rest. Anyway. He wants to celebrate." Laz raises an eyebrow. "If you know what I mean."

"Riiight," says Tess, nodding.

"Now?" I say.

"Mmm-hm," says Laz. "At his place. Before my uni lecture."

"Okay. Well, have fun," says Tess.

"Um. Yeah. The thing is . . . I need a ride." He looks at Tess, stares into her soul.

"From me." Tess stares back, unblinking.

"Always so smart." Laz grins and taps Tess's nose.

"Is it far?"

"It's almost at your place. Just a little bit sideways from your place. Ten minutes. Fifteen minutes out of your way. It's nothing."

Tess and I look at each other. Laz's sense of direction isn't prize-winning. There are stories we could tell.

Tess sighs. "All right," she says. "You better not get us lost. I'm so baby-brained, I might crash into a tree."

"You're not going to crash into anything," says Laz, pulling Tess out of her chair. "I trust you with my life."

I get up and notice the two and a half leftover pastries. "Who wants these?" I point to the plate.

Laz shakes his head. "You take them. Too full. We ordered too much, Tess. We don't even have money and we always order too much."

"They were two for one!"

"They were?" says Laz.

"Yeah—they were a day old. Maybe two? Bargain."

"Seriously? Yuck."

"Come on, you couldn't tell the difference—"

"You could have told me!"

They've turned for the door; they're walking away.

I wrap the pastries in napkins and ask at the counter for a bag. I'll have them later when I'm drawing, or doing one of the random online uni courses I started because my gap year got boring, or after my next paddling session . . . or at some moment in the undefined future when eating a leftover, unknown-days-old pastry will feel like a great idea.

On the café veranda, Tess jiggles her keys, beeps open the car. Pokes my shoulder with a finger.

"Want a ride?"

"Um." I hesitate. My house is only a fifteen-minute jog away. If I ride with Tess and Laz, I'll have to listen to all their noise . . .

I look out at the road, the space above the road. The air beats with promise.

"George?" says Laz, already by the passenger door. "An answer today, please."

"Oh! Uh. No, thanks. I really like—" I begin.

Tess laughs. "Fine, go on then, weirdo," she says, and pecks me on the cheek.

I glance down at her belly. "You could come with me if you like," I say. "I've heard it's good for people in their millionth trimester to have a little run. Laz could drive the car. Shout out the window. Be your hype man."

"I could do those things." Laz nods.

"Very funny," Tess says. She eases herself into the driver's seat.

Laz grins. "No? Okay. See you tomorrow, Georgie." He waves and climbs in.

I wave and watch them drive away. The radio is blaring already, music thumping out of the open windows. I can see Laz's and Tess's hands moving as they talk. Notes thrum and shimmer—I feel their colors in the air. Down the road they go. The car goes left; the colors turn, and follow the car out of sight.

3

I jog from the café, jacket tied around my waist, pastries bouncing in the bag in my hand.

I zigzag right and left, up and around the familiar paths, past parked BMWs and wrought-iron fences and gnarled jacaranda trees and cats slow-blinking from veranda chairs. Sunlight slinks along, dappled and broad, the path heating under my feet.

Tess and I have run this way, from our café to my place, for years. We've run everywhere since we were little, since our mums bonded in mothers' group, then drank coffees while we crawled and walked and played, then sent us to the same local school. Tess and I have run all around our neighborhoods. Done athletics together. Run on beaches, kicking up froth like in all those 1970s inspirational horse posters. Now I'm heading home alone, and Tess is in a car with a whole human waiting to exit her womb.

Tess and I are like the poem I just read for my online literature class: *Two roads diverged in a yellow wood* . . . But Tess and I aren't just diverging; Tess went and built a whole other road while I wasn't looking.

Nine months ago, Tess decided she wanted to get pregnant. Then she went and got pregnant. Now she's speeding towards motherhood without looking back, and I haven't asked Tess specifically, but I think she is expecting me to hop from my road onto hers, like we're still going the same way.

Tess is always saying, "When the baby comes we'll—" like we've planned to do this together. One time she even said, "When we have the baby—" as though I had been involved in conception. I don't know a whole lot of science, but I am pretty sure I'm *sans* sperm.

I have thought of telling her, "When *you* have the baby, Tess. You." But I think Tess sees us as one person, wearing the same skin.

I picture saying to her: *I'm thinking about having my own skin, for a change, Tess.* And: *I don't know about babies or raising them and maybe I'm not the baby-raising partner for you?* And: *I'm not sure, Tess, that I want to do this.*

I picture myself saying it all. That is, I try to picture it—the shape and line of my words, the colors.

But I've seen Tess upset. I've watched her break into pieces I've helped put back together.

I picture being the one who upsets her. Picture her face, changing—

I run and run. My words lose their grip, drip, and disappear.

I keep running. And the heat gathers inside me, where all my silence sits.

The summer I was eight, I was over at Tess's house for a sleepover. Tess was in the shower and I was in her bedroom. We only ever had sleepovers at Tess's place, which was fine with me. I liked it there better than at home.

We'd slathered our milk-white skin in sunscreen and swum for hours at the local pool. We'd eaten pizza for dinner and played dolls like always. I'd had my shower and was in my pajamas, reading a book about an elephant family. Mum and Tess's mum were drinking tea in the living room. That's when Tess started screaming.

Like: Loud, bone-shredding, horror-movie screams.

Like: I jumped out of bed and ran in a panic straight into Tess's door frame.

Like: I ran into the bathroom at the same time as Mum and Tess's mum, my lip red and swelling, and all we needed then was someone coming out of the drain with knife-hands to really make the moment sing.

When Tess could finally talk—after she'd been wrapped in a towel and the shower turned off—she said only one thing: *"I'm going to die."*

My mouth dropped open. My lip dripped a spot of blood on the floor.

"I'm going to die," Tess said. "I'm going to die. I'm going to die." She couldn't get a breath in. She was shaking all over.

No one knew what to do. What do you say to that? "No, you're not"? I looked at Mum. I looked at Tess's mum. They crooned over her, dried her off, helped dress her, then tucked her into bed with her dolls. They got ice for my lip; I sat next to Tess on the bed.

Mum said to Tess's mum, "Lydia, I can take Georgia home if you need."

Tess said from her bed: "No. I want her to stay."

That night, we lay together. Nose to nose. The dolls watched us with their plastic eyes. We breathed as the dolls breathed, hearts beating together, all hands clasped.

. . .

Tess panicked about death almost every day for two weeks, and then Tess's mum took her to a psychologist.

Next day I asked Tess how it went.

We were back at the local pool, drying out, our fingers touching. Lydia sat away in the shade, reading a book.

"Tess? Was it okay?"

Tess shrugged. She had her cheek pressed to her towel, and when she lifted her face, I could see the weave imprinted there. "Yeah," she said. "Mum was with me. I kind of wanted her to leave, but I didn't know how to tell her."

I nodded. I had been to a psychologist the year before, after a bad time with Dad. Mum sat next to me and cried. The psychologist said, "Maybe I could talk to Georgia alone?" But after Mum left, I felt like someone had reached into my throat and plucked my voice out, so the psychologist and I just kind of looked at each other like two snow leopards meeting in the Himalayas. I'd watched a documentary about them once, and I knew snow leopards liked their alone time.

"Did you talk, or did you draw?" I asked Tess.

My psychologist had had me draw—she handed me some stubby colored pencils and I drew a bunch of wonky snow leopards, all looking away from each other.

Tess glanced at me. "No. I just told her I was okay. I think I am. I just don't want to die, you know?"

"Yeah. I don't want to die either." I rubbed her pinkie finger with mine and thought about death. That is, I tried. It was too big for my brain to understand, but I thought if I said I was afraid too, maybe Tess would feel better.

"When I think about it, everything inside me starts wriggling."

I nodded again. I could relate. My stomach squiggled whenever Dad drank.

"The lady gave me these worry doll things and said to tell the dolls my thoughts. And she told me how to breathe, like I didn't know how."

"That's weird."

"Yeah. The dolls are really small. I don't know if they're big enough."

I looked at Tess. I didn't know what to say. I pictured her pouring her worries into tiny dolls. I pictured them being too small and the worries spilling out and oozing over Tess's carpet.

Wind licked our skin. Someone ran past, flicking drops on our backs. Tess shivered. "Let's go home. Want to go home?"

"Sure."

Back in her bedroom, Tess showed me the worry dolls: each one matchstick-sized and made of wool. They sat in a jar. Maybe the jar was the answer—if the worry dolls overflowed, the jar could catch the rest. We unscrewed the lid. Tess held a little doll to her lips. She whispered into its imaginary ear, then she dropped the doll into the jar and I slammed the lid shut.

There. Trapped.

That night, Tess yelled out once, in her sleep. She didn't wake up this time, so maybe the worry doll worked? I reached over, just in case it hadn't. I held her hand till morning.

4

I'm halfway home on my run when the sun flicks a switch and *blats* in.

The air cooks, sweat pools in my pits. Heat swims over my skin. The sun chases me down the road, swearing when I slalom into the shade of the trees. The sun thinks this is the best game.

I cross a small park. A dog lies by a bench in the shade, tongue out. Its owner checks her phone, maybe booking an Uber to get home. I think about Tess's car. I would have had five minutes of noise. Would it really have been too much?

I am actually dripping. I think my shoes are squelching with sweat.

The sun laughs.

When I get home, sweat is coming from places I didn't know sweated. I am basically a waterfall. I jog to the backyard, grab a towel off the line. Mum is on the deck, kneeling and scrubbing something from the wood.

"Hey there," she says as I come up the stairs.

"Hey."

"You're very sweaty," she says.

"Observant," I say. I look down at the deck. Beside Mum's knee is a dark patch. "What's that?"

"Blood," says Mum.

"Oh?" And now I see feathers on the deck too.

"A bird hit the windows while you were out. Poor thing."

I glance over at the sliding glass doors—there's a pale smudge on one.

"Is it all right?"

"No. It died." Mum sits back on her heels. Wipes away a strand of hair and blinks, hard. Is she crying? Mum is always so emotional. At least, that's what Dad always used to say: *So emotional, your mother.*

"I'm sorry," I say.

"Did you get bread?"

"Bread?"

"We texted you."

I pull my stuff out of my jacket pocket—house key, inhaler, phone—and see the messages I missed while I was with Tess and Laz.

MUM: *We're out of bread. Can you get some on your way home?*

GRAMPS: *George, have you seen my teeth?*

MEL: *Your mum says I've eaten all the bread. I have not. She lies!*

DAD: *Georgia. I can call you instead. Let me know what time suits you.*

I look at Mum.

"I didn't see these," I say.

"Oh," she says.

"But I have pastries?" I lift the packet up.

Mum's face brightens.

I peer into the bag—inside is a mess of chocolate and mashed pastry. "Um. They might be a bit smooshed?"

Mum's face falls.

"But I'm sure they're still delicious." I smile at her.

"Well, I'm willing to risk it—I'm starving." She stands up.

"Good," I say. I look around. "Where's the bird?"

Mum frowns. "Ugh. It's in the freezer. Can you believe it? Mel says she's going to paint it."

"Really? What kind of bird?"

"A gull. A young one, I think? It isn't very big."

A gull. Huh. I feel the tug of the bird, calling from the freezer. I want to see it.

"Have you had coffee yet?" I ask, stepping towards the doors.

"No. And somehow I'm the one out here, cleaning up. I am such a putz."

I step back and hug Mum, planting sweat onto her shirt. "You're not a putz. Just a pushover."

"Great!" she laughs. She pulls away. "You're really quite—"

"Smelly?"

Mum laughs. "Sure."

"Fine. I'll go have a shower."

"You do that, sweetie," Mum says, and hugs me again.

Inside, it smells like paint. Mum heads to the kitchen. Mel stands in the living room, working on a canvas. She's a professional artist—her warehouse studio is getting its electricity fixed, so she's taken over the house. Sculptures sit on shelves and tables. Sketches lie taped to the hallway walls.

The canvas in the living room is taller than she is. On it lie two enormous, pendulous testicles.

"Wow," I say.

Mel looks up, raises an eyebrow. "It's not like you haven't seen a testicle before, George. What's the internet for, if not to educate?"

"I haven't seen a testicle the size of my *body*."

"Your loss, darling," Mel says. She looks me over. "God. You're sweaty."

"That I am," I say.

"You need a towel?" Mel gestures to the rag beside her, the one she's been using to dry her brushes. It's shiny with paint.

"No, I'm good." I hold up the towel in my hands. "I'm going to have a shower."

"Okay. Don't leave your clothes on the floor!"

"I won't."

Mel turns back to the canvas. Peers at it, peers back at me. "Hey, did you hear about the bird?"

"Yeah."

"Poor bugger. I took a photo. Want to see?"

"Of the bird?"

"Yes, after it crashed." Mel pulls out her phone, swipes at it, holds it up. I step forward. See the broken body of the bird, its beak and wings akimbo, its neck a funny angle. I look at Mel.

"Should never have put in those doors," she says. Two years ago,

Mel sold a painting of a famous actor's bum. The money got us sliding glass doors, one repaired deck, and a kiln for Mel's studio.

She sighs, tucks away the phone. "Anyway, I'm going to paint it." She touches my arm. "You should too, George. Then we can give it a proper burial. I have a spot picked out in the garden. We can name him. I'm thinking Earl."

"Sure. Okay." I shake my head. Mel and her ideas.

Gramps wanders in, sees me. "Hey. Hab you seem my teep?" he begins, and stops when he spots the testicles. *"Oh,"* he says.

"Come on, John," says Mel, turning back to the painting. "You've *definitely* seen a pair of these, so there'll be none of that."

I start to walk away. Mel says, "Wait. Did you get bread, George?"

"No."

Mel opens her mouth to say, *Jesushowhardisittogetonething?*

"Chocolate pastries," I add. "In the kitchen."

"Ah!" Mel drops her brush in a turps jar, wipes her hands on the rag. "Perfect child!" She squeezes my cheeks and wanders out of the room calling, "Don't eat them all, Sara, you greedy bitch!"

Gramps tugs at my sleeve. "Teep?" he says.

"I think I saw them in the containers drawer, Gramps."

"—anks." Gramps nods and wanders off.

Now it's just me, a pair of hairy balls, and the sound of my mums in the kitchen tussling over melted pastry and Gramps clattering open all the drawers.

I leave their noise and head to the bathroom. Shower off sweat and paint from Mel's hands. Stand in cool water, run it over my head like a waterfall; like I'm in a rainforest; like I'm alone.

Upstairs, the cat meets me on the landing. Susan looks like she's been sleeping—she's got that rumpled, dozy look I love. Susan was Mel's cat when we moved in, but now we all agree she is mine.

Where were you? she says, pushing herself against my leg.

"Paddling," I say. "Running. Talking."

Susan sniffs. She doesn't think much of water. Or the other things, probably; way too much effort. She padpaws to my room.

I follow her. Pull on clothes, turn on the electric fan, flop on the bed, and prop my notebook on my knees. I have an assignment to do, but first I want to draw. Maybe I'll sketch the girl I saw cartwheeling in the water earlier? Upside down or maybe flying . . . Or perhaps I'll do the bird. Kinked neck, blood on the deck . . .

Susan jumps onto the bed. She steps into the crook of my armpit, shoves her face into mine. Sniffs me over. Approves. Kneads the sheets and starts to purr. I reach over and smooth the fur between her ears with the tip of my pen.

My phone vibrates on the bed—I glance down. Another message from Dad.

I really do need to talk to you, Georgia.

Now Gramps thuds up the stairs to his room. He's yelling: "What do you mean you cancelled my eye appointment? I am a geriatric! I could be going blind right now! Oh, *you're* sorry? I'll tell you sorry—"

The phone vibrates again. It's Tess.

Hey, I need to do my birth plan! Want to work on it tomorrow?

I breathe out, breathe in the cat's purr.

Sure, I text Tess back.

I put the phone facedown on the bed. Lay my pen and notebook beside it. Stroke Susan's back. "How has your day been, Susan? Any dramas? Any babies or testicles or dads in your day? Did you see the bird?"

Her left ear flicks. She adjusts her body, rolls onto her side, and exposes her chin for scratching.

The fan whirrs, cool air, left to right.

My grandmother's clock *tick-tocks* on the shelf above us.

I scratch Susan's chin. Pet her side. Lay an arm around her body. Susan releases her breath in a thick rumble. We breathe in and out till our breath is the same.

Together, we fall asleep.

FROZEN

(acrylic on canvas)

Berries and ice cubes and peas.

Feathers stuck to sides when once flapped.

Fish: no. Scraps: no. Only beak and eye and dead wings pinned.

Once, the bird flew over the chilled tips of waves.

The sun rose and called out to him—

he, a bird, a bird! Wind-filled wings, blood quick, eyes bright.

Once.

He?

> *Once—*

>> *was*

>> *peas and cubes*

>>> *he*

>> *Once—*

5

Mid-afternoon.

The sun beats at the bus window where my face leans against the glass. It's the day after I saw the cartwheel girl. I am on my way to work at the Art House. Strangers squeeze together, scrolling their phones. The air feels claggy, pre-breathed.

I watch houses slip by: blue house, white house, green house. Corrugated tin roofs, tiny porches, brick fence, picket fence, brick fence. Narrow houses press against each other and whisper secrets. I'd listen, but the bus has already moved on.

A hundred years ago, this peninsula was filled with steel workers and gas fitters, crusty children running, rickety wagons and flagstones, women pinning clothes to lines. Now the houses are glossed and stocked with millionaires. Two hundred and fifty years ago, these paths were uncut. People walked on songlines, the eucalypts dense. The land rose and fell, telling stories.

I close my eyes, try to imagine it back then:

the feel of the earth, the songs, the trees, the rocks.

I lean in with my mind, try to see—

and the bus heaves around a corner. Beside me, a woman's thigh presses into mine.

We whoosh off the peninsula towards the Anzac Bridge—all cement spires and gleaming wires, boats docked in bays below.

Now we're curving down the sloping freeway, turning right and left, lurching and trundling into the city.

On the second bus, I'm cramped in the back and thirsty. I am tempted to drink some of Tess's smoothie—she messaged me this morning, after I'd gone for a paddle: *George! Can you make me one of your smoothies and bring it to work? I'll love you forever!*

Today's drink is spinach, strawberries, almond milk, and some vanilla-flavored protein for added *oomph*. When I was making it, I reached in the freezer for ice and bumped my fingers on the plastic-wrapped body of the bird. It rocked, frozen, up against the peas.

"Sorry," I said. It felt important, to stop and say that.

After my nap yesterday, I pulled the bag out of the freezer to get a better look at the bird. Mum had left for work at her old-people's home. Mel was at her studio trying to get the electricians to work faster, and Gramps was upstairs in his room, listening to his old-people music. A moment of peace.

I stared down at the bird. Mottled-brown feathers, white, gray, and black feathers. Toes scrunched up against its chest. One dark eye gazed up at me through the clear plastic. *I used to fly,* the bird said. *I could see everything.*

"I am really sorry," I said. "About you dying. And, about the window."

Susan stood on the counter, wanting to see too. We looked down at the gull, held a moment's silence for the dead. Then Susan hopped down. I suppose when they're frozen, the dead don't hold much appeal for a cat.

I thought about taking a picture and texting it to Tess. But I didn't think she'd be into it. When Tess talks about death, she's very particular. Tess is particular about a lot of things.

After I went out on the lake when I was nine and Dad left me there, Tess talked a lot about drowning—she slathered me in statistics and sad stories. In her dreams she said she saw me dead on the lakebed, bones picked clean by the fish. But when I tried to talk about Dad leaving me, her eyes welled up and she got the shakes. Another time, when we were thirteen and I went to visit Dad in Seattle, Tess told me about plane crashes. She told me which airplanes were best; she messaged me a dozen times to make sure I'd landed safely. But when I came back four days later, she didn't ask what happened with Dad or why I'd come home so soon.

If I ever bring up my father, Tess will say, "Oh, George. Can we not? Please?" She'll slide over to me on the couch and kiss my cheek, loop her arm with mine, and say, "Let's do something fun. Let's watch that stupid dating show again."

If a hard memory about Dad ever comes, I don't bring it to Tess. I tuck it under a rib, with the others. Dad is like an eel sliding around our lives—quick and slippery. We don't talk about him. We don't remember him. If you don't look for him, maybe he's not even here.

But Dad has sent more messages. They crept in while I napped yesterday, while I paddled this morning.

Please call me, Georgia.

It's important, Georgia.

Let's talk, Georgia.

I don't want to talk to Dad. I never know what is coming with him. And the feeling of never knowing and being afraid slides around me, quick and slippery. My chest spikes. My fingers fuzz.

I am my own person, I think. *I don't have to call Dad. I don't have to do anything I don't want to.*

The bus revs and brakes. We swoop around corners, lurch through beat and haze. Strangers get on, get off, leaving holes where their stories were. And my story groans and stretches, coming back to life.

● ● ●

When Dad left the first time, I was seven years old.

I thought he'd be back the next day, the way you do when you're small and you don't understand the word *gone.*

I kept asking Mum, "Where's Dad?"

and she kept saying, "He's gone away for a bit, sweetheart,"

and I kept asking, "Where's Dad?"

and she kept saying, "He's on a trip. He'll be gone a while,"

and I kept asking, "Where's Dad?"

and she kept saying, "Please stop asking me, George. I have a headache."

When Dad came back, I didn't understand how long he had been away, but I watched Mum's face, collapsing in on itself, and I saw them holding each other for longer than they ever had and Dad saying, "I won't fuck up again, Sara, I promise," into my mother's hair. Then they went into the shower together and made noises in there I didn't understand.

When Dad left the second time, I was almost ten, and old enough to know what it meant.

Mum said, "It's for the best," and "Now it's just us two girls," and "Remember, this is our private business, George," and "Please don't talk about it at school, okay?" So we rattled about the house, two girls adjusting—settling into our silence and our secrets.

First Dad was here, and then he wasn't, and I kept walking into Dad-shaped holes in the house, like the doorway of the living room where some nights Dad used to stand and sway, or the space on the living room floor where he used to lie down and fall asleep, or the air on the couch where he used to sit and drink, watching us move—me and Mum—his eyes following and pinning.

The house felt different without Dad's voice in it, without the beer-soaked boom of him, without the coiled silence when he slept. The floors softened, the doors loosened, paper peeled off the walls—I'd rip it in long strips from the corners of my room.

Dad didn't call and he wasn't here and I didn't know how to soften myself, how to peel myself from the menace. I went to friends' houses and didn't talk about Dad. I tore tiny strips of wallpaper from their bathroom walls or tiny corners from their books. Once, someone's mother caught me. She stood over me and said: "Georgia! What do you think you're doing!"

I stared up at her. I wanted to explain. I couldn't.

At night, Mum and I lay in our beds. The Dad-shaped air sucked at us, pushed through the holes he'd made. The walls sagged, the windows creaked, and the house breathed and rattled where it stood, trying to become something new.

6

The bus door heaves open; I step from heat to heat. Walk to the traffic lights, wait to cross the road. Opposite me, the Art House flashes hello with its windows, waiting to welcome me inside.

The Art House is bright pink and almost a hundred years old. It sits sandwiched between a vegan burger shop and a boutique paper shop. The building has watched the street change clothes, put on new makeup, shine its shoes. Mel leased the store and the little upstairs studio fifteen years ago and started teaching art classes. That's how Mum and I met her.

I'd been to the psychologist again, after Dad left the second time. I couldn't seem to talk, so the woman gave me more paper and, this time, crayons. I drew swirling bats, night stars, a slice of moon, and a long sigh of water. I drew blue on blue on blue, all the colors wrestling.

Afterwards, the psychologist picked up my drawing. "How did you feel? To draw that?"

I shrugged. Maybe I smiled. Just a tiny bit. "Okay," I said.

At the end of our session, the woman said, "Do you want to take your picture with you, George?"

I glanced at it. "No, I'm good."

"Could I keep it? Put it on my wall?" She held the paper like it was precious, her fingers touching only the edges.

"Sure," I said.

When the psychologist suggested to Mum I might like art classes more than talking to her, Mum brought me to the Art House. And there was Mel, who made Mum laugh, and launched herself into our lives like a comet, or a runaway dog. And then they fell in love, the head-over-heels kind, and now they're married, and we live in a house by the water, which seems ridiculous sometimes, and I'm here at least twice a week to teach art classes, working with Laz and Tess—no lines at all between us.

The door of the Art House rings its little bell as it opens.

Cool air inside. Muted light. Hushed shelves stuffed with brushes, charcoal, oil paint. Canvases stacked along the back. Peace and calm—

"George!" shout Laz and Tess together.

I turn. "Hey." I wave.

My friends stand in the display area, setting up the new water-color paint and paper promotion. They're hanging painted flowers from the ceiling. At least, they're trying to. Laz is standing on a stepladder, Blu Tack in hand, getting it all wrong.

"No. Not like that!" says Tess, at his feet.

Laz looks down at her. "Like what, then? You get up here if you think it's so easy."

Tess glares up at him. "Have you seen me recently, Laz?" Then she remembers me. "George," she calls, "did you bring a smoothie?"

"Yep," I say.

"You beautiful life saver—" She starts to walk over.

"Hey! No leaving!" says Laz. "I need you to hold the flowers!"

A customer stands at the shop counter, graphite pencils in hand, staring at my friends, who are being loud. I go to the counter to help. I've got time—I always get here early to set up for class. "Lovely day, isn't it?" I say, ringing up the order.

"Not like that, Laz!" says Tess again.

"Oh, these are great pencils," I say.

"Shit!" says Laz, dropping a flower.

The customer shakes her head. She *tches* with her tongue as she goes out.

I walk over to Tess and Laz.

"Hey. No swearing at work," I say.

"Okay, Mum," says Laz, and rolls his eyes.

I hand Tess the thermos. "One smoothie, as ordered."

"Oh my god, thank you." Tess opens it straightaway—doesn't pour her smoothie into the cup, just guzzles from the bottle. "Want some?" she says, looking up. Her top lip is green.

"No. Got to get ready for class." Normally I teach with Mel but she texted from the studio just before I left for work: *George, they've stuffed up the wiring for my kiln. I have to sort it out. Don't worry, I've found a sub to teach with you. Enjoy the class!*

Laz glances towards the stairs. "Oh, that's right," he says. "The sub came in already. They're upstairs."

"Yeah?" God, I hope they're not making a mess. "What are they like?"

"Seems fine," says Laz. "Normal on the *outside*, anyway."

"Okay then."

Mel's subs are . . . shall we say . . . eclectic. I've taught with all kinds: Ginny the ceramicist who couldn't stop talking about Raku glazes, confusing the kids who were there to do lino prints. Then there was Fen, who described their scariest nightmare to the kids and then said, simply: "Draw." And Charlie told the class enormous lies about being Picasso's secret son.

Today, the sub and I will be helping the kids paint a still-life arrangement. I need to set up the display; I'll keep it simple. Mel might have reached too far with this lesson plan—watercoloring is hard, and these kids are only little. But Mel always says "Think big!" when she teaches, so I guess that's what we'll do.

"Wish me luck," I say to Tess and Laz, and head for the stairs.

"All the best and good tidings," says Laz.

"Oh!" Tess lowers the thermos. "Those pens you wanted just came in. I've put some in the drawer for you. You know, the fine-tip ones you said are better than sex?"

Laz laughs and the ladder wobbles.

"'Hypothetically better' is what I said. And thanks."

"You're welcome."

"Which color pens?" I say.

"All the colors, rainbow baby," says Tess.

"Perfect. Thank you, sweetums." I blow her a kiss.

She blows one back as I go up the stairs.

In the studio space, Mel's substitute stands at the center of the room, adjusting something on the display table. They turn as I walk in. And I see—almost in slow motion—that somehow, the sub for today is the girl I saw yesterday in the bay.

The upside-down girl.

Watery. Cartwheeling. Beautiful.

Holy shit.

She's *here*?

The girl is right-side up today, wearing soft green pants and a Beatles T-shirt. Her dark hair is tied into a loose ponytail and she's wearing scuffed sneakers. I instantly want to paint her.

"Hi," says the girl. And then her eyes widen. "Hey. It's *you*. Holy shit."

"Hi," I say.

"What are the chances?" she says.

"Haha. Yeah. That's wild."

And then I stare at her and think, *I know—what are the chances?*

Tess would call this Fate. I don't know what I'd call it. What do you call seeing a girl who was in your water one moment and in an art studio with you the next? Impossible. But true.

The girl puts out her hand. "Well, it's nice to meet you. I'm Calliope." Her voice ripples; her name sounds like a song—*Kal-eye-oh-pee.*

"I'm George," I say. I reach out and take her hand. Cool fingers. Soft skin. My brain goes blank. "Nice," I say. "Um. You. Too."

Calliope laughs. Even her laughter has music in it. I can picture Tess saying, "Have you fallen yet, George? Five, four, three . . ."

"It's a small world. Isn't it a small world?" says Calliope.

"Yeah. Definitely."

But we don't really have time to talk about the size of worlds—class is starting in a moment. Two kids are already walking in, sketchbooks under their arms.

Calliope gestures at the display table. "Mel said to set up the arrangement, so I think I've set it up? What do you think?"

I look at the table.

Huh. The whole thing is a wild vomit of color. There's a red leather boot. Plastic lemons inside a purple wicker basket. A brown-glass vase filled with red cloth tulips. A pink teddy bear, five stacked orange-and-teal plates, and Mel's favorite potted plant, its green leaves draped down like a naked person trying to be discreet.

Calliope sees my face. "Oh," she says. "Too much?" Then she leans towards me and whispers: "I've never run an art class before. I'm shitting my pants."

I look over the display. There's no time to change anything. All the kids have come in now and are sitting down. "No, it's fine! Really," I say.

"Okay, great." She looks relieved. She touches my arm. "Thanks, George," she says. Smiles.

Jesus. *Three, two, one . . .*

A kid at a table giggles.

I look over at them. I'm basically just staring at Calliope. *Get it together, George.* I turn towards the kids. "Hey, everyone. Meet Calliope!"

"Hi, Calliope," chorus the kids.

And now it's time to hand out the watercolor paints, the jars of water and brushes. It's time to stop thinking about Fate or music or lips. Time to look at the riot on the table and talk about color and line and the movement of water over paper. Time for the things on the table to tell us who they are.

. . .

Calliope and I teach two classes, back to back, which means three hours spent watching Calliope work. She moves through the room like a good witch—spinning the kids, dazzling me.

One kid knocks a jar of water over his paper; he looks like he's going to cry. Calliope's there with a towel in seconds, mopping it. She says, "We can turn it into something new. I love accidents! One time I rode my bike into a tree. I got this scar. See?" She pulls up her pants leg.

The kid leans over, fascinated. Then the two of them turn his mess into a watercolor monster. Crisis averted.

Calliope weaves between tables and points at everyone's paintings—the good, the not-so-good, and the paintings I'd crumple and put in the bin if they were mine—and says, "These are great!" She looks over kids' shoulders, says, "That's beautiful, Trudi," and "How clever to put the green there, Johan!" and "Want to add the boot there, in the corner? No room? Oh, I know—let's give it wings and have it fly over everything else. Yeah, like that. Fantastic!"

She's effortless. She smiles a lot. And she talks with an accent that sounds vaguely British. I've had a thing for British accents since I first watched *Mr. Bean*.

I can practically hear Tess say, "Well, that's your wish list ticked off, George."

Shush, Tess.

Class is over. The kids have said goodbye and filed out, and Calliope and I are cleaning up.

Calliope gathers up jars of water and says, "That went okay. I think? Was it? I was properly freaking out. I've taken art classes in school. I did ballet classes once for a month. I just finished my A levels. I do classes all the time. But yeah, I was losing my shit. Could you tell?"

"No," I say. I smile. "You were great. It was like you'd been teaching watercolor your whole life."

Calliope looks at me. "No."

"Okay. Well. At least, *half* your life."

Calliope laughs.

"So, A levels?" I say.

"Yeah. In England. I was there for two and a bit years. Just got back a month ago."

"Oh. Cool. And how do you know Mel?"

"My cousin knows her, I think? I think he gave her my number, but forgot to tell me about it. So I got this out-of-the-blue phone call from Mel today, asking if I could teach. She's funny."

"Yeah." That's one of the many words you could use to describe Mel. "She's my stepmum."

"Oh really?" Calliope pours the water out into the sink. "Do you like her?"

"Yeah."

"That's good. My mum's with this guy I can't stand. They're still in England with my little brother."

"Oh, I'm sorry."

"Yeah. What can you do." Calliope shrugs. "How long has Mel been your stepmum?"

"Well, Mum met Mel when I started classes here, when I was ten. They got married a couple of years ago."

Calliope glances over at me. "That's cool."

"Yeah." It *was* cool. Mel wore white overalls to the wedding; Mum wore a long wraparound dress. They looked so happy. We threw rice in the air, and the sun shone. It was a good day, with not a lick of Dad in it.

But I don't say any of that to Calliope, because we've only just met and you're not supposed to pour out your life story to strangers, even if you've seen them cartwheeling at dawn.

"It was a good wedding," I say. And I picture telling her about it, and then Calliope could tell me more about England and about jumping into bays, and anything else she wanted to talk about, but Laz shouts up from the bottom of the stairs.

"Jesus, are you ever coming down, George? Adesh is nearly here! I'm starving! Let's go eat!"

7

When we go downstairs, Laz isn't pacing by the front door about to throw himself at food. He's out in the back room, sprawled on an armchair near the little kitchen area, beside the coffee table stacked with unfiled receipts and art magazines.

So, no actual rush, then.

The room is chunky with heat; the back door is open to let in some air. Outside, the jacaranda tree drops fat purple blossoms on the courtyard stones. Tess has her feet up on the sagging orange couch and seems to be in the middle of telling Laz about her swollen ankles. "I think they're double in size, Laz. Feel them."

"I am not touching your weird ankles, Tess," Laz says. He looks up as we come in. "Oh, hey," he says to Calliope.

"Hi," she says, and smiles.

"I thought we were leaving?" I say.

"Soon, soon," says Laz languidly. "I just wanted you to be ready. Sometimes you take ages up there."

Tess waves at Calliope. "Hi. How'd you go? Did the children try to eat you?" Tess doesn't like teaching. She's tried it—says the children scare her. I have thought about the irony of someone afraid of small people, having a small person of her own. But I have kept that thought to myself.

"They were good," says Calliope. "Not *too* much biting today."

"Lucky you!" Tess says.

"I'm Laz," Laz says to Calliope. "Sorry, I should have introduced myself when you came in before. But I was trying not to fall off a ladder."

"And *I* was trying not to be fallen on," says Tess. "I'm Tess."

"Calliope," says Calliope, pointing to herself. And there it is—*Kal-eye-oh-pee*—the song again.

"That's funny," says Laz. "My boyfriend has a cousin called Calliope."

Calliope tilts her head. "How about that? My cousin has a boyfriend called Lazaros."

"No way."

Calliope grins, suddenly. "Wait. Are you—"

Laz says, "Did you just—"

"—dating Adesh?" finishes Calliope.

"—come home from England?" says Laz.

They look at each other.

"Shit! Yes!" says Laz.

"Yeah! A month ago." Calliope laughs.

"Ha!" says Laz. "What a fucking tiny world!"

It really is. Tiny, and filled with invisible, connecting strings. Tess looks at me. This is the kind of thing she likes to talk about in the middle of the night.

It turns out Mel was chatting with Adesh one time at the Art House, when he mentioned his cousin had just come home. Mel heard Calliope was creative, grabbed her number in case Mel had a use for her. And now, here she is.

"How random," says Laz.

"Not random," says Tess. "I've always said—"

Laz shakes his head. "Here it comes—"

"It's Fate," Tess continues. "Like, we're all being pulled by these invisible strings. Or stars, aligning. Or maybe it's God? All I know is—"

"—everything is meant to be," Laz and I chorus.

Calliope nods. "I like that theory."

"Thank you." Tess looks pleased.

"And now, here we are!" says Laz. He grins. "This is great. We should celebrate! We're going for kebabs! Want to come, Calliope? My shout."

"Sure," says Calliope.

"When's Adesh coming? I'm *so* hungry," says Tess.

"Five minutes," says Laz. "If you can't wait, I have these crackers—" He pulls a squished box out of his backpack.

"I don't think so, Laz. That box has been in your bag for weeks."

"Then maybe you're not that hungry."

"Or maybe I don't want to eat your moldy crackers. Have you thought of that?"

Calliope looks from Tess to Laz like she's watching a tennis game. She glances at me. Smiles.

I smile back. Everything feels loose suddenly, like when I'm running and in the zone and nothing hurts. Here we are—all of us together. Kebabs for dinner. Calliope, standing beside me, right-side up. Tess and Laz . . . being fairly mellow Tess and Laz. Nothing spiking. Nothing sinking. Nothing needing fixing.

It's a good feeling.

. . .

It's turning dark when we leave. Street lights blink on. The retail stores are mostly shut; a wrinkled man is already asleep in the paper-shop doorway, bags tucked by his feet and head. High-heeled girls trip-trap past. An Audi parallel parks in front of a Thai restaurant. A busker stands outside the supermarket, singing an anarchy song. People flit in and out of restaurants, roam the street like fireflies.

We weave through the crowd. Calliope walks with Adesh. Laz lopes along behind them, compact and wiry, plopping some coins in the busker's bucket. I follow with Tess, who walks slower because she could drop a baby anytime.

Three blocks down is the kebab shop—Laz loves this place because his family knows the owner's family, and he gets half-priced vegetarian kebabs. The shop is tiny, just three tables tucked under fluorescent light.

We stand at the counter to order and Laz says, "Oh, I've changed my mind about paying. There's too many of you now."

"Laz!" says Tess.

"Oh, sorry," says Calliope. "I can pay for mine."

"You don't need to apologize. He offered," says Tess.

"We're the same number of people as before, Laz, when you promised," I say.

"Oops," he says, putting his hands in the air, faking helplessness.

Adesh glances over at us. He looks ready for an actor photo shoot, tall and crisp in his button-down shirt, his hair swooshy. "Did he promise you guys free kebabs again?"

"Yep," I say.

Adesh squeezes Laz's arm. "You have to stop lying to the children, dearest."

"But it's so much *fun*," says Laz.

We stuff kebabs in our faces like we've never eaten in our lives. We're wedged around a small, laminated table and Tess is peppering Calliope with questions.

"So, you just came from London?"

"Well, Reading, actually. It's near London, like forty minutes on the train," Calliope says.

"What were you doing there?"

"Just finished my A levels, then did a bit of backpacking around."

"God, I'd love to do that," says Tess, maybe forgetting for a moment that she chose motherhood over travel. "Hey, was it weird, coming from winter to this? I've always thought that would be weird. You know—flipping seasons like a pancake."

"Yeah, definitely," says Calliope. "I forgot how hot it gets here! It was snowing when I left—and some rich girls from school are skiing in the Swiss Alps right now."

"That wouldn't suck," says Tess. She pauses. "What were your A levels in?"

"Film studies. And English lit. I'll be going to film school next year."

"That's cool! George is doing English lit right now," says Tess.

"And she's going to art school next year," adds Laz, his cheeks full of kebab.

"You are?" says Calliope to me.

"Yeah," I say. "I'm just on a gap year at the moment."

"But you're already doing uni?"

"Kind of—" I begin. "Just some online courses. An art history thing and an English thing. You get uni credits for them, so I thought I may as—"

"She got bored," Tess interrupts. "I told her she would, but she insisted on taking a year off." She gives me a long look, containing all the conversations we had last summer about *that* decision. "Anyway, she's going to the National Art School next year. She's a fucking art prodigy."

Calliope looks at me. Smiles. "Is that right?"

"Not even close," I say. "But Tess is my manager and she has to say that."

Tess straightens in her seat. "Lifelong companion, actually, joined by a blood pact."

"Oh. Cool." I watch Calliope's gears working—trying to make sense of me and Tess. Is she wondering if we're together? Is she thinking we are too much? Is she done with all of Tess's questions?

"How old are you?" Tess asks another one.

"Nineteen."

"Hey, same!" Tess says.

"And when are you due?" Calliope says.

"Oh this?" Tess gestures to her belly. "Just three weeks to go."

"Wow."

"The sooner the better," Laz says. "She's been a pain in the arse recently."

Tess scrunches up her nose. "That is another lie."

"You have been, though," says Laz, pressing.

"Don't, Laz. Don't poke the bear," says Adesh.

"I am not a bear!" Tess's voice rises. "George. Tell Calliope that's not true."

I open my mouth. Tess *has* been kind of a lot recently. Two nights ago, she asked me to come over to see if she was in labor. She sounded panicked. "I think this is it! You have to come! Everyone here is asleep."

It was after 11:00 p.m. I grabbed Mel's car keys and went. I watched Tess's belly, listened. I put my hands where she said.

By then, Tess was panicking even more because the baby wasn't moving. "Is she okay? George?" Her voice sounded whistley, like a kettle coming to the boil.

"The baby's fine, Tess. Probably sleeping. Like I should be."

Of course the baby was fine. Of course the baby wasn't coming out. But Tess fretted all night.

I look at her now, under the fluorescent light. She's pale. She's been on her feet most of the afternoon. I don't think she has showered today. She looks exhausted.

I am not going to poke this bear. "You've been fine, Tess. The same as anyone who's about to give birth."

Tess leans back in her seat. "See!"

Calliope says, "My mum just got pregnant."

"Really?" says Tess.

"She did?" says Adesh, looking at Calliope.

"She got knocked up by the guy she left my dad for."

Oh.

Calliope looks around at us. "Um. Sorry. Probably too much information."

"No, that's okay," Adesh says. "I'm sorry, *massina*. I didn't know—Mum didn't tell me." He bumps gently against Calliope's side.

The rest of us don't speak. The story of Calliope's mum sits awkwardly among the kebab wrappers, under the hard light. I look at Calliope, feel the story coming out of her skin: it's like indigo, drifting. I want, suddenly, for her not to be sad.

"That must be hard," I say.

She looks at me. Half smiles. "It is a bit." She lifts and drops her shoulders, like the feeling is a cloth she can flick off. "But, whatever. It's okay."

Tess says, "Well, I don't even have a baby daddy. It's just me. And George"—she gestures to me, then over at Laz—"and Laz."

Laz puts his palms up. "*I'm* not raising your baby, Tess."

"All right then, just me and George. Don't need you."

I look at my kebab. I want to say to Calliope: *We are not a couple. She didn't ask me. I never promised.* Although we did do a blood pact when we were eleven, so maybe I'm eternally bound to Tess, like a vampire bride?

But there's no space to explain. Not here. Not with the smell of meat spinning on its sticks and conversations scattering and people coming in and going out, and the clunk of the old air conditioner above our table. No space.

"That reminds me," says Tess. "We have to go, George."

"We do?" I haven't finished my food.

"Yeah. We're writing my birth plan tonight, remember?"

"Oh." That's right.

"You said you could, yesterday."

"Sure. Yes. I remember."

Adesh says, "Well, our movie starts in half an hour. Want to come, Cal?

"What's the movie?" says Calliope.

"It's about bees. Going extinct."

Calliope nods. "Okay. Sure."

I hesitate. Now *I* want to go with them to the bee movie. I've gone with Laz and Adesh to some of their documentaries before— they're pretty grim. Tess doesn't go anymore, not since she saw the dolphin-killing movie that one time and cried for a week. But Laz always says we shouldn't turn away from the hard stuff. He likes to look the hard stuff dead in the eye.

"You guys could come too," says Laz. "It's not like the baby's getting born tomorrow. And people have babies all the time without a plan. Some people give birth in *taxis*."

Tess rolls her eyes. "Thanks, Laz. But that's a no to the sad bee movie."

"The planet needs you, Tess. We all have to pay attention. Right, George?"

I shift in my seat like I've been caught napping in class. "Um? Sure."

Laz wants everyone to look, to *do* something. A few days ago at the Art House, he was talking about the big bushfire burning up north, and about the fire season, which started early and will be bad, everyone says. "Of course the fires are going to be shit," he said then. "What did we expect? Humans are like those frogs in the soup pot—except we *know* the water's boiling and we don't even care."

I didn't know what to say to Laz. I never quite know. I've marched in the marches with him and Tess and my mums and Gramps; I've signed the petitions and watched the movies and gone vegetarian with my family and we recycle all the things, but whenever I look closely at the end of the world, it feels too big, too chaotic, too loud. I feel tiny, like I want to hide under a bed till the danger passes . . . though everyone knows you can't hide under a bed from the end of the world.

And if I'm being honest, I want to go to the bee movie, not to save the planet, but to talk to Calliope more.

Which I definitely can't say to Laz.

Now Tess is out of her seat. "Maybe another time," she says, grabbing her bag. "See you guys later." She touches my shoulder. "George?"

I look up at her, look over at Laz. Who needs me the most?

Tess puts her palm on her belly. Her unborn child tugs at my heartstrings, whispers from the womb: *We do, George.*

I get up. "Sorry, Laz. I'll come to the next one. Promise."

He frowns. "Fine." He picks up his phone.

Tess heads to the door. Adesh slopes an arm over Laz's shoulders. "Good luck," he says to me, his eyes crinkling.

"Thanks." I tuck my re-wrapped kebab into my bag.

"It was good to meet you," says Calliope.

"Yeah, you too," I say. "Thanks for your help today."

"No worries. Anytime. Tell Mel I'm ready to teach Cubism next."

I laugh. "Got it."

At the doorway, I turn and look back. Adesh and Laz have their heads bent over Laz's phone. Only Calliope sees me turn. She smiles. Lifts her hand and waves.

8

Birth is way more complicated than you'd expect.

In the movies, the couple tumbles out of the taxi and into the hospital, everyone shouting and careening. Then you cut to the hospital room, where the woman is already pushing and screaming, squeezing people's hands. Then, voilà: a baby yowls off-screen, a gaggle of friends bursts in with balloons and tears and sitcom jokes, and seconds later the baby lies, clean and a good few weeks old, in the mum's arms.

But Tess has been going to birthing classes—dragging me and sometimes Laz along with her—and there's a lot more to it. First, a birth can take ages. You need to keep yourself busy and think of ways to distract yourself from the pain. Unless you decide to go for the no-pain option and take lots of drugs, which, of course, is not what Tess has picked. Tess is going for zero drugs.

When Tess told me, I said, "Are you sure?" and she said, "Of course I am," because Tess had googled and googled about natural births and just like all her other choices in life, she'd locked herself into this one.

So tonight, we are working on how to distract Tess from what the experts call "Level-10" pain.

Birthing balls are high on Tess's list. They're for sitting on and staying calm while a human tries to push itself out of a small hole in your body. Next on the list is lots of warm showers. Tess also wants there to be a certain *ambience*. "Would scented candles be too much?" she says.

I look over at her. I'm on the bed taking notes and she's at her desk brushing her hair.

"I don't know if you can have candles in a hospital."

"Why not?"

"Something might explode?"

"George, it's not a space shuttle."

"Just—it seems like a fire hazard."

"Hmmm." Tess considers. "How about some essential oils then? Like, they talked about pressure points last class—you know, the one you missed for no good reason?" I make a face at her. "Anyway, I googled after, and it said if you use essential oils while applying pressure points . . ."

I suddenly picture myself wafting oils around the room with one hand and prodding at Tess's pressure points with the other while she screams and pushes. My head starts to ache.

"That seems like a lot, Tess."

"I'm going to be in Level-10 pain, George. It doesn't seem like a lot to me."

When Tess talks about pain, her voice turns pinched, like someone is squeezing *her* out of a small hole. It's all fine choosing to have a baby and then googling your way into having a natural birth, but whenever Tess actually looks closely at her decision, she gets freaked.

"Tess, you can always get the drugs. It's not a test—you're not getting marked. There's no law against changing your mind."

Tess is sitting behind a curtain of her hair. "No," she says. "It'll be fine." She takes the brush and smooths her hair into a soothing red river. She sounds like she's trying to convince herself.

I wonder if this is what Tess does at night when I'm not here. I picture her lying in bed, holding her own hand, saying, "It's okay. It's okay." How does she keep going when everything scares her, but she keeps deciding to do scary things? Tess is a conundrum.

Like, choosing to get pregnant. Who does that at eighteen?

Tess does.

● ● ●

Last summer, Tess and I were at a music festival. Laz had come with us, but within half an hour he'd found someone more interesting to hang out with and was riding their shoulders. He'd be up there for a while. Tess and I took a break from dancing and went wandering through the food tents and market stalls. Wedged between a hemp T-shirt tent and a mango smoothie tent was a palm reader.

"Hey," said Tess. "Want to go in?"

"No," I said. It looked like trouble.

"Come on! It'll be fun!"

So, we went in and sat together in the clammy heat. A pallid woman sat opposite us, smothered in beads. Her cropped-blond hair lay limp, her top lip sweated, and dark circles bloomed under her pits. An incense stick burned in the corner.

"Am I reading you both?" said the woman, sounding as tired as her hair.

"No, just her," I said, thumbing over at Tess.

The woman raised her eyebrows, looked behind my ribs, rummaged around. "Are you sure?" she said.

"Yep," I said, slamming my ribs closed, shutting the gates, lifting the drawbridge, battening down the hatches, like in all those submarine medieval murder movies.

"Up to you, sweetie," said the woman and held out her hand for Tess.

The woman ticked all the palm-reader boxes: *I see a handsome dark-eyed stranger. Tall. Mysterious. Dead grandfather, oh no, great-uncle, of course, of course.* Tess was all smiles and openings, but then the palm reader pulled a swiftie and told Tess when she was going to die.

"Young," is what the woman said, specifically.

"What do you mean?" Tess said.

When the palm reader didn't answer, Tess pressed and pressed, until finally the woman sighed, checked Tess's palm again, and said, "Early twenties. Sorry, darl." And then she said our time was up.

We stumbled out of the tent, Tess crying and crying.

"Early twenties?" she said. "Early twenties? Like, that's basically now! Fuck!"

"Tess, listen to me. That woman was being a bitch. It's ridiculous."

But Tess wouldn't listen.

When Laz found us, Tess could hardly breathe. We found the medical tent, laid her out on the cot bed, and the first-aid people thought she was on drugs.

We dragged her out of there, Laz saying, "Tess, seriously, don't worry about her. Jesus, why did you even go in? What kind of a dumb—"

"Not helping," I said. We were on the bus. Tess was glassy-eyed.

"Let's get her a drink. You want a beer, Tess?"

"Laz, that's the last thing she needs."

We argued the whole way back and when we got to Tess's house, she crawled into bed and fell asleep. Didn't get up for fifteen hours.

A month later, Tess told me about Lukas. She'd seen him at some flea market a week before and introduced herself. They went out for coffee. He was traveling around Australia, he was getting a degree in linguistics, he was Lithuanian, he spoke three languages. He had *potential*, Tess said. She went on to describe his physical features—*hot, great bone structure, good skin, not stupid*—like he was a horse she was thinking of riding or racing.

I didn't think much about it. One of Tess's many hobbies was spotting hot boys—she'd been doing it since she was about twelve. She always wanted me to spot them with her, but I never found them very interesting to look at.

"So," she said in her room, long legs crossed on the bed, brushing her hair. "You know that guy I told you about?"

"What guy?" I was on the floor, sketching her.

"From the markets. The guy, the traveler guy."

"Do you mean Lukas?"

"Yeah. That's him."

"And?" I said.

Tess grinned. "We went out!"

"Oh? When?" The night before, Tess had texted me from her room. I was at Mel's warehouse studio, painting with Mel. Tess was getting ready for her first week of uni, listening to punk music. She had sent a clip of herself singing one of the songs, giving it everything she had.

"We hung out last night. Like, late," said Tess. "*And* this morning." She waggled her eyebrows.

"You slept over?"

Tess looked triumphant. "Oh. We did not *sleep,* George."

"Ah."

"Did I mention his cheekbones?"

"You did."

Tess started working on another section of hair. "Solid DNA. Seriously good features. Excellent potential."

I stared at her. There she was again with that word. "Tess," I said. "What do you mean, 'potential'?"

"I mean, if I get pregnant."

"Excuse me?"

"Like, if I have a baby. I want to have a baby before I die." She said it as though she was saying: "I want to have mac and cheese for dinner tonight."

"Wait. Wait." I sat up. "Tell me you used protection."

Tess looked at me through her hair. "Um. We kind of just messed around? And then we were kind of doing it but, like, not for long and we didn't have a condom so we stopped—and then we started again—but then we stopped again, so, probably nothing happened."

"*Shit.*"

"It was fine, George. Don't stress."

"Tess!"

"It was fine. Nothing's going to happen. But if it does—I'm thinking this could be my legacy."

"Oh my god—*what?*"

Then Tess told me her idea: Get sort-of accidentally knocked up. Have a baby. Love it till she died.

Result? A life not wasted.

I said she was being ridiculous. I told her to get the morning-after pill. I told her to get tested for STDs.

Tess refused the first part.

"You're eighteen," I said, then. "You're not meant to make babies at eighteen. Not sort-of accidentally on purpose."

"Who says?" Tess flicked her hair up and over, sending it down her back. She looked at me. "Who made the rules?"

When Laz found out about Lukas and the not-sleeping and the messing-around, he said, "Tess. You are missing a screw. What if you get a disease? What if you get pregnant?"

We were in the pizza place near Laz's house, sharing a large vegetarian with extra olives. Tess said, "I'm going to get tested." Then she smiled. "And I'm okay with pregnant."

"Sorry? You're okay to get pregnant?" Laz looked stunned.

"Yeah." Tess shrugged, the way she often did when something really big was happening and she didn't want to think about it.

"Wait. You want a kid?"

"I think so. Yeah. I want one."

"Tess. Fuck's sake. You're eighteen."

"That's what I told her," I said, as though they were listening to me.

"I know how old I am," said Tess, bristling.

"What about the guy?

"He's gone back home, I think? I don't have his socials. I don't even know his last name."

"Holy shit."

Tess picked an olive off her pizza, put it down. "It's not about him. It's about me."

"Are you kidding me?" Laz's voice had risen. "Are you serious right now?"

"Shh," I said. We were in our corner in the back, but we were filling the room with our sound. An old couple looked across at us, frowning.

"I need this, Laz. You don't understand," said Tess.

"Tess, you are out of your *fucking* mind."

"Shh," I said again, uselessly. The old couple lifted a finger for the waiter.

Tess tried to explain. *Legacy,* she said. *Leave something behind,* she said.

Laz wouldn't have a bar of it. "Jesus. You're barely grown. And besides, this planet does not need any more babies. Haven't you noticed we're killing the Earth? We are dying."

Poor choice of words. Tess's eyes filled with tears. "I know."

Laz shouted: "Oh my god! *You're* not dying! I'm talking about the fucking planet. Look around you! We're on fire."

The waiter came over. Coughed. "You're making a disturbance. People have complained. You need to be quiet or leave."

"Happy to go," said Laz. He shoved back his chair and strode out of the restaurant. Tess rushed after him. I went to the front to pay. "Can I take the rest of the pizza?" I asked the waiter. I waited while he got a box.

I came out on the street in time to hear Tess say: "But the children are our future, Laz."

"There *is* no future."

"Teach them well. Let them lead the way."

"No, no, no," said Laz, putting up a hand. "You are *not* going to convince me with Whitney."

Tess peed on a stick three weeks later. I was doing sprints at the park.

Shit!!! said Tess's text. And then came GIFs of babies. And storks.

Then she texted: *Café. Now. Please.*

At our café, Tess spoke very quickly. She had already written out her plans, calculated how much money she would need, how she would survive.

"I'll live at home," she said. "It's not like Mum and Dad will chuck me out. I'll do uni and work at the Art House and save up—and have the baby at the end of the year—and then I'll hang out with her all summer—Ruthie can help, she loves little things—and then I'll put the baby into daycare and do uni part time—and you'll catch up to me and we'll end up in the same year again! It'll be perfect."

I don't think she breathed once as she spoke.

. . .

None of it made sense. I told her so, but Tess had no room for logic. She tucked herself into a space I couldn't reach. She got excited, even: a baby, a baby, a *baby* of her own. Talking sense to her was like trying to convince a boulder to stop rolling downhill.

When Laz heard, his lips pinched together. He said, "That's so fucking stupid." He couldn't get Tess to change her mind, no matter how much he shouted.

When Tess's parents heard, they were stunned. David, Tess's dad, suggested she think things through. Lydia suggested Tess go back to her psychologist. Both her parents talked about options and the future and *did she really want* and *did she understand* and *what about*—

Tess shut them down.

Ruthie, Tess's six-year-old sister, lost her mind. "I'm going to be a *sister*?" she yelled.

"No, Ruthie," Tess said. "You'll be an *aunt*!"

Ruthie goggled. Tess grinned. Then the two of them laughed, like Tess having a baby was the very best and cleverest thing in the whole world.

● ● ●

It's late.

I've written down *Essential Oils*. I've written down *Pressure Points*. We have a playlist—Elton John and heavy metal and '80s synth *and* Beethoven, because Tess wants to be prepared for all moods. We're finally done with the birth plan and I'm ready for sleep, but Tess has twisted her hair into a top knot and her eyes are bright. "Want to go for a drive?"

I look at her. "Aren't you tired? I thought you were tired."

Tess shrugs. "Second wind."

We leave her sleeping family and take Tess's mum's car. We cross the city—drive over the Anzac Bridge, through the tunnel and past the fancy eastern suburbs, stopping at a 7-Eleven on the way for a bar of chocolate and a packet of jelly snakes.

It's almost midnight when we arrive at South Head, one of the two headlands guarding the harbor. North and South Head are probably visible from space, the cliffs are that huge. Tess and I have been coming here since we could drive, drawn here like moths.

We walk up the steps to The Gap—a fifty-meter cliff that faces the Tasman Sea. We lean against the curved fence, suspended above nothing and everything, and say hello to the water.

The waves don't stop to answer—they flip and crash, snarl over flat, jagged rocks and smash, phosphorescent, into the cliff face. The sound is wild and the wind is wild and we spread out our arms and holler into the empty space like hooligans.

I look over at Tess; her face is lit up and all her worry is gone. I must look the same. Here, nothing can harm us, because we belong to this air, this sea, this wind. We are just girls, just specks in the froth, free.

After we're done with hollering, Tess and I walk up the path that goes around the headland, not far because Tess is full of baby and swollen feet. We sit on a bench on a landing and open the chocolate bar—always rum-and-raisin—and the packet of snakes—always red for Tess and green for me, even though Tess thinks green snakes are an abomination and should be banned.

We eat. We press our shoulders together. We listen to the sea.

Tess says, "I wonder how many people have jumped from here."

I look over at her. Tess and death—never far from each other. "Um . . . I don't know."

"It's so sad. It must be horrible for them."

All around this headland are printed signs, about hope and talking, numbers to call. Mum always says, "You went where?" whenever I tell her we've come here at night. I know these cliffs hold the hardest stories, but somehow, this place isn't sad for me. I don't know how to explain it—when I'm here, everything feels possible, electric blue. Maybe I'm weird.

I'm quiet for a bit. Then I say, "Mmm-hmm," to Tess. I've learned not to say much when Tess starts speaking her death thoughts. If I pick them up and talk about them, they get louder.

Tess bites into a piece of chocolate. Chews. Looks over at me. "Do you ever think we should buy a different chocolate?"

I shake my head. "Never."

She leans against me. "Correct answer."

We don't say anything more, not for ages. Just float here, together. Stars click from place to place. The cliffs shift imperceptibly. Waves pound in. Sandstone hums beneath our feet. And for a moment—here, now—we aren't the pregnant girl or the quiet girl. We aren't scared of death, or of memories oozing out of the dark.

We are two girls, suspended.

Timeless. Immense. Untouchable.

9

I head home from Tess's the next morning. The bus swooshes along the highway, cars and trucks belching smoke into an exhausted sky. It's going to be another hot day.

Tess wanted me to stay but I wanted to go. I had an image of the water; I wanted to be on it.

"I have an art history essay. It's due in a sec," I told her, over cereal.

"Can't you come to the thrift shop with me first? I need some baby clothes."

"You have enough clothes. You could dress five babies. Are you having five babies?"

"I might be. You never know."

"Oh, I think you would know."

"The ultrasound could have missed some. You never know until you know. You know?"

I lifted the bowl to drink the last of my milk. "I'm not enabling you, Tess."

She sighed. "Fine."

Tess is sure she's having a girl. She's already three-drawers deep in op-shop magenta onesies, fuchsia dresses, and tiny pink socks.

I could straighten her out—I was at the ultrasound where you could find out the sex of the baby. Tess and her mum wanted to be surprised, so I was the only one looking when the penis floated into view.

I've heard Tess plan her little girl's name, the games they'd play, the way they would bond—two girls against the world. One night a few months ago, I said, "You sure you don't want to know what I saw in the ultrasound?"

Tess was tired and kind of snappy that night. "I already told you, George. I want to be surprised."

"Okay." I lay on her rug. We were listening to Ethiopian jazz. Tess wanted her baby girl to know all kinds of music. I closed my eyes.

Then Tess poked me. I looked up at her—she was leaning on her side, her hair sweeping over the bed. "George. Is there something I should know? Did you see a problem?"

Tess looked sick. She reached down. Grabbed my hand.

I squeezed her fingers. "The midwife would have told you if anything was wrong. You're all good, Tess." I looked at her pinched lips, fear in her eyes, worry waiting at the edge of everything. "Really. You're going to be fine."

Would she be? Who was I to promise these things? In flickered an old memory: Tess and me hiding; Tess scared, and me whispering in the dark, saying, "It'll be okay, it's okay, Tess—"

I switched channels then, turned the screen to black. I kicked the memory away.

. . .

On the bus, my phone buzzes in my lap.

I glance down—is it Tess? Do I need to add something else to her birth plan? A string quartet? An ice-cream van?

Oh. It's another message from Dad.

Georgia. I really do need to talk to you. I will call you tomorrow night your time. Speak to you at 10.

Shit.

What if I don't want to talk to you at ten, Dad?

The bus stutters, lurches.

I feel the past rippling round the bus—through the window, pooling up from my feet—all the stories wanting in. I stare hard out the window. Feel the old swell of fear, a slash of hurt, the itch of rebellion, a shoving back—

I write: *I'll be busy, Dad. Don't call me.*

I delete it. I write: *I don't want to talk to you. Leave me alone.*

I delete that too. I write: *When I think about you, my body feels brittle. My bones feel picked clean.*

I delete everything. The bus reels around a corner. The sky puckers with clouds.

When I get home, I go straight to the shed. Pull out the kayak. Go to the water. Thank God, or the universe, or a vast and unknown something, for the water. For movement on and birds above and fish under,

and all the secret, blind, sweet doings through the water,

for being a clean line on the water,

for being a girl in a boat in the wild on the water.

The first time I went out on the harbor, I was twelve.

It was Mel's idea. She had a double kayak. She dragged it out of the shed and down to the dock, where it sat like a shark, seats gaping.

I'd known Mel for a couple of years by then—first as my art teacher, then as Mum's girlfriend, then the person whose place we had moved into, boxes lugged out of our tired, sad house to Mel's ramshackle house on the peninsula.

I liked it here. I had my little room at the top of the stairs, freshly painted with new curtains. When Tess first stepped in and saw the view through my window, she made a sound—it was a "holy shit" sound, except Tess was going through a polite phase, so she just said, "Holy shorts! Holy monkey-plucking SHORTS." Then Tess and I leaned out my window and tried to spit into the harbor.

My new life had music and color and two women in the kitchen, laughing and kissing and dancing. Then Mel got an idea in her head.

"Come on, George. Let's go!" she said, beside the kayak.

I hadn't been in a boat since the time with Dad, just over two years before.

"Uh—" I said.

Mum tried to explain. "It's not for her—" she began, but Mel put up a hand.

"Sara. Sweetheart. You have to run *straight* at fear." Mel held up a life jacket she'd fossicked out of the shed. The jacket looked sickly, disheveled, like a bear yanked out of hibernation.

I said, "Um. I'm not—"

Mum said, "Mel, you can't make a child—"

Mel said, "I'm not making her. Who wouldn't want to go out on this? Look."

Mum and I looked. The harbor murmured, sun-glinted and glittery. Birds swooped low, wings almost touching the waves. Water rippled against the poles of the dock. *Want to try this again?* the water said.

I didn't.

Did I?

I looked up at Mel. She was like a force—could I say no to her? I hadn't tried it yet. I hadn't really tried saying no to anyone.

Mel handed me the life jacket. "Here you go, George. I promise you'll be okay."

I put it on. I kissed Mum goodbye forever.

Out on the kayak, the water was still. I sat behind Mel, shivering. I waited for us to trip on a wave and tip over, for the jaws of the harbor to open, for a ferry to mow us down.

Mel paddled steadily around the tucks and hollows of the shoreline. She pointed to a heron on a pole. She pointed out jellyfish. Other than that, she didn't talk. She was like a different person. At some point, she turned her head and smiled at me. It was like being dipped in warm chocolate.

A boat zipped by, kicking up a wake. The water lifted us up and down; I gripped the kayak sides. Mel turned the boat so we rode the swell forward, which made me think of riding a seesaw in the park, even though I hadn't done that in years. I felt the thrill of rising and falling.

Mel glanced at me. Saw my face. Smiled again. "Want to paddle?"

My face closed. "No."

"All righty," said Mel, and she took us home.

Mum was waiting for us in the backyard. She ran down to meet us at the dock and swooped me up in my damp life vest, wrapped her arms around me.

"Was it good? Are you okay? Was it okay? I love you, sweetie." Mum wouldn't let me go. She smooshed me into her jacket; I was still shorter than her then. I breathed her in.

"I'm fine," I muffled through the fabric. "It was good." I didn't know if she could hear me. She was trembling—I squeezed her tighter to get the tremble out.

Mel came up and wrapped her broad arms around us both. Now I was squished in a Mel and Mum sandwich. It wasn't terrible.

"My beauties," Mel said. "Fuck, I'm grateful for you!"

The following morning, I sat on the dock with my bowl of cereal. It was early. No one else was awake.

The water sloshed at the poles of the dock. Moored boats tilted in a little wind, a gull flew overhead. I watched light dapple the harbor. I remembered the rise and fall of the kayak, the buttery smoothness of the sea. Felt the new memory of water slide over the old, like tissue paper.

Next weekend, Mel and I went out again. And the next, and the next.

Rise and fall, fish under the hull, the kayak skimming.

One weekend, Mel turned her head, saw my face. She asked: "Want to paddle?"

"Okay," I said, and smiled.

My paddles dipped into the liquid and out. We moved forward and forward, over the silk of the harbor.

10

Afternoon.

I've been out in the kayak for hours. Now, the wind is picking up, the tide has turned, and I'm heading home. I lift and drop, my paddles cutting in, water dripping into water. Ferries and yachts and fishing tinnies slide past. Birds glide and dive.

I am just passing the park near the harbor baths when I see Calliope again.

Again? Three times in three days? I squint. Yes—it's really her. This time she's on the hill near the ancient fig trees. She stands by a rocky outcrop high above me, bending over a camera and tripod.

I can hear Fate saying: *"Look, George! Pay attention, this minute! Stop dropping into the past! There's a GIRRRRRL!"*

I know what Tess would say, except I haven't told her yet that Calliope was the cartwheel girl I saw in the water two days ago. Tess was so focused on baby plans last night, I forgot. Or maybe this time, I wanted to keep the story for myself.

I've already sketched Calliope a couple of times. All right, four times. Calliope is in my notebook, upside down and right-side up, all curls and curves. Maybe I'll draw her again when I get home— this time under a tree, bending, absorbed. Maybe I'll draw her *as* a tree. She could have been one in a past life—she has that vibe.

I slow the kayak. Stop. Float in place. Watch.

Calliope leans and adjusts the camera lens. Her hair is up and tousled; she's in overalls. Wind ripples the cloth above her black boots. She looks like someone from a period film—like one of those women who strides hilltops and gazes over windswept moors, saying no to suitors.

I take in a breath.

I drift and stare.

I wonder if I am in Calliope's camera shot, wonder if I should leave—

and so I don't see the wake of the boat coming towards me, don't feel the swell of it until it's here. The kayak tips and, just like that, I am flipped upside down into the harbor, which hasn't happened in years.

Now comes the shock of salt in my mouth, a blinking, brackish blackness, the fear of a bull shark coming to bite my head off—*and is it over, is this it?*—but then instinct kicks in, all the training in the quiet bays with Mel, the patience of rolling and righting, over and over. And I heave myself sideways, bring myself back into the dripping light and blink.

I look up, see Calliope staring out at me.

I hear her shout: *OH MY GOD! GEORGE! ARE YOU OKAY?*

Shit. She can tell it's me? She saw me splat into the water? She sees me here, frazzled and sogged?

My body ripples with embarrassment.

I shout across to her: "Yeah. Sure. Sorry!"

And then—*God! Sorry?*—I'm mortified by the spill and mess of it all, by me stopping to gawp at Calliope. I barely know this

girl—why did I stop? Why did I stare? She must think I'm the stu-
pidest, the most—

I drop my head, lift my paddle, dig into the water—

even as Calliope shouts *HEY, THAT WAS AMAZING*, even then—

I haul myself away. Dripping, flicking water out of my eyes,
scooping water from the boat, spitting and flicking and bailing and
wobble-paddling home before I die of river muck,

or embarrassment,

or the sudden, waking-up lurch of love.

I have been in love before. A few times. Maybe more. Tess has
heard about my walloping crushes, always on impossible girls.
When those girls have broken my heart, Tess has said, "Run it out,
George." So I've run, and paddled, and painted out Vera and Juniper
and Zafi, and the last girl who Tess calls *She who shall not be named,*
because that one had me miserable for a month. But still, the heart
wants what it wants—and my heart can't seem to stop wanting.

When I was younger, girls were just curious things to draw. I
was pulled towards their faces, fingers, mouths, all their shapes
and sizes. I watched how they moved in the playground, at swim
practice and gymnastics, watched them in the library and on the
bus home. I drew girls in my notebook: bodies round, reedy, stiff,
and soft. Bodies sitting, bodies bending. Bodies running, turning,
thinking. Bodies half-asleep.

At recess and lunch, the girls in school sat in clumps and talked
about boys. Boys and boys and boys. So, I tried thinking about boys
too. I watched how they fidgeted, how they poked each other, how

they walked with a slouch. I tried drawing them in my notebook, but they didn't look right—I kept rubbing them out and starting over.

Then when I was almost fourteen, Vera came to the Art House, and shit, wasn't that the end of me? Vera was seventeen and doing Year 12. She was smart. She had long, slender fingers I imagined touching me. I drew her in my notebook, wrote poems for her, in the style of all the old, dead poets: Devotion. Darkness. Death. I gave one of them to Vera and she said, *Oh, isn't that sweet? Aren't you the cutest!* She may as well have patted me on the head.

I drew the feeling into my notebook.

Vera was straight. She finished high school. She moved to Queensland for university. I mourned, hard. Mum saw a page once in my notebook, during that time. She'd come into my room with some laundry. I slammed the notebook closed, too late, and Mum said, "Oh my god, George. Are you all right?"

I told Mum and Mel about liking girls when I was fourteen and a half.

They said, "Okay," and "We love you." They hugged me, and then we got takeaway Moroccan food for dinner. It was that simple.

Tess already knew about me, because, "Duh, George." Not long after that, she started to look for girls for me: girls I might kiss, girls I might grow old with.

"As long as they know I'm your number one, ride or die, George," Tess likes to say, I can fall in love with any girl I want.

11

My family doesn't notice I'm soaking wet when I walk in from the back deck.

Mel and Mum and Gramps are in the living room, having one of their "discussions." The chairs rattle, the cushions shiver and trill, and sketches pull from the wall where they've been pinned. The cat knows better than to be here and is elsewhere.

Mum and Mel are in a flap about the dead bird. Which, it turns out, is in the bath, defrosting. Or as Mel puts it: "There is a goddamn corpse, decomposing" right where Mel likes to take a soak at night.

"What the hell, John?" Mel stands nose to nose with Gramps.

"I'm going to stuff it!" says Gramps. "I'm taking it to my taxidermy guy. He's got a license to do native birds. It's perfect!"

Last month, Gramps did a two-day class where he learned to stuff a rabbit. He did it from start to finish—we heard every detail over dinner. The rabbit came home in a half-standing position, weird glassy eyes staring at us, front paws up as though she'd spent her last minutes pleading for her life. The rabbit lived with us for three days, whispering stories of her death from the mantelpiece as I sketched her. Then Mum got the heebie-jeebies, and off the rabbit went to my uncle in Perth, along with a birthday card.

"John, I don't think we need a whole spree of stuffing dead things—"

Gramps says, "You painted it, Mel! What's the difference?"

Mel and I painted the bird two nights ago—while it was frozen, Mel might add. "Keep me company, George?" she'd said late at night, leaning in through my doorway. My painting is in my room; Mel's is on the mantelpiece—gray toes curled against a white chest, green haze around the bird like an aura, a single magenta eye, staring out. The bird looks at me from the canvas: *I was lord of the air. Why was there a window where the sky was supposed to be?*

Mel scrunches her nose at Gramps. "My paintings don't smell of terror and formaldehyde."

"Dad. Seriously. No," says Mum.

"Yes, yes, yes," says Gramps. "Come on, don't be such fuddy-duddy diddle-shits."

"Did you just call us diddle-shits, Dad?"

"I said what I said."

Mum and Mel sigh.

"Anyway. I need it thawed by tomorrow," says Gramps. "He said it can't be frozen."

Mel says, "Jesus. You don't need that much time to defrost a bird!"

"How do you know?"

"It's common sense. Have you never eaten a turkey?"

"Not recently. You lot with your vegetables. And where the fuck is my yellow shirt? I know those arseholes next door took it. My favorite shirt!"

"Did you check your laundry basket?" asks Mel. "Go look in your laundry basket, John. And we are not leaving that bird in the bath!"

I cough. Do they even know I am here? I am literally dripping all over the floor.

The three of them turn to me. "Talk some sense into your grandfather," says Mum.

"I don't need more sense. I have plenty," says Gramps. He goes upstairs to look for his shirt.

"This makes him happy," I say. "Besides, you paint testicles, Mel."

"Yes, but there's a *thing* rotting in my bath. It will not be usable if he leaves it much longer."

"Our bath," says Mum, correcting Mel.

"Yes. Of course. *Our* bath. For God's sake, Sara."

Gramps comes downstairs, wearing his shirt: yellow, pin-striped, and wrinkled all over.

"Found it!" He grins. "It was in my laundry basket!"

"Oh, Dad, you can't go out like that," says Mum.

"There's such a thing as an iron, John," says Mel.

"No time!" says Gramps. "Got to go to polka class!" He grabs his suit jacket off his armchair—puts it on, buttons it. Nods, satisfied. "Perfect, can't see a thing."

And away he goes.

Mel says, "Dear God."

Mum sighs. "Mel."

"I'm putting that bird back in the freezer—"

"Well, it's half-thawed now." Mum sees Mel's face. "How about we put it out in the shed. In a bucket. With some ice." She steps towards Mel.

Mel softens. "Okay."

This is the part where they unrumple. This is where they make up. This is the part where they always kiss.

They glance at me. Finally take me in.

"Shit, George," says Mel. "What happened to *you*?"

In the bathroom, I stare into the old, clawfoot tub—the bird looks about the same as he did fully frozen. A little softer. Damper.

I am not quite myself, the bird says.

"I get that," I say.

I wash off the harbor brine in the little shower stall beside the bath. The bird keeps his eye on the ceiling. I wonder what he makes of the four of us, clattering around? Mel is always in a tizz about her paintings. Mum always cries about her old people. And the two of them fret constantly over Gramps, who is not firing on all cylinders right now. Tonight, he'll come home shnickered on gin and lipstick kisses, having burned through another retiree. He's been sleeping with all the women he can find since Grammie died.

Four years ago, we flew up to Queensland and I sat beside Gramps in the funeral chapel. Gramps gripped his knees through the service. Tears dropped in fat, wet splats on his thighs. When two neighbors stood at the front with guitars and sang "Moon River," Gramps began to moan. People's heads turned, just an inch, but no one said "Shh." A baby stared, its fist in its mouth.

I slipped my hand into Gramps's. Held it tight, tight.

A couple of months later, Gramps moved into the little room

opposite mine and began his dating spree. He has barely taken a breath since. Gramps doesn't talk about what he's doing—he just careens around the house, in and out of old ladies' hearts, breaking things, a bull in everyone's china shop.

Mum says Gramps will get better. Mel always rolls her eyes. If my mums ever split up, it will be because Gramps has driven them to it. And if I ever leave to go live in a cave by a secret river, it will be because of this rackety house and everyone inside it, and life making *all this noise*.

The house is calm by dinnertime.

Mum has made eggplant parmigiana and a walnut avocado salad—she is pleased with herself. Gramps is still out. And Mel wants to hear about Calliope subbing yesterday.

"How did she go?" Mel says. "I kind of threw her into the deep end. But I figured a film student would have some artistic bones."

"She was good," I say, forking up my food.

"Good, as in, I can ask her again to sub? Or good, as in, she wasn't great but at least she didn't give the kids nightmares?" Clearly that time with Fen still rankles for Mel.

I talk through a mouthful of eggplant: "Good, as in, she was great."

Mel brightens. "Really?"

"Yep." I nod.

"Wonderful. 'Cause I'm thinking of having her do the classes with you for a while. The studio is finally ready, and I have my exhibition coming up. If she's good, then I can just give you some instructions and leave you to it. Sound okay?"

I look at Mel. *Calliope, teach with me? Every time? In the Art House? Have her walk around in that room with me, for hours?*

I play it cool. "Um. That sounds good."

"Yeah? You sure?"

Holy shit yeah, I'm sure!

"Yes. That'd be fine."

"Great! I'll give you her number. Can you call her and set it up?"

At which point my body has two responses at the exact same time:

My heart

and

God. Will she even want to work with me? I looked ridiculous today. Why did I tip into the water? Why did I paddle away? What kind of person does that? Only someone who's lost their mind—

"Yep. Uh-huh. I can do that." I cough. Then cough again. Drink some water.

Mel looks at me for a long beat. Is she reading my thoughts? I picture her listening to what's going on inside my head right now. I try to shut down all thought. Chew my eggplant. Look as though I don't give even the slightest shit about Calliope.

Mel nods. "Okay then," she says.

"Okay!" I say brightly. Try to swallow my eggplant. Choke on it and cough so hard Mum has to whack my back to sort me out.

. . .

Dishes are washed. Mel and Mum have gone to bed, and I'm in my room with my phone and Calliope's number on a piece of paper. It's time to call.

I stare at the phone.

It buzzes. It's a text from Tess.

Hey. What are you doing? Want to come over and watch the end of that stupid dating show? Mum made cookies. They're terrible but not so terrible they can't be eaten

I leave her on read for a minute. If I don't call Calliope now, I might not get the nerve.

I type in Calliope's number. Don't press the call button.

I breathe in, out.

My phone buzzes again.

It's my father.

Georgia. Just to confirm, I will call you tomorrow night at 10 pm your time. Please let me know if that doesn't work for you. It will be good to talk.

A ripple. A lurch.

I leave him on read too.

But now my insides feel queasy. Even more queasy than they were at the thought of calling Calliope.

I wish I could feel steady when I thought about Dad. Or Calliope, for that matter. I'd love to feel unrockable. Clean and solid and whole.

I'd love for my memories to stop stretching, yawning as they wake—

I'm holding Mum's phone and calling—It rings it rings—It rings *out—My voice squeaks into the nothing—Hurt!—Hospital!—*Please, Dad!

—but it's not that easy. Sometimes the past squiggles in, white-bellied and glistening. Sometimes it slicks over you, quick, before you can blink, and pulls you under.

● ● ●

When I was seven, I slammed Mum's hand in the car door, trapping her fingers.

I have never forgotten (will never forget) the sound of Mum's scream. And the sick gray of her face. And me pulling open the door, saying over and over, *I didn't mean to, Mum! Sorry! Mum! God, I'm sorry!*

We took a taxi to the hospital, and yes, I had broken two of Mum's fingers.

Who knew I had that much power?

I called Dad and kept calling, but he didn't answer. And we knew why . . . and wasn't that the reason we'd left in the first place, gone shopping and to the movies and then gotten doughnuts, because neither of us wanted to go home?

When we got back—Mum's fingers splinted and wrapped, a packet of codeine in her bag—there was Dad on the couch, asleep. Wine cask on the side table, shirt half open. Skin and stink and sweat and hair.

Mum sagged at the door.

We walked past Dad, to the dining table, where we sat down.

"I'm hungry, Mum. Do we have anything to eat?" I said.

Mum shook her head. She opened her mouth. She closed it. She sat with her wounded hand in her lap and wept.

● ● ●

Gramps comes back from his polka class at midnight—he wobbles against the living room doorway. "I'm home!" he says.

"Shh, Gramps!" I say.

"Shh yourself." He grins.

I get up from the couch where I've spent the night not calling anyone, just watching show after show tumble from the TV, blue light filling the room. I go over to Gramps, peel him from the doorway, pull off his jacket, and sniff the gin.

"Gramps."

"Yeah, yeah, yeah." Gramps waves me off.

I help him to his armchair. "I'll get you some water."

"Yes. And a ham sandwich. I'm starving!"

"We don't eat ham anymore."

"Jesus. This house—cheese, then."

I slap some cheese and bread together, but when I come back to the living room, Gramps is asleep.

I turn off the TV. Stand in the room, listening to my grandfather breathing. I wonder if he's dreaming of my grandmother. I wonder what it would be like to love someone for so long that when they stop being in your life, your world implodes?

If Gramps heard my thoughts he'd say: "No dwelling! Forward motion only! Who wants to go climb the Harbour Bridge?"

Gramps starts to snore. The sound fuzzes the chair, shunts

tired air through the room. And now, the skin between the past and present thins again, because Gramps sounds like Dad used to sound, flat on his back asleep, and Mum on her knees, sweeping something broken off the hardwood boards.

It was a week after I had broken Mum's fingers. I stood in the doorway, little hand wrapped around the doorframe.

Mum looked up, saw me.

"Mum?"

"Go to bed, sweetie." She sounded like paper, like butterfly wings. She kept sweeping.

Glint of glass in the dustpan. Mum's face all lines and hollows. And maybe it was wet too, but it was hard to see in that light.

I watched for a bit longer. Sweep of the brush, crackle of glass into the dustpan, another sweep—

"Please. George. *Go to bed*," said Mum. And this time she sounded like something else, something harder—

So I went to bed.

I pull a blanket over Gramps. Wrap his sandwich, put it in the fridge, and walk outside. Slip down the dark yard to the dock, sit on the edge, and dangle my feet. The harbor is thick-black and spotted with light—from buoys and boats, from buildings across the water.

I lean back on my hands. Close my eyes. Listen.

Sound of waves slapping the dock poles below.

Clink of rigging from a boat as it rocks.

The hum of fish underwater, bumping noses and telling bed-time stories to their children.

I breathe in. Focus on the hush, the clink, the slap, the hum. The whisper and the quiet.

DELIVERY

(fine-tip pen on paper)

Bird's head lolls and rolls.
Turn and stop and lift,
a glimpse of wrinkled sun, then cool inside.

Bird feels hands. He rises. Lowers.
Hard flat under body. Old man's eyes,
white sky ceiling, false pricks of light.
Then: new voice. New eyes.

Knife comes down,
cuts into Bird's belly, slicing it open.
New man and old man pull out Bird's insides and
lay them on the bench.
Their hands are gentle.

Now there is bird and his insides, and they are two things,
but Bird still feels he is a bird.
He lies on the bench
and waits to see what happens next.

12

Eight a.m.

Windows open. Cool air.

A magpie singsongs in a tree. Susan purrs, circled on my lap. My grandmother's clock ticks and tocks.

The clock is all I've kept of Grammie's things. After the funeral Gramps said, "You can take anything you want, George." He waved his hands to her wardrobe, where her clothes hung in loose, unoccupied lines. In the end I just took the clock, because the clothes smelled too much like Grammie, but I liked the idea of her time and my time becoming the same.

I am at my desk. I haven't quite started work on my art history essay. I've gone for a run and now I'm drawing the feel of morning. And—windows wide—I'm scooping cool into my room before the day heats up. It's going to be sweltering today. Like, *off-the-charts* hot. *Fry-an-egg-on-your car* kind of hot. Bushfire hot.

The fire up north is huge now. Mum and Mel have been looking at the footage on the news after dinner. "Awful," they've said. I have sat beside them, watched people with red eyes standing outside a shelter. Thick smoke. Animals and houses lost.

Everything looks terrible and far away, and I've watched the footage like a movie I want to turn off. Laz would say: "Don't turn away, George. We all need to look." But I don't know if I can.

Laz came over last week. We went to the park at the end point of the peninsula, lay on the grass under sandstone cliffs, and looked up at city-dimmed stars. Laz swigged from a bottle of vodka he'd brought from home, passed it over to me. I took a tiny sip and passed it back.

Laz said, "You know this park will be under water one day?"

"Mmm?" I looked over at him. Sometimes when Laz drank, he got goofy; sometimes he got sad. Which was it going to be?

Laz lifted onto his elbows. "Everything will be gone. We'll be in bunkers. If we're here at all."

"Laz."

He took another swig. "George." He mimicked my voice. Scowled. Sadness, then.

Pre-pregnancy, Tess always came with us for the night drinking and talking under the cliff. If she were here, she and Laz would probably start debating the collapse of society, and I would listen to the fish singing, the planet rotating, the buzzing skin of the earth. But now, I was all Laz had.

Laz could roll himself into a vortex once he got started. He was like Tess, always thinking about death, only Tess's fears were personal, and Laz's took in the whole world.

He sat up. "It's hopeless, George. We're all going to die."

I sat up too. "We've still got time—"

"No, we don't. Nothing's changing fast enough." And then out of his mouth, sliding and sucking, came all the facts:

Did I know about the mining? The drilling? The oil? The fires?

Everywhere's burning, and

Think of the fish, the reefs, the coal,

the fracking, the heating, the cutting, the killing, and

No one gives a fuck, George! We're screaming into the void!

When Laz stopped to take a breath, his truth had rolled us flat. I was silent, trapped under Laz's words.

He sighed. "Shit. I'm sorry, mate."

I tried to speak. Cleared my throat. Tried again: "It's true, though. Don't be sorry. It's fine."

"*Nothing* is fine," Laz said brokenly.

"I know." He was right. What more could I say?

Laz was too sad to fix right now. And there was no point trying to talk to him when he was drunk.

So, I helped him up.

We tottered silently around the foreshore—past the stone steps where off-leash dogs liked to leap into the water in the daytime, past the playground where kids tried to swing and kick the sky— and down to the road. The last bus had gone. I called Adesh. He was at work; he delivered pizza when he wasn't studying drama or being naked in plays.

"Shit," he said. "Wait there, George. I'll come get him between deliveries."

By the time he came, Laz was asleep on the grass.

Adesh opened the car door. "Don't throw up, Lazaros," he warned as I bundled Laz in.

"Yes, sir!" said Laz. He sprawled over the back seat and fell asleep again.

Adesh looked at me, made a face. "Messy."

"Yeah," I said. I wanted to add, "I don't think I can take it," but Adesh didn't know about Dad and he wouldn't know what I meant. And what kind of friend couldn't handle a boy who was sad about the state of the world? "Thanks for coming to get him," I said instead, and shut the door.

I started to turn away, but Adesh called over: "Aren't you getting in?"

"No," I said. "I'm just a quick run from here."

Adesh fixed me with a look. "George. It's the middle of the night. It's not safe. I'm giving you a ride."

So I got into his car. It smelled like pizza. We didn't talk much as he drove. Just watched the streets roll by, feeling the earth twist under us. Creaking, groaning, coming to an end.

Warm air shoves in through the window. It ripples my notebook. I have stopped drawing. Somewhere up north, a living thing burns. My insides squeeze.

Mel knocks on my door. She doesn't wait, just comes in. "George! Your mother is making waffles. Want some? It's a big batch. Woman's going wild. It's going to be a scorcher today. God, imagine if we had AC in this house—would be *glorious*—but then we'd have to rewire the whole place. Maybe after the next commission—"

"Okay. Yep. Sure," I say, in answer to everything Mel's just said and wants to keep saying. I feel like adding: "Also, can you not just barge into my room? I could have been naked in here." But Mel would probably say, "You should lock your door then," or "Good idea, we should all be naked!" or maybe she'd just laugh.

Mel leans over my notebook. "Oh, I like that sketch!" she says.

"Thanks," I say, shutting the book.

"Have you called Calliope, about the teaching?" Mel's picking up some things off my floor and folding them. She doesn't wait for me to answer. "I've also got some work for you at the studio today, if you want. I need a bunch of canvases stretched, but I've got admin stuff to do at home. You could ask Calliope to help? She seems a good egg."

I turn and look at Mel. *Oh?*

Mel goes on. "And can you empty your bin? It's not supposed to overflow, that's not how bins work. Which reminds me—I found an apple core on your bookshelf the other day. It had fossilized."

I let out a long breath.

"I can do the canvases," I say. "I haven't called Calliope yet—I can do it after breakfast. She might be busy though. Sorry about the apple."

"Never hurts to ask!" Mel comes across and hugs me, hard. "Thanks, George. Love you."

"Love you too, Mel," I say.

At breakfast, Gramps gulps down his third waffle like he's carbing up for a marathon. You would never know this guy came home gin-sloppy after midnight last night. Maybe he's not really eighty-four—maybe he lied and is actually in his twenties.

Gramps pours more maple syrup onto his plate. "Hey, who's taking me to the taxidermist guy today?" he says.

Mum and Mel look at each other. "I have a trillion things to do," says Mel.

"I've got to go to work," says Mum.

Everyone looks at me—even Susan, who wouldn't mind a bit

of waffle or more breakfast of any kind. She stares at me from her station by the cat food cupboard.

"Fine," I say. "I'll do it."

"Thanks, Georgie," says Gramps. "You're my favorite of all the women in this house."

Mum rolls her eyes. "Do you want another waffle, Dad?"

"Sure, Sara." He grins. "Now *you're* my favorite of all the women in this house!"

Tess texts while I'm washing the dishes. Mum has gone to work, Mel's on the couch with her laptop, the upright fan on blast, and Gramps is banging around upstairs, probably looking for something he's lost.

Hey, writes Tess. *You didn't write back last night. You all right? You missed out on some really bad cookies*

I towel-dry my hands. Reply: *Sorry. Kind of a weird night*

Yeah? Want to talk about it? I got the farts last night. I think the baby's making me fart. Can babies do that? Or maybe it was the cookies

I look at the screen. I've got a choice. Do I write:

It's okay. Just some stuff happening here. Sorry you've got the farts

or *Yeah, I do want to talk about it. My dad has been messaging, like, constantly. He says he has news. I'm having all these memories. I'm kind of freaking out. Oh, and I might be in love. Sorry you've got the farts*

I picture writing the second option.

Picture Tess not coping with me talking about Dad. Picture her asking a thousand questions about Calliope.

I send Tess the first option.

Tess starts writing back. I see dots dancing. See dots stop. See dots dancing. The dots stop.

She doesn't reply for an hour. At which point the dishes are done, and I'm sitting on my bed, summoning the nerve to call Calliope.

Tess writes: *Sorry, had to go with Mum to get some baby stuff. We picked up a change table for $20 can you believe it? I'm STILL FARTING. Got to go. Have a uni lecture. Love you*

Love you too, I write. I wait for a moment. *Hope the farts settle*

PRAY FOR ME, Tess writes back.

I have typed in Calliope's number. Now all I have to do is call. I stare down at my phone and will it to do the work for me: *Ring Calliope and ask her about all the things. Be charming.*

My phone buzzes in my hand. My insides instantly squiggle—*is it Dad, is it Tess?*—but it's a text from an unknown number.

Wait.

It's from Calliope.

Hi George how are you? This is Calliope. Mel just texted and said you had something to ask me? She gave me your number. Are we going on a spy mission? Will it make my phone self-destruct?

Oh my god. Mel is probably the most impatient woman to ever walk the earth.

I write back: *Hi yeah, I do have something to ask. I was going to get to it, but Mel likes jumping in haha*

OK, she says. *Who are we assassinating?*

ME: *Haha sadly no contract killing today* ☺ *Mel wants to know if you'd like some more work teaching at the Art House?*

Calliope's answer comes in almost before I've pressed send:

SHIT YEAH! ARE YOU KIDDING? OF COURSE!!

ME: *Great! It would be a couple of days a week with me*

CALLIOPE: *Yes, that would be perfect. Can you tell her thank you?*

ME: *Sure and also she has some work today if it's not too short notice?*

CALLIOPE: *Really??? I'd love that. I have less than no money. Is it at the Art House? Your stepmum is like a fairy godmother tbh*

ME: *It's at her studio, stretching canvases*

CALLIOPE: *Okay what's that*

ME: *Haha that's like making canvases. You put the frame together and fix canvas over it. It's not hard*

CALLIOPE: *I've never done it but it sounds good. Yeah I'm 100% in*

ME: *Great! I'll send you the address*

CALLIOPE: *Thanks a lot George!*

I text Calliope the address for Mel's studio.

She replies: *Thanks! btw I loved what you did with your boat yesterday. I got it on film! I'll show you later. See you soon!*

Ah.

Calliope caught me on film, thwacking into the water like a robot dolphin? She has it on *record*, me looking stupid? I have no idea what to say. So I just loveheart the message, and then sit in my room and squirm.

13

Gramps doesn't talk much on the ride to the taxidermy guy. He holds the dead bird in a box on his lap. The bird lies wrapped in thin plastic, freezer bricks at his sides. When we turn corners, the bird's body shifts right, left. His head wobbles, and one gauzy eye stares at the car ceiling.

Once, I flew, the bird says to me. *I coasted beside boats. I hardly had to move my wings.*

We turn another corner. The bird rolls and says: *I will never fly again.*

"Gramps," I say. "I'm not sure this bird wants to be stuffed. Have you considered just burying it? I could take it out in the kayak. I could say a few words."

Gramps shakes his head. "It will be good, George. Just wait and see—this guy is great. He's done full-grown kangaroos. He goes along the highway and finds the least-mashed ones. There's always plenty of them, poor buggers."

"That's really sad."

"Yeah. It is." Gramps nods. A moment passes, then another. I glance across at Gramps. Maybe he's thinking about how sad death is. He gestures to the box. "Want to stuff this bird with us?"

Okay, then.

I consider his offer for about one second. I picture Gramps's dead rabbit, its glass eyes sending despair across the living room. Picture myself standing by Gramps, watching a stranger cut the insides out of the bird. Picture the bird becoming a not-bird, made of wire and stuffing and glue. Picture telling Tess about it . . . and her recoiling.

"No thanks, Gramps. I really do have to get Mel's canvases done."

Gramps shrugs. "Your loss."

At the taxidermist's house, Gramps practically skips down the path.

I'll see you on the other side, calls the bird from his box.

"Good luck," I say, to both of them.

No one replies.

I get to Mel's warehouse space ten minutes early, park the car, and wait for Calliope. It's a maze inside the building—if I don't guide Calliope to Mel's studio, she might get lost forever. Artists and designers and small film companies all work here. Some days when the rooms are all full, I feel the stories thrumming, every color.

Mel brought me here for the first time when I was twelve. It was before we'd gone out in the kayak—we had only just moved into her house. She showed up at my bedroom door one Saturday and said, "Want to make some art with me, George?"

Of course I didn't say no.

I walked into the warehouse building with Mel. Our feet tapped on concrete, steps echoing. We twisted down corridors—right, left, right, right. I thought about leaving crumbs for myself, thought about string; I didn't have either, so I just followed Mel's red coat.

When we got to her studio, I looked up, all around.

Vaulted ceiling. Light lilting in from high windows. Different smells: something acrid, something smoky, something sweet. The floor had dings in it and long streaks of dried paint. Shelves rose up one wall, holding paint tubes and turpentine and brushes in jars. On a long desk, disheveled drawings sat in stacks beside a vase of dead flowers and a tower of books. Against the far wall, canvases stood with their backs to me.

"Want to see some paintings?" said Mel.

I nodded.

Mel flipped a few canvases around—they were as tall as Mel, and five times as wide as me.

Mouths.

All mouths.

Mouths open and shut. Tongues, teeth, lips. Mouths grimacing on blurred faces, lips pressed onto lips. Mouths sneering, smiling, kissing, spitting.

I squeaked. The sound just came out.

Mel put her hand on my shoulder. Laughed. "Yeah, they're a lot to take all together, even for me. That's why I keep them mostly looking at the wall."

She turned the canvases back. I let out my breath.

"Okay, kiddo," she said. "Let's make some art."

We walked through wrinkled light to Mel's long table. She cleared a space, set up some things for us to sketch. She gave me a few sticks of charcoal, didn't tell me what to do or how to do it. We just drew.

We went so long, Mum came by the studio.

"I rang and rang," she said.

Light had started to seep out of the room. I looked up at my mother, charcoal on a cheek, far away.

"Sorry," said Mel.

"Sorry," I repeated.

Mum looked from one to the other. And perhaps we had the same eyes then, like thieves, like people holding secrets, like artists. Mum smiled, her edges soft. She touched my head, bent forward, and kissed it.

Calliope knocks on the car window. "Hey!"

I look up, startled. "Oh hey!" I say, opening the window.

"Aren't you boiling in there? It's so hot." Calliope's in a tank top and shorts today. She looks effortlessly cool.

"Oh, no, I've got the AC going."

Her eyebrows raise. "I see how it is." She smiles.

I flush, embarrassed. I must seem like a climate killer. "Yeah, I guess I shouldn't have—"

"It's okay, George. You wouldn't want to die in there."

But still. I shouldn't have kept the car running. I could have waited inside the warehouse entryway. I didn't think of that. I feel like apologizing. I feel like explaining. But Calliope's already walking in; she's already let it go. I follow her and her red shirt inside.

. . .

Deep in the warehouse space, I open Mel's studio door for Calliope. She steps in, looks up, all around.

I look around too, take it in like I'm Calliope, seeing it for the first time. Then I look at her. Does she like it? Is it magical for her the way it was for me?

"Wow," she says, walking in further. "Wow. This is great."

I smile.

Calliope looks at me. "This space is just for Mel?"

"Yeah. Though I paint here too sometimes."

"Oh, cool." Calliope pauses. "I googled her. Your stepmum's kind of a big deal."

I laugh. "I guess so," I say, but Calliope is right. People study Mel at art school. Last year, she sold a nude self-portrait for what Gramps called a "shit-ton of money." Mel used the money to fix the roof.

Against the far wall, near the kiln, clay and wire sculptures sit on more shelves—all body parts. Tall canvases stand in a stack, facing inwards.

"Want to see one?" I say, pointing to the paintings.

"Sure." Calliope nods.

I cross to the paintings. Flip one around.

It's another pair of testicles. Fleshy and flattened like they're smooshed against glass. Hairy and big as the world.

Calliope squeaks. "Sorry," she says, covering her mouth. "It's just—um—so—"

"I know. They're all like this. Mel likes to get up close. Wait till you see the penises."

Calliope makes a face. "Do I need to see the penises?"

"Well, no. No one ever needs to see penises."

Calliope laughs.

"There are plenty of vulvas too. Just so you know. Equal representation."

"That's a relief." She motions to the canvas. "You can turn that around any time—"

"Oh, yeah," I say, and flip the painting back.

"When does the exhibition open?"

"In a couple of months—after New Year's, I think. Mel's going to basically disappear until then. She's got us teaching classes, and Laz and some of her old subs managing the store. Hopefully no one will destroy the place while she's gone."

Calliope laughs again. She wanders around, looks at some of Mel's sculptures. Her eyebrows rise, keep rising.

Mel's art is intense. And she's going through an even more, shall we say, *intimate* phase than usual. Last month, she described her exhibition concept to us over dinner. "We have such an aversion to our bits," Mel said. "We should be familiar with everything, don't you think? Our body parts shouldn't be strangers to us. *Love yourself! Know your vagina! I say.*"

I focused on my food. God. This family—

Gramps frowned. "Do we need to talk about vaginas tonight, Mel?"

"We've talked about your projects, John, plenty of times." Mel said. "Your bonsais were the center of conversation for weeks, remember?"

"A bonsai and a vagina are not the same thing."

"Depends on your perspective," said Mel.

I didn't even know what that meant. I looked over at Mum.

Mum looked at me. A tiny smile had started forming.

"I'm not just doing genitalia, John. I'll be doing boobs too. So you'll be happy."

"I am not a boob man. Give me a nice, round bottom, I say—" Gramps began.

Mum couldn't help herself. She started to laugh. "Oh my god. The two of you are ridiculous," she said.

"It's your fault!" said Mel, looking over at Mum.

"For forcing us to live together," finished Gramps.

Mum nodded, unfazed. "Yes. That I did. Well done, me." She reached over and squeezed Mel's hand. She suddenly looked really happy.

I loved it when she looked like that.

Inside the studio, I tell Calliope: "Mel's calling the exhibition *LOOK*. All caps. She's planning to set it up so people have to stand really close to everything."

"Sounds special." Calliope smiles. She has moved across to another, smaller stack of canvases, their faces to the wall. "Are these for the exhibition too?"

I step forward. "Oh. No. Those are mine."

Calliope's face lights up. "Can I see?"

"Um." Panic floods my body. I don't show my art to anyone but Tess and Mel, and sometimes Mum.

Calliope sees my face. "I don't have to if you don't want."

"No. No. It's fine," and I feel my *fine* come out glittery like when Tess says it.

Calliope steps away from the canvases. "No. That's okay. I'll see them another time. We have work to do, right?"

"Yeah, we do," I say, relieved. I don't know how I'd explain my art to Calliope. How would I tell her I mostly paint the unpaintable? Like the feel of silence. And the secret thoughts of animals. And the shiver of water under a boat. And the way the sky turns colors so fast, you can't catch it when it changes.

Calliope might look at my canvases and just see a mess.

She steps away from my paintings, and I'm so grateful she isn't looking at them, it takes me a minute to catch the fact she just said, "Another time," as though there'll be one.

For the next hour or so, I teach Calliope how to stretch a canvas. How to slot the stretcher bars together, use the canvas pliers to get tension in the fabric, staple it down, work from the outside in, and finally, tap the canvas to hear the satisfying *whump* of fabric stretched just right.

Calliope is a fast learner; she bends forward and watches my hands move. She says, "Oh, it's like *that*," like I'm a magician showing her my secrets. Then I work on the bigger canvases while Calliope does the smaller ones. The studio fills with the sound of our staple guns firing into the frames and sometimes, Calliope saying, "Oops."

Some of her canvases need a redo, but that's all right. Calliope says, "Thanks, George," so many times I feel like I've done something bigger than put a canvas together. I've taught her a skill; I've solved a problem for her. I know something she doesn't. I'm cool.

We leave the studio with seven new canvases stretched for Mel. My muscles feel good, the same as after a paddle.

Calliope lifts her arms in the air. "I think I pulled something—can you break your arms making canvases? And I think I've got a blister. Look, George." She holds out a hand.

I look, laugh. "It can be like that. The first time I did it I had to rest for a day."

We step outside. It's so hot, our bodies sag as we hit the sunshine.

"Wow. I need a swim," I say.

"Same," says Calliope. She looks at me. "Want to go to the baths?"

"Which ones?"

"The ones near where you flipped your boat like a boss." Calliope grins. "My flat is, like, ten minutes from there. I can lend you a swimming costume, if you want?"

Turns out, Calliope and I live on the same peninsula, only fifteen minutes' walk away from each other.

Another impossible thing. But also true.

Far out. What are the chances?

Fate! Fate! Fate! shouts the shape of Tess on the wind.

14

Calliope and I float like cooled ducks in the harbor baths. The water is delicious.

We both went home first to get our swimmers. "My spare suit might not work, actually. I kind of have . . . a lot of boob going on," Calliope had said, looking down at herself.

I looked at my chest. "Well, I kind of don't have *any* going on," I said, which made her laugh. I dropped her off at her apartment, dashed home, and met Calliope back at the pool, walking too fast in the heat to meet her.

Here in the baths, the harbor is unwilded—a stilted building fences the pool, ropes mark the lanes, and a net stops the sharks. Calliope and I did some fast laps when we first got in. Now, we're just bobbing around, telling each other about ourselves.

I've told her about Mum and Mel, how they found each other at the Art House, how we moved into Mel's house, and how Gramps came to live with us after Grammie died. And I've mentioned—almost as an aside—that my dad lives overseas.

Now, Calliope starts telling me about having a mum and a younger brother overseas, and her dad here. "We went two years ago because Mum got homesick. Her family are Sinhalese, from Sri Lanka, but she grew up in Reading. Dad's family is Sinhalese too, but he grew up here. Anyway, when Mum suggested we go over, Dad was like, 'Sure, let's have an adventure.' It was just meant to be for a few months, and we talked about going to Sri Lanka after that, but then my grandma had a stroke. So we stayed so Mum could look after her . . . and then my grandma died."

"Oh. I'm really sorry," I say.

"It's okay. I didn't know her that well," says Calliope. "She was pretty conservative . . . like, *Marriage is between a man and a woman,* and *Boys can't be girls,* you know? But when she died, Mum got really sad. She enrolled in uni to do her doctorate, which Dad thought would be good for her. Me and Ari got sent to school. He liked it. I didn't, and Dad didn't either. He and Mum started fighting, and then Mum went and fell in love with Terry."

Calliope says the name like it's something stuck to her shoe.

"Terry?"

"Her PhD supervisor." She rolls her eyes. "Such a cliché."

"Oh."

"Yeah, and now Terry and Mum are over there, writing about dead poets, and Mum's pregnant, which is wild. She's forty-five years old. And Ari has made all these friends and never wants to leave. But last month Dad said he wanted to go home. And I didn't want him to be alone, so I came back with him."

"Wow."

"Yeah."

"That sounds really rough."

"Yeah . . . it's not great."

"I'm sorry, Calliope," I say.

Calliope kind of shrugs. We've been kicking lazily up and down the pool as Calliope talks, but now she says, "Thanks, George," and ducks underwater. She cruises, holding her breath, while I think about what it would be like to be separate from Mum. I know how I feel being separate from Dad: anxious sometimes, relieved most of the time. Does Calliope feel even slightly the same way as me? Is it too soon to ask a question like that?

I watch Calliope's legs kick. The water pushes, pulls.

Yeah. It's too soon. I don't talk about Dad to anyone. Of course it's too soon.

So when Calliope bobs back up, I say, "Hey, let's get ice cream," because ice cream makes everything okay.

● ● ●

Dad and I got ice cream in the mountains once. I was six, or maybe five. Mum wasn't with us—I think she was doing a course for her job. So Dad and I took a train west without her. It was winter.

We walked along a gray street in a gray mountain town. I saw shops and bare-boned trees. A steady flit-flit of tourists. A black bird cruising a white sky.

People trudged past with beanies and gloves and heavy coats. Dad talked about *something something* beside me. His words slipped away; wind knifed into my lungs. We didn't have beanies or gloves. We hadn't understood how cold it would be.

We walked past cafés and antiques stores and shops selling hats and honey. There was a bookstore. I wanted to go in. Dad wanted to keep walking,

"It's cold, Dad," I think I said.

"We'll warm up if we walk," I think he said.

Then we were standing at a lookout. The view was endless: green, shadowed canyons and red-ochre cliffs, and closer up, three sky-scraping rocks in a line. Dad had me stand at the fence and smile for a photo.

"I'm cold," I said.

"I'm cold too," he said, and then he started to star jump. "Come on, Georgie, jump with me!"

We did star jumps on the lookout landing. Tourists came by, glanced at us, took photos of the view. I stopped jumping but Dad kept on. Then I started jumping again.

An ice cream van came.

"That's weird," said Dad. "An ice cream van in the middle of winter."

The van sang its ice cream song, trying to lure people in. No one came.

But Dad looked at me and I looked at him and we sent a message to each other with our eyes. Then we were beside the van. Then we were ordering.

Vanilla swirl, dipped in chocolate, for both of us.

I was so little, maybe this memory isn't real? Maybe it's actually a memory of Mum. Maybe I've painted a different story just to have some good colors in here.

But I think Dad and I stood at a lookout in the mountains that day, in the whip of wind, staring out at the wide-open everything. The sky an icy wash above us, the land a crease of shadows below. And I think Dad and I laughed together, and licked and licked the ice cream from our cones.

15

Strawberry for Calliope, chocolate for me.

Our ice cream starts melting the instant we have it in our hands.

We're walking to the park by the ferry wharf, Calliope licking around her cone, trying to catch the drips before they fall. I got a cup for mine—I'm watching it turn to soup before my eyes.

"Hey," she says. "Thanks for this."

I think she means the ice cream first, but then I realize she means the work. "You're welcome. You did great today."

"No"—she glances at me—"I mean, it's nice to hang out with someone besides Dad and my aunt and cousins—I kind of don't know anyone here anymore. We lived further north before we left. Everyone I knew two years ago has basically moved on."

I nod. Pause. "It's been kind of the same for me. I've only been out of school for a year. But Tess and I were this . . . pod. We didn't really know anyone else that well."

Calliope nods. "You two are close, hey."

"Blood pact," I say, and smile.

"How did she get pregnant? If you don't mind me asking?"

"She just kind of decided," I say. "She's pretty impulsive."

"She just decided? At eighteen? That's a bit . . . different."

I hesitate. I want to tell her the story of Tess. But should I tell Calliope the story of Tess? Would Tess mind me telling it? Is it a secret? Does my secrecy extend to Tess too? God, is there anything I can ever say to anyone?

All the thoughts come in a rush, and maybe I look buffeted by the wind of them, because Calliope touches my arm and says, "Long story?"

I let out a breath, half laugh. "Yup."

"Well, I have a minute."

"Do you have a few hours?" I smile.

Calliope looks at me. And it's like she reads through the smile, gets a whiff of the worry, the folded-away stories, all the flinty tucked-in things, because she says, "Yeah, actually, I do."

We are in the park by the water, on a bench in the shade. Our ice cream has gone or melted.

"Huh," says Calliope, after I finish talking about Tess. She nods, really slowly.

My fingers are sticky. My face feels sticky. I glance over at Calliope. Did I share too much? Is she thinking Tess is the weirdest? Or that I should have done more, fixed all the breaks, stopped Tess's boulder rolling?

"I'm sorry," I say. "That was a lot, I know."

"No. It wasn't. It's just—" Calliope shakes her head.

"What?"

"Nothing . . . just, I guess people do funny things sometimes. When they're sad. Or scared."

I am quiet for a bit. "Like your mum?"

Calliope nods. "Yeah, like my mum."

A ferry crosses the water. Something in me feels open, like I've taken out something hard and turned it over, given it a little light. I wonder if Calliope feels the same way?

Calliope looks at me. "Does Tess still think she's going to die super young?"

"I'm not sure. She doesn't really talk about it anymore. I kind of don't want to ask. I mean, Tess always has a list ready, of the things that might kill her."

"Hmmm. Well, our days *are* numbered," she says, like she's sitting under a tree having a Zen moment.

I smile. "Yeah. And Tess acts like hers have almost run out. Like it's going to be over any second, and she's trying to cram everything in now."

Calliope nods. "It can be like that," she says. "When my grandma died, Mum went all . . . *busy*. Like, she wouldn't stop doing things and she wanted to clear out my grandma's stuff and put it in storage and sell the house before we'd even taken a breath, you know? And then suddenly it was all about doing her doctorate, and then, she wasn't really with us after that."

I nod.

"I don't even know if she's happy," finishes Calliope.

"Yeah," I say. "Same with Tess. She *says* she is, but—"

"—but maybe they're just saying it. With Mum, I kind of don't feel like digging to find out if it's a lie."

I look at Calliope. That's it. Like, here's Tess, careening, not wanting to look at what she's doing . . . she's just going and going.

And now that I think about it, Gramps is too. Maybe Calliope's mum is the same? And maybe Calliope and I are both doing our best to stay upright while the people we love boulder down hills getting pregnant or having sex with retirees.

But now Calliope shrugs, as if to say, *I'm done talking about my mum.* She says, "Is Tess all ready? For the birth?"

I nod, follow her lead. "I think so," I say. "As ready as anyone who's never done it before. Her mum will be there. And her aunt. And I'll be there. We've got this birth plan—"

"Oh, yeah. That's right."

"It's got essential oils on it. And a bouncy ball. And, like, a pretty wild playlist."

"That sounds cool. I'm glad she'll have you all there." Calliope pauses. "Don't suppose she needs someone to video it?"

I look at her. "Are you serious?"

Calliope laughs. "Well, not really. But I'm picturing it, as like a time-lapse. It would be amazing."

I picture the birth on film, sped up: Everyone rushing around, all of us busy puppets, Tess's mouth opening in a scream, her face going red, and a baby whooshing out like the sun from behind a cloud, only faster. And a lot gooier.

"I can see it now—" says Calliope.

"So can I—" I say, and smile. "I think Tess would say no."

"Understandable. Not everyone wants to see themselves launching out babies at high speed."

"Yeah."

We grin at each other. Then we're quiet. A ferry comes into the wharf. A bird hops on the grass in front of us, looking for lunch.

Calliope nudges my elbow. "Speaking of which," she says. "Want to see my film of you doing that thing?"

Ah. I was really hoping we'd never mention me doing that thing again.

Calliope pulls her camera out of her bag. "It's so great, George, wait till you see," she says, and finds the movie of me tipping over into the water.

She presses play. I watch myself splat and pop up. She plays it again. I splat. I pop up.

"Great," I say. "Um, thanks for showing me."

"It looks so cool." says Calliope. She plays it again, watches the screen. "How did you learn to do that?"

"Mel taught me."

"Yeah? She kayaks too? What can't she do?"

"Yeah." I pause, then say, "I don't normally flip, by the way. It was a mistake."

"A good mistake."

"Thanks." I try to laugh. "I felt pretty stupid."

"Ah." Calliope looks down at her camera. "Okay. But, just saying, your 'stupid' looked great to me. Maybe you can take me out on the water sometime? Teach me to do it too?"

I picture being out on the water, in the quiet, with her. "It takes a lot of practice. As you can see, it's not very elegant."

She shakes her head. "You're amazing out there. I don't know how you do it. You look like a ballet dancer. Or maybe like a seal, if it was kayaking."

I laugh, self-conscious. I look amazing? I . . . look like a seal?

Calliope continues. "Anyway, I'm never elegant. You saw my cartwheels, after all. Not exactly a thing of beauty." And then she smiles.

God.

Sunshine. Poetry. Unicorns.

This girl is lovely.

Late afternoon.

Calliope has filmed the ferry coming into the wharf and everyone getting on and off. It's a time-lapse. When she's finished filming, we bend our heads over the little screen and watch it back. It looks great—the ferry gliding in and people scurrying like ants on and off the boat and a sailboat crisscrossing the water behind the ferry and the water sparkling. It's how looking back at something should be: bright and the good kind of busy. Nothing fuzzy or pinching. No swirling eels.

Calliope tucks her camera into her bag. "Sad to say, I've got to go, George. I've got a trial shift at this pub tonight."

"Oh, for a job?"

"Yeah. If I get it that means I'll have scored two jobs in one day!"

"Legend."

"You know it." She grins.

We walk to a corner. "Well, I'm this way," she says, and points.

"And I'm that way." I point in the other direction.

"Okay," she says. We both don't move. "Thanks for today, George."

"No, thank *you*," I say. "You were great. Mel will probably text soon about paying you. Don't let her forget! She gets distracted. Like, she'd be a terrible pilot—everyone would end up in Tahiti or Paris, or basically, anywhere shiny."

"Got it." Calliope laughs. "And, hey, let me know when you want to flip me over in your boat."

I nod. "Sure. And maybe I can see more of your movies sometime."

"Okay. I do post my stuff online . . . I can send you a link, if you want to look"—she scrunches her nose—"if you haven't, um, got anything else to do?"

"I don't have anything else to do." I smile.

"Well. Cool. All right. I mean, they're just little things." And now she reaches forward and gives me a quick hug. "I'm going to go now," she says, "and not think about you looking at my movies. I'll see you at the Art House tomorrow? For teaching? Yeah?"

"Yeah. See you soon." I wave goodbye.

My body feels bright after the hug. Bright at the thought of taking Calliope out on the water. A thousand colors because today has been perfect.

16

Home.

Freshly showered—ice cream, salt, and sweat washed off—I plonk on the bed beside the cat and check my phone. Calliope has already sent a link to her account.

Enjoy! ☺ *I mean if you want to hahaha*

I click on the link so fast, the cat twitches.

Calliope's feed is filled with tiny, fifteen-second films. A lot of them are time-lapses—people and places turned into life at high speed. Some movies have little animated lines outlining the images, like a painting on top of a painting.

I see two old hands holding knitting needles. They clack together, spooling out a red-lined scarf. I watch cars zip around a roundabout, with what looks like the Eiffel Tower in the distance. I see a chess game start and finish. See the London Eye, night spinning. Wind tipples a sapphire sea, and the camera pans slowly across whitewashed houses, the windows blue-trimmed. Tall grass bends in a foggy field, cows blobbing indistinctly in the distance.

There are no photos, just movies. It looks like she's been all over the place. She must have filmed a lot while backpacking in Europe. And you can tell when she moved back here. Everything turns into harbor, harbor, harbor.

The second-to-last film is of her, cartwheeling from the other day. It's slowed right down. Animated water flies from her hands and feet. It's mesmerizing. The last film, posted last night, is of boats: a close-up of them passing each other. It looks like the same place I saw her, maybe just before I paddled into view and tipped over.

I'm glad Calliope didn't put me in the film. Maybe she knew, even before we talked, that I wouldn't like people watching me make a spectacle of myself.

Calliope's movies feel like windows, like I'm peering into a dolls' house, or a snow globe with living things inside it. This is what Calliope sees; this is *how* she sees. I could watch them over and over.

So I do.

Now it's night. Tepid air slouches in through the window. A possum scrabbles up a tree. I've done everything today except my art essay. I've watched Calliope's movies, sorted my notebooks, trimmed my terrible fringe, made it worse. I helped Mum make dinner, then ate it in my room—Gramps came back from the taxidermist's glowing and wanted to tell us over spaghetti about the bird's guts.

Mel was still at the studio. Mum pinched her nose with her fingers and said, "No, Dad. It's been a huge day. Another time." She looked headachey.

Gramps looked at me. "Want to hear about the bird, George?"

I hesitated. "Sorry, Gramps. I've got a uni assignment."

His face fell. "Fine," he said.

"Another time?" I kissed his weathery cheek, took my plate upstairs, and watched Calliope's movies again.

The clock clicks to 9:30. I put my phone on my bed, facedown, and force myself to look away from one screen and to another. Two days from now, by midnight, I need to have written two thousand words on the Lesser Known Dada-ists, and Their Influence on the Period as a Whole. I open my computer, open the essay. Look at my starting paragraph:

Duchamp is certainly the most well-known member of the Dada movement, but we must not forget those whose legacy he followed and those who followed him—

I read through what I've written. It's not great.

Am I almost finished, at least? I look at the word count.

Oh.

I try writing another sentence.

If one considers the tenets of Dadaism and the construct of deconstructionism, it could be argued—

The phone buzzes on my bed beside the cat. Susan wakes up, lifts her head. I roll my chair over to the bed and flip the phone over.

It's Dad. Calling at ten like he'd threatened.

I let the call ring out. Roll back to my desk. Look at my essay— and Dad calls again.

The cat looks across at me, says, *You going to get that?*

I let it ring out. One minute later, he calls again.

The phone buzzes through the bed, through the floor and down the wood frame of the house, into the earth, disturbing the worms, the memories, the once-upon-a-time, the always.

The cat hops off the bed, tail flicking, and leaves the room.

The earth groans. *Stop that racket, George.*

I roll my chair over to the bed. And send Dad a message.

I'm doing my assignment, Dad

He messages back: *When is it due?*

Soon. Very soon

Today?

No

Well, then. Let's talk. Please. Georgia. It's important.

My ribs clank. Last time I spoke to Dad we had a brief chat about nothing. I think he said *Happy birthday*. I think he said *I love you, Georgia* but I didn't say it back.

I don't reply.

I don't want to talk to my father.

A minute goes by. Maybe he's going to leave me alone?

Another minute.

The phone starts ringing again.

It rings and rings and rings and rings and rings and rings and rings.

The man is relentless. If I don't answer, he'll call until my phone combusts.

I reach for the phone. Press answer.

"Hello, Dad," I say.

"Hello, Georgia," Dad says.

His voice sounds like cardboard. His voice sounds like empty space. His voice lifts from his body in Seattle, shards up through clouds and the dead light of stars, thunks against a satellite, topples and tumbles towards me, ready to slam me flat.

17

Five minutes into the call, Dad tells me he is dying.

"What?" I say. "Sorry, what?"

"Yes. I hate to tell you over the phone—"

"Like, when?"

"Two years, three years maximum."

Shit. Really? Oh my god. Shit.

But all that comes out is:

"Oh."

He has heart disease, Dad says. The precise term for what will kill him is *alcoholic cardiomyopathy*.

"Incurable at this point, I'm sorry to say," he says.

"Does Mum know?" I ask.

"No," says Dad. "Don't tell her, please, Georgia. I don't want her to worry."

"Oh, so, just me then."

"Yes. I thought . . ." He coughs. "You've got a level head. You know your mother—so emotional."

I don't say anything. I know my mother. I know what we have seen.

Dad already died once, when I was nine. It was a heart attack. He was brought back to life by a stranger.

Dad had just left a restaurant after a boozy lunch with clients. The stranger was passing by when Dad fell onto the sidewalk. The man whacked at Dad's chest with his fists, huffed breath into Dad's blank lungs. He shouted Dad's clogged heart awake, kept it beating long enough for the paramedics to come and shoot drugs into Dad's veins.

After the surgery, Dad lay in his hospital bed—wires on his skin, delirious from the meds. I sat by the bed and stared at him.

Dad stared back. He didn't know who I was.

I remember Mum saying to Dad: "Karl, the doctors say you're very lucky." I remember her crying by his bedside as he slept.

The doctor said, "The operation was successful, Karl, but your heart is very vulnerable. You can't keep drinking—if you do, you will die." This was before he noticed me in the corner of the room and asked if there was someone who could look after me while he talked to Mum.

I remember thinking: *If you keep drinking, Dad, you'll die.* Before I left the room, I looked over at Dad in the bed. Tubes and wires, the monitor and its ratcheting hills, light beeping, light lifting and falling. My fingers tingled. Fear moved in sparks along my arms and legs. I remember thinking: *Will you die tonight? Are you dying? Will you die tonight?*

After his heart attack, Dad promised he wouldn't drink again, not a single drop. He said, "I'm sorry, Sara. I promise, I promise." There were kisses. There were talks and hugs. Mum walked around in a relief cloud for months.

And then the lake happened.

We'd set up camp, made sausages, burned our marshmallows. And sometimes I remember, sometimes I forget, how Mum saw Dad pop open his beer, and she sucked in a breath.

"You brought beer, Karl?" she said sharply.

"Just a six-pack, come on Sara, don't be like that, we're on holiday—"

Mum sat by the fire and stared into it. I sat opposite her. I watched the smoke roil around us. The smoke caught in my lungs. I choked and coughed until tears streamed.

Dad said, "Move away from the fire, silly. You'll keep coughing if you stay there."

I stepped around the fire, sat away from the smoke. Mum brought me my inhaler and a glass of water. I sucked in the medicine, gulped the water down. Then Mum touched my leg. "Time for bed," she said.

That wasn't the last time Dad drank while he and Mum were together.

The last time was two weeks after the lake. Mum and Dad had been having these hushed, endless fights—I could hear their voices, garbled and slithering through the gap under my door. I could hear the pinch and rise of Mum's voice, like a balloon with the air squeaking out. I could hear the jellied murmur of Dad. I pictured him on the couch with a beer in his hand.

Other nights, Mum's and Dad's voices would be hard, like rocks splitting and slamming. I'd pull up my sheets and blanket and put the pillow on my head, like I was crawling into a crack in a cave.

The last day Dad drank before he left, he had just been kicked out of a pub, taxi dumping him on the roadside by our front lawn. Dad was laughing and fumbling with his pockets. The taxi driver was yelling at him.

I ran down the driveway, Mum close behind. I stood on the grass by the road and Mum said, "Karl, go inside. I'll pay." But Dad didn't go inside; he teetered on the grass like a tilted windmill, still laughing.

The driver took Mum's money, looked at Dad. "You should be ashamed of yourself, mate. You've got a kid and a nice lady here. What are you doing?"

As the taxi drove away, Dad came to. He twisted and shouted at the taxi: "Fuck you!" And then he bolted down the road after it, past kids playing handball in the cul-de-sac—shouting *FUCK YOU, MATE!*

COME BACK!

I'LL FUCK YOU UP!

—and then around the corner he went and slipped out of sight.

Mum looked like she was going to run after him, but then she saw the neighbors' houses with their windows open and the children stopped and staring. She ran into the house for the car keys.

I was already in the front seat when she came back. "No, George, stay home," she said, but I wouldn't leave. So Mum and I drove around and around till we found Dad. He was still running.

"Get in, Karl. Come on, Karl, get in. Please stop, please," said Mum, but Dad wouldn't and Mum kept pleading and Dad kept running until the ground dipped and Dad tripped, and splat, fell down.

I remember looking out the window at him. He was sprawled on the grass like a squished bug.

I remember thinking: *Are you dead, Dad? Have you died yet?*

●　●　●

Over the phone I say, "I have to go."

And Dad says, "All right, Georgia." He coughs again, lightly. "Let's talk soon. There is a lot to discuss, don't you think? I was wondering—"

"Yeah. Yeah. Sure. Later?"

"Okay."

"Okay."

"Well, take care."

And I say, "You too."

I tap the button on my phone, and Dad's voice stops sucking the air from the room.

I click on my bedside lamp. Stand up.

I pull on my wind-jacket. Shove on my sneakers. Grab my phone, key, and inhaler. Go down the stairs and out the door and onto the path.

And run.

I run past fig trees and white-fenced yards, past chrome-and-concrete houses and cars tucked into their beds. I run uphill, downhill. I turn right, left, left. I run towards the park at the point of the peninsula. The sky is black on black on black.

I don't listen to music. It's not safe, everyone says, for a girl to run after dark, so I stay alert.

Fact: I am a girl, running alone at night. I might die.

Fact: My father will be dead in three years or less. He might die tomorrow. Maybe he's dying right now.

Tick tock. Foot thump, heart thump.

I try to focus on the movement of my body, my breath in, out.

Keep an eye out for murderers.

Don't think about:

Dad dying, Dad leaving, Dad falling, Dad drinking,

Dad drinking, Dad falling, Dad leaving, Dad dying—

I try and outrun it all.

I get to the park. I run the curling paths, past trees and bushes and rocks and the ghosts of gas tanks and fences and benches. I run down the steps and along the water until I reach the point where the land stops, stone-walled, and waves slap and lick. I lean against the wall. Try to catch my breath.

The harbor is a black sheet, dotted with distant light. I feel my blood move, my bones tick, my skin/fingertips/toes/hair fizz. I feel my body straining, leaning, like if I could, I'd leap over the wall and onto the water, gallop over it like Jesus, run under the Harbour Bridge and past the Opera House, heels flicking the wallowing ferries, into the chop and swell where the Heads part, race between the great cliffs and all the way out to sea.

My breath slows.

Blood pumps. My chest thrums.

Inside my body, memories turn over themselves, burning. Under the water, the fish move, swift silver bodies, rippling through the dark.

Seattle, *thirteen*

The last time I saw Dad was five years ago.

Dad had written from Seattle, a lot. He said he was doing well and he was sober. He sent letters and photos and sorrys via email for six months. We talked on the phone. He said he was going to therapy; he said he was working. He said he wanted me to visit him.

He said he couldn't wait to see me.

Mum wanted to believe him.

I did too.

So the plan was me + Dad + three weeks + a Seattle winter instead of my Australian summer, and maybe I'd see snow?

Mum stood at the airport gate and said, "If you need me, I'm just a phone call away, okay? And like, a flight. You can come back anytime." She felt paper thin when I hugged her.

Mel stood beside Mum. She leaned forward and hugged me, hard. "Don't put up with any shit, George," she said. "All right?"

"Okay." I nodded.

Mum kind of hiccupped then—she tried to turn it into laughter, but none of us was fooled.

I descended through cloud, landed under a grim and dripping sky.

At the airport, after Dad squeezed me hello and said how big I'd gotten, he said, "Did you see Mount Rainier?"

"No." There was a mountain, that I should have noticed?

"Oh, that's a shame!" said Dad. "What about the Olympic Mountains? No? They're gorgeous. You can hike up there in summer. Not now, of course. I mean, you don't really go in winter."

He was kind of babbling. *Dad, look outside,* I thought. *You can't even see the sun.*

But Dad was scattered, distracted, nervous. We got in a taxi. Dad kept looking at his phone, and reaching over and touching my knee, maybe to check I was real. He fidgeted with his watch, kept undoing it and doing it up. Tapped and tapped the side of the car where the door handle was, like he was thinking of jumping out.

I alternated between watching Dad jiggle and looking out the window. A big circle stadium. SUVs and trucks galloping over the ten-lane freeway. City buildings sliding by. Dad pointed out the Space Needle; I craned my neck to see.

We rode over a bridge and a lake—houseboats and boats on the water. Then we were off the freeway. I looked at streets with apartment blocks and clapboard houses and houses and sidewalks and more houses, and then the taxi stopped.

We got out in front of a bungalow. It was green and white. It had a porch out the front, a big tree in the yard, and a straight path to the door.

"Here we are!" Dad said. His voice was like a remote-controlled car, revving, bright.

Dad paid the driver; we got out of the car with my bags. A woman appeared in the doorway. Pink-flushed face. Loud orange hair. Purple-striped leggings.

"Oh! Here you are!" she said. She clapped her hands and flung herself down the path.

I looked at Dad. He hadn't mentioned a woman, not in all his emails and phone calls. Was the woman his neighbor? A second later, I was trapped in arms and boobs and the smell of something I couldn't catch.

"Hello, darling! It's so good to have you here," crooned the woman.

Over the woman's voice I could hear Dad laughing nervously, like he'd been found breaking or stealing something. I twisted my head to look at him—he stood on the path and twitched. When the woman released me, Dad said, "Francine, this is Georgia."

"Shit. I know that, babe," said the woman.

Francine. Her breath smelled like strawberries, that's what it was. I stepped back.

"Georgia," continued Dad, "this is Francine. My girlfriend."

I looked from one to the other to the other.

"You going to say anything, cricket?" said Francine.

When I didn't say anything, Francine laughed. Her voice was gravelly, like actual gravel was rolling around in her throat.

"Sorry. She's tired," said Dad.

"Oh! You're tired?" said Francine.

I nodded.

"Well, I've made pancakes! That'll fix you right up!"

Down the path we went—me lugging my bags, Dad and Francine walking ahead. Francine had her arm linked with Dad's and was whispering something into his ear. "She . . . So . . . Like you said . . ."

Dad looked over his shoulder at me.

"Want help with your things, sweetheart?" he said, but it was too late. We were already at the door. We were already inside.

Francine put three pancakes on my plate, plopped a mound of choc-chip ice cream on top, and smothered everything in syrup. Handed me a fork.

"Get that into you—you could use some plumping up." Francine smiled and then coughed suddenly, like a seal barking. "Sorry! Got a throat tickle!" She went over to the counter and glugged from a bottle of cough medicine, swigged it straight like it was juice. Then she leaned on the counter and glanced at Dad, who was standing next to the fridge. "You want some pancakes, babe?" she said.

"No, no," he said. He rubbed his arms.

"You cold? Let's turn up the heat!" Francine moved towards the thermostat on the wall.

Dad said, "No, Francine, I'm fine."

But Francine turned up the dial on the thermostat. "Can't have us all getting sick! Just me," and she cough-barked again. She picked up the bottle and swigged.

I forked a mouthful of pancake. It wasn't cooked inside, so basically, I bit into batter. While Francine was gulping her medicine, I grabbed a tissue and spat the goo out. I ate some ice cream off the top. Felt sick.

Dad leaned against the fridge. He looked sick too. Were we both going to puke on our first day? Was this how it would go?

He said, "Francine, how much of that have you had?"

"Oh, sweetie, just enough!" Francine laughed. Barked like a seal. Laughed again.

Turned out, Francine was, as Tess would say: "Shit-faced."

How about that?

At some point, Dad picked up the medicine bottle. "No more of this, okay?" He went to take it away.

Francine lunged for it like a cat. "Oh, buddy, that's not going to happen!" she said, and pulled it out of Dad's hand.

And then it looked like they might have an actual fight there in the kitchen, like two mud wrestlers—Francine snatching, Dad grabbing, Francine making this *squealing* sound and Dad grunting, which is when I threw up all over the floor.

And wasn't that a special beginning for us all?

Francine was some kind of assistant at Dad's work. Dad didn't see clients anymore, he said. He was a "consultant" now. He also helped at the front desk sometimes, taking phone calls and making appointments. "Small office," he said. "It's good to pitch in." Dad said he and Francine had been going out for a few months. Dad said his new job was much better, *much less stressful than the old one, haha!*

Dad sat on the arm of the couch and talked to me while Francine cleaned up the kitchen. I lay on the couch, wet cloth on my forehead.

I said, "Why didn't you tell us about her?"

"Oh, you know. Your mother gets so—" Dad waved his hands.

"Kind of an important detail, Dad."

"Yeah? Well, Francine and I haven't been all that serious, not until recently."

"How recently?"

"Oh, well. You know . . ." Dad waved his hands again.

This is how he always was: Wave a hand and maybe the questions would disappear. Wave a hand and turn a lie into something true.

Francine trotted in. "All cleaned up! No problem!" She smiled, her face flushed, fizzy. "You feeling better, kiddo?"

"Yes." I nodded, tried to smile.

A dog came wandering in behind Francine. Trembly legs and tangly fur. Old poodle with curls over its eyes.

Francine said, "Ah! Trixie, meet Georgia."

Trixie?

The dog looked up at me. Sniffed my outstretched hand.

Hello, she said.

"Hello, Trixie," I said.

For the record, the dog messaged with her tail, her eyes, her ears, *I would have preferred Boudica, Ancient Warrior.*

I looked deeply into her eyes. I promised I would never call her Trixie again.

Thank you, she said.

We breathed in. Breathed out.

"All right then!" Dad slapped his hands on his knees and stood up. "You look much better. Let's get you out and about!"

"Yay!" said Francine, grinning like a sparkler. "Georgia, we have so much to show you!"

. . .

We moved through Seattle in the rain, riding in another taxi, which stopped whenever Dad asked. Dad rode in the front and Francine sat in the back with me.

We drove past trees and yards and houses. Dad pointed at a café he liked. A bookstore. Then we saw a troll under a bridge— a big concrete thing with hubcaps for eyes. Dad asked the taxi to stop. Under one of the troll's huge hands sat an actual Volkswagen car, cemented in. Two kids in puffy pink jackets clambered up the troll's side. People took photos. One man lay under the troll's other hand and pretended he was about to be eaten.

Dad said, "Want to climb it, Georgia?"

"No, thank you," I said.

The taxi moved on. We went over a bridge. We went up a hill, wound around narrow streets, and stopped at a lookout. You could see the whole city. "Do you want to get out and look?" said Dad.

"Sure," I said. We stood outside in the wet while the taxi waited.

Dad pointed out all the things he thought were important. Francine told me the history of each important thing.

"Want to take a photo?" said Francine when she took a breath. She stopped a stranger walking past in a green jacket. "Can you take our photo?"

When the woman said of course, Francine said, "Oh, thank you!" And when the woman handed back the phone, Francine looked at her in her hijab and said, "And where are you visiting from?"

"Nowhere," said the woman. "Born right here." Her mouth set in a line.

The woman looked at me. I wanted to tell her: "I don't belong to these people," but there wasn't room in the air for me to speak.

After the lookout, we went to see a market by the water. Dad paid the cab and it splished away through puddles.

We walked in under a red neon sign. I stood and watched men in bloody aprons throw fish at each other. One threw the fish and the other caught it with his bare, hairy hands.

We walked around. Francine bought mussels and pomegranates.

All through the afternoon, Francine told me the history of the Troll and the Lakes and the Bridges and the Buildings and the Market and the History of Pomegranates, because that was also important, the history of pomegranates.

The markets were crowded, noisy—full of moving bodies and smells and sounds. My stomach squeezed.

Francine kept putting her arm around me.

Dad kept saying, "Are you having fun, sweet pea?"

"Sure," I said.

The dark sloped in, and we went home for dinner.

In the kitchen I said, "I'll just send Mum a message," and Dad and Francine glanced at each other.

"How about we eat first, sweetie?" said Francine.

"Help me with these bags will you, Georgia?" said Dad.

We unpacked the bags from the markets. Dad and Francine had not stopped at shellfish and pomegranates. There were candles— "Sandalwood is my favorite smell in the world!"—and earrings for my mother—did she wear earrings? "Oh, maybe she'll pierce her ears one day!"—and a teal shawl—"Such a gorgeous color!"—and some ceramic bowls for when they had miso, and didn't they have a funny story about the time they had miso?

Francine's face was red. The room was hot. The kitchen smelled like dead fish and Francine's breath.

At dinner, Dad served up creamy mussel fettucine.

I hadn't eaten seafood since I was ten.

Dad said, "Shit, sorry, Georgia. I forgot."

Francine said, "Oh, I didn't know! Just scoop them out, Georgie, put them on the side."

Dad poured lemonade into glasses. Francine said, "No wine?"

He gave her a Look.

Francine asked me about school. "Do you have lots of friends?"

"Um," I said, "I have friends."

"Are you as shy with them as you are with me? Haha!"

I looked at Dad. "I'm not—"

"I loved school," Francine said. "I never wanted to leave!" She scooped mussels and pasta into her mouth. Chewed.

"That's nice," I said.

"And do you know what you'd like to do when you finish?"

I drank my lemonade. I tried to think of an answer. I looked at Dad; he looked at his plate.

"Georgia?" Francine leaned forward.

I leaned back. "Um. I don't know yet."

"Oh, you don't know? I'm sure you have some ideas. I wanted to have my name on a building! I'm almost there, haha! You're a smart girl—do you get good grades?"

"Yes," I said.

Francine opened her mouth to say more. Closed it.

The mussel smell wafted from my plate. The house was too hot. I peeled off my sweater.

"You hot, darling?" said Francine. And off she leaped to the thermostat.

Then Francine asked me more questions about school and my friends and my future and did I do any sports? She had done gymnastics in high school; she could do a backflip once upon a time; had I ever tried a backflip?

Mel always said, whenever you were asked questions you didn't feel like answering, to "just be the breeze." So, I answered Francine in bite-size sentences. I nodded, smiled, moved my food across my plate. And Dad just sat and listened to Francine's questions go around and around.

Francine chugged her lemonade. Glass empty, she put it down. Blinked. And said, "Well, it sure is nice to meet you, Georgia."

"You too," I said.

Dad smiled, relieved. "I knew you girls would get along!" he said.

At nine, Francine and Dad showed me my room. My bed was the fold-out couch in their study. Did I have enough blankets and was the room warm enough and did I have enough pillows?

I looked over at the bed. It was buried in cushions.

"I sure do," I said.

Francine kissed me on the cheek. Dad hugged me.

"Good night, Georgia," they said, two faces like goblins at the door.

"Night."

The door shut and I heard Francine whisper: *"Jesus, Karl."*

"Shhh," said Dad.

I sat on the bed edge. It squeaked. I looked around: Framed prints of over-saturated sunsets on the wall. An old timber desk with little drawers. A whole set of old encyclopedias on a shelf. "Feel free to read these!" Francine had said when we walked in. "They were my dad's, *mayherestinpeace!*"

I pulled out my phone to message Mum and Mel. I had asked about the Wi-Fi password after dinner and Dad said, "We were actually thinking it might be nice to go screen-free this visit, Georgia." He reached out and held Francine's hand.

Francine said, "You must spend a lot of time on your phone, with all your chats and snaps and games. So, while you're here, let's be cave people!"

Dad said, "Francine read an article about the positive benefits of taking time away from your screen. It does wonders." He said it like he'd read the article too.

"Tomorrow we're going on a bike ride. Let's leave our phones behind!" said Francine.

"It'll be great!" said Dad.

Their voices had been full of *pep*, but their eyes gave it away. Both Dad and Francine were deeply unconvincing, terrible liars. They'd be bringing their phones tomorrow, and checking them too. But right then, they held hands on the couch and spoke like evangelists.

"Okay?" said Dad.

"Sure," I said.

I wandered around the study, found the Wi-Fi password on a Post-it note on the side of the bookshelf. Logged on, and sent a message to Mum and Mel:

Guess what . . .

They replied within two minutes.

MUM: *Seriously????????*

MEL: *Oh, no, George. Really?*

I wrote back: *Yeah, but it's okay. Really. It's kind of funny, you know?*

I imagined a story where this was funny. I imagined the drawing of it: Me meeting the secret girlfriend. Me puking on the kitchen floor. The taxi ride and the shopping and "Are you having fun?" and "Let's be cave people" and hands held on the couch.

My phone lit up. It was Mum and Mel, calling.

We whispered together under lamplight.

"Do you want to come home?" said Mum. She added, "God. I could cry." And then she did.

"No. It's all right. Really. I'm doing what you said, Mel."

Mel said, "What's that?"

"Being the breeze."

Mel laughed. "Good girl."

"George, just say the word and you can come home. Or if you need me to come to you, I'll do it."

I knew Mum would, even though we didn't have the money for a last-minute flight around the world. People only had that kind of money in movies.

"Will you be okay, sweetie?" said Mel.

"I'll be okay."

"I love you," said Mum.

"Love you," said Mel.

"I love you too," I said to them both, my voice flipping into space and down to them, landing on the couch or in the kitchen, landing safely in our house by the water.

Then they were gone, and I was alone.

I thought about telling Tess next. One day in, and I missed her with my entire body. She'd already sent a ton of messages, saying, *Did you land safely????* and *I MISS YOUUUU!!* But Tess wouldn't like my news. She would probably get upset, and I'd be too far away to help her. So I put the phone away. Tucked myself into bed and tried to sleep.

Middle of the night, I heard a scratch.

A whine. Then another scratch.

I crept out of bed—*squeakgroansqueak*—and opened the door.

Two dark, liquid eyes looked up. I put out my hand. The dog sniffed.

"Hey," I said.

The dog licked. Cold, wet, snuffle nose. Raspy tongue. It was the nicest thing that had happened all day.

I went back to bed. Dog followed. I got in—*squeaksqueak-groan*—and the dog put two paws up on the mattress.

Up?

I patted the space beside me. The old dog heaved herself up. The bed shrieked and rattled. I held my breath. The dog did too. Would we break the bed? Would Francine run in, brandishing her high school yearbook? Would the house come alive with shouts?

Silence outside.

Squeak-snuffle inside.

The dog settled in against my body. I ran my hands through her fur. In time we fell asleep, two bodies pressed together.

Francine woke me at eight.

"Good morning, sleepyhead!"

Francine's face hovered over mine like a moon. Her voice was glittery, like pepper in your eyes.

I blinked up at her.

Francine frowned. "Oh. I see Trixie found you."

I peered at the dog. The dog looked at me. *I am a noble breed,* she said. *Once upon a time, I would have eaten her.*

"Off you get, Trixie! Bad girl!" Francine flapped her hands.

The dog lumbered off the bed.

"She's not supposed to sleep on there," Francine said.

"Oh. I'm sorry."

The dog nosed the door open.

"Bad girl, Trixie!" said Francine again.

Fuck off, said the dog. And padded out.

The dog was sent to her bed in the alcove off the kitchen. She had been inherited from Francine's father last year. Her dad had died of emphysema—so sad!—and left Francine one old dog and—*haha*—a whole lot of bills! Francine didn't want to keep the dog but of course she couldn't put the dog down! Anyway, Trixie wouldn't last long. Look at her. It would be a mercy when the dog went. *Haha!*

Francine's breakfast skills were poor. She kept pulling things out of cupboards and putting them back. Burning oats on the stove. Saying "Fuck!" then saying "Oh, sorry, sweetie!"

"I can get my own breakfast," I said. "I don't mind."

Francine said, "But you're our guest! Sit back and relax!"

The porridge (third time lucky) tasted like watery cardboard. I covered it with sugar. Francine moved around the kitchen, filling the space with words.

Bike ride! Picnic! Did I know? History of Seattle? Had I been before?

Nice to have some days off work! Work was hard but important!

And what did I want to eat for lunch? Did I eat meat? Why not? Protein!

Where is your dad? He is such a sleepyhead! Funny!

Dad came in then, his face leaden, his ashy energy swamping the room.

"Georgia," he said. He stood over me. His bulk made the air thin. "I just heard from your mother."

Francine and the dog and I sucked in our breaths.

. . .

My phone went into a drawer in the study.

I could talk to Mum, of course I could talk to Mum, he told me. But how about we have a day without our phones, and perhaps we could reset, sweetie, make sure we are all on the same page? And you don't need to tell your mother everything, because remember it is my holiday with you, Georgia, remember that. We have taken time off work and let's make the most of it, shall we? It's not a punishment. No. No. Not a punishment. Of course you can have your phone back at the end of the day. Of *course*.

Three silver bikes stood on the front path. Gleaming water bottles in the holsters.

Francine and Dad stood in their Lycra, under a bleary sun.

"Look, Georgia, we bought you a bike," said Dad. And then he looked pained. "We got these bikes for the three of us. For our time together."

I dropped my head. "Thank you," I said.

We rode past weatherboard houses; we circled roundabouts, rode past a doughnut shop, past a toy store, past a coffee shop, a bike shop, a coffee shop, a coffee shop, and a coffee shop.

I saw pale water in glimpses, then more water and more until there was a lake: blue-green, trees leaning, a couple paddle-boating the water. People jogged the lake path. Dogs ran along-side the people. Groups yoga-ed on the lawns. Families sat on rugs. Frisbees flew.

"Such a lovely day!" Francine and Dad said.

I looked at them. I was wearing a beanie and gloves, my jacket zipped up. The sky was slushy, slate-colored. My nose tingled with cold. Was I the only one feeling it? It was like being in opposite land.

Mum and Mel would be asleep by now. I wanted to send them a picture of the lake. I wanted them to be here, feeling what I was feeling.

We rode around the lake and Francine told me its history. "Green Lake!" *Blahblahblahblahblah!*

All the way around the lake we went.

And then we turned right down a street. I was getting tired. Mel had warned me: "Jet lag is an arse, George. Remember that naps are your friends!"

"Are we stopping soon?" I asked.

Francine laughed. "We've only ridden a few miles, Georgia! We're just starting!"

So down we rode, along a long street, past shops and houses and coffee shops until I saw more pale glimpses and there was another lake, this one huge. Boats cruised the water. A bridge to the left, another to the right, the city in the distance. And in front of me: a big park, tall hill, children running.

Between me and the lake sat an industrial site. It looked like something out of a movie, like in the final scenes when people meet in the dark to murder each other. Metal silos and corrugated iron, rust and old steel bones. Tess would love to see this. But I didn't have my phone to take a picture.

"Welcome to Gasworks Park," said Dad. He smiled. He drank from his water bottle.

"Gasworks Park!" said Francine. *Blahblahblahblahblah!*

The gasworks hulked beside the water. People jogged the lake path. Clouds hunkered. Families on rugs. Frisbees.

Francine finished the history of the park.

I went to get off my bike. This place was full of shapes and buildings, lines I could follow and draw. Giant metal arches like croquet hoops stood in a row nearby. Kids slalomed through them. I wanted to see everything—memorize it, put it on paper—

"Oh, no, Georgia," said Francine. "We've got longer to go, sweetie!"

Francine's face was like a clown face. Like if you made a whack-a-mole out of her clown face, you could whack her.

We rode and rode for a thousand years along a trail—"Burke-Gilman Trail!"—*Blahblahblahblahblah!*—past houses and trees and trees and houses, and then we stopped.

Another park. Another lake.

I could not stop yawning.

Boats on the water. Joggers. Families. Frisbees. Slate sky.

Francine pulled a rug out of her bike pannier. Dad pulled out Tupperware.

Francine pulled out wine.

Dad pulled out glasses.

Apples. Sandwiches. A kite.

"For later!" said Francine.

She sat cross-legged on the rug and poured two glasses of wine.

"Isn't this lovely?!" she said.

I nodded. The wind nipped; I zipped my jacket tighter.

We ate. We drank—me from my water bottle, them from their glasses.

"A beautiful day."

"So nice to be screen free!"

Drink. Eat. Bite.

I answered all the questions. "Yes, no, yes." I could not stop yawning, kept glancing over at Dad, the glass in his hand.

Francine smiled at me with all her teeth. "You tired, sweetie?"

Dad said, "Jet lag must be hitting. You feeling jet-lagged, Georgia?"

I nodded. "Yup."

"But aren't you up all night anyway? On your computer?" said Francine. "Teenagers!"

"Yes, she is getting old, isn't she?"

"Any second, we'll just get grunts!"

"Haha!"

I turned my head and watched the boats move over the water. They moved so fast, they could go anywhere they wanted.

"You seem very far away, Georgia." Francine frowned. She had another glug of wine.

"I'm sorry," I said, and yawned.

Francine sighed. "You say that a lot. And not a whole lot else. Have you noticed, Karl? Not much of a talker. A lot of a yawner."

Dad looked at me. "Georgia. Do you want to try a bit harder?"

"Sorry. Yes." My head felt like concrete. Body too. I wanted to be in a boat on the water. I wanted to run over that water. I wanted to be asleep under the water.

They drank the wine down—Dad with two glasses and Francine with three. And Francine pulled out another bottle.

Dad said, "I didn't know you were bringing two bottles, Francine."

"It's a celebration, Karl!"

And then Dad and Francine got shit-faced by the water.

In time, they unstitched me, there, beside the water.

For picking at my food and not appreciating how hard Francine was trying and for not talking and for yawning and yawning.

And then Francine said, "But really! It's fine!" and she flicked her hair off her lipstick, and said, "We'll have lots of time to learn about each other, won't we? When your dad goes on his trip?"

And Dad nodded.

And I said, "His trip?"

And Francine smiled like a thin, drunk crocodile, and told me the plan. About Dad's job interview on the other side of the country and how it was "such a wonderful opportunity for him! And for us!" and how they only just found out about the interview, only last week, but wasn't it exciting, and he would be away for only four days, but we would have so much fun together, she and I!

It was going to be a Girls' Own Adventure!

We would be getting pedicures! And going to the movies!

And Francine would introduce me to her friends' children!

And wouldn't it be wonderful to meet new people my age? And get out of my shell? And become confident, because *even though you're so shy, we believe in you, Georgia!*

The sky oozed with gray. Boats lurched across the lake, and Francine's and Dad's faces looked like clowns, there by the water.

This is the part of the story where the girl got on her bike and left the shit-faced clowns.

I rode all the way back and got lost—but it was okay because I asked someone: *How do I get to Green Lake?* And I followed the way they pointed until I had to ask again. And somehow, I found my way back to the green-and-white bungalow, where all the windows and doors were locked.

The dog was inside. She looked up when I knocked on the back door. Dark liquid eyes.

"Let me in," I whispered.

The dog padded to the dog flap, came outside. Nose to hand, nose to face, licking the wet there.

Then the dog and I broke in—only a little glass on the basement floor. I pulled open the study drawer, got my phone, and called my mother.

Dad came in. Francine too. Shouting. Shouting. Shouting.

Francine said, "I have tried and tried!"

Dad said, "Francine has tried and tried!"

"We bought you a bike!"

"Made time for you!"

"Weekend snow trip planned!"

"Pedicures!"

I looked at their faces. Red and splotched and bent. What should I do?

Choose your own adventure, George. I could hear Mel in my head.

Should I stay or go? I looked into the dog's eyes.

Don't leave me, she said.

But of course I couldn't stay.

On the plane home, I drew how it felt into my notebook:

All the talks we did not have.

The snow trip we did not go on.

The dog's soft fur.

The kite we did not fly.

The walk we did not do by Puget Sound

(pebbles scritching underfoot,

a mountain range, a sweep of water).

The air between me and my father, and

the way everything ended in that air.

Sydney, *eighteen*

1

Early morning.

Spangled light, cool breeze ruffling the water.

I'm out paddling again, going upriver. It has been ten hours since Dad called to tell me he was dying. You would think he would give me a minute to process, but he has been sending messages.

Some of them are long. Some are short.

They all say something like:

Perhaps you could come and visit?

There are things to talk about.

I am sorry, Georgia.

Let's talk soon, okay?

Dad rang after I got back from Seattle five years ago.

"God. Georgia, I'm so sorry," he said. "It was unacceptable. I apologize. I promise to do better."

I nodded, listening. Words words words.

A few days later, he rang me again, drunk. "She's left me!" he said, and cried.

A few days later, he rang again. Still drunk, speech-slurring:

"ShitGeorgia I've beenfired fuckthey fired me—I just wanted one thing to go right jus-one-thing—was that too muchto ask?"

A few minutes later he said:

"GoddamnitGeorgia. Think of what I did for you. Ungrateful little shit."

A bit later:

"So—is [*long silence*] what? Shit. That. What? *[Long silence.]* Georgia. Shit. Shit."

After that, Mum told Dad he couldn't call me anymore.

So he didn't.

We've hardly spoken since. Even though he emailed over a year ago and told me and Mum he was sober, we still almost never talk. My father and I speak at appropriate events and at appropriate intervals. We peck at conversation like polite birds.

And now he's dying? What the hell am I supposed to do with that?

A cormorant dives for a fish, somewhere in the far away.

I pause, look around.

I've been out a while. I've gone much further than normal. I'm not far from the place where the RiverCat ferry starts to nose through the marshy narrows and other boats aren't allowed.

The cormorant lifts from the water, empty-beaked and flapping.

I don't know what to do.

I don't want to call Dad. I don't want to talk to him. I definitely don't want to go see him. But he's *dying*.

My body feels bruised. My breath comes hard. I've been going fast—cutting down with my paddles, pushing forward—trying to cover history with water.

The cormorant calls from its great height: *You can't keep going this way, Girl. I can see the sign. You'll have to turn.*

On all sides: Boats and parks and trees and houses.

Below me: Fish sucking air through their hollow gills.

Inside my ribs: Memory, making tiny cracks in the bone.

Tess told me once that you could see the harm done to someone's body, even after they died. "You can dig up a skeleton and physically see it," she said. "Not just broken bones, but, like, other illnesses and stuff."

"Yeah? Even stomachache?" I said then, when I was twelve. "What about sadness?"

Tess nodded. "I'm sure they'd find it."

Then we googled skeletons and grief. We drifted away on a tangent. We read about the Peat Man, a dead man preserved perfectly in a bog. We watched a video, got grossed out. Made popcorn. Went for a run.

The cormorant dives again. Its body is a dart, sure and certain. It emerges, fish in its mouth, the fish's body silvery and flapping. Together, the two rise. The bird tilts a wing, swoops left.

I have to head back. I have to teach at the Art House later. I have to finish my uni assignment. I have things to do. I have to turn.

Could a scientist see in my body how much I don't want to? How much I want to just keep going? Move away from everything that hurts?

I stop paddling.

Picture my bones.

Picture the places where Dad's phone call is marking them.

Turn around! says the bird, flying away.

I don't want to die! says the fish, sliding down the throat of the bird.

I lift my paddles.

Turn and head back downriver.

The water swirls with stories; time tick-tocks.

Above, a plane arcs the harbor. The cormorant slips silently into the distance. Below us, and inside the water, the fish tremble and whisper to their lovers. They swim under my kayak, hiding under the hull the whole ride home.

2

Outside the Art House, the air is thick and seething. Inside, everything is hushed, cool.

No one is at the counter when I walk in. A few customers wander around the store. I go through to the back room and find Laz at the kitchenette making coffee with Mel's espresso machine. Tess has her feet up on the couch, and Calliope is sitting in the sagging armchair. The AC doesn't quite reach back here, so a fan beats limp air around the room. In the cracked-tile courtyard, leaves wilt on the jacaranda tree.

Calliope smiles when she sees me. "Hey," she says.

"Hey," I say. I try to smile back. *Be perky, George.* I put down my backpack. "Is no one, um, watching the store?"

Laz pours frothed milk into his cup and looks pointedly at Tess. "I'm on my break. *She* should be out there. Maybe you should go home, Tess, if you're going to spend the day on the couch."

"Why? I'm just taking a break." Tess frowns. "Like you."

"I'm taking five minutes. You've been on the couch for half an hour."

"It's fine, Laz. It's not even busy."

Just then the countertop bell rings. I glance out of the room—a customer stands at the counter, notebooks in hand, looking impatient.

Laz motions towards the door. "Your turn, Tess." He's not smiling. He's in a mood. I'm guessing it's because of the fires—another one has just started, this time in the mountains an hour west of us. The fire is deep in one of the shadowy canyons. It's growing.

"But my feet *hurt*," says Tess. She sounds like a kid.

The bell rings again. We're about to lose a customer—Mel wouldn't like that. God. Just once, could these two not be at each other's throats?

I turn to deal with it.

"Don't, George," says Laz. "It's Tess's job."

Tess looks at me. "Oh, *can* you go? For, like, a minute? I just need a bit longer."

"Jesus," says Laz. "You shouldn't get paid for slacking off."

Tess glares at Laz. If she could send knives with her eyes, there'd be a bunch of metal in this room, flying.

I head out to the counter. "I'm sorry to keep you waiting," I say to the customer.

"I could have stolen these," the man says. "You wouldn't even have noticed."

"I'm sorry. Um—" And I think the customer is two seconds away from storming off when Calliope glides up beside me. She grabs a putty eraser from the display on the counter.

"Can I offer you a free sample?" she says. "These just came in. They're *wonderful*." She smiles so sweetly, the customer turns into a man-sized putty eraser.

"Okay. Yeah, well, thanks," he says. He holds up the two

notebooks, each a differently weighted paper. "Which one of these is best for watercolor?"

Calliope doesn't even hesitate. "Oh, both are fine," she says. "The 250 is perfect, though. If you can't have both."

She smiles at him again; the man buys both notebooks, and pads out of the store like a puppy.

I stare at Calliope. "Wait. How'd you do that? How'd you know about the paper?"

"Oh, I just made it up," laughs Calliope. Her laugh sounds like a fork *tinging* against glass. "Did I do okay?"

"Uh, yeah? Like, you got it exactly right." I look over the rest of the store. "Okay, what would you say are the best oils for a *plein air* painting?"

Calliope considers. "Oh, well, those would be the Excalibur paints. In the back. If you can't find them, we must be out."

"*Nice*," I say. "I'd totally buy them, even though they don't exist."

She bows a little. "Thank you. Your resident bullshit artist, at your service."

I laugh. It feels nice—a ripple of something good in the mix and mess.

Calliope bumps my arm with hers. "Your friends are kind of intense. I needed to get out before Laz started chucking coffee."

I glance towards the back. "Oh, yeah. They can get like that."

"That must be interesting."

"Mmm, yep," I say. I think of the tangles Laz and Tess have gotten themselves into over the years, all the troubles I've tried to fix. When Tess got pregnant and Laz was furious, it took me going to both their houses to sort it out—to Laz's to talk him down from his parapet, un-notch the arrow from his bow, and to Tess's to convince her Laz wasn't the worst for being unsupportive.

In the end, they made up. But Tess and Laz are like complementary colors—like orange and blue, purple and yellow—dissonant and shivery when they are side by side. Hungry for chaos, for fizz and trouble. And I'm the muted gray between them—the noncolor that settles your eyes when you look at the painting of us. Or maybe I'm just beige, like a carpet.

The art class kids will be here any minute. Laz and Tess still haven't come out of the back room. Luckily, Calliope and I don't have to set up—we're still doing watercolor paintings.

I peer towards the back. "I think we need to head upstairs."

"Yeah." Calliope looks over. "Should I *coooeee* to get them to come?"

I glance at her, ready to say "No!" But she's smiling.

"I wouldn't shout across the store, George. Just so you know. I am a sensible girl."

"Damn. And there I was, planning to rob a bank later. You'll be no use to me."

Calliope grins—she's about to reply when Laz appears, scowling. He walks towards us with his coffee. "Okay, I'm here," he says. "You can go up."

A second later, Tess comes waddling after him. She looks like she's been crying. "I'm here too. I can work. I'm not a slacker."

"Of course you aren't," says Calliope. "You're doing great."

Another lie? It's clear Tess isn't doing great at all. But Tess smiles at Calliope, who offers one of her golden smiles back, and it seems genuine.

Calliope heads upstairs. I follow her. I practically run to keep up with her light.

Today's watercolor class is with the older kids. Everyone has a go at Calliope's still-life arrangement—they carefully dab at the paper while Calliope zips around the room saying things like, "That's amazing, Soula" and "Great use of the red there, Jerome!"

I go around the room too. I wander about on little cat feet and say, "That looks good. Maybe more green? Do you think? In that corner?"

Calliope is a peppier teacher than me. When I talk, the kids nod and focus on their work. When Calliope talks, the kids lift their heads and brighten, ask questions, smile. Basically, I know who the students would pick if there was an apocalypse, and you had to eat someone or hand them over to an alien overlord.

Time ticks on. The kids don't talk much, and I don't even know if they're enjoying the class, but when they finish, they carry their paintings to the drying racks like the paper is made of glass, so maybe they're happy.

When we're done, the students wave goodbye. "Bye, Calliope. Bye, George."

"Bye!" Calliope waves. She's been great again, like she actually knows all about art. How does she do that?

We wipe down the tables. Pack away the paints and paper. "That was fun," says Calliope. "I think I'm getting the hang of it, maybe? A little? You'd tell me if I sucked, right?"

"Sure." We head down the stairs. "Or maybe I won't. I could just keep you here to entertain me."

Calliope laughs. "Great! You could set up a camera. I could be your blooper reel."

"Exactly." I smile.

We stand at the bottom of the stairs and look at each other. We don't move into the store or walk to the back room. We just . . . pause. And I want to stay here, hold this moment, feel light for a moment. It's almost nearly . . . like something good.

I say, "Hey, I watched your movies, by the way."

Calliope's eyes widen. "Oh? You did?"

"They're great. I wanted to know how you do the lines? The animated ones, they're so—"

Tess opens the door of the toilet, just beside the staircase. "Jesus!" she says, seeing us. "The kid is literally kicking my bladder!" She stops. Takes us in. "What are you guys talking about?"

"Nothing," I say quickly. "Just chatting about the class."

Calliope glances at me. "Yeah," she says. "Actually, I have to go. I got that job at the pub! I have my first full shift this afternoon."

"Oh, that's great!" I say. "Congratulations."

"Yeah, congratulations," says Tess.

"Thanks. I'll see you guys next time," Calliope says.

"Sure," I say. "See you. Thanks for today."

"You're welcome. It was fun." Calliope walks away.

Tess half waves, then turns to me. "Hey, I need to get some more folate from the chemist. Want to come and get it with me after I finish work?"

I don't reply. I watch Calliope head out of the store without looking back. I watch her go without me getting to finish my question, without her answering it, and without us talking for the rest of the day.

I look at Tess.

"What?" Tess shifts her feet. She probably needs to pee again. "What, George?"

I shake my head. "Nothing."

"Really? You okay? Want to come to the chemist with me after work?"

"Actually, I was going to go to the library—"

"You could stay and wait for me, maybe? You could study here?"

I pause. I brought my laptop—I was going to do my essay in the library's ice-cold AC, but I pause, take in Tess's *I need you* face. "Okay, sure. I'll wait."

"Great! We can get some bubble tea after. You want bubble tea?"

"I will always want bubble tea."

Tess smiles, then suddenly flinches. Puts her hand on her belly. "God. She just kicked me so hard." She takes my hand. "Feel this, George."

I lay my hand on Tess's belly. I feel everything she tells me to.

3

It's two p.m.

I'm in the back room, fan up close and trying to work, but it's hard to concentrate—I can hear Laz and Tess bickering in the store like midges, buzzing and throwing themselves into each other's flight paths. Laz is fritzing about the fires, and Tess's sore feet are all she can think about.

I feel like getting up and shouting from the door: "Hey, some of us could do with a little peace! You're not the only ones carrying heavy things. Some of us have a dying dad!"

I picture what that would be like. The customers all turning, rattled to see me yelling from the doorway, sweaty and unhinged. Then me walking over to Tess and Laz to tell them Dad's news—my words pooling across the floor, the bruised shame of Dad climbing the white canvases. I picture Tess's shock. Picture Laz, who I've never talked to about Dad, trying to take it in. And I picture Mum's face later . . . finding out I've told the story no one is supposed to know.

Dad is the hard little secret Mum and I carry. Dad is a burn, a scar in his shape.

"No one needs to be in our business, George," Mum said when I was six. I'd been to a birthday party and told everyone my dad fell asleep on our driveway after drinking two bottles of wine. Mum told the birthday boy's mum I'd made a mistake. Three years later, after the lake happened and Dad ran around drunk in front of the neighbors' houses, Mum went to everyone's door with caramel slice to apologize. She told them he'd had a bad reaction to some medicine. That same day she called his work: "Karl can't come in. Stomach flu," she said, like they didn't know who Dad was.

Then she told Dad to move out.

Dad packed his stuff and slunk out at night, so the neighbors wouldn't see.

I remember I did not cry when he left. I remember visiting him in his new flat, and Dad saying he'd fix everything between him and Mum. Then he got busy with work and didn't call. Then he called me, drunk. Then he stopped calling again. Then Mum told me he moved to America. When he invited me to Seattle, I thought that might be the beginning of something new, but instead, it was just another ending.

After Seattle, I shoved Dad deep underwater, somewhere even those fish with their light tentacles couldn't reach. I put Dad under a rock. I swam up to the surface and tried to breathe.

A month after I got back, I wasn't saying much at dinner, and was hardly eating. Mel said, "Do you want to go see someone, George? Talk about it?"

I looked at Mum. I remembered how nervy she had been about my therapy when I was ten. After each session she would ask: "So, what did you say?" and "What did she say to you?" and "Did you tell her—" and "Are you sure you want—"

Mum had looked so relieved when the psychologist said to try art classes instead.

So at dinner I told Mel: "No. I'm fine."

I wanted to believe I was. I paddled, swam, ran, kept moving. I listened for stories; I painted and drew, went to school, laughed with Tess. I made life Dad-free.

There's no Dad in my paintings. No Dad in my notebooks.

There's no Dad anywhere.

Which should mean I'm okay. Right? Even if he's dying?

He's under a rock. He's under the water. He's not here.

I hear something breaking in the store.

"Fuck!" says Laz.

"Sorry!" says Tess.

I hear a bell tinkle as a customer leaves.

I get up. "Hey, you two," I say, walking to the counter, "maybe give each other a break today? I can hear you on the other side of the store. And, seriously, no swearing."

"I just don't get why she's here," says Laz, sweeping up a mess of glass and smashed charcoal.

Tess says, "I'm doing my best, Laz, you shit."

"Tess, your best is not sitting at the counter scrolling your phone and dropping jars."

"It was an accident. And my feet really hurt."

"Maybe stop working then?"

"I need the money. For the baby."

Laz sighs. "You should have thought of that before—"

"I *did* think of that." Tess bristles. "Which is why I'm here."

Jesus. This again. I interrupt: "Laz, go easy on her. You aren't carrying a watermelon-sized human in your uterus." Tess brightens, looking avenged. I turn to her. "And Tess, maybe you should go home? Just . . . it's so hot. And you're really uncomfortable. Hardly anyone's here, anyway. I'm sure Laz can cover for you."

Laz nods. "I *definitely* can."

Tess looks hurt. "Don't you think I can do it, George?"

"Of course I do," I say. "But you seem pretty tired."

Tess sags. "I am. I'm *so* tired. Is it normal to be this tired?"

"Yes," I say. "You have a whole person inside you, *kicking.* If it was me, I'd be in bed all day."

Tess looks at me, looks at Laz. Sighs. "Okay. Well, maybe I'll go home."

"Thank God," says Laz.

"Laz," I say.

He takes in a breath. "All right. Sorry," he says. "Yeah, go home and rest, Tess. It's the fucking End Times out there. Might as well wait for the shit-storm to hit in bed."

"Laz," I say. "It'll be okay."

He looks at me. "You can't promise that."

"I'm not promising. I'm just, hoping."

Laz shrugs. "Hope is fucking useless without action, George. I'll see you two later." He turns. His whole body is tense, fragile. I want to stay and fix him—or at least try—but Tess has grabbed her bag. She's already by the door.

"Let's go, George," she says. "Before I need to pee again."

. . .

We wander down the street, trying to stay in the shade, trying not to melt.

Tess doesn't talk much as we walk—she mostly holds her hand to her belly and stares ahead. In the side street, Tess beeps open her mum's car. "Shit," she says. "I need to pee again."

"Maybe we can go to the toilet in the shopping center," I say as we get in the car. "When we go to the chemist."

"The chemist?"

I look at her. She's forgotten already. "You wanted folate, right? And the bubble tea?"

"Oh, yeah." She stares at the steering wheel. Doesn't turn on the engine. It's a furnace in here. I can feel my blood actually begin to boil.

Tess says, suddenly: "I'm kind of spinning out, George."

I look at her. "Yeah?" I open the car door, just to get some air. We might be here a while.

"Maybe this was a mistake?" she says.

"Oh. Do you mean the baby?"

Tess blinks.

"Uh. Um." She tries to smile. "No, I'm just kidding."

"Yeah?"

"Yeah. Haha," she says without really laughing. Then she just sits there.

I stare at Tess. She's zingy with nerves too, like Laz but for a thousand different reasons. I guess it's the End Times for her too—the end of one time and the beginning of a completely unknown other.

We are silent for one beat, two, then I say, "Tess."

She looks at me. "Yeah?"

"Sorry, and I totally care about what you're saying, but can we open the windows or maybe get the fans going? I think I might be cooked through."

Tess and I go to the chemist, the bubble tea shop, and make three stops in the mall toilets.

The whole time, I can feel Dad's news under my skin, pushing to get out—but a) Tess won't want to hear it and b) Tess's favorite bubble tea flavor isn't available and she is sooooo tired and has she mentioned how much her feet hurt?

"You have, Tess," I say. "Like, maybe a thousand times."

"Well, they should make special shoes for pregnant women."

"I'm sure they do. Someone must."

"Maybe for *rich* pregnant women. If I was rich . . ." She sighs, sips her bubble tea, makes a face. "Hey, taste this. Does it seem sweet enough? Maybe I need more sugar. Or less sugar. God. I need to pee again."

I wait outside the toilets. Don't check my phone because another message from Dad might have sidled in.

The last time I really talked to Tess about Dad was a few weeks after Seattle. Tess started to cry, just thinking about Dad being drunk and terrible. I had to comfort *her*. Then she said, "It's so hard," like the story was her own.

I told Mum about it the next day, when she picked me up from Tess's place.

She said, "George, sometimes it's best to keep our stories to our-selves. You know? Not everyone can take what we have to say."

I looked at Mum. Her eyes got teary. I felt her sadness rise: a hard, ash-gray wave. I nodded. Reached over and touched her arm. "Okay. Okay, Mum." And I picked up the same stone as her and promised to keep carrying it.

Tess drops me home. She puts the car into park and turns to me. "What are you doing now? We could watch something? Or eat something? Or fill the bath with ice cubes and sit in it?"

"Tempting. But I really have to finish my essay. Due tomorrow," I say.

"Okay, fine," she says, then frowns. "*Shit.* I have an essay too. I forgot."

"When's it due?"

"Um? Like, maybe yesterday? Or in a week . . . I have to check."

I shake my head. "When are you done with uni?"

"Two weeks."

"Cutting it close, Tess."

She nods. "Always." She lowers the passenger window as I get out and leans towards me. "Love you, George. Thanks for, like, everything. Don't know how I'll ever repay you."

I bow in her direction. "I'll happily take a Porsche."

She laughs. "Okay. I'll have it here for you tomorrow." Then she pauses.

I can tell she doesn't want to go, or me to leave. Her need winds out of her, pale yellow and ribbony.

"Dude," I say, "go home and empty that tiny bladder. I'll see you soon."

When she's gone, I stand on the pavement. The air crackles with heat and memory. The afternoon gapes open. Inside my house, there's nothing for me but a uni essay. Driving away is my best friend, who seems to need help existing. And outside, inside, and everywhere else, my father hovers, waiting for me to call.

I don't bother going into the house. I step down the side path. Open the shed door, dump my bag on a shelf, and pull out the kayak. Move over the sweet ache of water, move fast and keep moving, until my arms hurt and the sun begins to drop, burning, over the drooping back of the city.

4

Evening. Windows wide open to let out the heat, cool-ish air sifting in.

I'm in the kitchen with Mum. The cat keeps sentry beside her food dish, hoping for more dinner. Mum is making soup. It makes no sense—the best thing on a night like this would be salad, or a bowl of ice. But Mum saw a soup recipe on some website: pumpkin, pear, and carrot. She wants to test it out on me.

"Don't diss it till you've tried it, young lady," she says, when I make a face at the pears.

Mel is at the studio and Gramps is out with a woman called Beverley who Mum knows from her old-people's home. "This one is fragile, Dad," she said, when Gramps was getting ready to go out.

"Aren't we all?" said Gramps. He saw Mum's face. "All right. Yes. No heartbreaking."

And off he went. Another wrinkled shirt, jacket on over it, his hair slicked back.

I look at Mum. She's singing along with an old R&B song, swaying as she slices the pumpkin. She looks happy. I picture speaking into her happiness, saying: "Mum. Dad's dying."

I picture the story of that—how she'll turn and say, "What?" and then: "What??"

I picture Mum hearing about Dad's heart. And how it will stop working in two years, maybe three.

I picture her face, changing.

I hear her voice, squeaking in the clammy dark.

Me under my blanket, the sound creeping in and rising round the
bed:

Please, Karl—

    The doctors said—

        If you just—   *Karl, stop—Karl!—*

            Please—

I picture our night blurring into water.

The last time Mum got news about Dad, he'd gotten remarried. I was fifteen. He sent me a brief email after it was done.

Mum stood in the kitchen and cried. "How hard would it have been to warn us?" She looked across at me. "He barely even told you, George."

I shrugged. "I don't care," I said.

It wasn't Francine. She was long gone. It was some lady he'd met in AA. He hadn't gone to AA once when we were his family, even though Mum had asked and asked.

The marriage didn't last, but Mum wept in the kitchen that night. Mel listened and nodded. I was making a snack, dry-eyed when Gramps came in. He saw Mum and sighed. "Jesus. Why do you still care about that man, Sara? It's over. He's out of your life. Good riddance." Gramps waved the air, wiping Dad out.

But the air wasn't where Dad was.

Mum started to cry harder. Mel gave Gramps a look that could level a city. "John. That's not how pain works. It resonates. Think of a fork, hitting a glass—"

Gramps put up a hand. "You don't need to tell me about pain."

"No. It's just—"

"I've had a hip replaced. I have been hit by a car. I have lost a wife."

Then Mum crumpled because, of course, she had lost a mum.

Mum said, "I'm not—It isn't—"

And she looked at me. The past rippled under our feet. I could see her, coaxing Dad off the floor. I saw her on the phone talking to the doctors. Saw her face open when he promised to be better, saw it close when he left.

I wanted to say, "I get it, Mum." The past was sticky-fingered, pushy, relentless. It came in flashes. It snuck up and swallowed you.

I looked across at her. Was the past swallowing her right now?

—a shout, the sound of something breaking,
slash of color, blur of lines,
a crash, a shape falling, eyes watching, a body shivering—

I stepped forward, onto Mum's eggshell island. "Mum," I said, "it's okay." I wrapped my arms around her. Stood as solidly as I could.

She wrapped her arms around me. And held on.

Mum and I sit at the counter, eating bright orange soup. It's practically neon. Mum has really gone for it with the turmeric.

She says, "It's good, isn't it?"

I spoon it in—it really is. "Mum, you've done it again."

"Thanks, George." She smiles.

We sit and eat.

I see the night spooling out from here—us finishing our dinner and me not bringing Dad into the room, and us not talking about Dad. Us washing our dishes and putting soup in a container for Mel and Gramps when they came home, and us watching our murder mystery series and the hard dark not rising, and the cat coming to sprawl on Mum's lap or mine.

I look outside. The sky has turned mauve. Possums rumble the tin roof and scuttle under the eaves.

I breathe in, out. Reach over, hold Mum's hand.

"Always be making your weird foods, dear mother," I say. "Always be surprising me."

She squeezes my fingers. "It needs more turmeric. But sure."

Marvin Gaye croons through the kitchen. Mum's feet tap and tap the kitchen stool in time.

5

Nine p.m.

Mum and Mel and Gramps and I are all in our rooms. Mel came home hot and tetchy—she has been wrangling with her genitalia series for weeks, and nothing is doing what she wants. She sniffed the soup when she got home. "You put pear in this? I don't know . . ." she said. She made herself Vegemite toast. Mum wasn't happy.

Gramps came back from his date, sat in his chair with a whiskey, and didn't want to talk. Not about the date, not even about the bird, who is in the middle of being taken apart and remade.

Mum and I turned off our murder show. Gramps sat, looking old and sad. Mum and Mel discussed, at length, the delicious soup vs. the toast.

Now I'm in my room, away from their rattling, not doing my assignment. I opened my laptop to do some work. Wrote some words. But then the cat came, pad-pawed the bed, turned round and around and now the two of us are watching a documentary about the Flat Earth Society.

My phone buzzes on its face, lighting my bed.

Is it Tess, asking me to come over and iron her wrinkles? *Can you make me a smoothie, George? I'll love you forever.*

Or is it Dad, writing—again—about his impending death? *We*

need to talk, Georgia. We need to discuss this. Stop everything. Listen to me.

My bones tighten and pinch.

Or maybe it's Laz, texting again from the pub. He asked me to come join him tonight—Adesh was working and Laz wanted company. *Sorry I was a shit today,* he texted. *Want to come and drink our feelings?*

I didn't want to watch Laz get unraveled by beer. I texted back: *Thanks, Laz. But I can't. Have an assignment due, sorry,* and left it at that.

I could have said, *Want to come over and talk? It looks like you're having a shit time. Is it the fires?* But I didn't. I felt like one of those sea urchins, curling into my shell. *Don't touch me. Don't talk to me. Be quiet. Be quiet.*

The phone buzzes again. The screen lights up, blue against my bed sheet.

Or maybe . . .

it's Calliope?

I pause the film, turn over the phone to check.

It *is*. It's her.

Hey, the first message says.

What are you doing right now? says the second one.

I reply:

Hey. I'm watching a show. What about you?

CALLIOPE: *That sounds good. I'm not doing anything . . . I just finished work. Want to catch a ferry?*

ME: *Wait. Now?*

CALLIOPE: *Yeah. I thought it would be good to talk more and you might like to be on the water, so how about a combo?*

ME: *Okay! Yes! Which wharf?*

CALLIOPE: *The main one? At the point? In twenty minutes?*

ME: *Sure! See you soon!*

CALLIOPE: ☺

I leap out of bed. Scare the cat. Scramble to find a jacket, my inhaler, my shoes. It's late. My phone is nearly out of battery. Who cares? What is time? I'm meeting Calliope.

We're going on a boat.

Lamplit ferry wharf, barnacled poles, *laplap* of waves.

I stand on the dock, waiting. The day has finally cooled—a breeze gusts under my jacket and pockmarks the water. Freckled light flicks from boats and buildings. In the distance I see the Harbour Bridge—the great arc of it, a spotlight on the flag at its top. No one else is here.

Calliope comes running. She swoops down the long ramp in a thin red hoodie, khaki pants, and yellow beanie. Hair down, curls everywhere. My breath catches in my throat like in those books where the main character says "She took my breath away." Or "She was a vision in red," or maybe just some sound people made before language was born.

"Hey!" she says. She steps forward and wraps me in a hug.

"Mmmf," I say. The hug is amazing—firm and soft, like pressing into a human-sized marshmallow.

Calliope doesn't let me go. She tilts her head back to look at me. We are about the same height. Her boobs are on my boobs. God.

"It's really nice to see you," she says.

"You too," I say.

We smile at each other. Calliope smells like vanilla. She feels incredible. She's still not letting me go.

What's going to happen now? In the movies, this is the part where two heads dip towards each other; this is the part where the lovers kiss. Right? I picture doing it—kissing Calliope. Would she mind? My head feels full of air and vanilla.

Before I can decide or just swoon into the harbor, the ferry cruises up.

Calliope releases me. My whole body pulses.

The two of us step across the gangway into an almost-empty boat.

Here we are. *Here we are.* It's our own boat to everywhere.

We ride the ferry to Circular Quay, past sleeping islands and houses with their curtains drawn and all the muted wharves.

"This is so nice," I say. We are outside, leaning against the prow.

"I love it," she says.

"Me too."

The ferry revs up and we don't talk. We just lean against the boat side, the wind whooshing past. My whole body feels goose-bumped and there's this other feeling too—a quickening, a feeling of something starting, something opening, something hopeful . . .

Our fingers slightly touch where they rest on the railing. Our hair swoops back. The ferry judders against the water. We zigzag from dock to dock, then scoot under the Harbour Bridge. I look up when we're directly beneath the great iron platform. Feel the air, pressing.

Calliope has pulled out her phone; she holds it above her head, filming. Then she pans down, onto my face. I look straight into the lens. Do I look poetic? Do I look mysterious?

Calliope sticks out her tongue.

Both of us laugh. The sound rises and gets caught, like balloons, on the underside of the bridge.

We get to Circular Quay at ten p.m. The city is thick with light—from the Opera House, from the bridge and bars and buildings, from the expressway and the camera flashes on the Opera House forecourt, from the tourists' wide eyes.

The ferry docks: a churn of green-white water as the engines reverse. We walk down the ramp to the floating wharf.

"What do you want to do?" Calliope says, turning to me.

"I don't mind."

"Me neither."

We stand, just looking at each other, until a wave jostles the wharf and rocks us. We stagger a bit and laugh, then slip up the long ramp and into the bustle of the quay.

On the esplanade, a busker plays didgeridoo. People stand in lines for restaurants, gather on outdoor seats, sift through tourist shops, swoop in and out of the train station. A little way down, a tin man stands motionless on a box. Further down, people line up at the gelateria.

"Maybe some more ice cream?" says Calliope.

"Perfect," I say.

The ferry to Manly comes in, regal and huge, just as we get our scoops—chocolate for me, strawberry for Calliope.

"Want to get on?" says Calliope. "Or do you want to just walk?"

"Oh. I pick boat," I say.

"Of course you do!" Calliope laughs.

We tap our cards, walk down the ramp, step onto the ferry. It can fit nine hundred, but right now the boat is almost deserted—a sleeping castle for two. The ride will be half an hour. We have nothing to do now but ride the water, eat our ice cream, lean against the railing, press our bodies into the dark and the wind. I can't think of anything better.

The ferry revs its engines, water churns, and out we cruise, past the Opera House, past the botanic gardens, past the military wharves and the navy ships, out and out and out. Gulls race beside us, wings barely moving. Froth speckles the boat sides. Calliope and I spoon ice cream from our cups and start calling more stories out to each other. Our words fling themselves into the wind, return.

Yeah, Tess and I have been friends since we were babies—

Mum and I talk every couple of weeks, it's kind of weird—

Mum runs an aged-care home and Gramps is dating all the women there—

Yeah, my parents knew about me liking girls before I told them—

Me too—

until we feel the water change as we pass the Heads, and the space where the sea swoops in. We can't see the cliffs in this dark, but we know we're beside the ocean because the swell lifts the ferry and drops us. Again, again—lift and *slap*—the bow plops back and thwacks the water. The feeling is stomach-lurching, heady. A slice of spray hits us both. We whoop, dazzled and alive.

"Fuck yeah!" Calliope shouts.

We are two girls, wave-tossed and wind-plucked. If we turned right, we'd go straight into the Tasman Sea. We could keep going then. We could go anywhere.

I reach for her hand, or does she reach for mine? We lean against the railing; we laugh into each other's eyes.

She wraps her arms around me, body pressed against body. I feel the warmth of Calliope's breath as she leans in close

and I lean in close—

and we're looking at each other like we're saying everything

and I lean closer and she leans closer

and now—

she's kissing me and I am kissing her.

I used to be able to breathe.

One second later, Calliope pulls back an inch. "This okay?" she whispers.

My body feels zapped, 1,000-volted. I grin, loose, like a spaniel. "Yes," I say. I nod, hard. "*Yes.*"

Calliope grins back. "Yeah? Cool! Great!"

And then the two of us lean forward—in the wild and wet, in all this wind—and kiss again.

KISS

(fine-tip pen on paper)

Once, a butterfly flew to a waterfall and swam up it—
or at least that's how this feels.

A kiss—this kiss—
feels like that butterfly
and that waterfall and the air trembling inside itself, and
can you imagine, can you see?

You could, if you have ever been a butterfly,
or a waterfall or everything in
the shivering inbetween.
Once, a butterfly slipped up water—
once a butter—
lips on lips— once a—
    again

        wings

    Once

6

We two butterfly girls walk away from the wharf, through the shuttered streets and to the sea. The waves are made of metal, moonlight grazes the water, and Calliope and I can't stop laughing; we can't stop telling each other small things about ourselves like we're picking up beach shells and handing them to each other.

"Wait," says Calliope. "Your cat is called Susan?"

"Yeah."

"Any reason why?"

"No. It just happened."

"My grandma has a dog called Ernest—I mean, Mum has him now. He farts all the time. Just sits on the couch and farts, right next to you."

"Gross. I don't think cats fart."

"Sure they do. All animals fart."

"Not worms."

"You sure?"

"I'm not sure of anything." I laugh. I would google worms and farting right now, but my phone has officially died. I'll check when I get home. If I ever go home.

I don't want to think about going home.

Calliope and I walk till we've gone all the way along the main beach, around the cliff and past the ocean pool, to a small cove. The beach is empty. The nearby café has its awnings closed, its seats stacked. We sit on the sand, two girls becoming something more to each other.

Calliope looks around. "I haven't been here since before we went away. We lived kind of close—I used to swim from the main beach to here with Dad—have you seen the swimmers doing that?"

"Yeah." I nod. Tess and I came here a year or so ago. We walked from the wharf to the sea, then around to this cove. We watched swimmers leave the big beach in clumps and head into the open ocean, arms and legs kicking, everyone thrashing around the point to get to the next safe place. Then Tess touched my arm and said, "What if a shark came right now? We'd see someone die."

"Maybe we could do it together sometime?" says Calliope.

I shake off the vision of us getting swallowed by sharks. "That sounds great," I say, and smile.

Calliope smiles back, then tucks her knees up to her chest. "I've missed this water. We were so . . . shut in, in Reading. Don't get me wrong, living near London was great, but the sea was hours away. We only went twice and the beach was all pebbles and the water didn't even have a color. And it was *freezing*. When Dad and I came back, I just wanted to climb inside the harbor, you know? I think that's why I jumped in, that time you saw me. Just wanted to really feel it again."

"Yep, I get that," I say. I think of how she looked cartwheeling that day. My body goes warm.

"The same with the surf," Calliope adds, "just multiplied by a thousand."

I nod. I think of the *whoosh* of the sea, the waves catapulting into the cliffs at South Head . . . and how the swell felt on the ferry just now. I think of the calm of the harbor at dawn, the stillness. I think of the rush and peace, the quiet and loud of the sea . . . and how I can't ever seem to leave its side—

"I could live in it, I reckon," says Calliope.

"Yeah," I say. And we're silent for a moment, just agreeing.

"But it means my movies are just harbor harbor harbor at this point."

"Makes sense."

"Not exactly varied content. Might not do so well at film school with that. *Oh, that Calliope Sanjeewa, she's the one with all the water, so limited—*"

"Your movies are amazing. They're going to love you," I say.

Calliope gives me a long, soft look. "Thanks." She bumps my shoulder. "It's only been a few months, but I kind of miss studying. I know that's weird—"

"No, I'm the same," I say. "My gap year got pretty ordinary. So I started the uni classes."

"Did you do any traveling first?"

"I was thinking of it . . . but then Tess got pregnant."

Calliope's eyebrows raise. "And that meant you couldn't travel?"

I pause. I remember that conversation with Tess—*You're going to leave, George? But . . . Why don't we go traveling together, after I have the baby? We can bring her, when she's a bit older*—and I remember how Tess got weepy and I agreed to stay, even though I'd already written up a plan of my own: how I'd save my money and all the places I would go.

I make a small up-down motion with my shoulders. "Tess was kind of stressed. So I figured I'd go later."

Calliope nods slowly. I'm sure it doesn't make sense to her. It hardly makes sense to me.

"Did you get to travel much while you were away?"

"Yeah. We took the train to Paris when Mum and Dad were together. And after school I backpacked in Greece, Italy, and Switzerland."

"That would have been great."

"It was. I hope you get to do it too, George."

I nod. I picture myself going to all the places in Calliope's films. Then I picture going there with her. Images fly in—the two of us kissing beside the fountains and mountains and on all the gondolas. I push the pictures away. *Too soon, George.*

And then we are quiet again. Calliope spirals a pattern into the sand with her finger. I shuck off my shoes and socks and dig into the sand with my toes.

"So, is it hard being here without your mum and brother?" I ask. I see Calliope's face change in the dark. "Sorry. You don't have to answer that."

She doesn't say anything for a bit. Then says, "I really miss them, but Terry is a dickhead, so I'm happy to be done with him. I think Dad's hoping Ari will wake up and come home too. But I've told him he shouldn't hold his breath."

"I'm sorry."

"Thanks. I don't know . . . Terry's just, really full of himself. He writes these huge poems about horses and war. I don't understand any of them. He calls modern poetry 'weak,' so he's trying to get Mum to change how she writes." Calliope rolls her eyes. "And he's a chronic mansplainer. Massive."

"Wow."

"Yeah, he's always like: *Let me tell you why you're wrong.* He once mansplained the word *queer* to me. For, like, an hour."

"Oh. That's sad."

Calliope nods. "He also says how much he loves people of color 'cause we're so *vibrant.*"

"Yuck. How did your mum end up with him?"

"Well, he's won all these prizes . . . I think he even got some award from the Queen? Mum thinks he's a genius, so she listens to him. But he's like a lemon pip. You know? Like when you're eating a curry and you bite into a pip that's fallen in—"

"That is the worst." I nod.

"Yeah."

And now I want to add: "My dad's a lemon pip too," because Calliope is an open book, and suddenly, I want to try being one.

I go to say something about Dad—just something small—but instantly, my mouth fills with the old, sour taste and then, the sick lurch that comes whenever I try to talk about Dad, or *to* him. And now, in comes the familiar swell of shame and—

blurry movement, a strange body,
a shout, and far away,
the look on Tess's face the night he—

Calliope touches my arm. "Hey, George," she says.

"Hey," I say, suddenly stuck.

"You okay?"

"Yes, yeah," I say, trying to come back to her.

"Sorry. I've been talking so much. You should tell me to just stop and breathe."

"No, it's fine. Really. It's just—" I want to explain. I can't. I reach across and take her hand. "It's fine. I really like listening to you, especially in that hot British accent."

Calliope smiles. "Thank you. Took me a while to get it just right."

She bumps my shoulder again. We stop talking and we are still and silent and listening to everything else: the hush of waves on the shore, a rumble-crash just beyond. Wind in the tall trees behind us. The plop of a fish or a mermaid in the distance.

Calliope stands up in a rush. "Hey. Let's go swimming!"

I look up at her. "Yeah?"

"Do you want to?" she asks, and I can see her biting her lip, and maybe she's thinking I don't want to be here, maybe she's thinking I'm quiet because I don't like her, or she thinks I'm boring? So I stand up and say, "Sure!" like someone who's sure of things, just for a moment.

We pull off our clothes and jump into the sea. Not all our clothes. Not all the way into the sea. Enough to stand in thigh-high water and splash at each other. Enough for our skin to fizz, to shiver in our bras and undies and feel the slap of the waves on our bellies.

And I'm standing right beside Calliope and we're looking at stars when a wave comes out of nowhere, pushes us backwards and under—*and now we're drowning, now we're going to get eaten*—and now we're two bodies blinking, two bodies twisting—*and is this the moment it all ends? Is this it?*—and we push up and stand, spitting salt, wiping the ocean from our eyes.

And now Calliope is laughing, reaching for my hand, steadying me. "Not today, sea!" she yells—and we are alive, and I'm with Calliope and she's shouting and unshakeable, fist in the air, fearless.

We run out of the surf. We tug on our clothes. We sit on the sand, squeeze the water out of our hair, shiver with the rush and thrill of it.

Calliope looks at me. "Terrible idea?"

"No, the *best* idea," I say.

And then we sit and watch the water miss us, miss the shapes our bodies just made.

And I know logically we have only a short time before the last ferry leaves to go back to Circular Quay and we should go and catch it, but something steals time and slows it, or turns it to air, because now we are kissing again.

And I can't quite think straight, can't quite get the air in, can't quite figure out if gravity is still on or someone switched it off. We can't keep our hands off each other. It's like in those movies where the couple can't keep their hands off each other, except we're the only ones who can hear the music swooping in and we are two girls, and they almost never make movies like that about two girls.

Cold hands
and lips and hushed laughter into mouths
and the feel of fingers and soft-brushed skin and
there's no *what if we are*
seen or *what if we are*
caught or *what about the ferry*—

and when we look up and blink, time has melted into a puddle. Of course we have missed the last boat.

Both our phones are out of battery. And I don't care.

The sea slides closer to our feet, wanting what we have in this moment, hungry for it—it might suck us up and turn us both into mermaids if we aren't careful. And I think that might not be the worst thing to happen, because I never want to feel anything other than this.

7

It's just after seven a.m., and we're sitting at the wharf, eating hash browns from McDonald's.

"Delicious. Best food in existence," says Calliope, her mouth full.

We have bought five hash browns each. We eat like we've been lost at sea. Maybe we have?

We've stayed out all night and my insides skitter. I have stayed up all night before; I've come home from parties just as my mums were waking, but this time Mum and Mel didn't even know I was going out.

My parents will get up and I won't be home, and Susan will be yowling for breakfast. And Gramps will probably have lost something he needs found.

I am going to be in so much shit.

That, or they'll think I've been murdered. I might arrive to lights going around the tops of police cars. Mum might be a heap on the floor. Mel too.

"My parents are going to freak out," I say to Calliope, to the air.

"Yeah?" says Calliope. "Maybe you'll get home before they get up? It's the weekend, maybe they'll sleep in."

"No—Mum's an early bird. I think she'll notice."

"Oh. I'm sorry."

She rubs her thumb over mine. I feel the memory of her hands, her mouth, the draw of time. "Don't be sorry," I say, pressing my thumb onto hers. "I'm not. It was perfect."

"Yeah? Okay," she says. "Well, I agree. It was."

We're on the ferry at 7:30. We stand at the front of the boat, along with a handful of bleary-eyed weekend commuters. The sun has crawled out of the sea. My skin zings where it was touched.

We pitch up and down as we hit the ocean swell. Our hair flies into our eyes. The city is an imprint in the distance. The seagulls croon and cry.

Calliope turns to me. "Maybe we shouldn't go home. Let's steal a ship, George. Become pirates. Want to become a pirate?" She kisses me on the lips in front of the other passengers. Some of them stare.

My insides cartwheel.

Calliope pulls back, her slow smile dissolving me.

God.

I lean towards her.

"Yes. Let's," I say.

Lips on lips, we kiss and dip. We rise and fall. We roll and tilt.

When I get home, I expect everything and anything. Away from Calliope and her hands and smile, I'm nervous again. My body feels scrunched tight with anticipation. How much shit am I in?

I walk into the kitchen.

I find Mum alone, standing at the counter, holding her phone.

"George," she says. "Oh my god."

Something in the way Mum stills her body, the way she puts the phone on the counter, the way her voice sounds like it's collapsing in on itself, makes my bones go cold.

"Tess was in a car accident," Mum says. "Someone rear-ended her when she went to get some food. She's okay. But she had her baby last night."

DELIVERY, 2

(oil on canvas)

midnight

two bodies/one car

headlights arcing over red taillights, and

the shape of something crossing the road

(a possum or a cat or a ghost the girl says, later, to her friend)

 and her foot punches the brakes

car hits car—baby hits womb wall—girl hits airbag

pulse and crunch and flash

and is it her mouth opening and closing like

a fish under fearwater?

girl can't be sure but now there's hurt, pinching everywhere

and noises all around

and a baby wanting to leave

rightthisminute because

it is suddenly too tight

 in

 here

8

Mid-morning. Smell of disinfectant. Fluorescent lights.

Tess sits up in her hospital bed, holding a baby.

She stares blankly at me when I walk in the door. She looks steamrolled. Three other mothers sit on three other beds—they have babies in arms, partners beside beds, and siblings peering at babies and playing on iPads. Everyone turns to check out the young girl visiting the young girl.

Tess is alone. Maybe her parents are getting some coffee; maybe they've gone to get supplies. All I know is, it's just me here with Tess and a human she just launched out of her vagina. There's a *CONGRATULATIONS!* card on the table.

I stare at her. How did it come to this? Tess is a *mum.*

"Hi—" I begin.

"Hey," she says. "You're here."

"Yeah. I'm glad you're okay. I'm so sorry I wasn't—"

She looks down at the baby. "He's a boy."

I lean forward, look down. "He's beautiful, Tess," I say. The baby's face looks scrunched, narrow, and blotchy. Which makes sense—he's just made his way through a very small opening. It's kind of a miracle he didn't come out like a strand of spaghetti.

"Did you know? That he wasn't a girl?"

"Um." I pause. "Yes?"

Tess nods. "Huh." She seems muddy, spaced out, like she's not quite here. Now she looks at me. "You missed it all, George."

I suck in a breath. "I know. I'm so sorry—"

"Mum called you. Where were you?"

"You weren't due for weeks—I didn't think—I was—"

"It was really scary. Did they tell you? About the crash?"

"Yeah. It sounds awful."

Tess's eyes fill with tears. "It was the worst. When we got hit, I thought, *God, my baby's dead.* And then everything started hurting. Like, *so* much. And in the ambulance, it started hurting even more. As if that was possible. You wouldn't believe. And then I got to the room and I started pushing, just like that. And everyone was running around, and then he came out and started screaming, which they said was good, but *oh my god.*"

Tess looks at her baby—the one she's been planning for all this time but today is a total surprise. "And then they washed him, I think? Or, like they wrapped him up and said to try and feed him but I didn't know how, and they showed me and then he hooked on and sucked—on my *boob*, George. It felt *so* weird."

"Wow," I say. I try to picture it all. Can't.

Tess's nose starts to dribble—she doesn't wipe it. "Why weren't you *here*?"

"I—" I say. "I—"

I don't know what to tell her. Tess needed me, and I wasn't there. I can't change that or fix it.

I feel the air turn gray. I look back at the ferry ride, but it is filtered now by the harsh hospital light, the white walls, the sound of Tess. It paints the night over with gray.

And now the baby squawks awake.

Both of us jump.

Tess looks down. The baby's mouth opens and he starts to squall. Tess looks at me, scared. "Do you think he needs feeding?"

"I don't know." How would I know? The baby's mouth widens— he lets out a cry that could topple a forest. *Oh my god*, I think. *I am never having a kid.*

"What do I do?" says Tess. "Should I feed him?"

"Yeah, do that."

Tess fumbles around with her shirt, lifts it, points her boob at the baby. The baby moves his head like an earthworm reaching blindly through dirt. Then somehow, mouth finds nipple; some kind of magic makes the two of them click and lock together; the baby stops shrieking, and sucks.

Tess stares down at her baby. Her face softens. She shakes her head. "How did this happen?"

I know Tess doesn't need a science lesson. "Some kind of magic," I say.

Tess gives me a lopsided smile. "You didn't tell me he was a boy."

"You said not to."

"I got all those dresses—"

"He can still wear them, right?"

"Hmmm." Tess blinks. She sniffs. "Can you pass me a tissue?"

"Sure."

Tess honks out a blow, startling the baby, who falls off Tess's boob and then she has to fumble him back on. And then the baby sucks again and Tess starts crying again and I see time stretching out like this: Tess weeping and offering up her boob and smiling and weeping, over and over and over, like in those movies where the day repeats and repeats and the best friend sits beside her friend and watches her feed a baby and cry, and feed her baby and cry, and feed and cry, forever.

After the baby is fed, he's burped. A nurse glides in to show Tess how to do it and Tess says, "Like this?" and the nurse says, "Not quite—more like this." The baby lets out a microscopic belch. Then he falls back asleep. The nurse lays him in his bassinet, then goes to check another mum.

Tess looks at me. "Holy shit."

"Yeah."

"This is so weird." She can't seem to stop saying that word. I don't blame her.

I nod. "It's the weirdest."

"I'm so tired."

"You should sleep, Tess."

"All right," she says. "Can you be here when I wake up?"

"Sure."

Tess closes her eyes and falls asleep instantly.

I watch her, I watch the baby—two bodies breathing. I watch life change, like a river moving across the land of me and Tess, parting us. On one side: a girl who just kissed a girl on a ferry. On the other: a girl who just pushed an actual human out of her body, without her best friend by her side.

I feel squirmy with guilt. Achy too, with fatigue and overwhelm, and too many feelings to explain. Maybe I'd paint them when I got home. I pull out my phone to text Calliope, but it is still out of battery. I lean back in the vinyl hospital chair. In seconds I am asleep.

Ruthie runs into the hospital room. "George!" she yells, waking me. "Have you seen my brother?"

Tess's mum and dad follow behind her. "Nephew, Ruthie! Nephew!" says Lydia. They're carrying bags and flowers.

I sit up. "Hey," I say.

Tess wakes, blinks, looks around for a second like maybe she's forgotten she's a mum and can't figure out what she's doing here. Then she remembers. "Oh," she says. "Hi, everyone."

Tess's mum kisses her on the forehead, peers over at the baby, then looks at me in my seat. "Hi, George," she says. "You good?"

"Hi, Lydia. Yeah," I say, avoiding the look in her eyes that says, *You missed it all, George. Where were you?* I'm used to dodging Lydia's looks; I've done it for years. Like the time Tess decided to have a kid and wouldn't change her mind. And the time Tess threw up in the dog's bed after drinking too much tequila, and the time Tess pierced her septum . . . and all the times Tess did things that didn't make sense, and I didn't stop her.

"We tried calling you," says Lydia.

"I know. I'm sorry, I was out—"

"Oh? In the middle of—" Lydia starts to say, but Ruthie says, "Can I hold the baby? I've been practicing with my dolls!" and Tess says, "Only if you're careful," and "Mum, did you bring my clothes?" and Tess's dad says, "Who wants a muffin? I brought muffins," and everyone bustles and clatters around like they always do, like they've clattered and bustled the whole time I've known them.

Tess spends the morning alternating between weeping, smiling, holding up the baby's fingers and feet for a look, eating muffins, weeping some more, telling Ruthie to be careful holding the baby, and remembering I wasn't at the birth.

"It doesn't make sense," she says, and then she says, "Look at his little feet," and then she says, "You missed it *all*, George."

Finally I say, "I was on a boat—"

and Tess says, "What?"

and in comes the nurse to check on Tess's insides (*doing nicely*) and the baby's belly button (*also doing nicely*),

and Lydia tries to show Tess how to swaddle the baby and Tess cries because she can't get it right,

and David goes for coffee (*want one, George? You look like you could use a double*),

and people come with their carts (*you can buy a teddy bear for the baby, dear, money goes to charity*),

and people come with tea and coffee (*one sugar or two, love?*),

and Tess keeps crying and her mum says, "Don't worry, it's your milk coming in," and Tess says, "What's the baby drinking *now*, then?" like she doesn't know, like she hasn't read every baby book in the universe,

and Tess's aunt comes to take Ruthie to play at the park,

and Tess's mum and dad go home to get ready for the baby to come home tomorrow, and Lydia says, "George, you can hold down the fort, right?"

and Tess cries again,

and the baby squawks,

and then comes more feeding and swaddling and crying and poo,

and at some point, Tess falls asleep again

and the baby sleeps too.

I am exhausted. The day has been long and loud. Should I have another nap, or should I keep watch like a tower guard—*Hark! Who goes there?*—just in case?

My phone is finally charged. I check for messages. Three texts from Tess last night, five missed calls from Mum, two missed calls from Lydia, three texts from Mum, two texts from Dad, and one text from Calliope.

TESS: *Hey, I need a burger. You want a midnight burger?*

TESS: *I'm thinking pineapple egg and bacon. Is that too gross?*

TESS: *Ugh delivery costs so much! You could pick it up on the way? Promise I'll pay you back*

MUM: *George, where are you? Please call me*

MUM: *Tess is in hospital. She is having her baby!!*

MUM: *WHERE ARE YOU??? CALL ME!!!*

DAD: *Georgia. Shall we talk tomorrow?*

DAD: *We do need to discuss all this.*

CALLIOPE: *Hey, that was so great. What are you doing tonight?*

Far out. I missed so much.

I stare down at the phone. I need to write back to Calliope, but what would I say? My brain feels gluey—my words are in there somewhere, but might come out like papier mâché mush.

I tuck the phone away.

Tess wakes, she's drooled a bit on herself.

Holy shit, I think, for the thousandth time. *She's a mum.*

I stare at her from across the river.

"Hey," she says. She half smiles. She sees the baby in his bassinet and frowns. *Holy shit,* she's probably thinking. *I'm a mum.*

"How long was I sleeping?"

"I don't know."

"My boobs hurt."

"Yeah?"

"Everything kind of hurts." She sits up. Looks over at the baby, and her face softens again. "God, George. Look at him."

I look at the baby. "Definitely cute," I say. He looks a bit naked-mole-ratty. His lips are chapped. He has tiny, perfect eyelashes. "Have you thought of a name yet?"

"Not yet." Tess starts counting off on her fingers. "Johan. Mortimer. Tintinabula. Zippy." She looks at me. "Thoughts?"

"Those are your options?"

"Those are some possibilities. Just from the top of my head."

"Would you seriously call your son Tintinabula?"

"Maybe. I want him to be unique." Tess pauses. "I really like Serendipity—that was in my top five for girl names. Maybe I'll still call him that. What do you think?"

"Mmm. What about Seren?"

Tess's eyes go wide.

"Seren! Shit. That's fantastic!" She leans over her sleeping newborn. "Dude. Wake up. You have a name."

"No rush," I say. "Take a minute, pal."

"No need. It's decided." Tess looks happy for a second.

Tess and I google the baby's name on our phones.

Tess says, "Hey, it's a top girl's name in Wales!"

I say, "And it's a top boy's name in Turkey."

We look at each other. Perfect.

Mel and Mum come to visit the baby at five.

"Tess!" they say, faces wide open. "Congratulations, sweetheart!"

Me, they look at coolly. "Hello, George," they say.

Mel and Mum were not pleased about my escapade. When I got home, they plonked me in Gramps's chair and sat opposite me on the couch, wearing identical faces.

"I need to go see Tess," I said.

"Just a minute," they said. Then they took turns telling me off.

"You should have told us! What were you thinking?" and,

"What if something had happened to you?" and,

"You could have been in trouble! We wouldn't have known!" and,

"Who even were you with?"

I opened my mouth.

Empty bubbles. Water. Kisses. Finding our feet. The shapes we made in that water.

"I was out," I said.

Mel sighed. "We know that, George."

Mum said, "Who with? We know it wasn't with Tess. Was it Laz? Come on, George. Talk to us."

I looked at her. If I didn't talk now, I knew Mum would ask and ask and ask until I gave her something. Mum was only good with silence and secrets outside this house.

"Okay," I said. "I was with a girl."

Mum and Mel looked confused. "A girl? What girl?"

I hesitated. Then: "Calliope."

Mel raised her eyebrows. "Calliope? Who just started work with you?"

"Yeah."

"*Kal-eye-oh-pea?*" When Mum said it, Calliope's name sounded rubbery, song-less.

I nodded.

Mel said, "And you went out with her? I didn't know you had become close."

"Oh, well . . . we're not—" I paused. Calliope and I had gone from strangers to friends to girls who kissed on midnight beaches, all in the space of a week. It would take some explaining. So I just said, "Yeah."

"Huh." Mel sat back, processing.

Mum said, "Why didn't you tell us?"

"You were asleep."

"Why didn't you leave a note?" asked Mel.

"I just—"

Why didn't I leave a note? I thought back to last night. Remembered running down the stairs, remembered running all the way to the wharf. I didn't think of notes or telling people I was leaving or anything else. I didn't know I was going to be out all night.

"You need to think about these things, George," said Mel.

"I do. I wasn't—" I sighed. "I really have to go see Tess. I can talk about it later. But I have to go."

Gramps wandered into the living room just then. "Hey. Who's going to drive me to the eye doctor?"

Mum and Mel looked at each other. They'd forgotten about his appointment.

"Can't you catch a bus, Dad?" said Mum.

"I won't be able to *see* afterwards, Sara," said Gramps. "You want me to walk into traffic?"

"We're having a conversation here, John," said Mel.

Gramps glanced over at me. "About Georgie? And her escapade?"

Mum sighed. "Yes."

Gramps grinned. "Nicely done. Showing some real spunk, kiddo."

"*John,*" said Mel.

"Thanks, Gramps," I said.

"Well, I'll be by the door, waiting," he said pointedly, and wandered out of the room.

Then Mel and Mum had to leave the conversation there, because I had to use one of the cars to visit a baby, and they had to decide who'd be using the other car to take Gramps. They jangled down the corridor—I could hear them in the hallway. "You know I have to be at the studio, Sara," and "You know I have to be at work, Mel."

"Okay. Rock paper scissors."

I heard Mum laughing. "Oh my god, you're ridiculous—"

And then silence, which was either them rock-paper-scissoring or kissing. Gramps was probably standing there rolling his eyes.

"Ha! Beat you."

"*Fine,*" Mum said.

And out the door they went, all still talking—the walls, the couch, the windows vibrating with their sound even after they had left.

Mum and Mel have brought flowers into the hospital room. They lean over Seren and look at his fingers and toes and sniff the top of his head (which every adult has done so far). They have brought their phones out and taken photos. Their voices have gone up an octave. They have melted into puddles.

"So how are you feeling, sweetie?" says Mel.

Tess says, "Sore," and grimaces.

Mum holds the baby. "He's beautiful, darling. He looks like you."

Tess smiles.

Mum stares down at Seren, and a look crosses her face.

I wonder if she's thinking about when she became a mum with me? About the time I was a baby and life had promise and she was in love with Dad?

When I was almost eleven, I asked her: "What was he like, Mum?"

Mum and I were in a fancy restaurant. It was Mum's birthday. It was our life just before Mel, and life "after" Dad.

"What was he like?" Mum repeated back to me.

"Yeah, when you first met him." I had a picture in my head. Dad new and sparkling. Dad clean and sober. Dad young. Dad like a statue when it first goes up in a park, before pigeons come and crap on its head and people stub cigarettes out on its feet.

"He was . . ." I could see Mum trying to form gentle words. "He was charming. And funny."

I thought about him being those things. It was pre-Seattle, so I still thought I might love Dad and the broken parts might mend. I remembered the time Dad took us to an ice-skating show when I was eight. Afterwards, he pretended to skate the sidewalk, twirling with his arms up. He pretended to do a double axel; Mum and I laughed, and Mum was charmed. She must have been, because when he came up to kiss her, she kissed him back.

And now here she is. Holding the baby of a teenager and feeling all the feelings, her emotions moving over her face like time-lapse clouds—from happiness to sadness to regret to a dragon to a rabbit to love.

Mum sniffs. She starts to cry. "He's just so lovely, Tess."

"Thank you," says Tess. And then she starts too.

"You two," says Mel. But her voice is wobbly, and in a second she's at it.

I look at them. God. They're all puddles.

Laz comes late. Visiting hours are nearly over. He sits beside Tess's bed.

Tess blows her nose. She's been leaking tears all day. "Isn't he beautiful?" she says to Laz.

"Yeah," he says, and smiles, but it's half-hearted. He looks drained and hedge-pulled like Tess. Hair on end, shirt wrinkled. He glances across the bed at me.

I take him in—in just two days Laz has gone from bright to dim, like someone turned his screen to low-light to save energy. And maybe it's just a hangover from last night, but I think it's a deeper trench than that. Laz has folded into himself, turned dark-clouded. I want to walk outside with him and ask: *Is it the fires? Is it Tess and the baby? Is it the impending end of the world?* I want to say sorry for not coming to the pub last night when he asked. I want to tell him about Calliope. I want—

The baby squawks. Laz jumps in his seat.

Tess says, "You want to hold him?" but Laz shakes his head.

"No. I'm good." He tries to smile. "Um. Sorry. Got to go, actually." He stands up, touches Tess's shoulder. "Good job, T," he says. Then leaves.

He's been here all of ten minutes.

. . .

Tess and I sit together. It's been a long day. A huge day. There's a new human here now—four new humans, if you count all the other babies squawking in their mums' arms in this room.

Tess looks over at me. "He barely glanced at him. And then he just bolted, because Seren started crying—"

"Oh," I say. "It wasn't like that." A hollowdark part of me wants to say, "Can you blame him? You could use that scream as a weapon. Your baby could overthrow a dictatorship." But of course I don't say that.

"What's it like, then?" Tess asks.

"Laz is just, um, he—" I pause. And I try to find the right words. I feel them forming like phantom animals in the shadows. When they arrive, the words will settle Tess like they always do. I want to throw them to her, build a bridge of words and walk over the river with them and join her. I want to sew good words into her clothes.

Nothing comes. Tess sighs. Then yawns, deeply. "Do you know if Mum is coming back tonight?" She reaches for her phone to check messages. The river rolls on.

The day is over. Lydia has arrived and is bustling around, sorting Tess out for her first night as a mother. It's time for me to go.

I lean over Tess, give her a kiss on the forehead. "See you," I say.

"Yeah, see you tomorrow."

I pause. "Yeah. Okay, sure."

I was planning to see Calliope tomorrow. How is it possible Tess doesn't know about me and Calliope? How have I not told her? I guess I waited for the right time for so long today, time slid on by.

"We'll be taking Tess and the baby home in the morning, George," says Lydia. "So why don't you come at eleven?"

"All right."

Of course I'm going to Tess's tomorrow. I'll see her the next day too, and the next day and the next, for the rest of my life. Life will spool out and I'll be Tess's companion animal, following her wants, endlessly.

But how can I complain? I've never said I wanted anything different.

I drive home, trying not to fall asleep. I open the windows, wrap my hands tight around the steering wheel, put on music—I blast it the whole way back. When I walk in, Mum and Mel want to talk.

"George? Just for a minute, please?" says Mum in the living room.

But, "I can't," I say, because of course, my uni assignment is due. The one I haven't finished yet, the one due at midnight tonight.

I slog up the stairs, open my laptop, write words. Push out an essay. Slide in citations. Don't even proof it.

I submit the essay at 11:57 p.m.

It's genuinely terrible.

I lie on the bed. My phone blinks on. I look at it for the first time in hours.

God. So many messages.

CALLIOPE: *Oh my god I'm so tired hahaha*

CALLIOPE: *Want to go get some food tonight?*

DAD: *Georgia. It's important we talk some more.*

CALLIOPE: *Hey. U ok? Did you get in trouble with your mums?*

DAD: *Georgia, I'm thinking perhaps you could come and visit. I could pay for your flights. You could come for Christmas? It's been a long time.*

CALLIOPE: *Everything okay?*

CALLIOPE: *Okay . . . you're not answering me . . . that's fine . . .*

DAD: *There is a lot to talk about, I know.*

CALLIOPE: *Please call. I really hope you are okay*

I don't know how to answer these. I'm so tired I can barely see. I'm so full of unspoken news and new things, my brain has clunked to a stop. The idea of writing back to Dad feels enormous, impossible. And the idea of calling Calliope and explaining any of this day turns me into fog.

I put down my phone.

Close my eyes. And sleep.

9

Seren comes home from hospital in his capsule.

Tess prods her boob at him and looks at me like I'm a made-up thing. She's frazzled as fuck.

The baby feeds. The baby burbs. The baby poops. The baby sleeps. The baby wakes. Arms flail through his swaddle cloth. Tess wraps him in thin muslin, but he manages to bust out like an alien. Life must be a rude shock. The baby yowls: *Where am I? What will happen? Where are we going?*

Same, kiddo.

Seren screams, his mouth open like a tiny, furious cave.

He pukes half-digested milk all over Tess.

Oh my god, I think.

"George," Tess pleads. "Help."

I try. I hold the baby. I jiggle him a little and Tess says, "Don't do it like that!"

"Like what?"

"You'll drop him! Support his head!"

"I won't! How? Okay!"

God. Maybe I can't be trusted with babies.

I tell Tess and she starts to cry.

. . .

Laz doesn't come to visit.

"Doesn't he care?" Tess says, and cries.

The baby won't "latch on"—a term the nurses used in hospital, like Tess was prepping for a space launch. Tess flounders with her boobs, and cries.

Ruthie comes into the living room and says, "Can I hold him? Maybe I can fix him?"

Tess says, "I can fix him too," and cries.

Tess's dad says, "Would you like a cup of tea, Tess?"

"Yes please," she says, and cries.

The baby falls asleep. Tess walks into the kitchen to make a piece of toast. Ruthie hops along beside her and pokes a finger sideways into Tess's tummy.

"You're so big and squishy!" she says. "Maybe there's still a baby inside you?"

And Tess cries.

Early evening. The end of Seren's second day being alive.

I am on the bus, halfway home. The bus shunts left and right, all bodies pressing. Everything feels cluttered—it's too busy in here. Too squiggly, too smelly, too hot, so I get off the bus and run.

I run through the fuzz of car exhaust, past traffic lights and lights turning on in houses. Run through heat-thick wind, along the up-down cracked pavements, weaving past walkers carrying their groceries.

I run and breathe. I breathe out the baby crying and Tess's dark-rimmed eyes and me not calling Calliope and Laz not coming by and Tess crying and my dad dying.

I breathe out the feeling of my body. I move so quickly, feet hitting the pavement, I stop being human. I become the path to the water, the choppy waves, all the hooded boats. I become parks and trees, leaves and fences and bikes and bins and houses getting knocked down or built. I become breath and bone. Over and under and away.

My mind opens, splays itself as I run. This is all there is.

I tumble into the house, into the jumble of rain jackets on hooks in the hall, the side table piled with junk mail, the smell of paint and something frying, and shoes in a turmoil on the floor.

From the kitchen Mum calls out, "That you, George?"

"Yep," I call back.

"Have you had dinner?"

"No."

"Want some?"

"Yes, please."

Mel comes out into the hall where I'm pulling off my shoes. "Did you remember the rice?"

Bent over, I look up at her. "No."

"Shit. George forgot the rice!" she calls towards the kitchen.

I say, "I didn't forget. No one asked me to get it."

"Your mother asked."

"Didn't."

Mum pokes her head out. "Oh," she says. "I forgot to ask."

"Shit," says Mel.

Gramps calls from the kitchen. "The lentils are burning!"

"Shit!" says Mum.

In the kitchen, the dead gull stands on the counter, freshly stuffed.

Two wings pinned, two glazed eyes staring.

This is what I've been brought to, it says. *I flew over oceans. I had brothers and sisters. I was Master of the air.*

Gramps tells us about the bird over dinner. He and the taxidermy guy found a lot of things inside the bird's stomach: a strip of plastic straw, a small fish head, a candy wrapper scrap, a fleck of balloon.

"Poor birds. They don't know what's food anymore," he says.

Over charred lentils and potatoes, Gramps tells us about the fleshing and stripping. He spoons in his food and talks about guts.

Mel says, "We're *eating,* John."

"Yes!" says Gramps. "And it's delicious!"

Gramps describes the taxidermy process from start to finish. He makes sure we get all the details. I move food around my plate. Guts and lentils aren't a great mix, no matter what anyone says.

When Gramps is done, the rest of us take a collective sigh of relief.

Then Mum looks at me. "How is the baby?"

"Noisy," I say. "He screams a lot. And he puked on Tess."

"Ah." Mum nods, like that all makes sense to her.

"Is Tess all right?" Mel asks.

"Kind of. Maybe." I pause, thinking of Tess's tears. "Um. I don't know?"

"I'll call Lydia tomorrow to see how I can help," says Mum.

"Okay." I nod.

Mum pauses. "George, I still think we need to talk about it."

"Yes," says Mel, looking at me.

You'd think Gramps's bird talk would have pushed my business out of Mum's and Mel's heads. But they are two determined, tenacious barnacles.

"Talk about what?" says Gramps. He looks at me. "Oh. The *escapade*."

"No need to call it that, Dad," says Mum. "George isn't a prisoner. It's just—she could have been hurt. We didn't know where she was."

I sigh. "I didn't mean to be out all night, Mum. We missed the ferry."

"The ferry?"

"We went to Manly."

"In the middle of the night?"

Gramps grins. *"Nice."*

"It was an accident, Mum." Which sounds like I'm saying it was a mistake. My stomach hurts.

"So, is Calliope . . . Is she—" Mel stops short of asking whether Calliope is my girlfriend. Mel and Mum don't like to intrude. They're cool mums. At least they like to think so. All mums like to think so.

"She's—" I stop. What is she? I haven't spoken to Calliope in two days. "I don't know. *God.*"

"It's okay, George." Mel reaches out and touches my hand.

I'm holding my fork like I'm about to stab it into the table. I look down at Mel's hand and pull mine away. It's too much. Dinner with this lot is always too much. Too many dead birds and squabbles and questions.

"Leave George alone, you two," says Gramps.

Mel and Mum look at Gramps. "We're just talking, Dad," says Mum. "You want us not to talk?"

"Too many questions," Gramps says. "You're always poking."

I look at Gramps. He smiles. I smile back. "Yeah," I say.

Mel turns to me. "Really? It's like that?"

Mum looks hurt. "But we talk. Do you not like talking, George?"

Ha. When have I *ever* liked talking? Does Mum even know me? And I haven't seen her do a bunch of talking, either, not about our knotty, shrouded things.

I look across at her. She seems so sad, suddenly.

"I'm just tired, Mum. It's been really intense with the baby. And Laz is kind of having a hard time too—"

"Oh," Mum says. "What's happening with Laz?"

Mel leans forward. "Is he okay? What's wrong?"

I blink at them.

Gramps barks out a laugh. "Too many questions!" he yells.

"Oh my *god*, John," says Mel.

And round and round they go.

. . .

Eight p.m.

We have dispersed: four seeds spread through the old house.

Mel has gone to write emails in the bedroom. Mum is in the living room, watching the news—the fires north and west of us are spreading. Gramps is in his room, arranging a date with someone new. Fragile Beverley is out of the picture; Gramps promised he let her down gently. I'm in the kitchen, scrubbing a burned lentil pan, and Susan is on the kitchen counter, sniffing the bird.

Susan breathes in the top of the bird's head, like everyone did with Seren yesterday. She half opens her mouth to let the smell in better. Now's she's taking a bite, which nobody did with the baby.

"No, Susan!" I dart sideways, lift the cat up with my sudsy hands, put her on the floor.

I look at the bird, look at the cat. Susan licks her side, then flicks her tongue, trying to get the suds off.

I am not for eating, says the bird.

"I'm sorry," I say to the bird. "I won't let it happen again." I look at the cat. "This bird is not for eating, Susan."

You're not the boss of me, Susan says. Her tail whaps. She stalks out of the kitchen.

I take the bird up to my room to keep an eye on him. Prop him on the shelf next to my grandmother's clock.

I check my phone. Sometime in the middle of today's muddle, I sent Calliope a quick text. *Hey sorry for not answering. I'll call u soon.* I got an *Okay* in reply. And then I didn't call her. And she didn't send any more messages.

She must think I'm the most confusing, the most unreliable, the least kissable—

Before I scrunch myself too tight, I send Calliope another text:

Hey, I'm really sorry for disappearing. Tess just had her baby and things have been kind of wild

My phone buzzes, three minutes later.

"She had her baby?" Calliope says. "Shit! All right. I forgive you. And I'm glad you're not locked in some dungeon—you had me worried. Tell me *everything*."

I half laugh. Just hearing her voice, the quick and bright of it, helps me breathe. "It's a boy. She had him two nights ago. She went to get some food and her car got rear-ended."

"Oh my god. Is the baby okay? Is Tess okay?"

"Yeah, he's fine. Tess is all right, considering everything. I can't believe I missed the birth. I was supposed to be there, but my phone died . . . and we were on the ferry—"

"Wait. You missed it 'cause we were out?"

"Yeah."

"Wow. I'm sorry."

"Don't be. It's not your fault. That was on me."

"Well, I am. I know you planned to be there. That really sucks."

"Thanks. I'm really sorry for worrying you. It's been full-on. Seren screams so loud."

"Is that his name?"

"Yeah. Tess and I came up with it."

"I love it." She pauses. "How about you, George. Are you okay?"

"I'm—" I pause.

I'm not. And I want to tell Calliope about it, about the baby screaming and Tess crying and the way the future feels right now—locked into Tess's life, wobbly with Dad's news, the rooms echoing with my family's sound. The future feels heavy, huge. I look over the heap. Don't know how to explain it.

So I say, "Yeah, I'm okay," because that answer is always the easiest.

Before she can ask me anything more, I add, "My grandpa just stuffed a bird that flew into our window. He brought it home tonight."

"He did what, now?"

"He took it to his taxidermy guy and they stuffed it. He told us all about it at dinner."

"Was it gross?"

"Yup," I say (*and thank you, Calliope, for swerving with me*). "He found some junk inside the bird's stomach. He brought it all back in a jar." Which is now sitting beside my grandma's urn on the mantlepiece, I don't add.

"Oh, poor thing," Calliope says. Then: "I need to see this bird."

"Okay." I kneel on my bed and take a photo of the dead gull: glass eyes baleful, flat, matted wings. Send it to Calliope.

"Oh. Pretty," she says.

I laugh. "The cat wanted to eat him today."

"Is that why he's in your room? Will you take him everywhere now? Like in that school experiment, where girls used to carry eggs around to see if they'd be good mums—"

I laugh again, which feels odd and good in my body at the same time. "Definitely, that's the plan."

"That makes me think of something. Here," she says.

My phone buzzes, and up comes a video.

"You want me to watch this?" I say.

"Yes please."

I press play.

It's water. Waves glint. Sun spangles. We're zooming in on a pelican.

The pelican bobs on the harbor. It looks Zen and peaceful, like a Buddhist or a boat.

Now the bird stirs—works its great wings, first in slow motion, then normal speed. The pelican rises, animated lines shivering over its wings, and beats away over the blue.

I say, "Wow, Calliope. That's beautiful."

"Thank you. Birds are like medicine in my opinion. Even a stuffed one . . . if you remember it was alive once." I picture her smiling.

"True." I look up at the gull—he'd nod, I think, if he could. "Thanks for showing me."

"You're welcome."

Now there's a tick of silence, and another. Two nights ago, Calliope and I sat in the sand, not talking. That quiet felt serene. This feels like . . . something else.

"So, do you want to do something tomorrow, maybe?" she says.

"Um." And I feel my chest fill with the space of having Calliope so close but not here. With me wanting to see her but not being able to.

"If you're busy, we can just leave it. It sounds like you've got a lot going on." Calliope sounds unsure. I picture her, sitting there, doubtful, not smiling. I want to run over to her place right this second. I want her to be sure about me.

Suddenly I blurt: "Things are kind of crazy right now, actually. Tess won't stop crying. And the baby won't stop crying. Everyone's losing their shit. And I just found out my dad is sick. In America. He's really sick."

Silence. One beat. Two.

What did I just do?

"Well, shit," says Calliope.

"I'm sorry. That was probably too much."

"You don't need to be sorry. I didn't realize—"

"It's okay."

"Is it? Are you all right? Jesus, that sucks about your dad. Do you want to meet up and talk? There's this Lebanese place—it's open late."

I want to say yes. I want to meet Calliope and talk to her and have her kiss all the noise away.

But I don't speak. My head feels blurry. I've pulled a secret out of myself; maybe I wasn't ready? I feel like one of those astronauts in the movies who has let go their line to the spaceship and is drifting backwards into the impossible deep.

Into my quiet Calliope says, "It's okay if you're not up for it right now."

I blink. "I'm sorry. I don't know what I'm doing."

"Hey, don't worry, it's okay. Thanks for telling me, though. I'm here if you want to talk. Like, don't worry if it's late. Okay?"

"Thank you."

More silence. I want to speak. I can't.

"All right, I'm going to go now. I'll see you at the Art House?"

"Okay," I say.

"Take care, George."

And those three words hang in the air a long time after she has gone.

BURN

(acrylic on canvas)

The smoke starts here:
in the base and body of a tree,
with fire and flame, the
panic of possums, and
insects racing in neat, fearful lines.

The smoke lifts, rises above the forest,
surveys.
It moves with the wind.
Rolls, twists. Curious.
It moves east, from the mountains to the sea.

The city glitters, turquoise and silver.
The smoke rolls in. Touches,
smears. Smothers. Squats.
And waits for the city to wake.

10

Inside my dream, the cat is running. Or maybe I am the cat, running?

We move through fuzz and haze. We don't know what is happening, but we run anyway. Running is best.

We go downstairs. House feels oozy. Air feels like cloth. We sniff for the Trouble. Is it in this room? Or this? We go to the kitchen to see if the air is nicer here.

It isn't.

Up down, here there, we're back in the room with the bird.

He stands on his made-up legs.

"Did you bring this?" we say.

"No," says the bird. "I don't think so. I don't remember. Birds don't—I—"

Inside my dream, Bird tries to remember. Or maybe I am the bird, remembering?

Was there—ever—like this?

Bird and I do not know. We remember other things—a silver railing, a shadowy ledge, a wave—glimpsed in ripped fragments. We fly after our torn past, snatching pieces in our beak.

Tree, heat, fuzz, and fug.

A feeling of something sliding down our throat.

We lean towards the past as best a dead bird can, trying to find the story of ourselves.

I wake up coughing. Outside the window, the sky pulses, eerie orange and foggy brown. The room smells like campfire.

"Shit. Shit." I get out of bed, shut the window. I start to cough and can't stop.

I dig in the bedside table for my inhaler and spacer. I hardly ever have to use them, but I *can't breathe.*

Two puffs.

Two more puffs.

I sit on the edge of the bed, sucking air in ragged clumps. Look at the smoke outside. It's like being encased in cloud, in weird, muffled light. It's like being in the middle of nothing.

My phone lights up.

It's Laz.

Well. Here's the apocalypse, he says.

I go to text back. Take a breath.

In crawls the smoke. I begin to cough.

The city is made of muck and smoke and musk. The news sites blare panicked updates—toxic air quality and health warnings and catastrophic fire danger. Monster fires rush towards each other, combine, incinerate, destroy.

The news sites show walls of flame. Burned-out cars. Houses collapsing. Blackened sky, crimson embers flecking, trees falling, ashy faces of firefighters, creatures charred, and people weeping.

The smoke spreads and smothers.

"Unprecedented!" bleat the newscasters. Everyone's beside themselves—they are used to such peace, sitting in their glass towers, looking over the glittering sea. Fires don't come to this clean city. Smoke doesn't squat *here*.

Mel and Mum move through the house, shutting windows, fussing and flustered.

"Have you seen the air quality? It's hazardous. The worst ranking," says Mel.

"This is unbelievable," says Mum.

I go to the cupboard to feed the cat—she is under my feet, yowling. I feel the smoke wrinkling my throat. The house, all gaps and cracks, smells like ash.

My phone rings. It's Tess.

"Oh my god, George! Seren's going to get brain cancer. Come. Please."

We have shut everything that can be shut. We have run around with towels and tape and ripped cloths and stopped as many gaps as we can.

Gramps has sat in his chair, swearing. "Fuckin' politicians with their fuckin' hands in their money-grubbing pockets. That's why we're in the shit now!" He looks at me as I move past. "Georgie, have you seen my bird? I've lost him."

"He's in my room, Gramps," I say.

"Oh. Okay," he says.

There's no time to explain.

When we've done our best at home, I grab my backpack, ready to take the bus to Tess's place.

Mum says, "You can't go on a bus in this! You're high risk, George."

"Mum. I've just got a bit of asthma." And I have, but it's barely a thing, if you don't count the time I had to go on oxygen two years ago after getting influenza and the time I got campfire smoke in my lungs when I was nine and the times I can't stop coughing when I get sick and, um, this morning. It's nothing. I just have to bring my inhaler everywhere I go; I just have to always have it with me in case of emergencies. Tess used to say I could drop dead anytime. But that was then. The point is, "high risk" isn't me. That's for old people and smokers and people with lung disease. Not girls in their prime who run everywhere and can't seem to stop moving.

"I'll be fine," I say.

"This is not a normal situation," Mum says. "I'll drive you." She grabs her keys.

Mel stops us at the door. "Wait you two, wear these." She hands us two masks—they're the kind she wears when she's making plaster vulvas for her sculptures.

I turn mine over in my hands. The mask is made of some thick, molded material, with a plastic nob in the front and elastic straps on the sides.

"It keeps out the P2 and P10 particles," Mel says.

I don't have a clue what she's talking about.

"That's the invisible shit that will choke you, George," she explains. "Cloth masks don't work in this."

I put on the mask. Mel fusses around me. She adjusts the seal at the bridge of my nose, fixes the straps. Then she does the same for Mum.

Mum drives her old Toyota to Tess's house. The windows are shut, but the car vents are broken and let the smoke in. The sun grinds overhead: hulking, burning red. Mum turns on the radio. News announcers give more details on the fire in the mountains, the smoke in the city, the spread and reach and harm of the fires. They update the death toll—people are *dying*, in their cars and houses. Mum and I don't talk. We just listen. The road looks blurry. My chest feels clunky. Mum has her car lights on like it's night. Every now and then Mum shakes her head.

Calliope texts:

U ok? I tried calling

ME: *Yeah. Well, no. We had to seal up our house. This is crazy*

CALLIOPE: *Do you want to talk?*

ME: *I'm going to Tess's house. She's freaking out. Maybe tonight?*

CALLIOPE: *I have to work tonight*

ME: *Okay later then?*

CALLIOPE: *Sure*

And then we just sort of stop texting and it only occurs to me five minutes later that I could have asked how she was and what time did she finish work and did she have a mask that stopped the P2 and P10 particles?

I text again: *I hope you are alright—*

But Calliope doesn't answer.

"Who's that?" says Mum, glancing over.

"Oh. Um. It's Calliope," I say, flipping the phone facedown.

"The one who made you miss the birth?" Mum frowns.

"Yeah. I mean, no. She didn't make me miss it, Mum. That was on me."

Mum shakes her head. "Still—"

I wait, but she doesn't finish her sentence.

Time slides forward. Mum turns left, right, and what does that even mean: "Still"?

Still, you shouldn't see Calliope? Still, you don't have time to fall in love? Still, remember you're supposed to be looking after a baby you never asked for? Still, remember what you're carrying, George? Remember, remember, remember—

My breath feels hot behind my mask. The elastic pinches. I look out the window at the beaten sky, fences and limp trees slipping past. Mum and I don't talk, and then we are at Tess's house.

Mum pulls up to the curb. I open the door. We've been silent for the past five minutes, both of us elsewhere.

"Call me when you need a ride back, all right?" She reaches over, squeezes my hand.

"Okay." I give her a thumbs-up. I'm smiling at her, but she can't see that through my mask.

Mum drives off. I stand on the pavement, watching her leave. All around me the air eddies, waiting for my mother to come back and finish her sentence.

Inside Tess's house, everyone is bustling—Tess, Lydia, and Laz. He's finally visiting the baby. Sort of.

"Hey, Laz," I say when I see him.

He glances over at me. "Welcome to hell, George. Population: eight billion." His hair stands on end. Has he slept at all? There is no time to ask.

Towels and rags line the base of every window. Tess's house is old like ours, so there's a lot to do. Laz tapes the window sides. I roll rags. We're all wearing masks—Tess's dad went to get protective gear this morning. Now we're kitted out like fledgling firefighters, dealing with smoke most of us didn't think about until it traveled here.

The baby, not even three days old, is too small for a mask.

So Tess stands over him and frets.

At some point, Lydia goes out to try and find an air purifier. David and Ruthie are at work and school—Ruthie wore a tea towel clipped around her face because she was too small for a mask too.

Laz comes into the living room. "I'm out of tape," he says.

Tess says, "There's more on the kitchen counter, I think."

No one's joking around. No one's teasing each other. Nothing feels normal. Today, I almost miss the bickering.

We seal up the house like we're entombing ourselves. Once we're done, all Tess will need to do is get into her sarcophagus with her baby and close her eyes. I wonder if Tess would like that—Laz and I standing guard as she and Seren sleep, warding off all the danger.

When we're done, we sit on the living room floor. I make peanut butter sandwiches at the coffee table and hand them over. We pull off our masks. The hard edges have left red marks on our noses and cheeks. Smoke taps and pokes at the windows, trying to get in.

Tess doesn't eat. She's too upset. She sits by Seren, who's asleep in his little cloth bassinet—her hand on his chest. "I can't believe this is happening. What if he gets sick? What if he gets brain cancer?"

Tess read about inhaled smoke and cancer and lung disease this morning while she waited for me and Laz to come over. She's full of information and huge, walloping fear.

Laz isn't eating either. He looks over at Tess. "Well. He might."

Tess looks at him. "He might?"

I hold myself very still.

"Yeah. This has been happening for weeks, Tess. The fires up north—have you seen the air up there? People have been sucking this in since September. And air pollution isn't new. Think about other countries. Think about Delhi. Think about Mexico City. Air pollution has been killing people a lot longer than it's been scaring white teen mums."

"Harsh, Laz," I say.

"Yeah? It's true, though." Laz rubs his face.

"Seren might get cancer? Are you saying he'll get brain cancer?" says Tess. She's like a machine—stuck, whirring in place.

"It's okay, Tess," I say. "You haven't even gone outside. And it's only been a day."

But Laz says, "I mean, yeah, he might get cancer. We all might. The poison's everywhere."

And it is. It's all over the news: Smoke has crawled through the whole city already, slithered into office buildings, into buses and hospitals and hundreds of frail lungs.

"*Shit.*" Tess starts to cry. Not the leaky kind she's done for the past couple of days. Loud, big sobs.

"That's fucked up," she says, shaking her head. "I've killed him."

Laz waves a hand. "I told you—" he begins.

I stare at him. "Laz, don't."

"But I told her!" he says. He gestures at the baby. "I told her!"

And then he starts to cry too, and it's not pretty. Two mouths sagging open. Two people I love falling into grief holes, as the smoke spins and laughs outside.

I sit on the floor—I don't know who to comfort. I don't know how to fix it. So I just sit and say nothing. Nothing, nothing, nothing. I turn to smoke and stone.

Tess stares into her lap. "Laz," she says.

"What?" Laz looks over at Tess.

"Get the fuck out of my house."

Laz blinks. "Wait. You want me to leave? Jesus, Tess. I'm just saying—"

But then Tess lifts her hands and screams. It's stunning. A proper take-the-roof-off, murder-scene scream. Laz and I shrink back. His mouth falls open. Mine too. And if I could draw it, the sound would be a jagged line going through our bodies, piercing the windows, spiking through the smoke, looping around the fires in the mountains, coming back to us as terrible as it began.

Laz puts up his palms. "Okay. Tess, stop!"

But then the baby wakes up and starts going too, and *oh my god.* The walls are shaking and Tess is shaking and then Laz is standing up, and I'm standing up and sitting down again in a muddle.

"All right. I'm leaving. I'm leaving," Laz says. He goes to the front door, opens it, lets in more smoke. *"Fuck,"* he says. And the sound of his voice is like the earth and sky flinging themselves at each other, breaking each other's bones.

The door closes behind him.

And I crawl over to Tess and try to rock the scream out of her but it is so loud, we lose ourselves in it for a while, the two of us like stones thrown so high, maybe we will always be falling.

11

Time splinters into life before and after the scream.

I sit with Tess.

Tess doesn't speak.

"Do you want some tea, Tess? Some food, maybe? I could make you a smoothie—"

Tess shakes her head.

I sit beside her. I get up to do something useful. I sit down.

Tess's mum comes home fifteen minutes later. She takes one look at Tess and says, "Oh, sweetie."

Lydia looks after the baby all afternoon, except for the feeding. I sit with Tess; she barely speaks. We try to watch a cooking show, then a bad romance, then a dog show, but Tess doesn't really watch—she scrolls her phone, won't talk about what just happened. Whenever she looks at Seren, her eyes fill with tears.

Ruthie comes home from school. She hovers around the baby.

She says, "Tess, it was so smoky at school! We all had to stay inside! It was so *boring!*"

Tess nods, mute.

Ruthie sits on the couch. "What's this show? Can we watch something else?" She grabs the remote, flicks the channels round and round and round, till Tess says, "Ruthie, stop," like she's made of cement and Ruthie huffs off to play with her dolls.

We watch the show Ruthie landed on—a car race. We stare at the screen and watch the cars go round and round and round.

Mum messages at four: *I'm free to come and get you now. Is it a good time?*

I check with Tess. "Mum doesn't want me catching the bus. She can pick me up now. Do you need me to stay?"

Tess shakes her head. "No, it's fine. You can go."

Mum parks, pops in to see the baby.

"How's everyone doing in this hell smoke?" she says, stepping through the door. She sees Tess's face. "Oh, sweetie," she says.

For over an hour, Mum and Lydia murmur in the kitchen. I picture them, heads close. I picture Mum with her hand on Lydia's back, listening.

When Mum comes out from the kitchen, she says, "Tess, it'll be okay. We are all here to support you, sweetheart."

Tess just blinks at her.

Mum sits on the couch. "I can bring you soup this week. What's your favorite?"

Tess opens her mouth to answer. Shuts it. Starts to cry.

"Oh, Tess," says Mum. She tears up too because that's how she rolls, and now Lydia comes in. She and Mum sit beside Tess. No one speaks.

Ruthie walks in. "I'm hungry! Why are you all sitting here? Everyone's being boring!"

I make Ruthie some jam toast in the kitchen. She looks at her plate. "Why is everyone sad, George?"

I look at her. "I'm not sad, Ruthie." It's a lie, but Ruthie doesn't know that. Then I say, "Do you know I have a magic bird in my house?"

Her eyes go wide.

I tell her about the bird's special powers. I grab some scrap paper and a pen from the kitchen drawer and draw a story for her. When I draw the bird juggling a kitchen knife, a ladybug, and a carrot, Ruthie starts to laugh. And just for a moment, something in the world is not terrible.

When it's time to go, Mum and Lydia hug goodbye at the door.

Ruthie has gone back to her room to play with her toys. The new air purifier rattles in a corner, trying to fix things.

I stand beside Tess, who's feeding Seren. "Are you sure you don't want me to stay?"

Tess's eyes are closed, her head leaning back on the couch. "No," she says. "Go. It's fine."

I feel a beat of relief. I can't help it—the feeling slides in, blue-gray.

"Okay. I'll call you later. All right? Okay?"

Tess just waves me away.

12

Ten a.m.

Hazy street. Traffic gruntling.

I'm opposite the Art House in my mask, waiting to cross the road. It's day two of the apocalypse. The smoke squats over the city, seeping.

I took the bus today. Mum had to go to work early and Mel had to go to the studio. "I'm sorry, George," she said, "I really need to get things done for my exhibition. You'll be fine on the bus. Just wear your mask. Make sure it fits properly. Don't take it off or you'll *die*."

Across the road, the Art House tries to wave to me with its windows, but the smoke has smeared the glass. The best it can do is dully glint.

Tess messaged me this morning. *Can you bring some boob pads when you come today? My milk has come in. I'm like a burst water main*

I wrote back: *So sorry, Tess. I've got work. Helping in the store before I teach. I can come tonight, though?*

Oh, said Tess. Just, *Oh*

Inside those two letters, I felt the buzz of Tess's disappointment. Yesterday was terrible. I probably should have gone over there this morning. But I couldn't. I couldn't be with Tess all the time.

A motorbike passes, its muffler *blatting*. Truck, car, taxi, bus. Clatter and rattle. A sigh of brakes. The walk signal turns green. It *beep beep beeps* as I cross the road.

The bell tinkles.

I step inside the hush of the Art House.

Laz sits at the counter, on a stool. He looks up at me. "Hey," he says.

I can barely hear him, he's so quiet. "Hey," I say. I walk over. He's scrolling his phone. "Are you okay?"

He rubs an eye. "No," he says.

I stand beside him. I touch his hand. "I'm sorry about yesterday."

"It's not your fault."

"No. I mean—"

"It was going to happen, George. We all saw it coming."

Now I'm not sure if he means Tess or the fires. Maybe both?

"Want to talk about it?" I say.

"Not really—"

The bell on the door tinkles again.

Laz and I look over. Calliope's here. She's wearing a mask, but pulls it off inside, where the smell isn't much better. Everything feels acrid, gloamy—the smoke has made its way into the back of my throat and is refusing to move.

"Hi." Calliope smiles.

"Oh," I say, "I thought you were coming this afternoon?"

"And hello to you too," says Calliope. She laughs, but there's a pinch to it, like I've hurt her.

"I'm sorry," I say. "I didn't mean—"

"I asked her," says Laz. "I didn't know you were coming in."

"I messaged you."

"You did?" Laz flicks through his phone. "Ah. Sorry."

His voice is flat, his eyes dull. I want to spark him back up, but a) how, and b) my brain feels sandpapered too. I couldn't paddle this morning because of the smoke. I couldn't even go outside. Dad messaged three times before I got up—I haven't replied to him in days. I tried to draw in my notebook this morning to get the tangle out, but all I could manage were rows of flat, black lines.

The bushfire in the mountains is monstrous now. Everything is growing, raging, destroying. Fires have started in the south too. The whole state is burning.

Today at breakfast, Mum said, "We had to send Arthur to hospital yesterday. His asthma—"

Gramps said, "We should go and burn something in Parliament House. Then those arseholes would wake up!"

Mum and Mel didn't say anything. I didn't say anything. I felt so full. Tess. Dad. Noise. Future. Dying. How could I fit in *fire*? But life isn't a "Choose Your Own Adventure," even if they tell you it is at school.

The bell tinkles.

A customer comes in. Calliope steps out of their way. Laz stands up and tries to look like he's working. The customer goes to browse the oil paints.

Somehow, we're selling art supplies while the city is choking? It's ridiculous. There should be a law against having to act normal when nothing is.

Calliope comes to the counter. "Well, this is a garbage situation," she says. "How are you two doing?"

Laz and I blink back at her. Two sandpaper people.

As if she can feel our auras, Calliope holds up a brown paper bag. "I thought you guys could use some food therapy."

The bag's warm. I look inside. Flaky pastry, buttery smell. Three fresh croissants.

Calliope smiles at us, and it's a fairy-godmother, five-star smile. A smile like that could blind you, or maybe heal you, if you weren't prepared. I'm trying to get used to any of these smiles being directed at *me*.

Laz dives into the bag.

"Ohmygod, thank you," he says, his mouth full. "I was *starving*."

It's an hour before art class. I'm on the couch in the back room, unpacking art supplies. The back door is shut because of the smoke. The room is sticky and hot, even with two fans on.

Calliope and I haven't had a chance to talk today—for some reason, the store has been super busy. Maybe climate emergencies bring out the shoppers? Maybe everyone's ducking in to hide from the smoke. Or maybe people are stocking up on canvases so they can paint and cry while the country burns.

Calliope comes in; she goes over to the sink and fills her bottle with water. "How are you going in here?"

"I'm surviving." I smile.

She sits down on the arm of the couch. It's the closest she's been since we kissed. I feel jangly, on edge, full of unspoken things. Like: *Sorry for not being in touch* and *This is crazy, isn't it?* and *Did you like kissing me?*

"How's Tess?" Calliope says.

"Um. She's okay."

"Laz just said she's not doing so well."

"Oh, he did?"

"Well, he just said she's kind of freaking out . . . because of the smoke. That makes sense to me. I'd be losing it too if I'd just had a baby in all this—" She gestures to the back window.

"Okay. Well, yeah. She *is* kind of a mess." I feel a twinge, like I'm betraying Tess by admitting she doesn't have her shit fully together. But it's true.

Calliope leans towards me and says softly, "And how are you going?" just as Laz walks in.

"Hey, dickheads," he says.

Calliope leans back.

"Hey," we say, together.

Laz heads to the little espresso machine. It is way too hot for coffee, but maybe caffeine is the only thing keeping Laz standing. He pulls out milk from the little fridge, pours it into the jug, glances over at me. "What are you teaching the small people today?" He starts frothing the milk.

He won't hear me if I answer him now. Maybe that doesn't matter. Maybe Laz is just trying to get through his day with small talk. Maybe he's trying to drown out all *his* unspoken things, like: *I'm so sad I can barely move* and *Why the fuck isn't anyone saving the planet?* And *What the hell is wrong with Tess?*

I don't say anything. I don't really have a plan for teaching today. Mel was in a rush this morning and didn't give me any tips for the class. I've had to improvise.

So when Laz looks over at me, I just reach into my backpack, pull out the shoebox I brought from home, open the box, and place the dead bird on the coffee table.

Laz's mouth drops.

Calliope grins. "Ha! You brought your dead bird to work. That's a twist I didn't see coming."

"I didn't know what else to do. It's for the kids to draw."

"That's perfect, George."

"Not gross?"

"No."

Laz leans on the counter with his coffee. "Um," he says. "It's definitely gross."

"Oh."

"What's your backup for the kids who don't want to draw a bird corpse?" Laz says.

"I don't have one."

"Hmm." Calliope looks over at the little wireless printer, tucked into the counter of the kitchenette. "I have an idea."

In art class, I stand the dead gull in the center table.

All the children goggle. On their tables sit ink pots, nib pens, and A4 squares of thick Stonehenge paper.

"Hi everyone," I say. "Today we're drawing this bird." I look at the kids' faces. That doesn't sound interesting at all. I hesitate, glance at Calliope. "I mean, we're drawing the story of this bird." I try to be sparkly, like when Mel leads the class, or when Calliope says anything at all. "What is this bird thinking? How is he feeling? Where has he been?"

I'm hoping the kids will join me on my existential journey, like I joined Mel's, back when I was ten. It was one of my first lessons at the Art House—Mel placed an old boot on the table and said, "What has this boot done? Who has worn it? Where has it been?"

Back then, the whole class had squinted at the boot, looking kind of confused, exactly like the kids are doing now. But I understood. I bent over my paper—creamy, textured, nothing like the printer paper Mum had at home—and picked up the oil pastels. Out came the boot on the page. Wrinkled skin, curled laces. Drooping top. Scraped toe.

Afterwards, I touched the drawing, tracing the boot's lines. I pictured paths, bricks, mud, and worn feet, tramping. The boot seemed lonely. Maybe it missed its other boot? Or maybe it missed its owner. I had used dark brown for the boot's sadness, green for its secrets. I felt like leaning close to the paper, listening for more stories.

Mel came up behind me. Peered over my shoulder. "Shit, George," she said. "That's beautiful."

Now I stand in front of these kids and say, "Let's think about who this bird is, okay? You can write words too, if you like."

I lift my notebook and flick to my drawings of the bird. The last few days I've drawn him standing, flying, sleeping, sitting on the water.

I've even scratched words around his body, like little poems, I guess.

"You can write around your drawings if you want. Or you can just draw the bird. Remember—there are no wrong lines!" I say, which is what Mel always says.

Some of the kids smile, because they love it when Mel says that.

One kid puts up her hand. "Is that your bird?"

"It's my grandfather's," I say. "I mean, the bird is his own bird. But he flew into our window and my grandfather got him stuffed."

The kid says, "It's creepy. I don't want to draw a dead bird."

Another kid says, "It's not creepy. It's cool."

"It's gross." Another kid, wrinkling their nose.

Calliope says, "Remember. You don't have to draw it dead. You can draw it alive."

"But it *is* dead."

Calliope looks at me. Looks at the kids.

I say, "If you don't want to draw this bird, we've brought other pictures for you." I hold up the sheets of paper Calliope just printed out with all living birds. Birds in flight, birds resting on water, birds eating seeds, birds thinking about their lives and wondering if they should have done more with them.

"Okay," says the wrinkle-nose kid. "I want to do that."

"Can I have one too?"

"Can I have one too?"

Half the kids pick the living-bird pictures.

Half the kids pick the cool dead bird.

All of them bend their heads over the paper. Dip nibs into ink. Start drawing.

The room fills with *scratching*.

I look over at Calliope and smile.

When class finishes, everyone carefully carries their pictures to the racks. Some of the kids have written words around their living birds; some have drawn theirs looking stunned and super dead. Everyone seems happy.

A clutch of parents has come upstairs instead of waiting down in the store. One mum comes close: "I don't know if I can bring Leila if it's this smoky next week."

"Oh, it won't still be smoky!" says another mum, stepping forward.

"They're saying the smoke might be here for days."

"The air's worse here than in Delhi," adds a dad.

"Oh, that's terrible."

All the parents' faces scrunch up. Maybe they're worried about their baby's lungs, or about their shiny city being worse than Delhi, or about living in a world that's let itself go so badly.

I don't have answers for them. If Laz were here, he might say a few choice words about colonization and capitalism. There might be some swearing. But then he'd probably invite them to join the revolution.

I try to smile reassuringly. "I'm sure Mel will be in touch."

Calliope and I do the same dance for the second class. We offer the kids one dead bird and lots of living birds. The kids make their choices, then bend over their pages and scritch. Parents pop upstairs and fret about the smoke. I reassure them, and everyone leaves.

Calliope grins at me as we pack up. "You did it," she says.

"Ha. All thanks to you. That was a great idea."

She moves through the room, scooping up ink pots and pens. "No, you totally sold the whole dead bird thing. I wanted to draw him too."

"Yeah?"

"Definitely." She walks over to the bird, strokes his back. "Did you like that, Bird? Everyone listening to you?"

I picture the bird, melting at her touch. *I used to fly,* he says. *I could see everything—*

"It's like he's still alive, but just . . . stuck in time," Calliope says.

"I know."

"I wonder what he's thinking."

"Well, I have some ideas," I say. I touch my notebook.

Calliope raises her eyebrows. "Oh, hey. Are you actually going to show me some of that art of yours?"

"Maybe." The idea is terrifying, but she's walking towards me, smiling that billion-watt smile and—

Sure, I'll show you my drawings, Calliope. I'll show you my insides. I'll show you whatever you want to see—

I pick up my notebook, "Well, okay, so these are kind of rough. And pretty abstract . . ."

"Got it," she says.

I open the pages. Calliope bends forward, sees the bird, sees sketches of the cat, of the underside of water, of fish dreaming, of tilting trees and boats, and before I realize I'm on the page, she sees a sketch of her, cartwheeling. And on the opposite page: a drawing of her rising into the air.

Shit.

Calliope points to the page. "Wait. Is this me?"

"Um . . . yeah?" I say. "It was after I first saw you, that day in the water. Um." I can't read her face. I try to be cool. "Haha, probably weird, that I drew you before I knew you—"

Calliope just stares down at the page. "Far out." She says it softly, her fingers touching the page edges, like the psychologist did with my drawing when I was small. Now she turns to me and smiles. "Far out, George."

And now she is touching my arm—

she's leaning in, now she touches my face,

and now—

she's kissing me again.

I fall into the kiss, into endless, suspended time.

Here we are.

Nothing else matters. Nothing else exists.

13

Calliope and I have made our way downstairs. It's half past six; Laz is closing the register and I'm turning the store sign over on the door. Adesh walks in—he pulls off his mask, leans against the counter, and scrunches his nose. "It's disgusting outside," he says. "Have you seen the air rating? We are *doomed*." He says it like he's doing a soliloquy. "We still going to the pub?" he adds.

"Definitely," says Laz. He looks over at me and Calliope. "Want to come?"

I hesitate, glance at Calliope—is she going to say yes? I want to be with her, but I don't want to drink away the apocalypse with Laz. He spent most of the day gazing like a glazed stone at the smoke outside. I know he's about to ruin himself with beer.

Besides, I really have to visit Tess. She's already texted four times wanting to know when I'm coming. "Sorry," I say, "I'm off to see Tess."

Laz shrugs, as though I've said something like "Two-minute noodles are a viable food source" or "I scrubbed my shower yesterday."

"All right," he says. He turns to Calliope. "What about you?"

She hesitates, looks at me. "Well, I was thinking I might come with you, George. Would Tess mind? I haven't met the baby. I've heard he's cute."

I was not expecting that—Calliope come with me? What will

Tess say? She's so tender right now. But the idea of more time with Calliope overrides everything.

"Oh, sure!" I say. "Yeah, Tess won't mind."

Laz raises his eyebrows. He knows Tess. She will almost definitely mind. But he's not about to defend her now.

"Okay then. Good luck," he says. And then he and Adesh head into the smoky soup before I even get to hug Laz goodbye.

Calliope and I ride the bus to Tess's place.

Her leg presses against mine on the vinyl seat, both of us in shorts so our skin touches. Her skin is cool, mine is sticky, but she doesn't move her leg away.

"Hey, I hope it's okay I'm coming," Calliope says. "When I was in preschool, Mum says I invited myself to everyone's birthday parties. Like, *everyone's*. Mum said it was a little embarrassing." She looks at me. "Should I have waited?"

I smile. "Um. No."

"Will Tess be okay with it?"

"I think so. But she has been having a pretty tough time."

Calliope nods. "All right, maybe we can help out a bit? What's her favorite food? Does she like mangoes? I know this recipe—"

And now she starts telling me about a family recipe that's been passed down through generations. It sounds amazing.

Calliope's voice feels like honey in the crackle-heat of the bus. I lean back against my seat and listen. How does she do it? Make everything feel better for a moment?

And maybe it's all going to be okay. Maybe Tess will love

Calliope. And maybe the baby won't cry or get sick from inhaled particles and maybe the smoke will disappear and the world won't end. And maybe Dad's not even dying. Maybe that was a lie, just to get me to care about him.

● ● ●

When I was six, Dad got sick with the flu and Mum tended to him like he was a baby.

I hovered around trying to help too. I brought Dad water; I brought him cool cloths for his forehead. I wore a mask because Mum didn't want me catching what Dad had. I felt a bit stuck and funny behind it, like I couldn't see properly. But Dad said I looked like a superhero with it, so I kept it on.

"Thanks, Georgie," Dad said on my third trip in. He smiled into the fevery air. When I turned to go, he said, "Hey, want to stay and fight this bug with me?"

"Bug?"

"Yeah, the one inside me," he said.

That sounded gross, but I knew he meant a tiny bug—I wasn't a dummy. Mum had explained about infections and viruses when she gave me my mask.

"Okay," I said, and sat on the edge of the bed.

Dad didn't say anything then. I think he fell asleep. After a minute I said, "How do I fight the bug when it's inside you, Dad?"

Dad stirred. "Oh? The bug?" He blinked and looked up at the ceiling. "Well, you could get inside my Zappifer."

I smiled. Dad wasn't often silly, so this was nice. "Your Zappifer?"

"That's right, it *Zaps* you down and makes you tiny. Then I'll sniff you up and you can go fight. You can take my sword. Lop off its head."

I laughed. Dad and I talked about the Zappifer for ages. We pictured what the bug looked like: spectacular fangs and a blue mustache. Slithery. Spoke Norwegian. A bad singer. "The worst!" Dad said.

Dad said we had to be careful the bug didn't get into the Zappifer and turn itself huge. I said if it did, I'd explode it with my sword, and it would spray the room with purple goo. Dad laughed then and started coughing. He couldn't stop. The room filled with the rasp and hack of it, and I got scared.

I ran out to Mum. "Mum! Mum! Dad can't breathe," I said, and she ran in to save him. And everything was all right in the end.

But when Dad was better and could drink again, he didn't remember the Zappifer. Or the bug, or the goo. When I tried to remind him, he said, "Georgia, please, I need to take this call. Let's talk later, okay?"

And I remember getting into my bed and wishing he could get sick again so he could be fun again. So he would talk to me and notice me, and we could be friends.

● ● ●

Calliope and I stop at the grocery store for treats for Tess, and the things on Tess's list: boob pads and nipple cream and nappies.

"Nipple cream?" says Calliope.

"Yeah," I say. "I don't want to ask."

"Me neither."

In the fruit section, we get mangoes and grapes. Calliope says, "Do you think she'd like kiwi fruit too? I love kiwi fruit." She keeps adding things to the basket.

"Calliope, stop already!" I laugh.

"But look at this melon. Smell it!" She holds it up to my nose.

We practically buy out the whole fruit section for Tess.

It's a short walk from the shops to Tess's place. My eyes itch from the smoke. Calliope and I have our masks on, but it still feels like the smoke is creeping all over us, trying to find a way in.

"Hey," says Calliope, glancing at me. "How's your dad? I'm sorry I didn't ask before. You said he was sick?"

"Oh, yeah," I say. "Um. I haven't spoken to him since before Tess had her baby. I think I'll hear more soon."

I don't know how to tell her, moments from Tess's house, that my dad is in fact dying—that he is a lifelong alcoholic (at least, for the length of my life), who has forgotten my name, fallen asleep on driveways, and left me in the middle of a lake. That's more of a "sit down, I need to tell you something" conversation, not a walk-through-toxic-smoke chat while lugging a pineapple.

"All right," she says. "Well, if you want to talk about it, seriously, anytime, I'm here."

"Thanks." I smile at Calliope behind my mask, but she can't see.

She reaches out, takes my hand. "It's really nice to hang out. Even, like, in this," she says.

My insides get shivery. Just touching her makes me feel both grounded and like someone's shot me out of a party cannon.

"Yeah," I say. I look at her, and I think she's smiling too, behind her mask.

We get to Tess's house. "Okay"—I pause at the door—"so, Tess's family will probably all be home, 'cause it's kind of late. And the baby cries, really loud. And Tess is, well . . . you know. I need you to be prepared."

Calliope squeezes my hand. "Got it." She squeezes it again. "It'll be good—I'm sure they'll love me. I mean . . . I brought *nipple cream*."

We both grin behind our masks. I step forward and ring the bell.

Tess is in the living room when we walk in. Seren is feeding from her boob. She looks up—begins to say, "Hey, George"—then sees Calliope.

Her face falters, falls, then she scrapes on a smile. "Oh, hey, you guys," she says. I watch her straighten in her seat, see her slap on her "social" face, when a second ago I saw only flat-pack exhaustion. It occurs to me, not for the first time, that this visit might be a mistake.

"Hey, Tess," I say. "We brought you treats. And Calliope wanted to come and see the baby. I told her how cute he was. And we got your baby stuff." I don't leave room for Tess to answer; I just keep talking. "How are you? Did you have a good day? Did Seren go okay? We had a lot of customers today. It was really busy. Calliope brought us croissants."

I realize I'm babbling. I can't seem to stop.

Tess looks at Calliope, looks at me. Before she can say anything, Ruthie, who let us in, tugs at my shirt.

"You brought treats?" She hops from foot to foot. "What are they?"

"Well, they're kind of for Tess, but maybe she'll share, Ruthie," I say.

Calliope smiles at Tess. "Hi, Tess. Congratulations. I kind of invited myself over 'cause I heard your baby is the cutest in the world."

"Thanks," says Tess. She tries to smile again, but she's looking at me and I'm sure she's silently saying, *Shit, George. Why did you bring someone over to my house? Without telling me? I have not washed.*

Tess's eyes are dark and she's super pale. I wonder if she stayed up all night googling toxic smoke and brain cancer. I remember how Tess went on a sleepless googling spree after the palm reader, to see what might kill her. Now she's probably locked onto Seren's fate: all the terrible sicknesses he might get, the future lurking for him beyond the windows.

Calliope steps forward to peer at the baby—then realizes she'll also be peering at Tess's boob, and steps back.

"Um, we brought you mangoes?" I say, to fill the awkward space we seem to have made.

"And a pineapple," says Calliope. She holds up the pineapple.

Ruthie beams. "Yay! I love mangoes! But pineapple makes my lips fuzzy."

Tess's parents walk in from the kitchen. Tess's dad says, "Oh! We didn't know you were bringing someone over, George!"

I say, "Um, yeah. This is Calliope."

"Hi, Calliope," says Lydia. She says Calliope's name correctly, but she glances at me, and I think she's silently saying: *Uh, George, did you think this through? Yesterday Tess was in pieces. And now you've brought a stranger into our house?*

Tess's dad comes forward and puts his hand out. "Hi, Calliope, I'm David. How do you know Tess and George?"

"Oh, hi," she says, shaking David's hand. "We. Um, I'm George's, um—"

"We teach together at the Art House," I blurt, before we dive into what exactly Calliope is or how she might be my anything at all.

"Oh!" says David. "Great! Want to stay for dinner? We're having Chinese food, I'm sure we have enough—" He turns to Lydia.

Oh . . . dinner.

Why did I not think this through? How did I not compute that we were coming right at dinner time? I was so focused on sticking with Calliope and she was so focused on buying every fruit in the shop, we never really talked about the time.

Calliope and I look at each other, and I bet she's rethinking this whole adventure: *Dinner! Shit, George. We didn't think about dinner!*

Lydia says, "We might have to get a little more. I'm sorry, we didn't know—"

"Um," Calliope says.

"Um," I say.

Calliope suddenly turns to Tess and lifts up the bag of stuff from the store. "We got nipple cream too? Lots of nipple cream. Like, enough for everyone."

I can't help myself—I'm so nervous and this is all *so* awkward, I start to laugh. And now Lydia and David look confused, and Ruthie says, "What's nipple cream?" and Tess just kind of closes her eyes and Seren pulls off her boob with a shriek and Tess's milk goes wild (new fact: I did not know boob milk did that). And then Seren makes some kind of alien sound and pukes all over Tess.

At which point, the whole system collapses, or maybe goes into overdrive: cloths for boobs and laps, and a baby gets whisked off to be cleaned by Lydia, and Ruthie goes "Ew, that's so gross!" and David goes to the kitchen to cover up the take-away Chinese food before it gets cold.

Worst of all, Tess starts to cry.

It's a full-on shit show, as Laz would say.

And what about me and Calliope? Are we helping? No, we're just . . . standing here. Both of us useless. And we know it.

Outside the living room window, the smoke doubles over, laughing its head off at how ridiculous and flimsy we humans are. It can't wait to get inside us all.

14

We don't stay for dinner.

We politely excuse ourselves and say our goodbyes, first handing Tess the fruit and baby supplies, and giving a mango to Ruthie, who wishes we would stay, and saying, "Thank you, no, we actually have to go, thanks so much though," to Lydia and David.

As we leave, Tess says, "I thought you were staying over tonight, George?"

I look at her. Me, stay over? When did we agree to that? Or did Tess just decide, and assume I would read her mind? I picture myself staying, with a sleepless, crying baby and a sleepless, googling Tess. It sounds terrible . . . and I'm a terrible person for not wanting to do it.

"I'm sorry," I say, "I can't tonight, but I can come over tomorrow, after my uni class? And maybe I could stay on the weekend?"

"Okay, sure," says Tess, but she doesn't look sure at all. She looks run over. To Calliope she says, "Sorry for all the craziness."

"Oh, listen, hey, that's fine," says Calliope. "Like, this seems pretty normal to me. You're doing great, Tess. And Seren's gorgeous."

"Thanks." Tess smiles, but it's wobbly and she looks so fragile, I pause again at the door. I want to go over and tape over her cracks so she can stay together while I'm gone. But instead, I wave, and she waves back, and then I leave her to it.

. . .

Calliope and I walk to the bus stop. It's getting dark. Streetlights try to glow through the haze.

Calliope sits on the bench and says, "Well. Shit."

"Yeah. I'm really sorry."

I feel awful. I just made a whole family confused, made Tess sad, and made Calliope uncomfortable. "That was on me," I say. "I didn't think about dinner—I just, didn't think. I didn't even text her. That was dumb. I'm sorry for putting you on the spot like that."

Calliope glances at me. "Hey, don't beat yourself up. We both didn't really think, hey."

"No."

"Poor Tess."

I nod.

Calliope sits for a minute. Gazes out at the grunty traffic, the dusky lights, the Italian restaurant next to the grocery store, the maskless people walking past trying not to breathe too deeply. Then she looks at me. "Oh my god, George, I'm *starving.*"

We eat pizza in my room. The restaurant was full, so we took the pizza home—we were going to eat some pieces on the bus, but the driver spotted the box and said, "Don't even think of trying to eat that on my bus."

"Got it," said Calliope. She pulled her mask down, smiled sweetly at the driver, and gave him the peace sign.

We sit cross-legged on my floor, pizza box beside us, our knees touching. The cat circles the box and Calliope says, "Okay, this cat is a darling. Do you want some pizza, Susan?"

Yes, I do. Susan comes in for a nibble.

I palm her backwards. "No, Susan, don't listen to her. You can't have any."

The cat plants herself close by, in case I change my mind.

Miraculously, no one else was home when we got here—so I could take Calliope upstairs without her being interrogated. When we got to my house, she said, "Shit, you live *here*? Beside the water?" She looked at me. "Are you rich, George?" And then she said, "Actually, don't answer that till we've eaten. I have questions, but I'm so hungry, I won't understand a word you say."

We slam in two pieces each without stopping. I haven't eaten since Calliope's croissant this morning. I think the smoke and kissing Calliope and the world tilting sideways made me somehow forget I needed food.

Once we surface, Calliope says, "All right, George. Tell me. Are you a billionaire? Do you have a yacht?"

"No," I say. "Neither." I tell Calliope the story of Mel inheriting the house, and making enough to keep the house from falling down but not much more, and me and Mum moving in, and the weirdness of living by the water with all the rich people and kind of being like rich people, but without most of the money.

When I'm done, she says, "So. No yacht?"

I smile. "No yacht."

"But Mel is kind of famous. She's not rich?"

"Well, maybe artist rich. But not like investment-banker rich."

"But richer than that guy who sleeps in the paper-store doorway after it closes."

I nod. "Yeah."

"Same here." She stops. Processes. "I have thoughts."

"Same." We look at each other.

"I'm totally ready to talk about how shit our society is. But . . . I want to ask about your dad too, 'cause he's pretty sick, right?"

I nod.

"Okay. So . . . do you want to talk about him?" She touches my knee.

I think for a minute—do I want to talk about Dad? With Calliope? Right now? It's late. The story of Dad is long. But Calliope is smiling at me, and she has spinach in her teeth and it's completely adorable, and when I'm with her everything seems to be, just, easier—

So I lay myself out, like the cat sometimes does when she rolls over and shows her belly. And I tell Calliope about my father.

My grandmother's clock marks the time between Calliope not knowing about Dad and her knowing.

I feel the change in the air. I feel the weight of Dad here in the room: Dad lumbering and smothering, Dad's clogged heart heaving. I've told Calliope about Dad's drinking, and about his news, and about Dad being . . . Dad. I wait for Calliope to change the subject or make an excuse and leave.

"Hey," I say. "Sorry for dumping all this on you. It's fine, really. It's okay." My leg kind of jitters in place.

Calliope leans towards me. Our knees clunk together.

"George," she says. "Nothing about what you've just told me is okay. I'm so sorry you're dealing with this."

I nod. "Thank you."

"Who have you talked to about it? I mean, besides your mums and Tess—"

"Um. I haven't actually told anyone. About him dying. You're the first."

"Wait. Really?"

"Yeah, I don't know how to talk about it. I've never really told anyone about Dad drinking. I saw a psychologist a couple of times, but it didn't really work." I pause. "Mum says Dad's stuff is private anyway, like, I never talked about it at school and Laz doesn't even know. And Mum gets pretty upset when she talks about Dad. So does Tess. She saw some things, when we were little—"

Calliope's eyebrows raise. "So, you haven't said anything? You're just holding this stuff on your own?"

I nod. "Um. Yeah? It's a hard time for everyone, right? And Tess just had her baby."

"And you don't want to bother anyone."

"I guess."

"Do you ever? Bother people, I mean?" Calliope touches my hand where it rests on my leg. "Or are you just a smooth-butter girl?"

I half smile. "I think I annoy the shit out of Mel and Mum some-times. And Tess says I can be a real pain in the arse."

"Well, I think this is big enough to talk about. I don't think any-one would get mad at you." Calliope squeezes my fingers.

I look down at our hands. "I guess so. But still, like tonight,

I messed things up with Tess, and if I talk about Dad, it'll mess things up more . . . so I just feel really stuck, and I'm having all these memories, and it's like I'm carrying this, this—"

"It's a big fucking rock you're carrying around, George."

I nod. "Yeah." I try to shrug off the weight of the rock, and blink back whatever is in my eyes.

Calliope looks at me for a long moment. "I worked at this pub back home," she says, "I mean, in Reading. We got a lot of lifetime drinkers in there, all these old fellas who would be at the door when we opened. They liked to talk. They'd lost a lot of people, because of the drinking. It was pretty sad."

"Yeah."

Calliope's voice is gentle. "So it sounds like your dad lost you?"

"Um." My ribs pang. "Yeah."

"I'm so sorry."

"Thanks."

We sit together, both of us silent. The cat snores beside the pizza box. The clock *tick-tocks*. The bird looks down from the shelf, where I put him when we got home. Are we done with talking about Dad? I feel lighter for talking about him, but also kind of wrung through. Another reason why I don't talk about Dad—it is exhausting.

"So. Is he getting some care?" Calliope says. "Is he, like, in hospital? Sorry if I'm asking too much."

"No. I think he's all right for now. I haven't really talked to him. But he's been messaging a lot. I think he wants me to visit him in Seattle."

"He can't visit you?"

"The doctors told him he can't fly."

"What do you think about going?"

"I don't know. I don't want to go, but what kind of person doesn't want to see their sick dad?"

"Maybe a person who has been hurt, like, a lot."

I look at her. I don't know what to say.

She looks me over. "Maybe you need to look after yourself for a bit, before you decide? Like, before you keep on protecting everyone else, maybe you could treat yourself to a little love." She pauses. "Do I sound like a Hallmark card?

"No, you don't," I say. "You sound wise."

Calliope leans back on her hands. "Okay. Well. What's on your selfish list, George?"

"My what?"

"Your selfish list. Your just-for-you list."

"Um—"

Calliope smiles. "I've got so much on my list. That word isn't as bad as people think. Like, selfishness is basically self-care, just don't be a bitch while doing it."

I laugh. "Okay."

"Like, I love going to movies on my own—I do it all the time. And I love making red-velvet cakes, which sometimes I don't share. And, what else? Um, I could spend days filming people doing stuff and I wouldn't need company, or anything else. Except maybe food and water. And a place to sleep and pee. So, okay, I'd need a few things."

I smile.

Calliope pauses. "I saw a psychologist for a bit too. After Mum left Dad. They were nice. They said it was okay to feel everything—like, not to be hard on myself for feeling all the things I needed to."

"Yeah, my psychologist was nice too. It's just . . . I couldn't think of what to say. I'm not so great at talking."

"You seem fine at it to me." Calliope smiles. "I'm a fan of talking to people."

"I have seen that."

"Dad says I'm a pathological sharer."

"Well, this kind of talking is new for me." And it really is. It's the strangest feeling—I've let out into open air what I always keep in.

"Okay, then it means a lot that you're talking to me."

I nod. "Thanks for listening."

Calliope sits up again. She puts her hand on my chest, palm under my collarbone.

I smile.

Calliope doesn't say anything. She leans forward. Kisses me.

"You're welcome," she says.

She kisses me again.

And again.

And again.

And time turns golden, syrupy, divine.

15

This is how it feels to be in love when the world is ending:

What smoke?

What fires?

What sadness?

What dying?

What trouble?

It feels like Calliope and me kissing in my room until my family comes home, and me bringing her downstairs to meet them, and Mum saying, "Oh, it's nice to meet you!" and Calliope smiling and saying, "It's nice to meet you too, Mrs.—" and Mum saying, "Oh no, call me Sara," and Mel saying, "Hello! Now I can finally put a face to your voice!" and Calliope saying, "Thank you so much for the work, Mel," and Gramps stepping forward to shake Calliope's hand and saying, "Lovely to meet you," and Calliope saying, "Hello, Uncle, I heard about your cool dead bird"—and Gramps beaming and showing Calliope the jar of dead bird bits within five minutes of everyone walking in the door.

It feels like ignoring Dad's messages the next day and ignoring the news about the fires and ignoring the smoke and going to see Tess and ignoring how spent she looks and ignoring the sound of Seren crying and ignoring the world.

It feels like going to Calliope's the next night and getting a tour of the flat—not fussy, not fancy, just books everywhere and an old leather couch and Calliope's movie prints on the living room walls—and meeting her dad before he goes out to dinner—quiet, smiley like Calliope, offering me some of the lychees he just brought back from the shops—and kissing Calliope after he leaves, till we get hungry so we mask up and go out to the little Lebanese place that's open late—dolmas and hummus and olives and bread—and the two of us whispering into each other's ears till some stranger says, "Get a room" and we laugh and creep up her apartment stairs and get a room.

It feels like staying up till five a.m. because we can't stop kissing and talking.

It feels like walking home through the smoke the next day and none of it sticking or getting inside.

Love feels like a wild sea. Sleepless, electric, alive.

Love feels like telling Tess the first day and every day that I'll be there soon, but I get to her house late every time and her face makes patterns I don't want to read.

It feels like texting Laz to see if he's okay and him writing, *I'm fine,* and me forgetting to reply.

It feels like hearing my mums update me on the fires, the air quality, the deaths, the animals—but the news feels cloudy, like I can't quite hear it, like they are speaking through water.

It feels like Dad calling and me not answering and him writing *Can we please talk* and me not calling or writing to my father.

. . .

Love feels like Calliope coming over for dinner and her pulling gifts from her tote bag like Mary Poppins: a scented candle for Mum and Mel, a tortoiseshell comb for Gramps's beard, daisies for me. Love feels like pomegranate salad and pumpernickel bread and daisies in a glass tumbler and Calliope asking my family questions about themselves—Mel about her genitalia exhibition and Mum about her old people and Gramps about his old people classes. Love feels like seeing Mum and Mel and Gramps laugh for the first time in days, and finding Calliope in the living room looking at Gramps's scrapbooks of Grammie, and her looking up, saying, "Shit, George, your grandma was a badass," and Gramps smiling *this* big. It feels like the cat sauntering over and sitting on Calliope's lap like she's furniture. And Mum and Mel saying, "We like her, George," after Calliope leaves, and for once, for one hush-yellow evening, we don't talk about hard things.

Love feels like going over to Calliope's place with my mask fitted tight, through the smoke-clanged streets, away from the noise and the news and Tess's need and Dad's messages and fires roaring everywhere.

It feels like the smoke dimming, the fires receding, the hard things turning almost normal because I'm not looking at them.

It feels like an '80s movie montage, two bodies spinning, scenes flicking, making pink and silver lines in the air with our words, with our fingers touching, with the spark of our bodies, with our bodies.

It feels like a poem, like a room,

like hands, like her, like skin.

Like nothing beyond our four corners.

Like being wrapped in her.

Like being clean. Safe. Whole.

16

Sunday morning.

No alarm today. No paddling because of the smoke. No running, no swimming, no walking. So I'm just in bed, thinking.

The cat lies in the crook of my knee, Calliope lies in the crook of my arm—both asleep. Heat and blurred air press at the window. The fan purrs, left to right.

I already fed Susan. We crept downstairs, I gave her breakfast, then we padded back to bed. Both Calliope and the cat snore a little when they sleep. Calliope is dreaming—I can tell because she's twitching a little, like the cat. Funny.

I laugh, lightly, and Calliope wakes. Pushes against me suddenly.

"Oh!" Her eyes open wide.

I shift back, look at her. "Hey. It's me."

She relaxes. "Oh. Okay. Yeah. Yeah." She shuts her eyes. "Shit. What a dream."

"Yeah?"

"I was trying—" She stops. Frowns. "Oh, it's okay." Within a few minutes, she's back asleep.

Calliope doesn't always make sense in the mornings. She has slept over most nights the past ten days. It's like we've made a little hideaway home and are hibernating in it. We've gone to work—Calliope to the pub and me to the Art House to work in the shop. Calliope and I haven't been teaching because the studio upstairs started to smell like burned things, so Mel stopped the art classes for the year. I've gone to see Tess, Calliope has gone to see her dad, but then we have made our way back to each other like homing pigeons.

This morning, we have nowhere to be. My last uni assignment is due in a few days—an essay for my English lit class. I don't feel like working on it. I don't feel like doing anything until this afternoon, when I'm seeing Tess.

Tess knows about Calliope. I told her on the third day of being late to visit. That is, I told her about me and Calliope kissing in my room over pizza, and us being together now. I didn't tell her about the very first kiss on the ferry . . . or that I told Calliope about Dad . . . or about Dad being sick, even though Calliope said talking was good.

After I mentioned the kiss, Tess said: "That was fast"—as though she'd never kissed someone, or wanted to kiss someone, within seconds of seeing them . . . or had a hot Lithuanian guy impregnate her moments after they met.

But I didn't mention that. I just said: "Um, I guess so?"

You wouldn't be surprised if you knew her, Tess, I thought. *She's so great. She smells like vanilla. Her skin is this soft. She's funny and smart and did I mention her smile?*

I looked at Tess—her pallid skin, the maroon-dark circles under her eyes, the mauve blotches on her cheeks and arms. I didn't think she had space for me slamming into love right now, so—

"She's really nice," I added.

"She is that," said Tess. And then the baby squawked and Tess had to poke her boob at him. And she didn't ask any more questions about Calliope. She didn't scoot close and say, "Tell me *everything*"—and I didn't tell her *everything*—and she didn't laugh and say, "You know she's not perfect, right, George?" and shake her head like she always does.

This Tess is same-but-different—she doesn't ask about my love life, not even about me and Calliope showing up the other day like weird, fruit-bearing hobos. This Tess cries every day. She forgets to eat and forgets to wash and is limp with exhaustion. This Tess doesn't listen to music. And when the baby sleeps, Tess watches him, to see if he's going to die in the night.

And same-but-different me sits with Tess and watches her fade. This me doesn't know how to stop Tess fading. This me feels for the buzz of a message from Calliope, and wants to be in two places at once.

Tess messaged last night and said, *I think I am losing my mind. I haven't left the house in almost two weeks. I think Seren is breathing differently. Can you come over tomorrow morning and check? We have pancake mix if you want breakfast.*

I wrote back: *I'm hanging with Calliope in the morning. And then I have to work on my uni assignment, but I can come in the afternoon?*

Okay, she said. Nothing more.

I felt a ripple of guilt . . . then pushed it away, down and under a rib where all my other hard feelings sat. The guilt folded its brittle wings. And tucked itself in with everything else.

Calliope is awake.

She stretches. Opens her eyes.

She blinks at the ceiling for a moment, then rolls over to face me. "I dreamed about her again," she says.

I turn to face her. "Who?"

"Mum."

"Oh." I wait to see if she wants to say anything more.

"Yeah." Calliope rubs an eye. "She was walking with me to our old house, and we were going up a hill and I couldn't move my legs. It was like walking through wet concrete, and she kept saying, 'Hurry up! We don't have time!' I knew I had to go faster . . . but I couldn't."

"I hate those kinds of dreams."

Calliope rolls onto her back. "Yeah. Me too." She reaches out. Puts a hand on my hip. "Good morning."

"Good morning."

"What are we doing today?"

"Um . . . this?"

Calliope smiles. "Okay. I have a shift tonight, but I'm in for some slothing first."

We breathe in and out—same slow breaths. It's like being cocooned, like we've spun ourselves into the same silky space. Maybe we can stay here till the smoke clears?

"This show I want to see dropped last night," says Calliope. "If we don't leave the bed, we might get through the whole season before I go."

"What if we need to pee?"

"Okay . . . we can pee every two hours. Like in the contests where you have to keep your hand on the truck to win it."

"Oh, I love those. They're so stupid."

"But great."

"Yeah."

"And we should probably flip each other over a few times so we don't get bed sores."

I laugh. "It's a deal."

My phone buzzes.

I check it. Make a face.

Calliope glances over. "Who's that? Is it Tess? She okay?"

"Oh." I wave the phone as though to show her. "No. It's my dad. He's sent . . . a novel."

Dad is explaining himself, again. He is so very sorry. He wants to tell me—If I would please listen—If I came to visit, he could—

I picture Dad poking at his phone in the dark over there: alone, remorseful, sick. Something shifts and lurches in me. Is it love? Is it pity?

No. Don't think of him as a good guy, George. There lies danger.

The skin of the day abruptly changes. The fan grates; the heat beats. Smoke shoves against the windows. Outside our safe space, the world clangs and judders.

I put down the phone. Say suddenly: "God, I don't know what to do."

"About your dad?"

"About all of this." I move my arm through the claggy air.

"This current garbage time?"

"Yeah. I don't know how to turn it down."

Calliope nods. "It really is shit."

"Like, this smoke is just—And the fires—People are *dying*. I can't get my head around it. And Tess always needs—And Dad won't stop—"

"Yeah."

"It's so loud."

There's more to say, but my head feels scrambled.

Calliope rolls towards me. Puts her hand on my face. Kisses me. "Same, George. Just . . . same."

"Yeah?"

"Yeah." She looks at me for a slow second, two. Breathes in. "For example," she says, "my mum has started writing me letters, on paper, super old-school, you know? She's sending me her new poems and they're gorgeous, but I don't know what to write back. So I've been sending her my movies. And now she's writing poems to go with them. It's sweet, but sometimes I want to scream, 'Why'd you choose Terry over Dad?! Why the fuck are you pregnant?!' But I know she'd get upset. So we just keep . . . doing this." Calliope pauses. "I don't know how to talk about it with Dad."

I've met Calliope's dad a few times now. He makes great coffee. His sci-fi book collection fills a whole corner bookshelf. He's offered me something to eat, every time I have come over.

"What do you think he'd say?"

"Oh, he'd probably say something nice, like 'It's good you're in touch.' He never says anything negative about anyone, especially not Mum. He'd probably hug a puppy kicker."

"Hmmm."

"I don't know. I mean, Mum hasn't disappeared, you know? She's just not here. I should be okay. But I miss her and Ari, and I hate that she chose Terry over us."

I breathe that thought in—the idea of Mum picking a life that pushed me out. I can't imagine.

"It'll be okay," she continues. "I'm fine, really, not like—God—

everyone in the fires, but sometimes—I don't know, it just feels—"

"Like a weight," I say.

"Yeah."

"Like being smushed—"

"Yeah, and I know this is random, but my first day at the pub a couple of weeks ago, some guy asked me my name and when I told him, he said I shouldn't have taken a white girl's name. Like I'd stolen it or something."

"Wow. That's messed up."

"I got him chucked out of the pub after that."

"Yeah? *Good*."

"It didn't get to me, but it also did. Like, I'm used to it but it's shit that I'm used to it, you know? Anyway . . ." She pauses. "It's just . . . *life* . . . It's always, there's always—"

"Something."

"Yeah. But then sometimes, there's a moment where you can . . ."

"Breathe?"

She smiles. "Yeah."

I smile back.

I lean my head forward. She leans her head forward, and we press our heads together, forehead to forehead.

The cat wakes. Pushes her paws against my leg.

The fan blows cool on our skin. Time slows. Quiet wraps around our bodies and the outside fades, till there's nothing here in the world but us.

BREAK

(oil on canvas)

A koala staggers, bleating, across smoking ground,
paws and skin charred.

A woman runs to it, weeping; she takes off her shirt,
picks up the animal, cradles it.

Both of them broken, both breaking open.
Their sound crackles, crimson and bitter brown,
over the earth.

Bird feels the sound, sweeping,
sees from his shelf two girls: their heads together, dark eyes
and lilac mouths,

     not listening, for a moment, as everything cracks and burns.

17

Afternoon. Smoke-chunked sky.

Dirty air and muted sunlight.

Tess is sobbing in the bathtub as I run inside—after I get her phone call, after I take a taxi over, when I go up the stairs two at a time.

Tess is in the bath with her clothes on, the tub empty. Somewhere in the house, I hear Seren screaming.

I stand over the tub.

"Tess. *Tess, what's happening?*"

Tess is shaking, she's crying so hard.

"He won't sleep," she says. "And when he does, *I* can't. I shouldn't have had him, George. He might have cancer. He might be *poisoned*. Maybe that's why he can't sleep. Maybe he's dying! Laz was right. Oh my god. I can't do it, I can't do it, I can't do it anymore."

Tess's eyes are wild. Her clothes are twisted. She is made of snot and baby vomit and sweat. Tess looks like she has dragged herself up a mountain; she looks like she's fallen off.

I run to Tess's bedroom and there's the baby, screaming in his bassinet. His face is purple. He's going ballistic.

I pick him up. Seren's body vibrates, judders like one of those cars that's been souped up. He's unswaddled. He arcs backwards in my arms.

What do I do?

Tess's parents are an hour away, at a wedding. Ruthie is at her friend's house.

I call Mum at work. She says she can't hear me over the screaming. "God, what's happening, George?"

"It's Tess."

"Tess?"

"The baby."

"What?"

I have to shout to explain.

"Right. I'll be there in fifteen minutes," she says.

And then it's fifteen minutes of walking up and down, and the baby making a sound that maybe isn't legal? It feels like Seren's scream could bring down the whole block, like you could use it to crumple skyscrapers, or bomb your enemies in their caves.

Mum bangs on the front door. I let her in.

"I could hear him from the street, George. What's going on?"

"This is what's going on." I hold the baby out, arm's length, to Mum.

She takes him. He gulps, looks at Mum, stops crying for a long, blessed second.

And then he starts to scream again.

"Dear lord," says Mum. And then she gets to work. Fixing everything. Because isn't that what mums do?

I go to the bathroom, where Tess is, still. I get into the bath. I reach out for her, and hold her. Hold her. Hold her.

Eleven p.m.

I am home. Mum and Mel have gone to bed. The cat dozes beside me, paws tucked under herself. I am frazzled, wiped clean. How is it possible that more noise has come in?

At Tess's house, after the baby was settled, changed, fed, and calmed, Mum rang Lydia. She and Tess's dad came home early from the wedding, Lydia looking crinkled in her blue dress and heels.

"God, what's happening?" she said.

"This is happening," said Mum, and sat Tess's parents on the couch to talk.

After we got Tess settled, fed, and calmed, I helped her to bed.

Tess lay there and said, "I'm sorry" and "Will everything be okay?" She lay like a toy with its stuffing taken out.

Seren lay in his bassinet, asleep.

Tess looked over at him, started to cry. "Why can't *I* get him to do that?"

I smoothed her hair. "You do, all the time, you're doing so much, Tess."

"It's not enough," she said, and she kept crying and wiping her face with the back of her hand. "I'm doing it wrong. I'm wrong. It's all wrong."

And then she just sobbed in bed, silently, so she didn't wake the baby, and in time, her mum came in and hugged her, and then Mum came in and hugged her, and Tess's dad came in and went out again because almost everyone was crying, and maybe he didn't know what to do with so much water. And I could relate, because the room had too many feelings in it, and all I wanted to do was run.

Right after that thought came in, up came the old swoop of guilt, the old sweep of shame, my two familiar birds.

I lie in bed. Text Calliope and tell her about Tess. I'd rushed out and left her in my room this afternoon, after I got Tess's call.

She writes: *Wow. Well, that's awful*

I write: *It took ages to get her to calm down*

I'm so sorry, George. Is there anything I can do?

It's okay, I write. *Her mum and my mum are taking care of everything. Thank god for mums*—and press send before I stop to think about what I've written or how she will probably read it.

When I realize how it might feel for her—a millisecond after I send the message—of course it's too late.

She doesn't reply for a moment.

Then: *Okay*

Just, okay.

I'm sorry. That was stupid

She writes: *It's fine. I'm glad Tess is all right*

But it doesn't feel fine at all.

I'm really sorry

Calliope is writing back. The dots dance. Disappear. The dots dance again. Disappear.

Then: *I'm sorry Tess is having such a shit time. Tell her I'm sending love okay?*

Okay, I write.

And then, neither of us writes anything, and it's like we've hit a pocket of air where words have stopped working. We don't say anything for so long, we end up saying nothing for the rest of the night.

I try to sleep. Can't. Inside me sits the old hollow feeling of getting it wrong. I turn over, turn over. The cat wakes, irritated, and leaves. Outside, smoke churns against the window, aching to come in.

18

Afternoon.

Beige-gray office windows, beige-gray walls, beige-gray sky.

Tess, her baby, Lydia, and I sit in the psychiatrist's office. It's been a week of Tess needing me every day, Tess going to the doctor, Tess getting a referral, Tess being seen quickly because she's in crisis.

Tess insisted that I come. Lydia insisted that she come. We've sat together in a room with a mental health team—a counselor and a nurse. Tess has filled in forms; Tess has told them her hard, sad thoughts. Now we're in the psychiatrist's room, waiting.

The doctor opens the door. Her eyes widen a little at the sight of all of us, but she doesn't react. "Tess?" she says. She must be wondering who her patient is. Maybe we all look like we need her help.

Tess puts her hand up. "That's me."

"Hi there," the doctor says warmly. She sits down opposite us—her desk wide but not so wide the distance is impossible. But I can't speak for Tess. I look over at her—she looks like she's floating out in the middle of a lake at night, oar lost, turning in circles. My whole heart creaks. I want to swim over to her. I want to dive down, catch her as she drops.

. . .

Tess has postpartum depression, says the doctor. It's not because she is a young mother, not at all, the doctor says. She speaks to us so calmly, we all kind of sway to her voice. She says it's because Tess is a mum and mums sometimes experience this. And then the doctor talks about chemicals and sleeplessness and stress and *I mean, it's a very hard time* and *It's not uncommon to feel this way* and *It sounds like you had a very challenging birth experience* and *It happens* and *It's not your fault, Tess.*

Does Tess know it's not her fault?

Tess starts to cry.

The psychiatrist takes notes on her computer. She hears about Tess's history—Lydia says, "She's had some anxiety since she was small. She saw a psychologist before but then she stopped. We've been saying she should go back, but Tess has said she's fine and George has been so helpful—"

Lydia sounds ruffled, like she's trying to make a nest for herself, find a safe space to rest. I raise my eyebrows. The doctor catches it. She says, "Tess, do you feel like you've had anxiety since you were small?"

Tess squints. "Um. Yeah?" Her voice is pinched, like she can't quite get enough air in.

"All right. I think it will be good for you to get back into some regular therapy. We can talk about who would be a good fit for you." The psychiatrist smiles, then says gently, "It's going to be okay, Tess."

She asks more questions. Recommends a psychologist and writes a referral. Suggests some medication. A prescription zips out from the printer. The doctor hands the script to Tess. "This will lower your anxiety and help you sleep," because when did she last?

Tess can't remember.

Tess holds my hand.

I squeeze it. She squeezes back. Two of us in all this water.

At home, I text Laz. He calls me back.

He says, "So is she okay?"

"I think she will be, but she's not great right now. Can you come visit?"

"I'm pretty busy, George. Adesh and I are organizing a protest thing with our uni group. Tell her hi, all right? I don't think she'll want to see me anyway."

"She'd want to see you, Laz."

"I don't know . . ."

"Please?"

"Ask her. If she wants to see me, I can come on the weekend. Maybe next week. Actually, let me see when I'm free."

"When are you coming back to work?" I haven't seen Laz in ages—just Mel's old teaching subs who've been helping in the store. Laz has turned into a ghost.

"Oh, didn't Mel tell you? I got work at Adesh's pizza place. I'm not coming back."

"But what about managing the shop?"

"It's fine. Last time I was in, Fen said I was dimming their aura. So I don't think I'll be missed."

"Well . . . Shit."

"It's all right. They're a way better manager than me—so we're all good." He pauses. "Hey, George, sorry, but I really have to go. See you later, okay?"

And he's gone before I even get to say goodbye.

Another day:

My father sends me a photograph of Puget Sound.

Cloudless sunset.

Silvery water.

Mountains sprawled against a cornflower sky.

He texts: *I'd like to take you here, Georgia, when you come. Can you come?*

I text Calliope every night.

That is, I text her most nights—sometimes I'm so wiped out I forget.

Calliope hasn't slept over since Tess was in the bathtub. I've filled Calliope in on everything that's happened, but haven't seen her. I get home in time to sleep and then go back to see Tess. I feel untethered, bleary.

Calliope calls one morning. "Hey, do you want to come over? Dad just bought, like, a thousand mangoes. He wants to make lassis. We're going to be swimming in lassis. Want some?"

"That sounds great. But I have to be at Tess's in a bit 'cause her family's going out, and then she has her psych appointment tomorrow. So maybe tomorrow night?"

Calliope's voice shifts. "Tomorrow's Dad's birthday dinner."

"Oh—"

"I told you about it last week? It's at seven. I sent you the address."

"Oh sorry, of course."

"Will you be free?" she says.

"Yes, definitely. I think so."

"You think so?"

I shake my head to get the wrongness out. "Sorry, yeah, I can come."

"Well . . . we'll see you if we see you."

"You will. I'll be there. I'm sorry I'm being such a mess."

"You are, kind of."

"I'm—"

"It's just, I miss you, George. Things are a bit wild here. Mum rang last night, and she and Terry are—"

My phone vibrates. The screen flashes, green and red. Another call is coming in—it's Tess. "Oh, I'm sorry. Tess is calling. I have to get it, I think?"

A beat. Then Calliope says, "Okay. Well, I'll see you tomorrow?"

"Sure," I say. "I'll see you. Yes."

When I answer Tess, her voice is two octaves too high. "He's thrown up twice, George! I think he has a fever. Mum said he's fine but then she went to the shops and then she's got her dentist appointment and Dad's away and Ruthie's at school . . . Can you come right now? Please? I don't know what I'm doing."

So I go over.

. . .

Every morning, Tess takes a pill. She's exhausted.

"When will it be okay, George?" she says.

The baby has reflux. The baby has a rash. The baby might have smoke in his brain and might die of cancer. The baby waves his fist in the air and gurgles.

Lydia has taken time off work to help. She sits on the couch with Mum and says, "It's so bad. How did it get so bad?"

Mum holds her hand. "Sometimes it just happens. It can take a feather."

My father sends messages nearly every day.

I can buy you a plane ticket.

Will you come?

Maybe when you come we can go to that lookout. Do you remember? You could see the whole city.

I promise it will be better this time.

I am so sorry, Georgia.

At night, the baby falls asleep, finally. But Tess's mind can't seem to stop revving. The psychiatrist said the pills might take a while to work. So I stay up with Tess and listen as she says:

"What if he dies in his sleep?"

and: "What if I poisoned him when he was inside me?"

and: "What if he breathed all that smoke in?"

and: "Is he going to die of cancer, George? Laz said—"

The night oozes on.

I sit with Tess as she tries to slow-breathe the panic out.

Mum and Mel sit with their morning coffees and say: *How is she? How is the baby?*

I want to say: *Terrible. I'm terrible.*

I want to talk to them about Dad, but they don't even know about him being sick.

How can that be? Why haven't I told them?

Dad's voice loops in: *Let's keep it between us for now, Georgia. You know your mother. So emotional—*

Somehow, I listened to him, again. Tucked another secret behind my ribs. And I guess somewhere along the way, I got so used to the things I carried, I forgot they weren't mine?

Now it feels too late to give them back.

So you didn't come last night, Calliope texts.

It's the day after her dad's birthday dinner.

Oh my god.

I forgot to go.

Shit. I'm so sorry. Can I come and see you now? I'm so sorry I forgot

Calliope writes: *George. You're busy. You have a lot going on. I get it, but it hurts. Let's leave it for now okay? I have a ton of shifts at work. A lot of stuff to deal with. So let's take a break for a bit. I'll text you. Take care.*

I sit and look at the phone.

God. She's cut me loose.

The house tilts. The earth rolls and twists. I feel windblown, feel the smoke creak in. All around the city, the fires roar and wheeze and cry. The fires don't care about any of our human shit.

I sit on my bed.

I try to breathe the panic out.

19

Another morning.

Same smoke.

More fires.

Same, same, same, same.

The end of the world is so nigh I can taste it.

I've woken up, twisted in my bedsheet, sweating. It's not even eight a.m. and we are animals broiling in our burrows, the sky an enemy. My secrets clack around and rub themselves together, making sparks.

Breakfast? yowls Susan at the bedroom door.

Breakfast?

Breakfast?

"God, Susan, give me a break," I say. I want to throw the bird at her to make her be quiet.

You want to throw me at that cat? the bird says from his shelf, wounded.

I groan and put the pillow over my head.

I wake again to a terrible *BEEEEEEEEEEEP!*

BEEEEEEEEEEEP! BEEEEEEEEEEEP!

The smoke detector downstairs is losing its mind.

I crawl out of bed, go downstairs, find Mum and Mel and Gramps ricocheting about the kitchen, arguing over Gramps's burned toast.

"Oh my god, Dad, you have to check the number on the toaster before you put the bread in!" says Mum. She's got a broom and is waving it around the detector, trying to waft away the smoke. Above the stove, the fan buzzes waspishly, adding to the fuss.

"Jesus, we can't even open a window," says Mel.

"These stupid new toasters. They never work," says Gramps. "Give me the kind you could take to the repair shop. Better yet, send me back in time." He pulls out the charred bread, chucks it in the bin.

"Well, good morning to you all too," I say.

Gramps grunts.

Mum and Mel sigh.

The room smells cindered. I would leave, but I'm out of bed now, and need to eat. I grab smoothie makings from the fridge.

"George," says Mum, "are you going to Tess's place this morning? I have some things for the baby."

I chuck frozen berries into the blender. Shrug. "Sure, I'm going to Tess's this morning. Like I'll go every morning until the end of time. I'll probably get fossilized there, buried under all of Seren's shit."

Mel raises her eyebrows. "Ooo-kay," she says.

"Um. George?" Mum says. She looks shocked. "You all right?"

I scowl at the blender. "I'm fine."

I am not fine. I feel like running out the door and into the harbor. I feel like swimming underwater until this crinkled, miserable feeling passes and everything quiets down. But it won't, will it? I can't swim out Dad dying, or Tess unravelling, or Calliope letting me go, or these fires. So here we are.

Mum steps beside me. Puts her hand on my shoulder. "You sure?"

I look at her. She seems like she wants to listen, to hear what I'm dealing with. I open my mouth—I'm going to tell her about Calliope. I'm going to tell her about Dad. I'm going to pull out one of these stupid secrets. I'm going to finally talk—

BEEEEEEEEEEEP!

BEEEEEEEEEEEEP!

BEEEEEEEEEEEEP!

BEEEEEEEEEEEEP!

—but I can't, because Gramps has gone and burned his toast again.

Dad calls after breakfast. I see his name on my screen as I'm washing the dishes. I ignore the call.

He calls again as I'm brushing my teeth.

He calls again while I'm in the shower.

He calls again while I'm getting dressed.

I picture him calling, and calling, and calling. Picture my phone lighting up and buzzing red through the whole heat-sagged day.

When he calls again, I pick up the phone.

"Hello, Dad."

"Georgia," he says. "Thanks for picking up. I've bought you a ticket."

"Wait—you just decided? Without checking with me? Jesus, Dad."

"Okay." He pauses. "I know you're angry."

"You don't get to say how I feel."

"I'm not. I'm just—I know it's hard. I know I've been a terrible father."

I don't answer.

"If you came, you could get away from the smoke for a while. I've been watching the news. It looks horrible. The fires look hellish."

"They are," I say. "But I'm fine."

"Are you?"

"If I say I am, then I am." I feel snappable, a stripped twig that could break with a look.

"I'm sorry, George. I'm just trying—"

"What? What are you trying?"

"To be better."

"Are you? Or are you just trying to *look* better?"

"Georgia."

"Dad. Honestly, you can't buy me plane tickets before I've decided whether or not I'm coming. I haven't even talked to Mum about it."

"Oh, I thought you would have by now."

"You told me not to!"

"Ah. Yes, I did." He pauses. "Do you want to tell your mum?"

"Of course I do. But I know . . ." I trail off.

Dad finishes for me. "She'll get upset."

I don't want to agree with anything he says, but—"Yeah."

The two of us stood by the lake as Mum shouted.

"You could have drowned, Karl! George could have drowned! What were you thinking?"

She looked at me: "Why didn't you wake me, George?"

She said: "Why did you go with him?"

She said: "Why didn't you tell me?"

I didn't know what to say.

Mum stood alone by the tent, cried in the sloppy half-dark. The moon paled and bats churned. I wanted to run to Mum; I wanted to push away all the terrible. But I was the terrible. I had made her cry.

Dad says, "If you want to tell her, I won't stop you."

I pause. A tiny part of me wails: *I don't want to tell her! You should do it! You're never here for the hard things!*

But I know he'd fuck it up.

So I say, "You *can't* stop me, Dad."

"I know. And I can't make you fly over. I can't ask you for anything."

"Exactly."

That's right, Dad. No asking. No rights. You don't get to claim me. I'm not yours.

"Georgia."

"Dad."

"I'm so sorry," he says. "Truly. For everything." His voice gets scratchy, like there's something scraping his throat. "This is what I want to tell you when you come, but if I have to do it over the phone, I will. I'll do it again. And again."

. . .

Dad has told me he's been sober for nineteen months. He has the badges or pins or whatever they are—he can show me when I come. He is single. He's working on himself. He's going to therapy. He can show me everything. He can talk to me about it, when I come to visit. If I could just come. Please.

Dad wants to lay himself out in my forgiving light. He wants to be bathed in it. Blessed.

But it's not that simple. How do you forgive someone when you still carry the memory of everything, every wrong moment, inside your skin? I don't have new skin. I carry this old skin, these bones, with me everywhere.

This is what I'd like to tell Dad.

I carry you, Dad. The story of you, every place I go. I'm clogged and clagged by it. The past is always here. I can't escape you.

This is what I would tell you if I saw you.

Would you listen?

Would you hear me?

I say, "I have to go, Dad."

"Okay. Shall we talk again soon?"

"Sure," I say.

"That will be nice. I love you, Georgia."

"Bye, Dad," I say.

I press the red button and send Dad away.

20

Midday.

I find Tess on the couch. Smoky sunlight smears the living room floor. The rest of the family is out again. Lydia called me just before she left, to check I was coming. All of us taking turns so Tess doesn't have to be alone.

Seren lies on his back, looking fuzzily at a mobile. Tess sits beside a laundry basket, fuzzily folding Seren's clothes.

"Hey." I kiss Tess's cheek, hand her a thermos filled with smoothie.

"Oh. Great. Thanks, George." She even sounds fuzzy. Maybe it's the meds kicking in. She yawns. She looks like an out-of-focus photograph.

I sit on the couch. "Did you get some sleep last night?"

"Yeah, I did. I think? Four hours. If you add it all up."

"That's great. What about Seren?"

"Yeah, he slept, on and off," she says. Then she shrugs. "Fuck, I'm tired of talking about sleep. It's all anyone asks about."

"Okay, sorry. Well, I'm glad you got some."

"Mmm." Tess sips smoothie straight out of the thermos. Stares down at her baby.

And we sit and say nothing for a while.

I check my phone. No message from Calliope. It's been three

days. I refresh, in case I've missed something. Nothing. I click the screen off.

Why am I even expecting her to write? I have to sort myself out first, she said. I've spent a whole lifetime unsorted, so it's not like I would be done by now.

"George?" Tess says.

I look up. She has shifted to face me.

"Yeah?" I put the phone on my lap.

"What's happening?"

"With what?"

"With you," she says, gesturing at me with the thermos.

"What do you mean?"

"You're, like, a thousand billion miles away these days."

"I am?" I mentally check myself over. I thought I'd been present. Do I look like I'm far away?

"Yeah," Tess says. "What's going on?" The question sounds like the opening to a cave: tight, narrow, unknown.

I stare at her. "Do you want to know?" I say. "Really?"

"Of course. I'm your best friend."

"Okay. Um. Well."

I open my mouth. I close it. Where do I start? What can Tess take? I move the pieces of my story around in my mind. Try to order them from "least difficult to hear" to "most difficult." I should probably skip "most difficult." Can Tess even take "least difficult"?

Tess sighs, tired of my silence. "Is it Calliope? Trouble in paradise? A lover's spat?" She shakes her head. "You and your girls, George."

Wow. What does that even mean? Tess has seen me sad about

my girls—she's fed me chocolate as we sat on clifftops; she's seen me shredded and rejected. She should know better. And when did she start being cruel? I thought when you became a mum you softened, not the other way around.

The anger from this morning—that rumpled, miserable feeling—shoves in. "That's a shitty thing to say."

She sits back. Nods. "Okay. Yeah. Sorry. That was harsh. Tell me about it. Has Calliope dumped you? I had a feeling about her—"

"No," I say. "It's not like that. I mean, we're taking a break, I think. She's just tired of me being—"

"—friends with me? We've been friends forever, she should understand."

"No. She's actually been great about you. She sent her love. She said—"

"I don't even know her, George. Why is she sending me love?" Tess's voice spikes. "I barely know this girl you've been hiding out with, while I've been stuck here—"

My chest thumps. "That was your choice, Tess," I hear myself say. "And I wasn't hiding out, I've been here, more than anywhere else."

Tess laughs. "I don't think so."

"Seriously? Oh my god." I feel hot, jangled. "Tess, I've stopped everything for you."

"That's not true."

"I've been doing everything to support you, for . . . forever. I haven't seen anyone but you for weeks. And I love Calliope, and now she's dumped me—"

Tess's eyebrows go *up.* "Wait. You love her?"

Uh. I stop. Think . . . Do I love Calliope?

I feel around, check my heart, body, bones.

Shit. I do.

Tess takes in my face. "Wow. And you'd rather be with her than with me."

I would. I would. The truth of it blooms on my face.

"I knew it," says Tess, tearing up.

"No. Tess. Listen—"

"How long have you even been together? It's only been, like a minute, hasn't it?"

I pause. "Um. I—"

"George?" Tess suddenly sounds small, like when we were little and she needed me to walk her to the bathroom because the dark had pasted monsters onto the walls.

"It's been . . . a bit longer."

"Since when?"

"Since . . . um, just before Seren—I mean—the night he was—" Oh God. This is going to be hard.

"The night he was what?"

"Born," I finish.

Tess looks walloped. "Wait. You were with Calliope when Seren was born?"

"Yeah." There it is. The truth. It flops raggedly in the air between us. I don't like it. I want to take it back.

"And that's why you missed the birth?"

"Yeah, uh, there was this ferry—we went to Manly. Just a spur-of-the-moment thing. Then our phones ran out of battery. I had no idea you needed—I was always going to be there, Tess. I just—"

"Oh my god." Tess stares. "Were you ever going to tell me?"

"Yes. Of course. Just—I got distracted, because of the baby. And then Dad called again and he said—"

"Sorry. Wait. What?"

I don't know what I'm doing. I'm adding Dad to the mix now? I feel reckless, roaring—

"Tess. Listen. Dad is—"

"You want to talk about your dad right now? After you just told me this huge—" Tess lets out a sharp breath. "George. What the hell. You're too much."

Seren gurgles on the floor. Tess grips the thermos, white-knuckled. "I asked for one thing," she says. "One thing, only the biggest thing in my whole life, and you missed it. And now—"

"I'm really sorry, Tess. It wasn't—I didn't mean—" But then I stop myself. This is when I always apologize. This is where I always try and smooth the surfaces, do whatever I can—with anyone I'm with—to find peace.

I say, "You never asked me, Tess."

"What?" Her face is blotchy, like she's a second away from losing it.

"You never said, 'Can you please come to the birth? Will you please help me raise this baby?' You never said, 'Will you do this with me? Do you want to?'"

"Of course I did."

"You never, ever did."

"Don't you want to help?"

"Of course I do. But I have a life. Of my own. I have stuff to deal with, Tess. I need to talk to you about it. But you're always focused on your own shit."

"I'm not."

"You are."

I am out of control. I wonder if this is how Tess felt when she got pregnant? I'm a boulder, rolling, headlong. "Calliope listens to me. She checks in. She listens all the time."

"*Wow.*"

My chest pinches. My throat grinds. And Tess looks like I've slapped her.

"Why didn't you tell me this was too much for you?" she says.

"Would you have heard me?"

"Yeah. I would have."

"Really?"

"Yes. I would."

"Well then. Okay," I say.

"So go on. Talk to me. Tell me your *shit*." Tess waves a hand in the air.

I look at Tess. This is a terrible time to talk about anything.

"Uh—"

"*Tell me,*" says Tess. Her voice sounds mangled.

"All right. Fine." I suck in a breath. "Dad is dying, Tess. He has heart disease, because of all the drinking. He has two years to live, maybe three. It's unfixable. He's going to die. Not this second, but soon."

Tess's eyes go wide. "Oh my god."

"So. It's a lot to take—" I say. "And I feel . . . pretty shit. And confused. He keeps calling—He says he's sorry, but I don't know if he really is, you know? And I keep having these memories—"

But Tess isn't listening.

"Oh my god," she says. "Oh my god."

"Tess?"

"Shit, George. He's dying? He's going to die?"

"Yeah," I say. "I—"

Now Tess has started crying, hard.

I reach forward, touch her leg. Shit. Shit. "Tess. I'm sorry—" I begin. I don't care about the truth anymore. I want to go back to soothing, fixing, smoothing—

"No. Don't be—" She waves her hands, flapping them. "Thanks for telling—" She starts to cry harder. And now Tess is shaking uncontrollably.

She can't seem to stop.

Oh. God.

I have pulled Dad out of the place where Tess had boxed or buried him. I've dug him out and here he is—slithering and staggering into Tess's living room.

I put my arms around her. "Tess," I say. "Tess. It's okay. It's going to be okay."

But it's not.

Tess can't hear me.

"Oh my god," she says. "*Oh my god.*"

She shudders in my arms.

And suddenly we are back there, stuck in that slick night.

We are under the bed again.

21

We were so small.

Tess and I were seven and she had come for a sleepover. We were so excited; we were always excited. Tess brought her dolls. We were going to have a midnight feast! Tess had brought snacks: two apples, a half-eaten packet of Oreos, and a block of sliced cheese. I had an alarm clock I'd taken out of the spare room—where Mum slept sometimes because Dad snored, she said. Tess and I were going to wake up way after our bedtime and have a midnight picnic in the garden. We were going to be so sneaky.

We buzzed through the afternoon. Dad was tired from a hard week and having a rest on the couch. We kept running through the house. Our dolls were airplane pilots; we even made them tissue-box planes to ride in. The planes kept making jet sounds that Dad didn't like. "Stop it, girls," he said, once, twice, and then he shouted it. We stopped running through the house. We went to the back-yard and flew there.

Mum was making a big dinner. We were having guests over, some friends of Dad's. Dad said we didn't have the right wine. I heard him and Mum discussing the wine that wasn't right through the kitchen windows. Tess and I climbed the tree at the bottom of the yard and pretended we were pirates, or maybe koalas? Either way, our dolls got out of their planes and climbed with us and our clothes ripped like in those books about girls who climbed trees and ripped their clothes.

Tess said, "Oh no, we ripped our clothes," and I said, "Who cares!" because I was caught up in the excitement, the heady feeling of being a girl who climbed trees and ripped her clothes.

It was a beautiful day. The sun beamed. The birds twittered. Everything shone: the light, the birds, the tree, the tick-tock time carrying us towards midnight.

The guests came. They drank the right wine that Dad had gone out to get. They were two of Dad's old university friends. Tess and I had already eaten our dinner, so we watched a movie in my room on Mum's laptop. The guests drank all the right wine and then they opened the other wine Mum had already bought, and then they had whiskey and beer.

The house echoed with laughter, with the roar of it, the kind that swells up without you seeing it. The noise shook the roots of the house, the furniture, the walls. It boomed, thunderous, as Tess and I lay in our beds—me in my bed, her on the inflatable mattress. We tried to sleep. We looked at the alarm clock. We watched time slide towards midnight. We could hear Mum say, "Shh, the kids are sleeping, Karl," and we heard Dad say, "Who cares!" like in that book about fathers who didn't care.

Then it was midnight and the house rocked in its moorings, because Dad and his uni friends were out of control. They were shouting, laughing, arguing; they were fighting. I could hear things breaking. Noise tore through the house like a runaway plane. Tess looked at me.

"George?" she said.

I felt the house angle under us. I said, "Get up, Tess," and she got up. We opened my door. We heard a shout, another shout, a crash, a scream. There was no escape; they were right there, *right there.*

Tess shook next to me. The sound was so loud she covered her ears.

"Come on," I said. I got out of bed and lay down beside it. It had the slats above and just a little room underneath. "Come on," I said, more urgently.

"Under there?" she said.

"Yes," I said.

She went in first. We slid like quick snakes on our bellies under the bed—past a sock, a crumpled tissue, a book. It was dusty. I could feel the prickle of it in my nose.

I pressed against Tess. I took in a breath. Sneezed.

The door crashed open. Light flooded in. I could see legs standing there, light behind them. "Wake up, kiddos!" said a man, one of the friends. "Come and play!"

The floor rippled and rolled. I shook as Tess shook. The house shrank in on itself, cowering.

"Where the fuck are ya?" said the voice. One step forward. Then another.

"Hey! Wha the fuck you doing?" said two more legs, light behind them.

The stranger spun in place. "Just kidding round, Karl."

"Get the fuck out, kids are slupping," said Dad, who couldn't even say "sleeping" right. He pulled the man out of the room, two bodies stumbling. The door slammed. On the other side of the door,

I could hear Dad yelling, just a little wood between us. I heard the stranger being shoved against the door, and then the door burst open again. The stranger toppled in and fell to the floor.

He rolled on his side. "Fuck!" he said. His eyes opened. He could see me there and Tess too, hiding. Could he? Our eyes locked.

He started to laugh. Pointed to me, to us, to Tess crying behind me, pressed against my back. "Hahaha!" he said. "Caught you!"

And then Mum rushed in, saying, "Stop! Stop! Stop!" as though they might listen. She had a tea towel in her hands. Had she been washing dishes through the madness? Trying to pretend there was no madness at all?

Now all of them tumbled out, and I could hear Mum screaming at them and I could hear the fear of her, the wallpaper shake and peel of her, and I could hear Tess whimpering behind me and I could hear the front door open and slam shut. I could hear Mum crying and Dad yelling and the house breathing, ragged like it was running.

And then, a hush. A minute passed. Another minute. Another.

Were we safe? Was everything okay?

I turned towards Tess. "Tess. Tess. I think they've gone. It's okay."

But she couldn't speak. I couldn't see her properly under the bed, just a shape, like it was my shape, the body shivering there my own. I wanted to crawl into her skin and make it right.

I wrapped my arms around her. "Tess," I crooned, "Tess, it will be okay."

But of course it wasn't.

And wouldn't be.

. . .

We crawled out from under the bed. Tess had been so scared she'd peed her pants. She asked to go home. She dressed, silently, and Mum and I drove her home, leaving Dad to pass out on the couch/the bed/the floor. Mum had texted ahead, so when we got there Lydia was standing at the door in her pajamas, half-asleep.

She looked at Tess's face. "What happened, sweetie? What's wrong?" She touched Tess's messy hair.

Tess stood, mute at the doorstep. She hadn't said a word the whole way back.

Mum had kept turning in her seat to look at Tess as she drove. "I'm so sorry, sweetie. That will never happen again, okay? It will be okay. I promise, okay?"

I'd sat next to Tess and gripped her hand. Kept squeezing it three times, as if I was sending Morse code: *I'm sorry. I love you. I love you. I'm sorry.*

When Tess didn't answer Lydia, Mum stepped forward. Said, "We had a bad night. I—" She stopped, suddenly stuck.

"Did you have a nightmare, sweetheart?" Lydia looked down at Tess. She looked back at Mum. "Too much ice cream?" She smiled.

Tess looked at me. I looked at her.

Mum stared at Lydia. "I—Um—"

I felt the ripple of our story, undulating and ugly, underneath us. It felt like the world was ending. What would Mum say?

Tess looked up at her mum. "Yes," she said. "I got sick."

I stared at her. Wow. That was a really big lie. I didn't think we were allowed to tell a lie that big.

Lydia looked down at Tess, her face rumpled and sleepy. "All right, well, next time don't eat so much, Tessie. It's the middle of the night. You would have been okay at Sara's house."

Tess's eyes glistened. She nodded. She didn't say anything else.

And Mum didn't say anything. And I didn't say anything.

Lydia and Mum hugged goodbye. Tess and I hugged goodbye.

And then we drove home in the rolling dark, through the hot, hard shame of not saying anything, through the sick, thick shame of Dad being Dad, through the wallowing, underbelly shame of us keeping his secret safe.

Mum and I drove until we *were* shame, riddled through with it—one tiny person, one grown—twined up in someone else's story. Dad's story was ours, his harm ours.

And maybe I didn't know it then, but I can see it now.

How all we've done since then is stay quiet, stay small, stay good.

And try to atone endlessly for our terrible sins.

Tess has stopped crying.

We are sitting in the muted light, just breathing.

"Tess," I say.

She looks at me. "It's too much," she says. Her voice is flat, rubbed so thin you can see through it.

"Yeah. I know," I say. I reach out my hand. She doesn't take it.

She looks at her lap. "George. I'm really sorry about your dad."

"Thanks," I say. "I—"

"But I need some time," she says. "All this. I don't know how to—" She waves an arm through the air. "God. I'm so *tired*."

"Tess, I didn't mean to add more—" I begin.

Tess takes an enormous breath—she sucks in her tremble-tired days and Seren crying and all her sleepless nights and me keeping secrets from her; she sucks in our hard-packed memory and our years together and me holding her hand and us pinned in that shocked, underbed dark, and it's like she sucks in the smoke too, and all the people weeping, the burning animals and houses and trees—and she leans back on the couch and closes her eyes.

"George," she says. "I think you should go."

"But don't you think we—"

"I don't." Tess's fingers twist together. "I can't. I'm sorry. This was a lot. I can't right now. Please. I'm so fucking full. I *can't*." Her voice cracks.

"I—"

"George. Please. Just. Go."

I sit on the couch in the beat of her words, the heat of the room, the open, empty space of Tess not wanting me here. Two roads diverging. Two girls on two roads that maybe were never really one.

"Okay," I say.

I get up. My limbs feel far away.

The room is so quiet.

I feel Seren breathing in his invisible poison. Hear Tess sniff, once, twice. Feel the thin lime-green lines of Tess's overwhelm. Hear the hushed *tick* of a clock. Feel the pale, donging ache of being asked to leave my best friend's house.

The sounds are all so silent.

I stand at the front door, turn to look at Tess. Her eyes are still closed.

"Is your mum coming home soon?" I say. "I could wait for her—"

"You don't need to babysit me, George." She doesn't open her eyes.

"Sorry. Right. Okay. I'll see you later?"

Tess nods. The movement is so tiny maybe I imagined it.

So that's it, I guess?

I step outside. Walk to the bus stop. Get on my bus. Text Lydia that I've gone. Shove my phone deep into my bag so I don't have to read her replies. Sit with the strangers and all their stupid stories.

The bus turns right, turns left. Smoke writhes around us. It fills our lungs.

22

Evening.

I went to the library after leaving Tess. I didn't want to go home—I didn't want to do anything but run. But I couldn't, so to the air-conditioned library I went. I sat at the computers and pushed out my last uni assignment. Now it's done and I guess I'm finished with my online classes, and I guess all I have to look forward to this summer is . . . what?

I feel so bleak, I can't see even a day ahead.

When I get home, only Mel is up. She texted when I was on the bus, heading back from the library: *George, what do you want for dinner? I can't promise anything good. Your grandfather has gone to bed in a mood. Your mum has gone to bed with a headache. I blame the smoke. We're all losing our minds.* And then she sent a GIF of a monkey clanging cymbals together.

I wrote: *I'm fine for dinner. I'll just have whatever's in the fridge.*

Thank god, she said.

Mel is sitting at the kitchen counter when I come in. She's eating hummus and crackers, going through her emails, swearing under her breath about something.

She sees my face. "Oh, sweetie," she says. "Shit day?"

I plonk down onto a stool. "Shittiest. The most shit. A pile of shit." I don't even have words for how terrible this day—this entire week—has been. And at the same time I'm aware, with my whole body, that I'm living in a house by the water. I'm sheltered. I'm not burning.

Guilt pushes in on all sides. I've let down Calliope; I've let down Tess. I'm still barely answering Dad's messages. I'm not talking to Mum or Mel about anything. I'm complaining about my life and I am so lucky. More guilt sits on top of my Most-Shit mountain, and plants a flag.

Mel gets up. She comes over and wraps her arms around me. "All right, George. I'm making you a sandwich. We're taking it with us. It's time to paint."

Inside Mel's studio, her paintings and sculptures loom and stare—testicles and labias and penises and boobs. All the canvases are facing out for once. It's a cacophony of bits.

Mel moves around the space saying, "I know, I know they're a lot, George. Let me turn things around to give you a little peace."

I put up a hand. "It's okay, you don't need to." Mel is always turning things around for me. Or maybe I'm always the one turning? Maybe I am always looking away.

Mel scans me, trying to gauge my thoughts. "Well, how about I move the shoutiest ones for now? Baby steps. Then you can get up close and personal at the exhibition." She moves some of the larger canvases and faces them against the wall, then grabs her bucket of brushes. "I don't know what I was thinking with this series, George. Maybe I'll do landscapes next. Some tidy gardens. Maybe some cows, sleeping." But of course she won't. Mel loves to go deep into what makes humans tick; she loves to shock and awe. Mel has been a disco ball in my life since I met her.

I say, "Mel. You doing tidy anything would be like Van Gogh losing his yellow paint."

Mel doesn't even hesitate. "Or if O'Keefe stopped liking skulls."

"Or Picasso stopped objectifying women."

Mel laughs. When Mel and I did this at the Art House—back in the days when Mel was there all the time and life was mostly right-side up, Laz always called us nerds. Tess always rolled her eyes.

My insides clutch at the thought of Tess.

Mel sees my face change. "Okay," she says. "Listen. Here are some canvases. Have at it, George. I'm here if you want to talk. Otherwise, I'll be in my corner with this"—she gestures to a wall-sized labia—"and you can be over there, doing your thing."

"Thanks," I say.

"Want some music?"

"Sure."

The room fills with violins. Mel says she likes all kinds of music, but we always paint to classical. I think it's the one predictable thing about her. "Besides my love for you and your mum," she'd probably say.

I put a canvas on an easel. Squeeze paint from the tubes. Begin.

I use red ochre. Chromium green oxide. Raw sienna. The paint curls on the canvas; the colors throb and roil.

I don't look away.

A month after the under-the-bed thing happened, Mum told Lydia our secret.

Dad had left—he'd been gone for weeks. Mum had cried and cried. And I guess she couldn't contain it anymore. Shame was heavy. Secrets pinched and wriggled. Maybe Mum thought the truth would hurt less?

We were in the playground. Tess and I had climbed to the top of the tall rope structure. I could see for miles.

Mum and Lydia were on the bench. Mum leaned towards Lydia—I saw her stiffen as Mum spoke. I watched Lydia put her hands to her face. I watched Mum cry.

I felt fear, treacling through my body. The earth seemed to carve in two: On one side, our secret, and on the other side—

I watched Truth storm our castle. I watched Lydia stand, come over to the rope structure, and call up to Tess.

"Tess, come down, sweetie. We're going home."

"But we just got here!" said Tess.

"Tess. Come down *now*." And Lydia's voice was flinty, sharp. It could have sawed the ropes all the way through.

We climbed down.

Mum came over. "I'm so sorry, Lydia—"

"Unbelievable," Lydia said. The rage in her was white-hot. I could feel it where I stood.

We didn't see Lydia for three months. Tess and I only saw each other at school. We made the best of things—we held hands as we walked in the playground, sat together in the classroom, clung together like limpets, even when the teacher said, "Would you like to play with some other friends, girls?" When the teacher put us in separate class groups, Tess and I made our way back to each other, clicked together like gravity. We wrote each other notes to read at bedtime, while our mothers didn't speak.

Mum rang and rang Lydia to apologize, left long messages. She and I roamed around our old house, floated through a barren land where Lydia knew the worst side of Dad, where someone knew about Dad and had left us because of him.

Mum cried sometimes. I watched her cry. Sometimes, I cried.

Weeks passed.

And then Dad started calling. He started saying sorry, and that it wouldn't happen again.

More weeks passed. Dad made promises and promises and promises.

The door sat on its hinges, the glass swept up, lamp replaced. Memories faded.

Mum started to believe him.

Mum called Lydia. Promised her nothing bad would happen again.

Dad called Mum. Promised her nothing bad would happen again.

"Please," Mum said on the phone, and I didn't know who she was saying it to.

Then Lydia came to our house. She and Mum went into the kitchen and closed the door and they murmured to each other behind the wood.

And then Lydia invited us over. I ran down the path to Tess. We fell into each other's arms.

Months passed. Tess didn't come to our house for sleepovers, but I could go to hers for dinners and dolls and sleeping, and I made sure never to bring up Dad's name or talk about anything sad.

And then Dad came back.

He came down the path and through the door, opening it wide, all his light bold, sweeping in. He and Mum fell into each other's arms, and into the shower they went.

When Lydia heard Dad was back, Mum padded the news with Dad being better, with Dad trying, with Dad not drinking, with Dad not being sick anymore.

Lydia believed Mum. At least, she didn't disappear again. But it wasn't quite the same.

To keep us safe and unabandonable, Mum locked away her stories. I locked away mine. When Dad started drinking again, Mum didn't tell Lydia and I didn't tell Tess. Maybe we thought if we didn't say it, the truth wouldn't be true?

And when Dad left me in a lake, and when he went running down our street drunk and screaming, and when he left the house, the cold air whooshing behind him, Mum didn't have anyone to talk to. And neither did I.

Tess and I got older; Mum and Lydia drifted apart. I still went over to Tess's house and, when we moved, Tess came over to Mel's place. Lydia and David visited for polite dinners until they didn't, and they went to Mum's wedding and smiled and lifted their glasses for the toast, but then . . . nothing.

Until Tess got pregnant.

Lydia came over one night saying, "I don't know what to do, Sara," and they stayed up late, talking and talking in the living room like they used to.

And when Tess didn't listen to Lydia and didn't do anything to stop her boulder rolling, Lydia looked at me and said, "You'll keep an eye on her, won't you George?"

And inside those words I heard: *You let me down once, George. Maybe lots of times if I stop to think about it. In fact, if your father hadn't happened, I would have a happy, sensible girl.*

I looked back at Lydia. I promised her the world.

● ● ●

Mel and I paint until almost midnight.

I've poured my feelings onto canvas. After the old, mashed memory of Lydia and Mum, I kept on: I painted the tangle inside me, how "lost" tastes in your mouth, and then—kinks loosening— I painted the pulse of running, the flat-slap of wind, the sound of upside down, the jiggering pattern of flight.

In the end, Mel stops first. She stretches her arms in the air, yawns, says, "George, I hate to be first to quit, but I'm done."

I lower my brush, wipe it with a cloth, set it in the turps jar. I'm exhausted too, but also want to keep going—fall into the canvas and stay.

Mel comes over to my easel. I've somehow done five paintings, set them in a row along the wall. Mel sighs, soft. Touches my shoulder. "Well, that must have felt good to get out."

I nod. "I guess."

She steps over to her satchel, pulls out a tall thermos. "Coffee?"

"At midnight?"

Mel laughs. "I know. It doesn't make sense." She rummages a bit more. Pulls out a packet of chocolate biscuits. "Bikkies?"

"Sure. Who needs sleep?"

We sit in the middle of the studio, on two rickety chairs Mel sometimes gets naked people to sit on. She pours coffee into chipped mugs. It comes out steaming and milky. I take a sip—it's so sweet it makes my teeth fuzz. In other words, it's perfect.

"Cheers," she says, clinking my cup.

"Cheers," I say. Now that I've stopped painting, I am back in the real world again. I don't love it.

Mel looks me over. "George."

"Yeah?"

"Talk to me." Her voice is gentle.

I look at her. Here she is. Ready to listen. And I'm tired. I am suddenly so very tired of holding all this in.

I lift and drop a hand. "Where do you want me to start?"

Mel angles her head. "It's up to you. The beginning is always nice."

I think about beginnings. Once, I was born. Once, Dad had a drink and couldn't stop. Once, there was a Big Bang. Once, Tess got pregnant. Once, Mum and Dad fell in love. Once, we were all amoebas. Once, Tess and I were so scared she peed herself. Once, I started keeping secrets. Once, I loved my father.

Mel leans forward, touches my arm. "All right. How about you start with today. And we'll go backwards."

. . .

We talk and talk, Mel and I. About Tess and Calliope, about Dad, about my memories waking up, about Dad dying.

Mel listens and listens.

When I tell her Dad's news, she says, "Oh, George. That's really awful."

I nod.

"He's really dying?"

I nod again.

"And how long does he say he has?"

"Two to three years, he said."

"Is he sick, right this minute?"

"Maybe?" I say. "I mean. I don't know for sure. I haven't really talked to him."

"How long have you known?"

"Um."

When I tell Mel how long I've been holding on to Dad's news, she says, "Sweetheart. What a thing to carry on your own."

I don't know what to say.

"So Karl just handed this huge news to you? Without telling your mum?"

"I guess."

"Didn't even have the courtesy—" Mel mutters. "Jesus, that man—" She shakes her head. "George. It's too much."

My gut tightens. "I know. I'm sorry if I—"

"No. I mean for you. To deal with. Why didn't you talk to us?"

"I don't know." I half shrug. "I didn't want to upset Mum."

"It would be normal, for her to get upset," says Mel.

"It's just . . . I don't like upsetting her."

Mum in tears on the floor, sweeping glass—
Mum shaking and me shaking—
Please, Karl. Please—

Mel looks at me. "And you'd give anything to avoid that."

I pause. "Yeah," I say.

Mel sighs. She squeezes my hand. I didn't realize she was holding it.

"You and your mum have been through a lot. You deserve good things and you deserve peace. But your mum is going to want to know about your dad. And then, you'll have each other . . . and you'll both have me. I'm not going anywhere."

I nod.

Mel continues. "Your mum doesn't like to talk much about this either. But I'm a big fan of talking." She catches my eye, laughs. "I know you know that. But especially you and your mum talking to each other. What do we have, if not the people who love us?" She pauses. "And you might like to see someone else too, to sort through all this? Because I know we can be annoying sometimes."

I smile. "Only sometimes?"

"Ha."

I picture myself talking—telling Mum about Dad, me bringing up the past . . . and Mum reacting like Tess. I picture talking to a stranger about it all. The colors turn dark yellow and purple. I feel sick.

"I know it's hard, George," says Mel through the muck.

"It is. It's just—" Tears prick. I blink them away. I'm not a crier.

"Do you think maybe holding it all in is the worst part? Not being able to talk about it? It's not your stuff, remember, George. Your dad's story is not your story."

I look at Mel. How is that true? How is what happened to me not my story? How is the fear and the rumple and the shouting and the breaking of glass and swaying at doors and the tilting house and the underbed dark not my story?

It's as if Mel has read my mind. "I mean—your dad's addiction is sad. Like, really sad. But . . . or I should say, *and* . . . it's not yours to carry, George. His illness, this news—it's not yours. You don't have to hold it in or hide it. You don't have to look after everyone, or protect people who have hurt you. Not at your own expense. You've a right to be upset, to be wobbly as hell. Sweetheart, you don't have to be silent about this."

She's right.

She's right.

She's right, say the paintings and walls and the streaks of paint on the floor and the land beneath it.

Mel lets out an enormous yawn. "Okay, I want to talk more about this, but I think I'm about to turn into a pumpkin. Can you drive us home?"

"Sure."

"And in the morning, we can talk some more . . . and you can talk to your mum? About all this? What do you think?"

"Maybe." I see Mel's face. "Okay. Definitely maybe."

"All right," she says. "But listen—just so you know—your dad's news—you can always pass the ball to me. I can tell truths till the cows come home. Okay?"

"Okay. Thanks, Mel."

She nods, stands. Her knee cracks. "Oh my god, I'm getting old." She smiles down at me. And reaches out a hand to help me up.

Mel falls asleep on the car ride home. The streets are quiet, traffic lights all green, the smoke a haze that feels almost ordinary now.

I picture talking to Mum . . . I try not to picture her crying. I picture the words I want to say—to her, and Tess, and Calliope.

I'll probably say "I'm sorry" a thousand times.

I'm so sorry for holding this in,

I'm sorry for not telling you,

I'm sorry for disappearing—

and now, Dad's voice glides in, lopes alongside mine: *I'm so sorry I let you down, Georgia, I'm so sorry I didn't sort myself out, I'm so sorry I wasn't there for you—*

I grip the steering wheel tighter.

Sorry won't be enough. My story is larger than that. Louder, deeper, wilder . . . like every story there is.

It might take a while to figure mine out.

The car thrums. Mel shifts in her sleep. The road is gloamy, dreamlike. Streetlamps whirr—unworldly orange light bathing our bodies, reaching out endlessly into the blue-black.

LOST

(oil on canvas)

Muggy and close.
Girl can't sleep.
Toss. Turn. Hot and fitful.

On his shelf above her,
Bird feels the restlessness of the girl.
He remembers the feeling—of wanting, of turning,
of looking for something that needs to be found.

Girl twists. All around her: eels and embers.
Bellow and burn.
Teeth and rot and weeds and wings.
"Speak, Girl, speak." Voices shout, all invisible.

Girl opens her mouth—
and out of the bird's beak fall all the lost things.

23

Morning. Smoke at the windows.

Mum is pouring coffee. I'm making a smoothie. Gramps sits at the kitchen bench reading the newspaper, and Susan sits beside him on a stool, washing a thigh.

None of us talks. All of us are far away, lost in thought.

"Good morning, lovelies!" Mel busts into the kitchen, clapping her hands.

We all jump. The cat guns off the stool and out of the room. Mum spills her coffee.

"Oh my god, Mel!" she says.

"Sorry!" She grins. She doesn't sound it at all. "It's time for a family chat! We're going to sit at the dining table. Put away the paper, John, we all know the news. It's shit. Can you pour me a coffee, Sara?" She looks at me beside the blender. "George, have you ever heard of solid food?" She motions with her hands. "Come on! Let's go!"

Mel was so much gentler last night. I guess she's not tired anymore; she's back to full speed. And I guess I'm talking today? I glance outside. Unless I leap out of this window right now, and run to my cave—

Mel comes up beside me, touches my elbow. Whispers in my ear. "Georgie. It's going to be all right. You're going to be *great*."

· · ·

We sit at the table.

"What's going on, Mel?" says Gramps.

"Is everything okay?" says Mum, looking at Mel, then at me.

"Everything's fine," says Mel. "I just wanted to say—" She pauses. Glances at me. I must look panicky, because then she slows her roll, and says, "I just wanted some time together. I love you weirdos. When did we last really hang out?"

Gramps frowns. "Are you serious? I was about to do the crossword."

Mum says, "You had me worried, Mel." She visibly relaxes.

Until I say, "Actually, the thing is—"

And I tell them Dad's news.

The room has to make space for all the surprise and all the noise.

Gramps says, "He's dying? He's really dying?"

"He says he is," I tell him.

"Shit," says Gramps.

"How long have you known?" says Mum.

"A while," I say.

"Like, days?"

"Um. More like, weeks?"

"Oh, sweetheart. And you didn't tell us?"

"A lot's been happening, Mum."

"But you've had to deal with it by yourself—"

"I was going to tell you. I just . . . It wasn't—" I sigh. "It's exhausting."

"What? What's exhausting?" says Mum.

I lift my hands up and down. "Everything." And I mean, almost every single thing in my life. I would explain it but that could take hours . . . and I wouldn't even know where to start.

Mum's face is all emotions—clouds scudding over the sky, hell-bent. My chest clunks and pangs. "I'm sorry for not telling you," I say. "Dad said—I didn't want—"

"It's just a shock," says Mum. "The doctors always said—And I tried so hard—" She looks like she's going to cry.

I feel tiny again, seeing Mum in pain. *Fix it, George. Fix it.*

"Mum. It'll be okay."

"How will it be okay? Is it definite? Have you asked?" Mum says.

"I think it's definite." Have I asked? I think I did. I don't really remember.

Gramps shakes his head. "I never liked that man. But shit—poor fella."

I look at him. Part of me wants to scream, *Poor fella? He did this to himself!* Another part of me wants to say, *Don't fall for it, Gramps.* But another part of me twinges, remembering the sound of Dad's voice over the phone. How he's fumbled and fallen, over and over. How he's trying to get up and, this time, stay standing.

Now Mum starts crying, just like I knew she would.

"Mum—" I say. I want to paint over my words and start again.

Mum, nothing's wrong.

Mum, I didn't talk to him.

Mum, I didn't leave you to go nearly drown in a lake.

Mum, life never made us freeze up till we couldn't speak.

Mum, it wasn't, it didn't, it never—

"I'm sorry," I say. "I'm sorry, Mum."

"No, don't be." Mum flaps a hand at her face. "It's terrible news. But—" She reaches for a tissue from the box on the table. "The doctors said it would happen." She honks into the tissue. "So—It's a lot, but—I'm not surprised."

She sniffs. Honks again. I watch her trying to calm herself, straightening her body, breathing in and out slowly. Then she turns to me. "So, is he sick right now? What does he need? Does he have someone with him? Is he in hospital?" And for a moment she sounds like Mel, all bustle and business.

I open my mouth. Close it. It occurs to me I don't have answers for these questions. I haven't asked any. What kind of person doesn't ask?

Mum must see the shame swooping over my face, because she touches my hand. "George—" she says.

I pull my hand away. "I don't know!" I blurt. "All he's said is sorry and that he wants me to come see him. I don't know anything else."

"Wait. See him in Seattle?" says Mel.

I nod.

"Ha!" says Gramps, slapping the table. "As if."

I guess Gramps's sympathy only goes so far. And Mum looks like I've suggested driving into a tornado.

"Are you going to go?" she says.

"Maybe." I pause. "I should, probably. What kind of person wouldn't go?"

"Someone who's been through what you've been through, George."

Calliope said that too, I almost say. But Mum would hate that I've talked to someone about this before her.

She picks up her phone. Puts it down. "Well. Okay . . . I'll call him today."

My insides jitter. When did Mum and Dad last talk? What if he says—What if he makes her—

I lean forward. "Listen, you don't have to. I can sort it out. I know you don't like talking about this. You've always said—"

Mum stops me. "It's okay, George." She pauses. "I'm sorry for what I've always said. I've been . . ." She takes in a breath. "I was wrong. You should have been able to come to me. You should have been able to talk about your dad. I've been a total clam."

I stare at her. "No, you haven't—"

"I have, George. Seriously. I've been so stuck. I don't know why—" Mum hesitates. "Okay. That's not true." She pauses again. "Do you remember, George, how I lied to Lydia that time?"

"Uh . . . yeah?"

She sees my expression. "Right. Of course you do. Well, after Lydia found out, I felt so . . . ashamed. I thought I shouldn't ever talk about your dad again. Especially after I let him come back." A longer pause now—like it's taking effort for Mum to pull the words out. "I guess . . . I always thought I had to keep it private. No one else seemed as broken as us—I mean, as me." Her eyes well up again.

"Sara," says Mel.

"You're not broken, love," says Gramps gently.

Mum turns to look at him. "You and Mum kept telling me to leave."

"And then you did."

"And then you found *me*," adds Mel, and smiles.

"I know," Mum says. "I *know*. Just . . . these things are sticky. Like, I've been trying to help Lydia and Tess, but this whole time I've been thinking, *How do I help them when I'm so busted?* So, Mel and I have been talking, and . . . I've made an appointment to see someone."

I sit back in my chair. Try to process. My mother. Talking. To a stranger. Mum talking now. Mum weepy, but not in pieces.

She continues: "I should have talked to you about this sooner, Georgie, but I didn't want to add to your load. You've been dealing with so much."

I shake my head. "I didn't tell *you* about Dad." I pause. "I didn't want to add to your load either."

"Oh, sweetie." Mum wobble-smiles.

I half smile back. I think over the last month—all of Mum's headaches, the nights she and Mel went to bed early, the muffled conversations I never really registered until just now. I think about how focused I've been on Tess, on saying yes, on chasing quiet, on running away . . . and all the years Mum and I have stepped carefully around each other, tucking away our splinters and shards. Always light and tiptoe-quiet, trying to protect each other from the monsters under our beds.

"Would you like to talk to someone too?" Mum says.

"I did already."

"Yeah, but I didn't . . . encourage you to keep going when it got hard. And now, with your dad's news . . . it's big. There's a lot to process."

I picture sitting in a room again with someone I don't know, with all the blank paper and pens and soft furnishings and feelings. It makes my mind gooey. Mum has been practicing with Mel; she's turning into Mum 2.0 before my eyes. But my words aren't here yet. They're tender, still forming. "Maybe," I say. "I might." Then I touch her hand. "Thank you for talking to me, Mum."

"Thank you for talking to *me*, George," she says. She does a big, raggedy sniff.

Mel hands Mum a tissue. "You both deserve to talk!" She lets out a huge sigh. "Fuck, silence is exhausting. I don't know how you lot do it."

"I don't. I talk all the time," says Gramps.

Mel laughs. "In what world?"

"I'm sure I don't know what you mean."

"John. Mate. You're the biggest clam I've ever seen."

"You kind of are, Dad," says Mum.

"Fine." Gramps folds his arms. "Then what are you, Mel? If you're not a clam?"

Mel thinks for a second. Then grins. She leans forward and pats Gramps's cheeks with both hands. "I'm a goddamn dolphin, baby!"

Gramps can't help it—he does his loud laugh. Even Mum starts laughing, though she's still a bit leaky.

I stare around the table. I feel muddled and clear—Mum's talking and I can talk, finally, I think? And we're here together and people are laughing and the world isn't ending right this second. I don't know what to make of it, but I crack a smile to keep my family company.

"Is it okay that we're laughing right now?" Mum says, a second later.

"Karl's not dead yet," says Gramps. He leans over and lays his papery hand over Mum's. "Even the shittiest things in the world can take time."

24

We've stood up from our table portrait. Time has moved on.

We've hugged—at least, Mel has hugged us all, and then gone to the studio for the rest of the day. She's taken Gramps with her, dropping him off at his first French lesson, where I'm sure he'll *voulez vous coucher avec moi* himself into some kind of trouble.

Mum's still here—it's her day off. She's moving around the house replacing rags and tape around our windows.

"Do you want any help?" I say.

She looks at me. "Could you do some laundry? Just a little bit, 'cause we can't hang it outside."

"Sure." I go around the house, picking up everyone's limp things.

When the load starts running, I lean against the wall and text Calliope again, and Tess, and Laz. Wait for a reply.

Only Laz writes back. He tells me about the protest coming up.

Do you want to come?

Sure, I say.

He gives me the details. *See you there!* he says.

I put my phone in my pocket. Now what?

I walk up the stairs and sit on my bed and do nothing at all.

It's good that my family talked today, and I told Mum my news and she told me hers and we had a bonding moment and everyone laughed, but I still feel so . . . lost.

I've finished my online classes. I'm not teaching and Tess doesn't want to see me and Calliope is leaving me alone to sort out my shit. And Dad still needs me to make a decision and the fires are still burning and the smoke is still here and my whole body aches, and I can't *move*.

"George?" Mum stands at my doorway.

"Hey." I stare at her, wedged.

"I just spoke to your dad. Just to get more information."

"Okay."

"He's been quite sick, with the flu. There were some complications."

"He didn't tell me that," I say.

"Well, he said he didn't want to worry you. He was in hospital, just for a while. But he's out now, and he's stable. The damage from the drinking is irreversible and he's quite weak . . . but he's stable for now."

"Okay." I can't really register what Mum is saying. Dad was in hospital? Dad was sick? I try to focus.

"Main thing is, you don't need to make any sudden decisions, sweetheart. About going or not going. Not before you're ready. There's time."

"All right."

Mum hesitates. "Can I come in? Can I sit down?"

"Sure." I motion to the bed. Mum comes and sits right beside me, so I have to shift—I scooch over in the bed to make room for her.

She presses her shoulder into mine, looks at her knees. "I haven't spoken to your dad in years. It was so strange."

"Yeah," I say. "It's always weird for me."

Mum glances over. "Oh, George. You've been through so much."

I shrug. "So have you."

"He says he's very sorry."

"I know. But he's said that before."

"I know."

We sit. We remember all the sorrys, all the excuses, all the promises. Maybe we'll always remember? Maybe it will always hurt.

"There's a lot, Mum. Like, how do you let go of everything—" I wave my hands.

Mum nods. "I know. I know." She touches my hand. "I guess we're kind of banged up, you and me."

"Just a bit."

"Yeah. Well. I wanted to say, what I think, is, um—" Mum stops. We look at our knees.

God. We are both so worn—pulled and pinched by our shitty history. And now the history is here. Now we have to face it. No more running.

Finally, Mum says, "I'm sorry, for telling you to be quiet. For saying we shouldn't talk. For making you—"

She takes in a long, unsteady breath.

"I am *so* sorry I didn't protect you, George."

And her voice breaks with my name.

And I break with the break in her.

"Mum." I lean against her, touch her leg. Just like that, she's shaking. It's a full-body tremor.

I look at her. What is she picturing? She just spoke to Dad. All her memories—are they waking up like mine? God. I'm sure Mum is about to cry again. And all I want is to wrap her up—smooth her—smooth *us*—but the dark is the dark, and the past is ours, and maybe nothing in the world can change that.

● ● ●

It was night.

I was little.

I stood in the living room doorway.

Mum stood by the couch, bent over like a puppet with its strings loose.

Dad looked up, slow, sleepy—waving a droopy hand in my direction. The other hand held Mum down by her hair.

"Hey," he slurred. Slow smile.

I stepped forward.

Mum said, "Go to bed, Georgie." Her voice was scratchy, pan-icked.

I stepped forward instead.

Again, again, till I got to them.

I took the man's hand—his thick fingers—lifted each finger up.

Dad giggled. Like this was a game.

He giggled.

I undid the binds. Released Mum. Freed her.

Hand in hand, I took Mum to my room—or did she take me? At least: One led the other away.

I lay back down in my bed. Felt proud. *Saved you, Mum.* But Mum was shaking all over.

She kept saying, "It's okay, it's okay, it's okay." She kept stroking my hair, hand trembling, body trembling. So I sat up and held her.

I shook with her shaking.

I said: "It's okay, Mum. It's okay. It's okay."

But of course it wasn't. We sat, pinned. In the endless, the terrible, the howl. Together and alone.

● ● ●

Mum grips my hand.

"George," she says. "Sweetheart."

I come back to her, to this bed, this room, this day.

"Let's not say it's okay," Mum says. "Because it isn't."

I look at her. It hasn't ever been, has it? But here we are, still. Mum isn't crying. She's stopped trembling. The cat is here, at the foot of my bed. The bird is here, beside my grandmother's clock. My notebooks are on the desk. Somewhere above us, above all this smoke: clear sky.

"All right," I say.

"You deserve to be really happy, George," she says.

"The same—for you, Mum." I squeeze her fingers. "Like, you too."

Mum sighs. "Thanks, sweetheart."

We are quiet for a moment. The two of us, just, here. Holding all . . . *this*.

I suddenly picture going to South Head—standing on that great cliff with Mum, and us shouting our story out.

I picture the two of us screaming it, chucking out the worry and weight, heaving everything into the air, into the wide-open ocean. I picture doing it until we are free.

What would that be like?

I press my shoulder against Mum's. "I love you, Mum," I say.

"And I love you, George."

I picture our arms, lifting.

Picture the pull back, the throw.

Picture everything hovering, midair.

Picture the fall.

25

Heat. Noise. Smoke-stilled air.

What do we want?

Climate justice!

When do we want it?

Now!

It's the millionth day of smoke. Time has grunted forward. Everything around us is on fire.

Today we, the people, are out in the thick of it, shouting.

I'm here with Laz and Adesh. Thousands of us stand with our masks on in front of Town Hall, our fists thrust up.

Mum and Mel came for a bit, then left for work. Gramps wanted to come, but he has a sniffle. There was a "conversation" about his lungs this morning, and he's at home. There's also no Tess because of the baby/the smoke/her being done with me. And no Calliope, because even though I've texted every day and called, she's still taking a break from me and my disasters. Adesh said she was possibly coming, but she's not here, beside me, in the crowd.

I texted her last night. *Are you going to the protest tomorrow?*

She didn't reply until this morning. *I might,* is all she said. And then as if throwing me a mercy bone, she wrote: *I'll probably be working, but I wish I could.*

Now, Laz, Adesh, and I, and a thousand strangers hold up our painted signs and scream through our masks.

What do we want?

Climate justice!

When do we want it?

Now!

We scream until I can't, until the air in my mask turns close and hot. My eyes stream; I start to cough and have to go inside a mall to use my inhaler. Three floors up, in the bookstore overlooking Town Hall, I stare down at all the people. I can hear the yelling through the glass. I wonder if anyone is listening?

After it's over, Laz and Adesh meet me in the food court near the train station. "That was great," Adesh says. "Wasn't that great?"

"Yeah," I say. "Sorry I had to go inside."

"That's okay," says Laz. "Breathing *is* kind of important."

We go to the Thai food counter; Laz hands over a reusable container. "Pad Thai please."

I didn't bring a container. I brought a cheese sandwich, wrapped in paper.

We sit down to eat. Laz puts the container between him and Adesh to share. He looks at my sandwich, made with the crusts because we were out of bread again. "That looks sad, George."

I take a bite. "I know."

"No Pad Thai in the apocalypse for you?" says Adesh, slurping up a bean.

"Can't. I'm saving. I'm not teaching right now . . . because of the apocalypse."

"But you're working in the store—" says Laz.

"I know. I just need—" I start, but then I stop myself. If I really wanted, I could get Pad Thai right now. I have money. A home to go to after I leave this shiny food court. Nothing on fire.

Laz nods. "Yeah. I know," he says, as if he's read my mind. "The system has trained us well." He glugs from his water bottle. "You should come and make pizzas with me. If you need to accumulate more wealth." He nudges Adesh. "Can you get her a job, Desh?"

"I don't think I can squeeze another person into Pizza Heaven. I had to sleep with the boss to get *you* in, Laz."

Laz laughs. "You did not sleep with Marco."

Adesh nods, straight-faced. "True. I did not."

"That's fine," I say. "I really am okay at the shop." I look across at Laz. "Do you think you'll ever come back?"

His face changes. "No," he says. "I don't think so."

Adesh glances at him. Opens his mouth to say something. Shuts it.

"Is it because of Tess?" I say. "She won't be back till next year. And you guys have had tough times before—"

Laz shakes his head. "All we *were* were tough times. She's made decisions I can't stand. She doesn't care about the things I care about. And she's said stuff . . ." He takes in a breath. "I don't think Tess and I are a fit, George."

"But—"

Laz says, "People stop being friends all the time. It happens."

I stare down at my sandwich. Laz doesn't know that Tess isn't speaking to me either. Is this what's going to happen with me and her? Will we just . . . stop? Will it happen with Laz too? What about Calliope? *God.* Am I just going to end up completely alone except for a cat and a dead bird, muttering at walls and painting my feelings?

I must look miserable, because Adesh reaches over and thwaps my shoulder. "He's not letting *you* go, George. And you've got me too, if that's not too hard—I know my looks can be overwhelming." He lobs a square of tofu into his mouth.

I smile. "Thanks. If I don't look too closely at you, I think I'll be safe."

Laz says, "George. I'm not giving up on you. I'm just . . . giving up on Tess."

"Do you think you'll ever be friends again?" I sound so small. And Laz sounds so final.

Laz shrugs. "Well, I won't say never but it's unlikely. At least right now. I've got shit to do."

Adesh says, "Yes, we definitely have shit to do. Want to join us, G?"

And just like that, they leave Tess behind, and start telling me about the climate group they've joined.

It's the real deal—the flip-tables (non-violently) and fuck-shit-up (peacefully) kind of group that glues themselves to things and gets arrested. Well, Adesh doesn't plan to get arrested. "I'm not putting this brown body anywhere near a jail," he says. But he is going to fuck shit up.

"Adesh is going to do the gluing," Laz says.

I look at Adesh. "You'll be gluing people? To things?"

"Yes. I will *be* the glue," he says.

"And Calliope's going to film us," Laz adds.

"Oh—"

Laz catches the shift in my voice. His eyebrows raise. He'd make a good spy, or maybe a crime novelist. He leans forward. "She says you're super busy and probably won't be able to join us."

"I am kind of super busy."

"But she had this *tone*. You two in trouble? Desh won't tell me."

"Sorry. I am a vault." Adesh lifts his hands, palms up.

Laz turns his laser eyes on me.

"Well. It's just—I kind of—" I pause. God. Where to start? My face must have changed seasons, because Laz touches my hand.

"Are you okay, George?"

"Um. Not really? I just—" Ugh. Words. If only I could paint what I mean or turn it into water—then I could move over the surface of the story as it spoke.

I need to talk.

I *want* to talk.

Do I start with Calliope, or do I tell him about Dad? Laz has no idea about Dad. And just thinking about Calliope makes my insides twist.

How have I never told Laz about my father? We're *friends*.

"Okay," I say.

I put down my sad little sandwich. And let go some weight.

It's done.

I've done it.

Laz and Adesh know about Dad. The shortened version that is, where I say simply that my dad is a lifelong alcoholic, now dying of heart disease. (Turns out if you rip the Band-Aid off quickly, it's over in a second.)

Laz's sigh afterwards is long and empty. "Shit," he says. "Well, wow. That sucks."

"Yeah."

Adesh shakes his head. "I'm so sorry, George."

"Thank you."

Laz rubs his eyes. "Shit. Wow."

"I'm sorry if this is too much, Laz," I say. "I know you're really stressed about the fires and everything."

Laz says, "I can be here for you, and still be freaked out about the end of the world. I can multi-task."

"He really can," says Adesh, nudging Laz.

Laz soft-punches his shoulder. "That really is shit, George."

"I know. It's all shit."

"What are you going to do?"

"I want it to go away." I flutter my hands like I'm whisking Dad out of the air. Maybe I could, if I just wished hard enough.

"What does he want you to do?"

"He wants me to go see him in Seattle. He's bought me a ticket."

Laz blinks. "On a plane," he says.

"Yeah."

"Fuck."

My insides lurch. *I know, Laz.* I know what he's thinking. But he doesn't start—he doesn't talk about the carbon footprint of planes, or how flying on one is basically like taking a giant shit on the planet. He doesn't call me a climate murderer. We all just sit there. And then Laz reaches over and twines his fingers in mine.

"Well. If you decide to go—"

Adesh finishes for him. "You can always do that carbon trade thing."

"God, that trade thing," says Laz, rolling his eyes. "It's like those people who ask priests for forgiveness after doing something evil, instead of just *not doing* something evil—"

"Um. Laz—"

Laz looks from Adesh to me. "Right. Except in your case, George. If you decide to go see your dad, just plant three trees and I'll absolve you."

"Um. Thanks?"

"You're welcome." Laz starts to fork up the last of the noodles. Remembers something. "Hey, is this why you and Calliope—Did she—"

"No. No. She's been great. I've just been caught up with Tess. I've been a terrible girlfriend."

"Cal says she's just waiting for you to sort things out," says Adesh.

Laz looks at Adesh. "I thought you were a vault."

"I'm just saying . . . it might be a motivating factor for George to get her shit together."

"I have my shit together," I bristle. But then I think about it. Do I?

No, I do not.

"Well, I'm glad you do, George," says Adesh. "All I'm saying is, maybe you could get your shit a little *more* together, and then you can get your true love back."

"She's not—" I stop. Blush.

"Oh my god!" Laz leans back in his seat, gleeful. "You've gone and fallen," he crows.

"Shut up."

Laz laughs and laughs.

I look at him—face open, head tilted back. He's gone and found his light again. Or maybe he and Adesh found it together? Either way, it's gorgeous to see.

When we get up to go, Laz hugs me, hard. "Listen, George. I'm really, really sorry about your dad. Everything is going to hell. We're going to die on a cooked planet. All we have left is love."

"Sweet, Laz. Really comforting," says Adesh, beside him.

"It's true though," Laz says.

I look at them looking at each other. Holding each other up. Standing beside each other in the middle of all this. They kiss my cheek goodbye, then weave away through the food court—hands tucked into each other's back pockets, arms intertwined like vines. The two of them are going to change this whole cooked planet. Or at least, go down trying.

26

Morning. Air thick and hot.

The smoke sits—still and here—a flat plate over the city. It doesn't budge; it's been here for weeks now. I haven't spoken to Tess in ten days. Haven't spoken to Calliope in thirteen. The fires have spread down the entire state. On the fire maps, the whole east coast is red.

I miss Tess, I miss Calliope, I miss moving, I miss rain, I miss the air outside.

The heat is so intense at seven a.m., I can't take it anymore and go outside to swim in the harbor baths. I sneak out because I know Mum and Mel wouldn't like it. I haven't been outside properly since the smoke started—haven't moved properly—haven't paddled—haven't, haven't, haven't. Mum dragged me to her gym two days ago because me running up and down the stairs repeatedly wasn't *working for the family,* she said. I went to the gym, ran on a treadmill, and stared at a wall. Then I sat at a rowing machine and rowed to nowhere.

I walk through the park, past the fig trees, and down to the water. People are actually running maskless along the paths, filling their lungs with particles. At the baths, people swim maskless up and down their lanes.

Ten minutes, I promise myself. I pull off my mask, slip into the water, and put my head under.

God. The feeling is so perfect I might just stay here always. Here, there's no Dad, no decisions to make, no noisy family, no silent Tess, no empty space where Calliope once was, no fire. Here is only cool and wet, and my body moving through it.

I swim two laps, hard, fast.

I stop at the pool end and lift my head, look around. The surface is pocked black with charred specks—once bark, once trees, once leaves—flown from the fires to here. I pick up a fleck. It grinds to pulpy ash between my fingers.

I look up. The sun glows red, a monster watching over its children.

Should I keep swimming? Should I swim with my mask on? I can't bear the idea of leaving. I do two more laps. I try to breathe only ashless air, as though willpower alone can take the best bits of the sky and put them in my body.

Out of the pool and in the showers, my face and hands are sticky, speckled black. I have to rinse and rinse to get the ash off. I walk home, mask back on, checking my breath, checking I'm okay. My hair is almost dry by the time I get home.

Mum and Mel are in the kitchen with their coffees. They turn to see me when I walk in.

"Oh my god, George. You went out?" says Mum. "Do you know the air quality today?"

"Did you swim outside?" says Mel.

"I did. I had to. It's just so—"

"She can do what she likes!" Gramps calls from the living room. "It's like a prison in here! Also, where are my pants?!"

"It's not a prison, Dad," Mum calls back. "I just want everyone to be okay."

Mel bumps Mum's shoulder. "Sara—"

Mum looks at Mel. "What?"

Mel kisses Mum. "That." She looks into Mum's eyes and I guess she sends some kind of love note with her mind, because Mum smiles back, all gooey.

I think I'm free to leave.

I go in to see Gramps. He's sitting in his chair in just a shirt and underwear. "I think the neighbors stole my pants, Georgie," he says. "Those fuckers!"

"I saw them on the little clothesline in the bathroom, Gramps. I'll go get them."

Gramps looks at me. "I need to iron them. I have a date."

"Oh yeah?"

"With Dot."

I look blank.

"She was in my French lesson. She spoke to me in the language of love afterwards . . . if you know what I mean."

"God, Gramps." I kiss the top of his head. A second date? This is new for him. "I can iron them for you, if you want."

"Thank you, angel child," he says.

I'm ironing Gramps's pants when Mel finds me. "Hey," she says, "can you please stretch some more canvases for me? I went on a spree last night and finished my last big ones, and you used up my last small ones the other night. I'm going into the city to talk to some buyer. He wants me to do an installation for a bank. Do you think a bank would like a big, bronze vulva in their lobby?"

I smile. "I'm sure if you tell them it's something else, they won't know any different."

Mel kisses my cheek. "Thanks, George." She gives me a measuring look. "You okay? Have you talked to your dad?"

"I sent him a message. I'm talking to him tomorrow."

"You all right with that?"

"I think so. Mum and I are going to do it together."

Mel smiles. "That's really good. I'm so proud of you both."

I feel warm. Maybe a flicker of proud too. "Thanks, Mel."

Gramps waits in his chair for Dot to come pick him up. He tells me a bit about her. "She's been to Machu Pichu! She just retired. Legal secretary. Very smart. Loves dancing," he says.

"She sounds nice," I say.

"Lovely bottom," he says. He smiles fondly. "Just lovely."

I hear a honk outside. Gramps stands up to go.

"She's not coming in?" says Mum, wandering into the living room.

"I'm not a teenager, Sara. She doesn't need to meet the parents."

As he makes for the door, Mum follows. "Wait! You need a mask!"

"I'll be fine!" he says. "I'll be in a car for Christ's sake. And then a cinema."

Mel's in the hallway too now. She holds out one of her industrial masks. "No mask, no going out," she says, like Gramps is a preschooler.

"*Please*, Dad," says Mum. And maybe her voice pings Gramps's heart like a resonant string, because he sighs.

"Fine." He holds out a hand, takes the mask and puts it on. He looks like an old, white-beaked duck. "Now can I go?"

"Yes, John," says Mel.

He hesitates. "Do I look okay? The pants. Not too wrinkled?"

Mum smiles. Mel smiles. I smile.

"You look very handsome, Dad."

"Just don't knock her up," says Mel.

"Oh my god, Mel," I say.

"I'll do my best!" says Gramps, and he's out the door.

At Mel's studio, I'm bending over a canvas and punching staples into the wooden frame when I hear footsteps. I look up.

It's Calliope.

"Oh!" she says, and stops.

"Oh!" I straighten. I'm suddenly aware of my clothes (rumpled), my hair (messy), my skin (spotty), and my whole body (instantly electric).

Calliope stands in a square of light from one of the high windows. "Mel texted and asked me to come in and do some work for her. I should have guessed."

"I'm sorry. She's a total meddler." I pause. "She is the worst." I'm going to have some words with Mel when I get home.

"She told me she'd heard we weren't talking. She said we should start, sometime. I didn't realize that time was now."

"Mel loves to talk."

"Seems so."

We look at each other.

"I'm sorry she lured you here."

"It's okay." Calliope almost smiles. "We do need to talk. So, she's not the worst person in the world."

"All right." I hesitate, then say: "I'm really, really sorry, Calliope. For disappearing on you."

"Thank you," she says. "You kind of did. So thank you for saying that."

I look at her. What should I say next? Should I explain? Will it matter? She looks about ready to leave. Is she trying to decide if I'm worth staying for?

The idea of her leaving feels so terrible, I start to babble.

"I really am sorry. I've just been . . . overwhelmed. So much stuff has been happening—with Dad and Tess and Seren and Laz and all this smoke . . . and then everything got so . . . *full* . . . and I wanted to be with you, but then Tess crumpled and I clicked into 'Tess-care' mode. I've done it all my life. With, like, everyone, but especially her." I pause. "It's no excuse, I know. I didn't want to let you down, or let her down, but in the end, I managed to drop you both."

Calliope looks at me. "What do you mean . . . both?"

"Well, Tess isn't talking to me either."

Calliope's eyebrows raise.

"It's kind of a long story," I say.

"Huh," she says. I see her processing. "I thought you two were stitched together."

"We kind of are. Ever since we were little."

"Well, that's a hard space to fit into, George."

"I know." It always has been. Have I ever really let anyone else in?

Now Calliope says: "I have a lot going on too, George. I have big stuff happening too. I needed to talk to you about it, and you weren't there."

"You have stuff?" I take a step towards her. "What? What's been happening?"

Calliope looks around the studio, as if deciding whether it's worth filling me in. Finally, she says, "Mum's coming back, George. She's left Terry. Turns out, she wasn't the only one he was reading his shitty horse poems to, shall we say."

"Whoa. Really? That's horrible."

"Yeah. He's already moved in with *whoever* . . . and Mum's coming home. She's going to have her baby here. She and Ari are coming in two weeks. She's asked Dad if they can live with us."

"What did he say?"

"He said, 'Maybe.' I mean, obviously he said yes to Ari, but he's not sure about Mum. He wants to help, but I've told him, '*No one should be that noble.*' And our flat's pretty small. So we've been having a lot of talks. It's kind of intense."

"Wow. *Wow.* I'm so sorry, Calliope."

"Yeah," she says. "And I really wanted to talk to you, but you just faded out."

"I know."

"That was hard."

"I'm sorry."

Calliope sighs. "George, you can say sorry a thousand times, but you really do need to get your shit together."

"I know. That's what Adesh said too."

"Well. Exactly." Calliope hesitates, then says: "I don't mean you have to be a saint—no one is. Like . . . I may sound like I'm all sorted, but I'm not. I threw one of Terry's poetry books into the fire, a week before I left Reading. He was so angry, he turned blue."

"Really?"

"Yeah. It was a first edition."

"Oh."

Calliope looks almost embarrassed. "I didn't tell you . . . because . . . I'm trying not to be the angry girl who chucks books into fires."

"Right. Okay." I nod. Try to process. So. Not perfect, then.

Calliope looks at me. "Yeah."

We are silent for a second, taking each other in.

"Listen," Calliope says now. "I know the stuff with Tess and your dad is massive, but you're so . . . stuck, George. You just . . . keep dropping your own life to look after everyone else's. It's like you turned your yes switch to ON and can't switch it off. And it means you're not even deciding anymore—you're just on autopilot." She's sounding fierce now. "It's kind of fucked."

I nod again. "I know." I pause. "I am. It is."

I feel clanky and hollow, like Calliope has pulled out my clockwork pieces and is rummaging through them saying, "Dude, your gears are a mess." And I don't know how to fix it, how to unstick myself. Mum and Mel are all *Go talk to someone,* as though talking to a stranger is the holy grail, but maybe I'll go and talk and the therapist will say, "Dude, these gears are *smashed.* There's no hope for you." Or maybe I won't be able to talk, like always, and maybe I'll be like this forever—busted and silent and scared.

I must look tragic, because Calliope softens. "What I mean is, you never say what you want. I swear, if you just said it, life would be way easier."

I blink.

Me? Say what I want?

First, I'd have to figure that out.

What do I want?

Calliope is five feet away from me—hair slipping out of her ponytail, standing there in her op-shop sundress and high-top sneakers, looking earnest and open and true.

I want her. I want Calliope.

There. That's one thing.

And I want Tess to be okay.

And I want Mum to be okay.

And I don't want to always feel sick when Dad gets in touch.

And . . . I want him to be okay.

And I want the fires to stop. And the smoke to stop. And the end of the world to stop.

But maybe they won't and maybe it can't and maybe I can't control everything . . . and maybe I have to deal with that?

And maybe, if I just said what I wanted, and did what made me feel good and right, the noise would go down anyway? And maybe there'll even be noise I *like* in the mix—it's possible. Maybe that's what Laz has done, and that's why he's still standing and planning protests and kissing Adesh in food courts. Maybe that's how Mum is settling herself? And maybe all I have to do is find myself in all this mess and keep myself steady, and everything will be—

"George?" Calliope's looking at me.

"Uh. Yeah?" I think I've been staring at her without talking for a while, like a beached jellyfish.

"Did you fly to the moon just now?"

I half laugh. "No, I'm just . . . thinking. About what you just said. You're right. You're totally right."

Calliope gives a tiny bow. "Well. Thanks."

"So I'm trying to figure things out."

Calliope's eyebrows go up again. "Like, what part?" And she sounds really small.

And it occurs to me, suddenly, that I might have this all wrong.

Maybe Calliope is standing here wondering if *I'm* a second away from leaving *her*. Maybe she's had enough of people disappearing, and has been waiting this whole time for me to say I'd like to stay?

So I step forward. "Calliope. I know I have a lot of shit to sort out. But . . . I really, *really* like you. I want to be with you. I want to be there, *for* you. I want this. I want . . . *us*." I pause. Shake my head. "This probably sounds so cheesy."

"It doesn't." Then she smiles. "Okay. Yeah. It's pretty cheesy."

"Shit. Words are *hard*." And I gesture around the studio, to all the words I've tucked into paintings I haven't shown her yet, all the stories I want to tell her, all my lost and hidden things.

"George." Calliope half steps towards me. "I want to be with you too. I . . . really like you. I want to do this"—and now she waves around the space, scooping up her own story maybe, and offering it to me—"with you, too."

A beat. I register what she is saying.

"Wait." I look at her. "Really?"

Calliope smiles again. God—three thousand watts. "Yeah," she says. "I mean. If you can fit me in." She tilts her head. "I know you're very important. Busy schedule and all that."

"Oh, I can fit you in." I say, emphatic. "Definitely. Absolutely." And I start smiling too.

"Well, okay then," Calliope says.

"Okay then," I repeat. And then we stand there, not moving, just beaming like beacons at each other.

And the world stops clanging for a second. The noise lowers and the worry ebbs, as the two of us step forward and forward, into a new square of light.

27

It's late afternoon when Calliope and I get back to my house. We walk inside—it seems calm, potentially peaceful. Maybe no one's home? Or maybe everyone's just doing their own thing, in their own spaces, being silent. That would be a rare celestial event.

I'm ready to go upstairs and talk to Calliope and kiss her till the end of time, when Mum comes into the hallway.

"George—" she begins, then sees Calliope. "Oh! Calliope. You're here."

"Um, yes?" Calliope half laughs.

Mum shakes her head. "Sorry! I mean, hi, sweetheart. It's lovely to see you again." She comes and gives her a quick hug. Then turns to me. "Tess is here."

"Here?" I say. "In the house? Now?"

Mum nods.

Calliope says, "Oh." She looks at me. "I should go."

I look at her. "No. I don't want you to."

"George," says Mum. "She's been here all afternoon. I fed her soup. She's keen to talk to you."

Calliope nods. "I'll go." She moves to the door just as Tess steps into the hallway, holding Seren.

"Hi, Calliope," Tess says. We both turn, take in my pale friend, her baby drooling on her arm, both of them looking crinkled and tiny.

"Hey, Tess," says Calliope.

We stand awkwardly in the hall. Except for Mum—she steps out, and leaves us to it.

"Seren's almost six weeks old," Tess says. She gives me and Calliope a lopsided smile. "I can't believe we've survived this far."

Calliope smiles back. "He's really gorgeous, Tess. You've been amazing."

"Well . . . I haven't been *amazing*. But I'm on drugs now, haha, and I'm sleeping, like, more than an hour, so I'll kick some arse soon. I'll be so fucking amazing, they'll name a building after me."

Calliope laughs, then says, "I know it's been hard."

"Yeah." Tess nods.

"Maybe you can help me learn how to be around babies? My mum is about to come home and have one, and I've no idea how I'll even hold it."

"It's not hard," says Tess. "You just . . . here—" and she steps forward and hands Calliope her baby.

"Oh!" Calliope scoops up Seren like he's a pile of laundry she might drop.

"Wait, do it a bit more like this," says Tess, and adjusts things.

Calliope looks down at Seren. "Holy shit. He's even cuter than last time."

"Isn't he just?"

My oldest friend and my girlfriend smile down at the baby. Seren looks up at Calliope like she's someone he might end up loving. She puts her finger under his hand; he wraps his tiny fingers around hers.

"Awwwww," we all say. And then Seren shoves Calliope's

finger into his mouth and she's probably thinking: *Gross!* or maybe: *Adorable!* and then Tess smiles at Calliope, and Calliope grins back. Like maybe they're going to be friends.

Like maybe we're going to be okay.

Calliope heads home with promises to return and continue her baby training soon with Tess. Mum comes and takes Seren into the living room, and I take Tess up to my room. We sit cross-legged, facing each other on the bed.

"Hey," Tess says.

"Hey," I say.

"So . . ." Tess pauses.

I wait. My first instinct is to roll Tess up in a "Sorry" blanket, smooth her wrinkles and fix all the breaks. But for once, I don't.

"I'm sorry, George," Tess says.

"Okay," I say.

Tess looks at me. "Is it?"

"Well, what are you sorry for? And then I'll say if it actually is okay."

Tess looks at her knee. Rubs a freckle there. "Um. For being, um, kind of a shit friend."

"It's not like that, Tess. You've just been—"

"Everything's been about me. For ages."

"Yeah . . . Maybe. All right—yeah."

Tess nods. "My psychologist is getting me to do these reflections. Just noticing a feeling and spending time with it. We've been talking about you. And when I said how mad I was about you missing the birth and being with Calliope and you telling me about your dad, she had me sit with that. And then see . . . if there might be another way of looking at things." Tess laughs, self-conscious. "It probably sounds stupid. It's kind of new."

"It doesn't sound stupid," I say. "I'm probably going to have to do the same thing soon."

"You're going to see someone?"

"I think so."

"And talk about your dad?"

I nod. My chest aches. Yeah. I'm going to talk about him. How will it go? I have no idea.

Tess reaches forward and touches my knee. "I'm really sorry he's so sick."

"Thanks," I say. "It doesn't really feel real. There's been so much—" and I pause, because there's been *so*, so much.

"It's been a lot," says Tess.

"Yeah," I say.

"If my memories of him are garbage, yours must be royally shit, George."

"They are." I blink. It's like my body wants to cry, but has forgotten how. Maybe I'll learn? When I go and dump all my history onto a stranger and she has me spend time with it? Weirder things have happened.

"I'm really sorry, George. That you couldn't talk to me about him. And, everything else. I'm here now. And, like, you've got Calliope too. She's great. I'm sorry I was such a bitch about her."

"You weren't. You were kind of right. I didn't—I haven't known how to be with you both. I'm figuring it out."

"Well. I'm happy to have joint custody," says Tess. She smiles.

"Ha," I say.

"Maybe you, me and her, and Laz and Adesh . . . maybe we can all hang out sometime. When this smoke goes—" Tess says.

I look at her, see her dreaming of our rosy future. I open my mouth to tell Tess that Laz is gone, that Laz isn't coming back. But then . . . I don't.

Tess might show up at Laz's door next. Maybe they'll figure themselves out? Maybe that's for them to work out. Maybe that's their story.

Tess and I sit on my bed—Tess picturing a life where the smoke leaves and the fires stop and we all can have picnics together . . . and me picturing . . . well, a swirl of somethings. A feather. A wave. Hands holding. Open air.

I have no idea what's going to happen. Time does odd things. It moves on, it ripples, bends. The fires will stop—they have to, right?—and something else will start, something else will step in. More noise, more baby drool, more paint and kisses and mistakes and tears. And that's life, I guess? An endless parade of colors.

Tess says, "George? What are you thinking about?"

I shake my head, come back to her. "Um. Life . . . I think?"

Tess nods. "Sounds about right. You going to paint it?"

"Probably." I smile.

We look at each other. The earth spins, our knees touch, our story spools behind us and ahead, too.

And now we hear a cry downstairs.

Tess stares down at her chest. "Far out. I felt that in my boobs.

You wouldn't believe, George, how weird it is. Like he's a tractor beam, summoning me to feed him. With my *boobs*."

I get off the bed. "Please tell me more, Tess."

"Oh, you *know* I will."

I pull her up from the bed. She looks at me. "I love you, George. Like, a lot."

"I love you too, Tess."

She steps forward and hugs me. But not for long. "Shit," she says, pulling away and looking at her shirt. "We'd better hurry. I think my boobs are going to explode."

We step to the door—as the cat unfolds from the bed and leaps ahead of us, hoping maybe she'll get fed too—once time ticks on, and we make our way through it, and down the stairs.

A girl sits, phone in lap, her mother beside her—
two bodies perched on the edge of the bed.
Above their heads sit a bird and a cat and a clock.
All bodies poised.

"I'm not coming to visit, Dad," I say. "Not right now. I need time."

Dad's voice pings the satellites, comes down as tin and ache.

"Well . . . okay. That makes sense . . . I know there's a lot to process."

"Yeah, there is."

Everyone is quiet for a moment.

Bird, listening from the shelf, would nod if he could.
He knows sorrow. Knows glass. Once he—
Bird hears a rustle now, scouring the air.

"I'm walking by Puget Sound," Dad says. "It's beautiful. But so cold. Can I send you a photo?"

I nod.

Mum glances at me, says, "She's nodding, Karl."

"Yeah," I say.

"Oh! Okay."

The room tilts with wind and regret.

"I love you, Georgia," says Dad into our silence. "I know I hurt you. And you too, Sara. I know it's been incredibly hard for you both." He pauses. "I never owned it the way I needed to." He pauses again. I hear his breath going in, out, laboring a little. "I really am so sorry."

"Thank you, Dad."

"Thank you, Karl."

More quiet. More wind. More breath in and out.

"All right, I've just sent the photo," says Dad.

My phone lights with the incoming message.

I open the photo.

The sound, in blues and greens and grays.
Choppy water, tendrilled clouds,
mountains a blurred hint in the distance.
Girl can almost see the movement of the water,
the air sighing, fish undulating below the gray, and
a dark bird about to fly into the frame—

"It's beautiful, Karl," says Mum.

"Thanks, Sara," says Dad. "I'll show you, Georgia, when you come . . . When you're ready, I mean. And, Sara, you too, if you come along." His voice is tentative.

Mum nods.

I look over at her. "Mum's nodding, Dad."

"Oh! Okay."

A beat, two. Smoke shifts a little in its spot by the window.

Mum takes in a breath. "So, Karl, did George tell you she got into the National Art School for next year?"

"Oh, she did?"

"Yeah," I say.

"Well, that's wonderful. I'm not surprised, George, you're a great painter—"

Bird listens, feels through his glued bones the story start to move.

> *He feels a sense of things opening now,*
> *a kind of quickening,*
> *feather spreading from feather,*
> *a new feeling of flight.*

Bird remembers flight.
Once, he breathed, and lifted from a flecked sea
—rise and beat,
air and pull and memory.

> *Once he was—*
> *Once he will be*

> *Once,*
> *he—*

(oil on canvas)

Smoke-streaked windows. Hazy sky.

Tess calls me from her house. She's on her bed, watching our protest via livestream on a laptop. "I can't see you," she says. "Oh, wait! There you are!"

"Yeah," I say. I wave into the air. "I'm here."

I picture what she sees . . .

> *A girl, stepped away from the protest choir where*
> *she has been singing climate-crisis Christmas songs.*
> *A boy, crouched over another boy on the street,*
> *gluing his hand to the road.*
> *A bustle of masked bodies, some stuck to asphalt,*
> *others playing dead on the sidewalk, occupying*
> *space so cars and people can't move.*
> *Shouting. High-vis vests. Painted signs. Honking.*
> *People in business suits passing by.*
> *Police rushing in.*
> *And a girl moving like liquid through the tumble,*
> *camera focused on bodies and*
> *faces and hands.*

"Hey! I just saw Calliope!" says Tess. "And Adesh and Laz too, I think. You all look amazing." A beat, then: "Oh my god. Is that your gramps, lying down?"

I laugh. "Yeah. He's here with Dot. Can you believe?"

"Is he glued too?"

"No. He's just pretending to be dead. He was so excited."

"Far out."

"I know."

Later, Tess will tell me how it felt, watching us:

a pang of missing,

of wanting to be somewhere,

doing something different than this, and

how the feeling rolled, loose,

moved through her body, passed on—

and her son stirred in the bed beside her, ready for lunch.

"Got to go," says Tess. "Seren just woke up. My boobs are twitching."

"Okay."

I hear a small squeak through the phone—Seren practicing maybe, for when he might need to say something too.

I picture Tess, turning towards her baby. Kissing his cheek, pouring love, gold over his skin, like armor. I picture the smoke hanging limply outside her window, hoping to be noticed.

"Oh shit," says Tess. "I think Laz is getting arrested."

I look over. He is.

The police have unglued him. They hustle Laz up, muscle him over to a van. Calliope follows with her camera.

"It'll be okay," I say, reassuring Tess, even though my chest pangs. "He prepped for weeks for this."

I see Laz's face as he goes out of sight. He looks lit from the inside.

> *Voices all around,*
>
> *noise and movement, a flurry like stirred water,*
>
> *bodies crouched over bodies, all of us calling out—*
>
> *Here we are. Here we are.*
>
> *Here is the pulse of all of us, doing something—*

"Keep me updated, okay?" says Tess.

"I will. We'll see you tonight?"

"Yeah. Love you."

"Love you too."

I hang up. The choir has not stopped, in all this time.

Into the air, into the immensity, our voices rise. They loop and touch and turn.

(here, now)

It is two minutes to midnight.

New Year's Eve.

Mum and Mel headed to bed an hour ago; they didn't want to watch the Harbour Bridge fireworks. None of us did—even though today the smoke has thinned a bit and the view would probably be amazing from the end of the peninsula—we all boycotted.

Gramps is at Dot's place, like he is every night now. Adesh and Laz—released and waiting for his court date—are at the pub. Tess is home with Seren and her family, and Calliope came over from her mum's flat at ten. We set up snacks in my room and cued up a movie marathon, all black-and-white movies that Calliope prom-ised I would love.

We watched half a movie before Laz texted.

Look at the news, he wrote.

We turned on a live feed. And haven't looked away since.

A week ago, the bushfires came to the beaches down south. All along the coastline, in towns one, two, five hours south, people have fled the fires. They've slept in shelters till those shelters burned; they've run to the water and tried to hide in it. Families with no road out have been taken away on navy ships. The sky has melted into red and black.

Tonight, in a town seven hours south, flames roar through trees, over brush and dunes, down to the ocean's edge. Thousands of people crowd on the sand and in the water. Others huddle in boats, faces smeared with ash.

Fire spikes and explodes, trying to lick life clean.

Calliope and I press together on the bed.

We don't speak.

We sit in our safe house, in this safe room, watching the end of the world. Someone's end, someone's world. And it's not just a picture; it's here, it's life, it's real.

I imagine seeing it in person. I pour myself into other people's lives, lean towards the television. Will everything be okay?

Will these people on the burning beach who could be us, be okay?

Will anything be okay?

I don't know. Laz says maybe it can be, if we do something—if we at least try—while we are alive inside these human bodies, loving and careless, hopeless and hopeful and loud.

There is so much to do. There is so much to say.

The earth rolls and cracks.

Trees split, bare-boned.

Flames swarm, leach the living of their color.

Time loops over and into itself.

Once, I went out under a star-filled sky and almost drowned.

Once, my father took up all the space I had.

Once all I did was dodge (and bury and carry) his story.

Now I'm here, feeling the push of another terrible. There is always something—

Time flings me out, pulls me back, draws me to this house, this room, this bed, this girl beside me.

Calliope takes my hand, squeezes my palm with her thumb. She turns to me, leans forward, and presses her forehead against mine.

"Hey," she says.

"Hey," I say.

With her eyes she says: *Are you okay?*

No, I message back. *I'm not and you're not and none of us are. But we're still here, and there is still time, maybe? And I love you, I love you, I love you.*

I think she reads my mind then, or perhaps I said it all out loud? But Calliope nods, making my head nod too.

"Same, George," she says.

Her eyes are deep brown. Her eyes are universes.

She nods again. *"Same."*

author's note

This book is set in Sydney, Australia, at the start of summer in late 2019. During that summer, enormous wildfires swept Australia's coastlines and inland, destroying thousands of human lives and killing billions of animals. The book begins as those wildfires start to take hold, at the end of a year of significant climate protest. This was a year of voices rising—of hundreds of thousands of young people calling for climate justice, and of climate groups using peaceful, direct action to disrupt a complacent and complicit system.

The urgency I felt during those protests, along with the sadness and stress of the fires, and the climate grief I felt and continue to feel, made an enormous impact on me. I built a story out of those feelings, and my own past. I wrote about what it is like to keep painful secrets, to navigate grief, anxiety, and shame, and to feel like life is out of your control. Ultimately, I also wrote about how it feels to be understood, heard, and loved, and to finally feel free to tell your story.

Like George, I have experienced domestic violence and parental addiction, and since I was small, have had to manage the many symptoms and embedded trauma responses of Complex PTSD. Like Tess, I have dealt with the muddy, exhausting world of profound anxiety and post-partum depression. Like Calliope and George, I know how it feels to have a parent make big decisions that hurt.

And like Laz, I deal with climate grief every day. As someone who knows how deeply pain, fear, and silence can sit inside the body, I encourage anyone who is living with hard things to find their voice and speak it. Whether it is by talking to a trusted someone, or singing, painting, writing, creating something . . . or by standing in a street and shouting with a crowd of others, we deserve to let our stories out.

We also have a right to make choices about our future and our own bodies. When I decided to write about Tess becoming pregnant at eighteen, I did so because she seemed fascinating, vulnerable, and complicated to me, and her choice created curly, unique story paths for her and George. In writing about Tess, there was no agenda—no intention to lecture anyone about teen pregnancy, or debate abortion or reproductive rights. While Tess's decision brings with it many challenges, her right to make this decision is never up for discussion. Any person capable of becoming pregnant should have the right to decide what happens to their body. No one should be able to force another human to continue a pregnancy or have a baby against their will.

May we all have a voice. May our rights be protected, not erased. May we lean (and lean, and lean) towards kindness. May we be able to advocate for ourselves and others, or call for compassionate change, without being punished or silenced. May we love who we love freely and know that we deserve to be loved in return. May we listen to the stories around us, take care of this hurting planet, *and* heal our wounds. May we be loud in ways that bring us health, strength, and joy. May we all find the quiet we need.

acknowledgments

To the people who helped Book Two come into being, with all my heart, THANK YOU.

Thank you to my editors, Jessica Dandino Garrison and Claire Craig, for your kindness, patience, and incredible insight. Your support has meant the world to me, both professionally and personally. I am absolutely and utterly a better writer because of you.

To my agent, Catherine Drayton: Thank you for always reaching out, checking in, and championing me. It started with you, and continues with you, and for that I am so thankful.

A huge thank-you to Nash Weerasekera, Kristie Radwilowicz, and Cerise Steel for my stunning cover illustration, cover design, and interiors! You have made my book so beautiful. Thank you to Regina Castillo for your smart and thoughtful edits. And thank you to everyone at Dial/Penguin Random House and Pan Macmillan Australia for your enormous support, talent, and dedication.

Thank you to Derek Simmonds, kayak expert and clinical psychologist, for your helpful information about paddling, and for confirming the meditative, calming benefits of moving quietly over water. To Lyss Wickramasinghe, thank you so much for your sensitive, nuanced reading and all your suggestions—what a wise reader, editor, and friend you are.

Thank you from the bottom of my heart to all my first readers.

To my writing mentees (and friends!) Rhys Lorenc, Jerome des Preaux, Jamil Badi, and Sophie Miller, thank you for your generous and incredibly discerning feedback. Thank you to Tobias Dunan, Kit Fox, and Christine Fox, who read the very first version of this book and have cheered me on ever since. And to my dear, dear friend Hayley Scrivenor, thank you for your thoughts about the book and about writing, your belief in me, and your constant love and inspiration.

Thank you to my whole family for answering all my random questions on the family chat thread! And thank you, obviously, for being my cherished people. I love you very much.

To my friend and fellow writer Donna Waters, thank you for your openness, and for always listening. Thank you to Lucy Mills, lovely troubadour, for so steadfastly walking beside me as I wrote these words. Thank you to the creative community of the Illawarra—just so many talented inspiring friends—for your warmth, kindness, and support. Thank you to the beautiful writers in Australia and all around the world for your generosity and friendship from the beginning. To all my students and mentees, thank you for constantly delighting and moving me. And to my readers, thank you for all the book love and your incredible, heartfelt messages—they have meant the world.

I think we are who we are because of how we love and are loved in return. I would not have made it through the last few years without the steadfast love of the people in my life who buoyed me up and stayed with me, even as I dropped balls and faltered. Living with Complex trauma is hard. Living with triggered trauma is close to impossible. But with the compassionate, devoted care of my family and friends, I am here, still. And writing, still. And grateful to my bones, always.

A last, special shout-out to Tobias and Kit: My goodness, you are extraordinary. The literal lights of my life. I adore you and am inspired by you. Thank you for your compassion, humor, faith in me, and all your love.

Finally, to dear, best Mom: You know what we have walked through to get here. This book is dedicated to you. I will love you forever and ever, moon and back. Love you more than all the stars.

HELENA FOX lives by the ocean on Dharawal Country in Wollongong, Australia. She mentors young writers and runs writing workshops to support mental health. Helena's debut novel, *How It Feels to Float,* won the Prime Minister's Literary Award and Victorian Premier's Literary Award for Writing for Young Adults in Australia, and was a *Kirkus* Best Book of the Year and Chicago Public Library Best Book of the Year in the U.S. Helena received her MFA in Creative Writing from Warren Wilson College. She can be found mostly on Instagram at @helenafoxoz, posting pictures of the sea and talking about kindness.

**Don't miss Helena Fox's award-winning,
internationally lauded debut, *How It Feels to Float***

"I haven't been so dazzled by a YA in ages. . . . Biz's voice is wild
and rollicking, lyrical and hilarious, utterly authentic . . .
There isn't a false note." —Jandy Nelson, author of
I'll Give You the Sun (via *School Library Journal*)

A Kirkus Reviews Best Book of the Year

A Chicago Public Library Best of the Best

Winner of the Australian Prime Minister's Literary Award

Winner of the Australian Victorian Premier's Literary Award